WINKELSTERN

D0499144

Docker stood at the edge of the precipice where the over-hang was topped and spiked with bracken and frozen thornbushes. He swept the valley with his binoculars, hold-ing the scopes on an area where the fir trees swayed and bent underneath layers of fog. Lowering the glasses, he listened to distant grinding sounds that shook the ground beneath him. Something massive and powerful broke through a screen of trees a quarter of a mile from them, and Docker said, "Jesus Christ!" as he saw the dark shape of a tank. The tank clawed through the frozen timber toward the slopes, stopping in a grove of trees glittering with hoarfrost and ice. The tank was the most dangerous ground weapon in the German arsenal—a King Tiger Mark II. A Mark II was an awesome sight under any circum-stances, and the way it seemed to be hiding in the cover of the mist and trees charged it with an additional, an almost unnatural menace, as if it were more than a great engine of war but rather some species of intelligent, in-vincible beast . . .

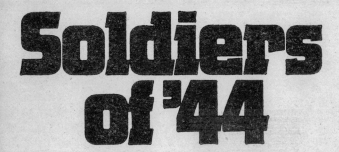

Soldiers of '44

William P. McGivern

BALLANTINE BOOKS • NEW YORK

Library of Congress Catalog Card Number: 78-72919

ISBN 0-345-28385-6

This edition published by arrangement with Arbor House
Publishing Co., Inc.

Manufactured in the United States of America

First Ballantine Books Edition: January 1980

To

the men of

Section Eight, Battery D,

789th Automatic Weapons Battalion

United States Army

World War II

Battles and Campaigns

Normandy	Ardennes
Rhineland	Central Europe

The following letter is classified Item 61-A in the Solvis Collection of Diaries and Letters donated to the College of Pennsylvania at Ardmore, Pennsylvania, by Edward G. Solvis.

The letter is part of an open collection which includes material dating from 1942 until the present.

To: Lieutenant Buell Docker ASN 36663864
APO 784
European Theatre of Operations

February 2, 1945

Dear Buell:

News of your promotion duly noted and long overdue, your fans here contend. Your pater-familias stopped by the college last week. Worn and tired as we all are by the war. But nothing physically serious. He asked me to mention that the cream-and-silver bitch—why did you name her Detroit?—is recovering from some kind of dysentery, and is again begging for snacks up and down your elm-lined paradiso street, and—what an irony—terrorizing the mailmen who must deliver those frightful telegrams. But not so frequently now, thank God.

And, irony—after all the pennants were flying for victory—stiff flags straining in the night-blasts cold—after all the terror and death you had seen, there was still to be more of it, still that last test of blood and fire in the Ardennes offensive. Did you know the newspapers are calling it the Battle of the Bulge? Well, too much. No tears left here. In the end, pessimists are always proven right, I expect.

As ever,
(signed) Dave

From: David Hamlin
       Associate Professor of English
       College of Pennsylvania
       Ardmore, Pennsylvania

This letter from David Hamlin is reprinted with the permission of Dr. Gerald Flood, Curator of Archives.

Chapter One

December 11, 1944. Eastern Belgium.
Monday, 1530 hours.

In an open jeep and two heavy trucks, the soldiers of D (Dog) Battery's Gun Section Eight followed a steep and twisting road to the crest of a hill layered with drifting fogs above a silent valley in the forests of the Ardennes.

Gusting winds shook the canvas sides of the laboring trucks and swept in erratic spirals around the sergeant driving the support jeep and the corporal scanning the white ravines below them through binoculars.

They had been out of contact with Battery headquarters for two days and nights, but knew that somewhere ahead of them in the mountains were divisions of German soldiers pulling back toward the Siegfried Line and the Rhine, the last barriers between the Allied forces and the heartland of Nazi Germany.

Sergeant Buell Docker raised a hand and Corporal Schmitzer in the lead truck acknowledged the gesture with his horn, the single beeping note lost almost instantly in the rasp of wind through the frozen trees. The small convoy slowed and stopped near a tangled mass of thorn bushes that gave them some relief from the winds.

Schmitzer swung his truck about in a circle and positioned its hood against the front of the second truck,

1

providing the cannon and machine guns behind them full fields of fire.

When Docker and the corporals turned off their engines, the silence that settled seemed intensified by the thick snow and rolling fogs. The sergeant listened for sounds of transport or planes, but heard only the rising winds and the occasional fragile snap of icicles.

Corporal Matt Larkin, in the passenger seat beside Docker, turned and looked at him.

"Well?"

"Well what?" Docker said.

"I don't know. What're you worried about?"

"You tell me."

Corporal Larkin smiled bleakly, his teeth white against black whiskers; dirt and grease smudged his forehead beneath the rim of his helmet.

"I mean our nonpareil leader," Larkin said. "I mean that ninety-day fuck-up, Whitter."

Docker picked up his binoculars and looked across the fogs toward hills almost lost in the shifting patterns of low clouds. "We'll break here," he said. "Take a few men and cover the east side of the hill. Keep your eyes open. I don't want any smiling faces missing when you come back."

Larkin had more to say but looked at the sergeant and decided against it. Climbing from the jeep, he yelled with ritual exasperation at three soldiers standing near the truck, and led them back down a narrow road to the floor of the valley.

The sergeant looped his binoculars around his neck, grabbed the windshield bar and swung himself from the jeep, his boots making splintering sounds as they broke through the crust of snow on the ground.

Docker was tall but not as slim as he appeared at a casual glance; there was a precision in his movements that masked the power and size of his body. He wore a field jacket with his stripes on it and a wool-lined canvas coat with a fur collar. A holstered .45 automatic was clipped to his cartridge belt and a carbine was looped across his shoulders.

Docker was twenty-seven but looked ten years older; his eyes were hard and there were flecks of gray in the dark hair at his temples. The single and obligatory requisite of his rank was responsibility, which had left its mark in his eyes and in his lined and weathered features.

From the top of the hill, Docker followed Corporal Larkin's detail down the slopes through his binoculars, checking to make sure the men were on opposite sides of the road, moving out with proper intervals between them.

Docker called to Schmitzer, who walked over frozen ground to the jeep, his thick and powerfully muscled shoulders leaning into the wind, his hands swinging almost down to his knees. In new units, Schmitzer was occasionally called Monk or Monkey, but seldom twice by the same person. With Section Eight only three weeks now, he had already booted Spinelli hard for rolling a rock at him and shouting, "Think fast! Live coconut!"

The sergeant told Schmitzer to take a second detail and cover the west side of the hill; the steep pitch of the ridge would protect the other two flanks of their position.

"I ask for volunteers?" Schmitzer said.

Docker glanced through the gathering dusk toward the guns. Joe Pitko and Ed Solvis were at the controls of the cannon, seated in the metal seats beside its wide breechblock. They were the oldest of Docker's men, in their middle thirties, and liked working together. Sensibly enough (in Docker's view) they preferred one another's company to that of the noisy youngsters in the section.

Docker answered Corporal Schmitzer with, "Take Linari, Pierce and the other kid, what's his name, Sonny Laurel. Linari is solid bone upstairs but he'll do what you tell him. Pierce and Sonny Laurel, I don't know."

"They ever see any action?"

"They shipped here as replacements a month ago. Fired at sleeve targets in England, that's about it. They know the manual of arms and how to unbutton their flys."

"I'll watch 'em," Schmitzer said.

The corporal went back to the trucks and called out the names of his detail, and three young soldiers hurried to join him at the top of the rutted pathway into the valley.

The sergeant watched them through his binoculars until their figures merged into the mists, then turned and studied the mountains and valleys stretching toward the Rhine, rolling and open country, fields bright with snow and occasional stands of pines that looked dull green through the fogs. He was searching for roads or farmhouses or signs of a village but the driving sleet had blurred the valleys into an opaque expanse of swirling white mists.

Over the years it seemed to Docker he had matured and hardened as a soldier in several distinct stages. At first he had tried to mask his anxiety and fears by pretending they didn't exist, because this seemed the only acceptable attitude to assume, the one he had absorbed from books and school and other recruits. Then he had learned something different from the panic they had all been seared with at Kasserine in North Africa, and in Sicily he had begun to trust his unrooted anxieties, to depend on unspecific suspicions about terrain and incongruous silences, examining these intuitive alarms as carefully as he would the condition of his weapons.

Eventually the instincts that caused him to be aware of danger escalated through repetition to a higher perception, a complex set of reflexes that were like physical sensors, monitoring devices as dependable as his eyes and ears. And now, standing alone on a sleeting hill in Belgium, Docker was paying close attention to the warning of his combat instincts.

Everybody was so goddamn sure the war was about

over. That was part of what disturbed and alerted him. ("Ah tell yuh, Dockah, this lil ole pig-stickin' is *over*," Whitter had told him just a week ago.) And it wasn't only green troops regretting they'd missed all the action, it was the noncoms talking about the jobs and women they were going back home to, and sewing new hash marks and stripes on their tunics, officers ordering Ike jackets and "pinks" run up by tailors in Paris and Brussels. Talk of eating and drinking, wistful discussions of glorious foods and beers and whiskeys; these had always been a traditional, time-honored preoccupation and fantasy of soldiers in all armies, but now there was a sense of the immediate in the leisurely discussions of crab and turkey gumbos, New England chowders, baked beans and hams and steaks and fried potatoes and pies and cakes and doughnuts, not as if these delights were waiting in the fantasy kitchens of towns like Duluth and Mobile and Boston and New York, but were in fact steaming and frying and bubbling for grateful soldiers just beyond the next range of hills.

Air Force Intelligence (according to Lieutenant Whitter again) insisted there were no German troops in the Ardennes. But Allied planes hadn't been flying for a week. And no one knew for sure what might be moving under that heavy cover of fog and clouds.

Nevertheless, everyone was certain it was winding down, even Dave Hamlin was convinced of it, Hamlin, three thousand miles away on a college campus in Pennsylvania, was just as complacent as everybody else. Only last month he had written: "It's not that I'm tired of being a surrogate cock for you heroes because I'm not. But fair is fair; wrap things up, come on home and get *yours*." . . .

Corporal John Trankic checked the breechblock of the cannon, climbed down from the firing platform and walked through the snow to Docker. Trankic's bulk was emphasized by the wool sweater and scarf he wore beneath a field jacket and overcoat as he studied Docker now with an appraising frown.

"What the fuck's bothering you?"

"We're taking a break here," Docker said. "Long enough for a piss call and chow."

"You worried about the new guy? What's his name—Schmitzer?"

"No, I think he's all right."

"I'd say it was pretty chicken shit of him kicking Spinelli in the ass that way. Live coconut. Hell, it was just a joke."

"Schmitzer didn't see it that way," Docker said. "Look, try to get a signal through to Battery or Battalion."

"I been trying all day, Bull."

"Unless you want to switch to smoke signals, stay on the radio. If you get through to Battery, I want to talk to Captain Grant."

Section Eight's X-42 radio receiver-transmitter was packed in its leather carrying case and strapped to the side of the jeep where its antenna had free play above the windshield and rear seats. It was essentially the same communications system used in command cars and spotter jeeps; it could monitor signals from the divisions on their flanks and occasionally—depending on the weather and configuration of the valleys and mountains in their immediate vicinity—could pick up German units ahead of them and transmitters operating to the north with Montgomery's British armies.

"Okay, let's get with it." Docker walked to the big trucks, ghostly shapes in the fogs now, and cupped a hand around his mouth and yelled for Dormund.

Private Chet Dormund climbed awkwardly over the tailgate of the truck and stood panting in front of Docker, his head hanging and his fingers moving nervously along the seams of his fatigue trousers. His mouth was open and his breath caused the heavy snow to melt and form drops of moisture on his chin and lips. When Docker told him this was a chow break, the section's cook shifted his weight uneasily, his boots making a liquid sound in the sleet and snow crusting the ground.

"The guys'll get on me, sarge," he said. "It'll be all cold. I can't light a fire, so the guys'll get on me."

"Start your fire between a couple of trees and put a tarp over it."

"You mean like tie it between the trees?"

"Right. Let's have some good hot food. Open a dozen cans of K-rations, beans and franks, roast beef hash, whatever you got. This may be the last meal today. Any biscuits left from breakfast?"

"They're cold and hard as wretched rocks, sarge. They'll get on me for it."

"The engine blocks are still warm. Start one of the trucks and put a pan of biscuits on the block and close the hood."

"You damn right, sarge." Dormund nodded vigorously and went to collect his supplies.

"Any luck?" Docker asked Corporal Trankic.

Trankic closed the top of the leather case to protect the radio from the snow and made a thumbs-down gesture with his hand.

"Not a fucking thing, Bull," he said. "Some yackety-yak from a civilian station in Brussels, could have been a resistance transmitter, and some shortwave static from God knows where."

Docker removed a map from a clip under the dashboard of the jeep and spread it across the frosted hood, securing two of its sides with his carbine and binoculars against the gusting winds. When one corner of the map continued to snap and flutter, Docker pinned it down with his helmet. The canvas straps in the helmet liner had made deep creases in his thick dark hair, and the settling snow formed patterns in them that matched the touches of gray at his temples.

"With a shave and a good night's sleep, you could pass for fifty," Trankic told him.

Docker studied the map, his eyes narrowing against
the stinging winds. He rubbed a hand over his head,
enjoying the pleasant discomfort of massaging hair and
scalp against the constriction caused by the canvas
straps of his helmet. With a gloved fingertip he drew a
line south from Liège to the Allied railhead at Bastogne. Fifty miles, perhaps sixty. He couldn't judge the
distance in terms of time; bridges might be down, narrow mountain roads packed and impassable with snowdrifts. His section was somewhere between those big
towns, traveling on a line roughly east of Trois-Ponts
and Malmédy.

"So what the hell's bugging you?" Trankic said.

"Take a look at the map."

The battalion had crossed the Meuse River at Namur
the first week of December, the mission of its thirty-two
gun sections to provide antiaircraft and antitank protection for various elements of the 28th and 106th Infantry
Divisions.

Docker and Trankic studied their line of march,
which curved in an easterly direction from Namur toward Germany. The towns of Werbomont, Manhay,
Vielsalm were behind them now. They had passed
through them at night, the houses and shops blacked
out, trucks and guns noisy in the narrow streets and
windswept squares, with Larkin at the wheel of the jeep
and Docker beside him plotting the course on a grid
map braced against his knees.

Bastogne, the site of VIII Corps headquarters, was
also behind them, but south by twenty or thirty miles.
They looked at the names of villages on the Salm
and Amblève Rivers—Stoumont, Foix and Lepont—and
in other directions—Spa and Malmédy and St. Vith
and Stavelot.

They studied the contour of the terrain, the bridges
and roads, the mountains and valleys where the other
guns of the 269th were posted in a thin north-south line
through this sector of the Ardennes.

"I can read maps all right," Trankic said, and looked

at Docker, "but I ain't any good at reading minds, Bull. So you better tell me about it."

"We've traveled about sixty miles the last few days," Docker said. "On the same line as the battery, according to our maps and orders. But if there was an error in parallax of only two or three degrees between the section and the battery at the IP, the error would be compounded fifty times by now. That's one thing. The second is that you haven't picked up any German units on the radio for the last thirty-six hours."

"So now we don't know where the battery is, and don't know what's in front of us. That about it, Bull?"

"That's about it," Docker said.

Trankic nodded again and uncapped his canteen. "You want a drink?"

"Sure."

Docker held the canteen in his gloved hand and took a swallow from it. The whiskey was ice cold and stained his lips blue-black but he was grateful for the swift and powerful heat it churned up in his stomach.

The whiskey came from Normandy, from the invasion area designated Utah Beach in France where the 269th had landed on the third week after D-Day. Utah was north of the other American invasion beach, which was code-named Omaha, and still farther north of the British beaches, which were coded Gold and Juno and Sword. Utah was divided into two sections, Tare Green and Uncle Red, and Dog Battery's guns had been on Beach Red with units of the 4th and 79th infantry divisions.

In the shatteringly noisy chaos of those landings and regroupings, with beachmasters shouting commands through bullhorns and 40- and 90-millimeter cannons pounding the skies at strafing Focke-Wulfs and Messerschmitts, Trankic had spotted and appropriated eleven five-gallon jerry cans of ethyl alcohol which (they'd decided later) had probably been ticketed for the engineers or medics.

Trankic, who had been a sandhog and bootlegger in

Chicago before the war, had distilled the alcohol to get
rid of contaminants, and then stirred oak chips in the
mixture to absorb its fusel oils. After adding color and
sweetness with sugar charred in a mess kit to the shade
of tawny molasses, Trankic had at last triumphantly
evolved a "whiskey" that tasted no better or worse than
a cheap, blended bar bourbon. The only flaw in his
eventual product (and everyone agreed it was a minor
one) was that on interaction with metal canteens and
cups the whiskey turned glossy and dark, as rich and
glowing as black satin. It was known throughout the
battalion as Trankic's "Old Black Jolt" and it had an
effect so intense that it seemed to explode like a series
of linked grenades from the back of the throat to the
top and bottom of the skeletal system.

As Docker studied the map and felt the winds becoming warmer on his numbing lips, he realized in some
curious warping of time that those tumultuous hours on
Utah Beach seemed more distant to him than Sicily,
where he had been hit, and Africa, where the Big Red
One had been blooded for the first time, and battle
flags of American units had been ground into the sands
in the scorched files of the Kasserine Pass.

He remembered that someone had been firing at
them on Utah in France, they didn't know who, they
saw only the explosions of dust and shale in the ground
beside their trucks, holes appearing magically as if
made by some invisible sewing machine, and that
Trankic was shouting, "Hold it, for Christ's sake, these
goddamn cans are full of alcohol . . ." And Larkin at
the wheel of the truck had yelled at him, "If you're
trying to be the first immortal, go fuck yourself . . ."
But Trankic, his face smudged with smoke and wet with
sweat, had stood fast in that noise and chaos and had
thrown can after can of the alcohol up to Shorty Kohler
and Tex Farrel, scrambling onto the tailgate himself
only a split second before Larkin floored the accelera-
tor . . .

Trankic took a drink now of his black liquor, wiped a

black blur from his lips, put the canteen in the canvas pouch hooked to his cartridge belt and said, "So now I know what you're worried about. But there's something else. We got a couple of guys in the section, Dormund and Gelnick, who'd be just as much good to us if they were back in the States peeling potatoes. And five to six kids who'd do fine if there was somebody 'round to change their diapers."

"So don't worry about Schmitzer pounding on Spinelli. It might help toilet train him."

Dormund came sloshing awkwardly through the snow. "Sarge, I got the biscuits hotting up on the engine block, but the guys are gonna get on me anyway 'cause I got trouble with the pump-stove and it's gonna take a long time to cut firewood."

"Where the hell is Gelnick?" Docker said, ignoring him. "Did he go down the hill with the other guys?"

"He didn't go with nobody. He's in the truck in his fart sack with a lot of blankets on top of him."

"Goddamn him." Docker replaced his helmet and walked through the snow to the trucks.

Dormund looked anxiously at Trankic. "I didn't mean to get him in trouble."

"Don't worry about it."

"Sarge won't send Gelnick back to the CP, will he?"

"He'll probably scare the shit out of him, but he won't transfer him back there."

"You sure he won't?"

"Shit, I just told you. Maybe I should have fixed you a head out of a tin can after all." Trankic rapped Dormund's helmet with his knuckles. "That one of yours got some holes in it."

"Come on, you're joking with me. It's just a wretched joke, okay, Trankic?"

Dormund had come on the word "wretched" in England. A girl in a pub had smiled pleasantly at him one night and called him a "wretched drunkard" and since then he had been addicted to the word.

"Sure, sure," Trankic said. "Now get a fire going."

Corporal Larkin sat perched on a cold tree stump in the valley below Section Eight's temporary gun position. He was reading a Rex Stout paperback and thinking, as he looked up to check around, that he liked Archie Goodwin better than Nero Wolfe. Not that he had anything against the fat detective and his beer and flowers, but Goodwin had the run of the city and that's what Larkin liked best, reading about neighborhoods he'd grown up in and worked in. Even the Village which was full of queers was all right. The upper Bronx was better and Yankee Stadium, where everybody said DiMag would be the first guy to hit a ball out. Ruth and Gehrig never did, and DiMag hadn't either, not yet anyway. But it was the bars on Third Avenue near where he lived that he liked best, all those Irish names with basements where they had steak rackets every month, all the steak you could eat and all the beer you could drink for three dollars, and fights by young brawlers trying to make it to St. Nick's or the Garden. And battle royals, the kind his uncles had the hots for. . . .

Private Irving Gruber, who somehow managed to remain overweight on GI field rations and was usually called Tubby, carefully packed a large snowball and lobbed it at Carmine Spinelli as he stood urinating with thoughtful precision into a rotted hole in the trunk of a tree. The snowball struck Spinelli just above the collar of his jacket, soaking and splattering his head and neck and shoulders. Wheeling around, his piss cutting a ginger arc in the white snow, he looked resentfully at Gruber.

"Goddamn it, Irv, that ain't funny!" Spinelli brushed the clinging snow from his shoulders. "It ain't funny at all." His lips were trembling. "Goddamn it, Tubby. It's melting down my back . . ."

"Put your cock away, Spinelli," Larkin said.

"A guy can't even take a piss without some lard-ass dumping snow on him."

Tubby Gruber was laughing at Spinelli's shivering

discomfort, but Shorty Kohler looked at him with disgust. "That's your trouble, you ginney bastard. You take shit from everybody."

Kohler had a forehead ridged with cartilage and a nose broken twice and reset both times by a rubber at Stillman's Gym in New York. He had been an amateur boxer before he was drafted and that, plus an explosive temper, had earned him an uneasy respect throughout the battalion.

"You know why you take your lumps from guys?" Kohler told Spinelli, "it's 'cause you don't have any belief. Like no character. You gotta stand up for yourself, know what I mean? Like that fucking Corporal Schmitzer. Goddamn baboon prick. Kicks you in the ass and you don't do nothing about it."

"So what's to do about it?" Spinelli said. His feelings were raw and his voice was breaking. "He's got the stripes, he's bigger than me, and lots older and everything."

"It don't make no difference," Kohler said. "Lemme tell you something. Fights are won two ways. The first is before anybody throws a punch. Lemme show you. A guy comes up to me in a bar, a big guy, he's got fifty pounds on me. So he wants to look good to his girl or his pals. So I move away from him, give him space at the bar, keep my eyes on my drink, he's already won the fucking fight. Acting that way, I give him balls. So the minute his elbow touches mine, what do I do . . ."

Larkin said, "You figure he's a queer so you ask him if he wants to go down on you, right, Shorty?"

Kohler looked pained. "Shit, corporal, this is for Spinelli's own good. What I do, Carmine, is I swing the edge of my palm against the guy's arm, hard. And I stare right into his eyes. Then I say something to him. No bullshit lines like you hear in movies. Just something quiet, like maybe . . . 'You looking for trouble, pal?' "

"That's great," Larkin said. "I heard John Wayne say that in a movie. But he said it to a girl."

Gruber was laughing because it was safe to now, but Spinelli's expression remained intent and serious.

"Okay, Shorty, that's one way," he said. "But you said two ways. What's the other one?"

Kohler rubbed the stubble on his jaw. "Well, you just win it, that's all. What the fuck you think? You come out of your corner fast, and you try to rock him with your best shots and no matter how hard he belts you, don't let him know it. If your eye's bleeding, fuck protecting it, keep wading in. Don't ever let the son of a bitch know he hurt you. Then he starts to worry and forgets what they tell him in his corner. And pretty soon, nothing's working for him."

Kohler raised his hands, shrugged and let them drop to his side. "That's all there is, Carmine. Just them two things."

Corporal Larkin regarded him with what seemed to be frank admiration; the smile beneath his smudge of beard suggested only an innocent sincerity.

"So tell me something, Shorty," he said. "Where was all them big fights of yours? At the Garden or was it maybe St. Nick's Arena?"

Kohler looked away from Larkin, his eyes moving across the white valley. "You know the fuck it wasn't no St. Nick's or the Garden. I fought at smokers and steak rackets and if you won you got maybe ten bucks and if you lost you got some beers and a steak on a poppy-seed bun. So it wasn't any fucking main event, but we didn't fight niggers."

"You got a real soft streak in you, Shorty," Larkin said. "I'm kind of surprised."

"What the hell you talking about?" Kohler's tone was uneasy; he could guess something was coming but knew no way to defend against it.

Larkin was black Irish, with black hair and dark eyes and a cough that bit into his lungs like the teeth of a saw, a condition which wasn't helped by sleeping on frozen ground for months and smoking several packs of cigarettes every day. Still, though he was wasted and thin, everyone except Docker treated him with a cautious, wary respect, because Larkin knew how to use words so they stung and hurt, sometimes worse. than blows.

"Shit, Kohler, you're a real patsy," Larkin said, but when he laughed there was just the flash of white teeth against his black beard. "A real lover, aren't you?"

Kohler looked at the low skies. "You gonna tell me what you're talking about? Is this Twenty Questions or something?"

"I mean, Shorty, you were so kind to all them spades. Kid Chocolate and Beau Jack and Sugar Ray. Imagine all those black assholes twitching and puckering with relief. Think of Jersey Joe Wolcott and Hank Armstrong and don't forget that clown Joe Louis, all of them on their knees thanking the good Lord because Shorty Kohler wasn't going to whip their asses for a stein of beer and a bowl of beans at some fucking mick steak racket."

"Look, I didn't say I could beat any of them guys." Kohler looked for support to Gruber and Spinelli. "Did I, for Christ's sake? Louis and Wolcott, shit, they're heavyweights. Sugar Ray and Armstrong, they're welters like me, but they're the best there ever was."

Corporal Larkin stuffed the Rex Stout into the outer pocket of his soiled, coffee-stained GI overcoat. The coat was singed black at knee level, charred streaks that circled the back and front of the coat like an extra hemline. The black singes, acquired from standing too close to glowing field stoves, were among the unissued insignia of combat field soldiers, along with bleeding gums and trench foot and hands blistered from cradling scalding canteen cups.

Larkin unhooked his canteen and took a sip of Trankic's black whiskey. It felt good, warming the coldness in his lungs that made him cough so much, but looking at Shorty Kohler didn't make him feel good, because Kohler was staring at him now like some dumb beaten dog. "Forget it, Shorty," Larkin said. "I saw you fight once. You were all right."

"Yeah? You're a big bullshit artist."

"You want to put next month's pay where your mouth is?"

Kohler looked uncertain. "No shit. You saw me fight?"

"Twenty-ninth Street between Lex and Third. Jimmy Ryan's bar, a steak racket in the basement. You fought an Italian kid, his name was Bonelli or Bottelli, something like that. Your cut man was drunk and the referee was that old priest from St. Stanislaus, he'd been a light-weight contender, and a chaplain in World War One. So, big mouth, I see you fight or I didn't see you fight?"

Kohler had begun to smile; his eyes were small and bright under the ridge of cartilage. "Shit, yes, you saw me fight. Hey, Carmine! Hey, Tubby! You hear Larkin? He saw me fight Don Bonavinci."

"Bonavinci, right," Larkin said.

"But, wait a minute. How come you never mentioned it before? Something like that, it figures you'd mention."

"Some things you remember, some things you forget." The look in Larkin's eyes made Kohler decide to change the subject. "It happened to me once with a girl," he said. "I forgot her name and I knew her all my life, seen her for years sitting out on the steps and playing in the street. But then I took her out, and I'm calling her 'hey' and 'you' and 'babe'. . . . It was funny because I never thought of her one way or another when she was just a kid on the block. But I'm out with her, she's a different person and I don't know her name anymore." Kohler shrugged and feinted a flurry of rapid punches at the trunk of a tree . . .

Private Tubby Gruber saw them first as they came out of the woods and down a twisting lane that brought them to the road where they stopped and stared at the soldiers. "Hey, corporal!" Gruber swung his M-1 around to cover an old man in a black overcoat and a little girl whose face was almost completely concealed by a coarse red scarf. The man carried a burlap sack in one hand, and with his other had a firm grip on the child's shoulder. As he stared and blinked at the Americans, standing now and silhouetted against the valley, his smile became uncertain.

"Yanks," he said. "Yanks. *Amis* . . ."

"That's right, Yanks." Larkin's eyes swept the woods behind the bearded man and the small girl. Nothing moved except the swaying crowns of the winter-black trees. The silence was broken only by a distant cry of birds.

"All right, get this the first time." Larkin stared at the three private soldiers. "I don't want any more fucking snowball fights and no more goddamn talk about who pounded John Doe's ears down to his hips. Keep your mouths shut and your eyes open."

In English and then halting French Larkin tried to find out where the pair had come from, but the old man only nodded at the questions, repeated the words "Yank" and "*Amis*," and then held out the burlap bag.

Larkin took the sack and spilled its contents on the ground—potatoes, leeks, bunches of shriveled carrots and a half dozen large purple and white turnips. The old man studied him and made an age-old gesture with his thumb and forefinger.

"Maybe we can do some business later, pop," Larkin said, and jerked a thumb at Gruber. "Go get Docker, he can talk to this guy."

When Gruber started up the slopes, the man pulled a brown bottle from his coat pocket and offered it to Larkin with a tentative smile. Larkin nodded his thanks, but then noticed that the child was staring off across the valley, her dark eyes very round and intent.

Glancing in the same direction, Larkin saw—or believed he saw—a slim flash of light on the horizon, a fiery ball that disappeared almost instantly into a background of driving sleet and low black clouds.

"You see that, Kohler?" Larkin said.

"I see what?"

"Something funny across those fields. Some kind of light."

But Kohler hadn't seen anything strange in those shifting gray mists. Nor had Spinelli.

From where he stood on an adjacent flank of the hill, Corporal Schmitzer looked through his binoculars and watched Tubby Gruber hiking up to the ridge, where Dormund was building a fire and the sergeant was standing with Gelnick, whose nickname, Schmitzer thought, was pretty goddamn appropriate. The Hogman . . . Swinging his binoculars the other way, Schmitzer saw Larkin talking to some farmer and a kid wearing a bright scarf.

"Hey, corporal, what do you think that was?"

Schmitzer lowered the binoculars and looked at Sonny Laurel. "What do I think *what* was?"

"You didn't see it?"

"See what?"

"I don't know. I'm not sure."

Sonny Laurel pointed to a stand of trees on the horizon where the winds were rising and the snow and fogs were torn into shreds by the force of convulsively spinning thermals.

"What do you mean, you don't know?"

"I'm not sure. It was like a flash of light behind those trees."

Schmitzer looked at the black trees that were in shrouded relief against the white mountainside. "Could be you're getting snow-blind. Happened to us in the desert in Tunisia from the heat on the sand. What they call an optical delusion."

"No, I saw it, whatever it was."

Schmitzer frowned and wondered what Laurel might have seen behind that stand of dark trees. He knew the Russians had developed multiple rocket launchers

called "Katyushas"—recoilless weapons firing thirty-six
to thirty-eight projectiles simultaneously. He had read
they were called "Stalin's organ music," which was
probably a lot of crap, a cozy nickname for the dumb
peasants. But Schmitzer knew the nearest Russians were
at least a thousand miles north and east of there, so it
was damned unlikely there were any rocket launchers in
the Ardennes.

"You sure you didn't hear nothing, Sonny?"

"Not a sound. It went by so fast, it looked like a bolt
of lightning on its side." Laurel pushed his helmet back
and absently rubbed his fair, curly hair, staring at the
trees where he had seen the streaking lights. "I don't
know, corporal, I never saw anything moving that fast
before."

Corporal Schmitzer had been in the army almost five
years. With a gut instinct for survival, he knew that
staying alive now depended to a significant extent on
how much their section could rely on these youngsters;
but standing stiff and heavy in the spiraling snow,
Schmitzer was betrayed by a distracting thought, a wish
that his father and brother and Uncle Ernie could have
had some of his guts and instincts.

Pushing those shadows from his mind, Schmitzer
said, "Laurel, you damn sure you didn't hear anything—no engines, no prop-vibes, no nothing?"

"I may be wrong but I don't think so, corporal."

"Well, don't worry about it. You could be trying too
hard."

Goldilocks, that's what the youngsters in the section
called Sonny Laurel, Schmitzer knew . . . Goldilocks
because of his blond hair and his slim, quick-moving
body, and the blue eyes that got darker when he was
serious or worried about something, working on the
guns or writing letters home. Laurel always looked fresh
and clean even with a fine beading of sweat on his forehead and throat.

Telling him to stay alert, Schmitzer walked abruptly off into the fogs, knowing that what he was feeling would embarrass or disturb the boy if it showed in his face or eyes.

Chapter Two

December 11, 1944. Eastern Belgium.
Monday, 1700 Hours.

___

The sergeant climbed into the jeep and drove to the base of the ridge where Larkin was waiting with the old Belgian and the little girl.

The pair stood close together, watching Docker anxiously through a darkness relieved now by only a filigree of white snowflakes. The sergeant could see the girl's intent eyes, round and polished like marbles, and the jagged black bangs on her forehead, but the lower half of her face was concealed by a red wool scarf. The old man looked to be in his sixties, short and stocky with ragged gray hair and chin whiskers. His dark overcoat was worn at the lapels and elbows, but his woolen cap struck an incongruous note of cheer, coarse and white with a blue tassel that hung down alongside his tobacco-stained whiskers. It was the only cheerful thing about them, Docker thought, because they were both obviously afraid, the old man like a dog at a strange campfire, eyes tense and wary, his old body coiled as if to dodge a blow.

"He wants a hundred francs for them," Larkin said, nodding at the heap of vegetables. "The bottle of booze is on the house, I guess."

"Fair enough." Docker glanced at Spinelli and Kohler. "You guys got some chocolate for the kid?"

Shorty Kohler took half a D-bar from his field jacket and offered it to the girl, but she wouldn't take it, hiding her hands in the scarf and pressing closer to the old man.

"Comment s'appelle?" Docker said.

The sergeant had learned French from his mother, who had grown up in Montreal, but she had died in an automobile accident when he was ten and so his knowledge of the language was limited to a simple vocabulary and a few songs and nursery rhymes.

The old man's smile became easier, relaxing the tension about his eyes.

"Je m'appelle Claude Girard."

"Et la jeune fille?"

"Margret. Elle est ma petit-fille."

The sound of her name seemed to reassure the child, who suddenly reached out and plucked the bar of chocolate from Kohler's hand. He laughed. "Sarge, I could make a contender out of her. See them reflexes?"

Claude Girard told Docker that he lived on his brother's farm near Verviers and was taking his grandchild to her cousins in a village on the Salm River.

When Docker asked him if he had seen any German soldiers in the area, the old man shook his head quickly and emphatically.

Docker opened his wallet and took out some French and Belgian francs, a few American dollars. The old man smiled and pointed insistently at the Belgian francs, the smile doing little to relieve the anxiety in his seamed face.

To test a sharpening suspicion, Docker pulled out a slim sheaf of Allied Invasion scrip from his wallet. The old man backed away from him and shook his head.

"Hell, he wants the Belgian gelt," Larkin said. "Why not give it to him?"

"He's sure as hell earned it."

"What does that mean?"

"Think about it." Docker put the Invasion scrip back in his wallet and gave the old man a hundred Belgian francs. Monsieur Girard smiled gratefully and bowed from the waist, the blue tassel on his cap swinging about like an antic little bird.

"If he's picked up, he doesn't want any American loot on him," Larkin said. "Is that it?"

"That's what he just told us," Docker said.

Spinelli and Shorty Kohler collected the vegetables and piled them in the rear of the jeep. The old man waved a good-bye but the little girl kept her arms tight at her sides as her red scarf and the old man's stocky figure soon disappeared into the snow-white darkness.

"So what now? We wait for Whitter, or we push on east?" Larkin said.

Docker looked up the hill through the swirling snow, observed the silhouettes of their guns and the tiny orange glow of Dormund's wood fire.

"We'll wait for the lieutenant," he said.

After a hot meal of fresh vegetables and K-rations, Docker ordered the fires out and split the section into two shifts. Half the men were now asleep in the trucks or stretched out on the ground under blankets and overcoats. The rest were manning the guns and standing guard posts at twenty-yard intervals below the crest of the hill.

The night was bitterly cold. Snow and sleet had stopped but the winds were high and fogs rolled in heavy masses over their position, cutting like damp knives through heavy GI overcoats and curling in lacy patterns around the barrels of the cannon and machine guns.

Stretched out in one of the trucks, Private Edward Solvis brought his diary up-to-date, using a small flashlight to track his pencil across the page of a ruled notebook.

He wrote the date, December 11th, and then: "A quiet day. Covered 18 miles, going north by east. Good chow tonight. No mail this past week. It's hard on the young guys."

The tarpaulin Solvis was lying on had bunched into a
hard ridge under his hips. Twisting around to a more
comfortable position, he pushed Spinelli's cold, damp
boots away from his face. Spinelli grunted but didn't
wake. The slender beam of the flashlight palely coated
the vulnerable faces of the other men sleeping in the
truck, Private Leo Pierce, knobby wrists locked around
his knees, and Tubby Gruber, slack and content on his
back, tiny bubbles of saliva collapsing on his lips in
rhythm with his soft, shallow breathing.

Solvis wet the tip of his pencil and wrote: "Docker is
worried. Half the section is on guard now and he said
no fires or cigarettes. I asked Pitko if he knew what was
up but got the answer I'd expected, which was that our
lives are in the hands of the Lord and we must put our
trust in His infinite wisdom and mercy. I envy Pitko"—
Solvis paused, thinking for words—"his faith, for him,
is like a deep river, running calm to the sea, his God.
He prays every morning and evening and isn't upset by
profanity and the lack of faith of Kohler and Linari and
some of the others. Faith is a fine thing, but I didn't
find Pitko's answer much help. Will turn in now. On
guard in three hours." . . .

Corporal Larkin was trying to sleep in the cab of the
other truck, lying under an overcoat and blankets that
smelled of wood-smoke. Heavy winds banged the canvas sides of the truck; he looked up for stars but saw
only heavy banks of fog drifting under the clouds. He
closed his eyes again, forcing himself to breathe carefully . . . gulping the cold, damp air could trigger one
of his coughing spells.

In the crook of his arm, Larkin cradled a canteen of
Trankic's black whiskey. The other hand rested on the
stock of his rifle. His eyes ached, maybe from the glare
of the snow, or maybe he was coming down with something. Too restless to sleep, he sat up and drank some
whiskey.

The talk with Shorty Kohler had brought back times
he despised, and with them a millrace of unwelcome

memory and emotion; his uncles and cousins on pay-days, tearing up dollar bills and throwing them into gutters or into the wind because they couldn't stand taking those paper symbols of slavery home to their women and children in bleak cold-water flats. Or so they claimed. But it was a justification born of self-pity, because they would spend money at steak rackets, swilling booze and beer, heaping noisy abuse or approval on a slob like Kohler getting his brains beat out, raising their dumb immigrant laughter in chorus with other hopeless losers, krauts and polacks and wops. Then, for the ultimate explosion of good sport, there were the free-for-alls, the battle royals where eight or ten blindfolded niggers would celebrate their fucking emancipation by battering each other senseless with a double sawbuck going to the bloody, reeling black who was still on his feet at the end of three rounds . . . Kohler brought all that back, and the old Belgian and the little kid, with knots of hunger and fear in their stomachs, they brought it back too. They were all pathetic fucking losers, buying cold withered vegetables for pennies and drinking black whiskey made out of goddamn rubbing alcohol.

Pathetic assholes, he thought, and drank more whiskey . . . And Hogman Gelnick, he knew that poor fuck's secret, afraid the guys would start riding him if they knew he was married, landing on him with their dumb fucking jokes, call her a schmuck-fucker or a Hebe-jeebie . . . sure, that was his secret, hidden from everybody but old Matt Larkin, not even a picture of her in his wallet or footlocker, and maybe he was smart to be scared, because Korbick had pounded on him around the clock all through basic just because he wasn't a Christer . . .

Larkin was suddenly drowsy and his thoughts had become erratic . . . What the hell did he care about the Hogman? "Hup-tup-thrup-four," he began shouting. "Left, tup, three, four! Your left, two, three, four—"

"Goddamn it, shut up, Matt," Docker called from the darkness.

Larkin blinked and realized with sodden surprise that he had finished off most of the black whiskey. . . .

Sergeant Docker made a check of the guard mount, exchanging a word with Corporal Trankic before joining the cook, Dormund, who sat on an outcropping of rock staring down a narrow trail leading into the valley. "Sarge, remember when we looked at planes on movie screens at Camp Stewart?"

"Dormund, when you were at Camp Stewart I was in Sicily."

"I keep forgetting that." Dormund frowned and rubbed his finger up and down his soft cheek. "We were in England when you took over, right after you got out of the hospital." Dormund turned and looked at Docker, a worried frown clouding his lumpy face. "I could never figure out them planes, sarge. They'd show little pictures on the screens and ask us what they were, and I never knew."

"All right, Chet, what did you see tonight?"

"Look, sarge, where'd you get hit in Sicily?"

"A place called Licata, the fourteenth of July, by a sniper I didn't see. I've told you that. Now cut this fucking crap. Did you see the same thing Larkin and Sonny Laurel reported to me tonight?"

Docker was on to him now, Dormund knew, and that brought a guilty heat to his face. But he wasn't going to tell him, not about a shape in the air that looked like it didn't have propellers, because that was crazy and if he told Sarge they'd get on him about it with the jokes that really scared him, about Trankic making a new head for him . . .

It had started in basic training. Trankic got mad at him about something and threatened to make a new head for him out of a tin can. Dormund remembered watching with growing nervousness while Trankic, with

a big metal shears, cut and fashioned a mouth and eyes
in a number ten can he'd got from the mess sergeant.
Dormund knew it wouldn't work, it was crazy, but it
scared him anyway when the other guys laughed and
Trankic began welding nuts and bolts and cartridge casings inside the big can. One night, after some beers,
Trankic, to Dormund's great relief, dumped the tin can
and its contents into the trash bins behind the mess
halls. But the fear stayed with Dormund and he'd decided to be sure to keep out of trouble after that and try
not to attract attention . . .

Avoiding Docker's eyes now, he said, "I didn't see
any wretched thing, sarge. I was getting the wretched
chow ready. That's a fact."

Footsteps sounded on the frozen ground as Trankic
walked up toward them from the guns. "Laurel's getting
something on the radio," he said. "You better check it
out, Bull."

Sonny Laurel and Kohler stood at the jeep listening
to a mix of static and voices sounding from the X-42.
When Trankic and Docker joined them, Laurel said, "I
thought it was England, sarge, because it was a British
voice. But that faded away to this."

They heard a sibilant voice saying, "*Amis, amis
. . .*" A brief tempest of static, then a new voice, a
deeper voice saying, "*Venez*—" After another eruption,
the French word for "come" was repeated several
times.

Then they distinctly heard the words "*La Chance, La
Chance . . .*"

"What's it mean, Bull?"

"I don't know. But *La Chance* means luck . . ."

After a stretch of whistling and windy silences, there
was a German word, spoken by a voice they hadn't
heard before.

The word was "*Vergeltung,*" followed by the numeral
four in French, repeated three times—"*quatre . . .*

quatre . . . quatre . . ." Then came an initial and
numeral—"*V-quatre.*" And again came the word:
"*Venez . . .*"

Docker knew the German word "*Vergeltung*" meant
"vengeance," and knew also that the Germans presently
had two operational V-weapons, the pilotless V-1 buzz
bombs and the V-2 rockets, which had been pounding
Liège and Antwerp and most of England for months.

And the V-3, Docker knew, had been a quarter-mile
system of cannons emplaced in massive concrete bunk-
ers at Calais, designed to fire salvos into the heart of
London at twelve-second intervals. Allied bombers
had destroyed the V-3 emplacements before the systems
were functional.

The next burst of words listed French and Belgian
towns—Malmédy, Nancy, Lepont, Houffalize—and
spaced emphatically between these place names were
the repeated initials and numerals: V-4 . . . V-4 . . .
V-4 . . .

The broadcast was interrupted by the unexpected ar-
rival of Corporal Larkin, who swayed drunkenly around
the side of a truck near the jeep, a canteen of whiskey
in his hand and only one arm through a sleeve of his
overcoat so that it trailed behind him on the ground like
a long, muddy skirt.

"I'll tell you assholes something," he was shouting.

Docker cut him off with an angry gesture. "Goddamn
it, shut up!"

"I'll tell you fuckers why Gelnick burned his fancy
uniform," Larkin said, and in tipping his head back to
drink from the canteen he lost his balance and fell in a
tangle of arms and legs against the side of the truck,
and from there in a heap to the ice-splintered ground.

Docker told Kohler and Sonny Laurel to take him
back to the jeep and when they were gone, the sergeant
and Trankic bent their heads again to the sputtering radio. They listened for another hour in the stinging winds
until the set went dead, but in that time they heard only
bursts of static and the word "luck" repeated over and

over again in French, and Docker could only hope that this was an omen for all of them that night, the fifteen soldiers detached and isolated in the vast white storms over the Ardennes.

Chapter Three

December 12, 1944. Koblenz, Germany.
Tuesday, 1900 Hours.

With an escort of flanking motorcycles, the convoy of military vehicles drove at speed through the blacked-out and empty streets of Koblenz, an industrial city fifty miles from the eastern borders of Belgium. In the first three cars with their drivers and aides were General Hasso Frieherr von Manteuffel (Fifth Panzer Army), General Erich Brandenberger (Seventh Army) and General Josef "Sepp" Dietrich (Sixth SS Panzer Army).

Trailing the tri-axled Mercedes-Benz command cars at orderly intervals were a dozen more staff vehicles carrying twenty-two generals of varying ranks who commanded the corps and divisions of Field Marshal Walter Model's Army Group B.

Security was maximum. Each intersection was guarded by troops from Department Four of the Reich Security Division, the Geheime Staats Polizei (Gestapo). Batteries of Panzer-IV tanks stood at alert formations in the fields and squares along the convoy's line of march. Antiaircraft cannons, 88-millimeter giants, had been emplaced at quarter-mile intervals along the route of the command cars.

The illumination was ghostly. Headlights tinted a deep night-blue made the curving roads barely visible in the diffused glow that glinted through spirals of heavy sleet and snow.

At a village the convoy was halted by details of Schutzstaffel (SS) troops standing guard near rows of parked trucks, swinging blackout lanterns.

There the generals and aides were escorted to trucks and when tailgates had been secured, the vans moved out on a circuitous route designed to bring them, after dozens of miles and many deliberately confusing stops and turns, to a courtyard facing a massive bunker built against the side of a mountain outside the city of Ziegenberg in Hesse—temporary headquarters of the OKW (Oberkommando der Wehrmacht), the "headquarters" being defined by the presence of the Reichsführer of Germany, Adolf Hitler. . . .

Colonel Karl Jaeger climbed across the tailgate of the truck that had brought him through the winter night from Koblenz. Dropping lightly onto the packed snow covering the courtyard, he gave an arm to his superior officer, Generalmajor Heinrich Kroll, a ranking commander of the Second SS Panzer Division (Das Reich) of General Josef "Sepp" Dietrich's Sixth SS Panzer Army.

Karl Jaeger's rank was the equivalent of a lieutenant colonel in the United States Army, but since Jaeger was a member of the SS Armed Forces, his title was that of an Obersturmbannführer, Waffen SS. (In the diaries of Edward G. Solvis, there is no mention of Jaeger's Waffen SS rank; he is referred to as "the Lieutenant Colonel" and on some occasions simply as "the Colonel.")

The convoy was quickly emptied of its high-ranking cargo.

Double ranks of SS troops were stationed at the entrance to the massive bunker, rifles at port arms, standards straining in high winds behind them. The Führer's personal flag was prominent, a swastika circled in gold leaf with a golden eagle in each quadrant. Flanking these pennants were flags displaying single black swastikas against fields of white and scarlet, emblems of the

First Company of the SS Leibstandarte, the Führer's
personal bodyguard.

An aide of Field Marshal Walter Model came
through the blackout curtains and instructed groups of
general officers to stand by to have their personal effects checked by security troops.

"There is no way to guess how long this will take,"
General Kroll said to Jaeger. "As far as I know, there is
not yet a final commitment to Christrose." The general
adjusted his Iron Cross so it hung neatly between the
lapels of his field-gray greatcoat. "I can only suggest
you make yourself as comfortable as possible."

The general returned Jaeger's salute and walked
across the crowded courtyard to join the other officers
who were opening briefcases and emptying their pockets
under the surveillance of SS guards.

Lieutenant Colonel Jaeger walked to the far side of
the enclosure where he found a wooden bench under a
windbreak of linden trees. Seating himself, he stared at
the great face of the bunker and the soldiers of Hitler's
personal bodyguard.

Snow and sleet fell through the blue headlights of the
trucks. The illumination coated the packed white snow
and spread across the courtyard to the flags and emblems of the Third Reich, gleaming on the red piping
running down the trousers of the general officers standing in line to be searched.

Karl Jaeger removed his gloves and opened the lapels
of his greatcoat to feel the winds on his muscular throat.
The blue lights touched the Iron Cross on his tunic, the
silver runes of the SS and the three emblems of his rank
on the collar tabs of his jacket. On the sleeve of his
tunic was the shoulder patch of Das Reich, a crusader's
shield with three horizontal bars within its borders.

Jaeger was tall and slender with coarse, fair hair and
luminous gray eyes in an angular face that was scored
with tensions. He would be thirty within a month and
had not smoked a cigarette for three hundred and
twenty days. This wasn't simply a matter of personal

health or fastidiousness, he was certain. But on the
other hand he wasn't quite sure why he had quit smoking. Whatever was wrong with him (why else quit
smoking?) Jaeger figured it wasn't physical. He had
been a soldier almost a third of his life and he had
fought for thirty-one months on the Russian fronts in
the campaigns code-named Barbarossa and Citadel,
the first attack in '41, the second in the massive clash of
armor at Kursk in '43. And in the invasion summer of
'44, he had been at Normandy and Avranches, when all
their divisions were at half strength, not like Barbarossa
where Goebbels had been able to proclaim: "The eastern continent of Europe lies like a limp virgin in the
arms of a mighty German Mars." Gross Deutschland
had been on the line then. With SS Totenkopf and SS
Leibstandarte, and to the south, Spain's Blue Division.

No, he still had the strength and stamina for war, but
in some fashion he had lost his ability to concentrate.
Or more accurately, he couldn't stop concentrating,
couldn't stop feeling and remembering things in the
past. It was the pressure of memory that created the
anxieties in him, that forced him to study the world with
what had become a bewildering and frustrating intensity . . .

Karl Jaeger still did have an occasional insidious
need for nicotine, and to distract himself had taken to
smoking a dry pipe. Feeling restless now, he took an old
black briar from his pocket and dug the stem into the
back of his hand until the pressure sent a searing pain
down into his numb fingers.

He just could not watch at ease and at peace, like a
dumb beast in a field, while the Gestapo searched officers whose names rang with honor down hundreds of
years of Prussian and German history. Kroll, von
Seeckt, Krueger, Lutz, von Manteuffel, Beck and Brandenberger and Guderian and Scheer and Jodl and von
Rundstedt . . . Yet if such security was necessary, his
thoughts were disloyal. Since von Faustenberg had
placed a bomb under the Führer's desk in East Prussia,

everyone in Germany had become a potential traitor and enemy. Von Faustenberg was dead, shot without a trial along with hundreds implicated in the plot, with even Field Marshal Rommel, the hero of the African desert campaigns, accepting a pellet of cyanide in return for a hero's funeral and a pension for his widow.

Hitler was damned by the world because he was absolute, because his character reduced principle to action. If that were cause for damnation, then what of Eamon de Valera and Simón Bolívar and Oliver Cromwell? Sanctified "heroes" now, Jaeger thought, like the American patriot, Abraham Lincoln, because they had all reduced their principles to ruthless action to preserve the strength and union of their countries . . .

When the search of the generals was completed, they filed through the blackout drapes into the bunker, which was known as Adlerhorst. Eagle's Aerie. A command car entered the courtyard and stopped with a whine of brakes in front of the Führer's personal guard.

Jaeger recognized the giant figure stepping from the car, Colonel Otto Skorzeny, presently the Führer's favorite among the junior officers in the Waffen SS. Skorzeny wore a black leather overcoat that fell in clean lines to his booted calves and against whose rich, dark lapels his Knight's Cross with diamonds glittered like a star. Accompanying the colonel was one of his senior aides, Captain Walter Brecht, a former Bavarian schoolteacher who savored the nickname he had acquired in Skorzeny's service—"Der Henker," "The Hangman."

There was no nonsense about a body search of Colonel Skorzeny. With Brecht at his side, the colonel greeted Hitler's personal bodyguard with a broad smile and swept past them into the Führer's bunker.

From the depths of Adlerhorst, the soldiers in the courtyard could hear the voice of the Führer, not as strong as it once had been, breaking now when he gasped for breath, but still dynamic and compelling when it rose high in the familiar, exalting cadences.

The meeting had gone on for hours; some of the drivers and junior officers were sleeping in the trucks. Others laughed and talked softly in groups, smoking and making late suppers of hot tea and spiced potato sandwiches.

Jaeger sat alone on the cold wooden bench thinking of Operation Greif, which logic dictated would be linked to Christrose if the latter became functional, and examining his dislike of Captain Brecht. He had met Skorzeny briefly on several occasions, but had spent almost three months with Brecht at the Military Academy in Berlin. Brecht was vain and supercilious, but that was hardly reason to be especially critical of him. Jaeger's thoughts troubled him; he had no right to sit in judgment of his country's soldiers, or Operation Greif.

He pressed the bit of his pipe into the back of his hand; on occasion physical pain was the only antidote for such disturbing concerns. Lately his mind had been driven constantly to embrace—or attempt to embrace—a variety of opposed concepts. He thought of the sacred and profane, tried to hold in mind at once the concepts of building and destroying, of flourishing and declining, belief and doubt, pleasure and pain . . . He abruptly realized with alarm that he had begun to breathe rapidly, the moisture on his forehead a mixture of sleeting snow and his own perspiration. His thoughts had involuntarily turned to Rudi Geldman and that had created other contradictions, Rudi in their home at Christmas, amused but envious in the presence of fir trees sparkling with candles and marzipan animals, or studying under the eye of Jaeger's father, but then later had come the persistent irreverence . . . "the sleep of reason in Germany, in which the beast in the blood stirs and wakens." The mocking of the Cornet Rilke . . . "The pale, romantic men of Germany seeking honor in death? *No.* The bayonets they sought were the cocks of

their fathers and what they yearned for were emasculat-
ing wounds to make them one with their mothers . . ."

Jaeger felt a spasm of anger. He had warned Rudi.
Even after they had taken him away, he had made inquiries. Guarded, of necessity, but the clerk at the Weimar camp had been in a gossiping mood: Rudi Geldman was a juicy capon, he had told Jaeger, and a lucky
one, sharing rations and bed with a senior officer, Captain Sturmer . . .

Jaeger was sweating in the cold winds. Another
wrenching thought . . . how could he be proud of
Christrose and ashamed of Operation Greif . . . ?

The heavy air raid curtains parted at the entrance to
the bunker, and Brecht—"Der Henker"—came through
the doors. When he noticed Jaeger seated alone under
the lindens, he crossed the courtyard to join him.

Brecht was in his late thirties, in excellent physical
condition; his slender body set off his uniform smartly.
His features were usually informed with a pleasantly
sardonic smile.

In an American Deep-South accent, he said, "Colonel, they ain't just whistlin' 'Dixie' in there. And you
can play that on your Jew's harp. It won't be magnolia
and honeysuckle for the Johnny Rebs holding Cemetery
Ridge."

Jaeger's own English was stiff but functional; he had
spent the equivalent of his high school years at a prepa-
ratory school in England. He glanced at Brecht now,
realizing that this could be one of "Der Henker" 's pa-
tronizing little traps. "Johnny Reb, as you probably
know, Captain, wasn't defending Cemetery Ridge. The
Confederate Army of Virginia, commanded by Long-
street and Pickett, was attacking it."

"It's good of you to set me straight, colonel, but the
metaphor stands. There'll be no old buttermilk sky for
Yanks *or* Rebs in the Ardennes next week." He studied
Jaeger. "I gather you don't approve of Operation Greif,
colonel. Is that correct?"

"That's correct, captain. I don't approve."

Still there was a troubling ambivalence in his thoughts. Operation Greif was necessary for the success of Christrose. And Operation Christrose would buy time and save German lives and might very possibly put an end to the enemy's shrill, irrational demands for unconditional surrender. He had been briefed on Greif by General Kroll: it would be commanded by Skorzeny and had been carefully designed to create terror and chaos behind the American lines in the Ardennes. Thousands of elite German troops, fluent in English, at ease with American slang, would infiltrate the fronts held loosely by General Middleton's VIII Corps. Wearing American uniforms and driving captured American jeeps and trucks, they would disrupt communications and destroy units already smashed or reeling under the striking force of Christrose . . .

"Colonel," Brecht was saying, "what disturbs you about it?"

"The fact that German soldiers captured in American uniforms will forfeit their rights as combatants. We can expect them to be shot in open fields after summary courts-martial or no hearings at all."

"Colonel, American soldiers have escaped from POW camps wearing German uniforms. The maquis have worn our uniforms. They've dressed as women to infiltrate our lines. Resistance groups pretend to be farmers or railroad workers to sabotage our transport and trains. It's deception, a ruse of war, nothing more. With respect, sir, you take the so-called conventions of warfare too seriously. Let me show you something . . ."

The captain pushed back the sleeve of his greatcoat. On "Der Henker"'s wrist was tattooed the slender figure of a woman with bright yellow hair, naked except for blue plumed fans positioned in front of her body. Underneath the tiny figure was the legend: "Chicago World's Fair: Miss Sally Rand."

Jaeger shrugged; it meant nothing to him. Brecht smiled. "It's a pleasure to repay the courtesy of your lecture on Johnny Reb, colonel. Sally Rand is an

American folk heroine, a striptease artiste, if you understand the term. So imagine a lecherous American soldier, a second-generation Slav, perhaps, who saw and lusted for Sally Rand in Chicago. Think of the stir in his balls when we hail each other in the Ardennes and I show him this tattoo, a living reminder of Chicago with its Drake Hotel and Palmer House, Polish sausage and Al Capone and the stench of the stockyards. You can see, colonel, that while that Polski is leering at Sally Rand's little red nipples, I'll have no trouble at all blowing his head off."

"You may find that personally very amusing, Brecht. But it is not honorable and it is not warfare."

Brecht laughed softly. "You criticize us for not playing fair? Let me give you some advice. If we lose this war, the verdict returned against us will be monstrous. So, as soldiers and patriots, I think we should do everything in our power to *deserve* that verdict. I find it unfortunate that so many German soldiers are now beginning to pretend that this or that event did not take place. For one example, the reprisals by your own division at Oradour-sur-Glane this year. Already the quasi-official line is blaming that on a few overly zealous hotheads."

Jaeger shrugged. "My battalion wasn't at Oradour, we were under forced march to the Normandy beachheads."

"But thank God there were other soldiers ready and willing to put a torch to the village. I know, I know"— he made a dismissing gesture with his hand—"there's pious talk of women and children, but do you seriously believe, colonel, that Allied airmen are concerned about the age or sex of the Germans they are killing by the thousands with their bombs? Do you honestly think those pilots distinguish between schools and hospitals and marshaling areas? Well, I suppose those are the facts of war. And the fact is that the maquis attacked the flanks of Das Reich and the village of Oradour paid for it. The only medals the Resistance can expect are the tears of their women. Do you think that's a callous attitude?"

"No, I think it's sentimental and cheap." Jaeger saw he had scored a point; a quick anger strained the captain's face.

"You disapprove of me, which I find strange at this stage of the game. If we aren't all sinners by now, we haven't been trying." His voice sharpened a bit. "You knew Rudi Geldman, I believe?"

The talk of Oradour had stirred Jaeger's anxiety. The mention of Rudi intensified it.

"As a matter of fact, yes."

"You know then that he's dead."

"Yes, someone mentioned it to me."

"He had an impressive mind." Brecht's tone became more casual. "Quite sinuous. I read a few of his articles when such activity was permissible. You know, it might have been all for the best if we'd bombed the concentration camps into the dust when they were first filled, the guards as well as the inmates." He studied Jaeger thoughtfully. "You understand, colonel, I'm being whimsical, not heretical. Still, there must be a symbiotic relationship between the jailer and his prisoner. I taught history, you know, and such matters interest me. After the war I would like to produce the plays of Lope de Vega and Lorca in German. I was at Guernica. There is something fascinating and paradoxical in the Spanish character, a merciless cruelty rooted in a fierce intolerance of spiritual error. But that's not my point. Who was it attracted whom in our camps, I wonder? Did the inmates act as magnets to a certain type of guard? Or did our death-head commandants with their whips and pederasty have an irresistible lure for a certain type of victim?"

A soft ridge of snow was dislodged from a tree limb by a gusting wind. It fell on the collar of Jaeger's greatcoat, and when he brushed it off his fingers touched the frozen metal of his SS runes.

"It was odious and reprehensible what they did to

young Geldman," the captain said. "But considering his name, there was a certain irony to it." Taking a silver flask from the inner pocket of his greatcoat, Brecht turned the cap back with his thumb. "Would you care for a drink?"

"No, thank you." Jaeger glanced at his watch. "You obviously want to tell me something, Brecht. So you'd better get on with it."

"Do you know how Geldman died, colonel?"

"There was no reason for anyone to make a report of the matter to me."

"Didn't you try to find out what happened? I understood you were friends."

"For a time we were students together in Dresden."

"Ah, that lovely city. It was at your father's school that you were classmates, I've been told."

"That's quite true." Jaeger stood and walked under the lindens, pressing the stem of his pipe into the back of his hand and remembering in shifting images the prize books in his father's classroom at graduation, the look of the river and wooded parks in Dresden, and some words from *The Death of Cornet Rilke* . . . "Mother, be proud, I carry the flag, I carry the flag."

The captain strolled beside him, the reflections from the snowy limbs of the trees touching the braid on their uniforms. As if sensing Jaeger's thoughts he said, "A pity there is no longer time for such loyalties, colonel."

It was obvious he intended to say more, but Jaeger heard a stir in the dark courtyard and saw with relief that the meeting at Adlerhorst was over, the generals filing through the bunker's blackout curtains.

"Another time, Brecht," Jaeger said, and walked quickly to join General Kroll, feeling the wind searing the sweat on the backs of his hands.

Chapter Four

First Lieutenant Whitter arrived at Section Eight's gun position as first light was beginning to spread across the valley. The heavy-weather front was holding; fogs and snow continued to produce visibility-zero conditions throughout the Ardennes.

Whitter was accompanied by a corporal from the battery motor pool, Cleve Haskell, and his junior officer, Second Lieutenant Donald Longworth, a career soldier with nine years in the regular Army.

Lieutenant Bart Whitter had been in the Army three years. A vertical white stripe was painted on the front of his helmet, and the silver single bars of his rank were clipped to the epaulets on his field overcoat. He was short and stocky, with light brown hair and a fair complexion that had reddened and peeled painfully in the battalion's basic training at Camp Stewart near Hinesville, Georgia. Although born and raised in the Deep South in Mobile, Alabama, Lieutenant Whitter never tanned, even when he smeared himself with cocoa butter. Still, he had always been proud of his pink and sensitive skin; in a state whose white majorities applied visual litmus paper tests to everyone as a matter of course, Whitter had decided early in life that it was no asset to tan darkly or display a tolerance for strong sunlight.

41

The lieutenant was twenty-nine. He believed in the customs and traditions of the service, military courtesy and discipline, and in RHIP—initials embodying the army concept that "rank has its privileges." Whitter enjoyed rolling the letters on his tongue and lips, seeming to taste them there like warm molasses, and in his native accent they came drawling out as, "Ah, Aich, Ah, Pee."

His father was a county sheriff whose family had been planters and soldiers before the Civil War. Whitter was fond of quoting his father. "Pappy believed in full bellies for them that worked and did right, and full prisons for them 'at din't. He tol' me, 'Pessimists say prisons are only half-full. Optimists know they just half-*empty.*' "

Some of Whitter's plantation mannerisms were employed for what he obviously hoped would be a humorous effect. His accent was not always consistent; it tended toward canebrake darky rhythms and resonances when he was in a frivolous or good-old-boy mood and was also pronounced when he spoke of more serious matters such as the value of regular church attendance and personal hygiene and white virginity. When he was impatient or angry, the accent tended to disappear.

Whitter climbed down now from the jeep and returned Docker's salute. "All your men okay, sergeant?"

"Yes, sir."

"And how about supplies? Got plenty of ammo and gasoline?"

"We're in good shape, lieutenant."

"Then I'd like to know why in hell you stopped here. My last orders to you were to continue moving east." Whitter stared at the cannon and machine guns, which were masked with camouflage netting. "Now it looks like you bedded down for the fucking duration. How come?"

When Docker explained why he had decided to stop, Whitter said, "You got your wind up because some old Belgian fart wouldn't take Army money? Shit, you should know better. These people don't know what they want anymore. Used to be every whore and bartender wanted Invasion loot. Now you're spooked 'cause an old fool wants Belgian money that don't even make good craphouse paper."

"I didn't see any point in taking a chance," Docker said.

"Well, sometimes that makes sense. And sometimes it sure as hell don't. Now fall your section in."

Docker gave the orders to Larkin and accompanied Whitter and Lieutenant Longworth on an inspection of the gun position. When they had completed the tour, Larkin had formed the section into two columns in front of the trucks.

Whitter looked them over. "All right, men, I know it's snowing, and colder than a witch's tit, but we still got to try to look like soldiers. Let's dress down and get to attention now."

Corporal Larkin slowly spit on the ground and looked with eloquent blankness at the low, drifting fogs.

"You heard the lieutenant, goddamn it," he said. "Try to remember there's a fucking war on. Drop your cocks and grab your socks and try to look like soldiers. You want a fucking example, look at Haskell here. There's some spit and polish for you."

Corporal Haskell was built widely and massively, with sloping shoulders and a bulging stomach that looked like blubber but was actually hard as a tree trunk. His fatigue uniforms were usually oil-stained from his work at the motor pool and he seldom shaved more than twice a week, a dispensation from Captain Grant because of a persistent rash that mottled the skin under his heavy whiskers.

When Larkin pointed at him and said, "Just look at the fine figure of the corporal there," Spinelli and Tubby Gruber looked at the ground and tried to suppress their laughter.

Haskell stared at Larkin, tight little grin bunching rubbery cheeks around his eyes.

"Jesus, you're a real clown," he said. "I guess Fred Allen and them other funny guys pay you hush money to keep you off the radio."

Docker knew that Haskell was no one for Larkin to antagonize; Haskell could be violent, brutal, and a streak in him relished it.

"At ease," Docker said to the section. "Settle down now."

The men dressed right and came to attention. Whitter was puzzled and relieved; something had been starting between Haskell and that sarcastic son of a bitch Larkin, and Docker had put a stop to it with just a few words.

"All right, let's get this I and E bullshit over with," the lieutenant said. "For your Information and Education, you're up to your ass in snow and shit somewhere in Belgium. I hope that don't come as no big surprise. We just got word at Battalion that our B-29s are flying daylight raids for the first time and pounding the honorable shit out of Tokyo. In Italy—our boys there just rammed a big firecracker up Mussolini's ass and they're holding a match to the fuse right this minute."

Whitter grinned at the men, encouraging them, for the moment, to forget his silver bars and the wall of rank between them, to relax and join him in a bit of soldier-to-soldier camaraderie. The men declined the invitation; their faces remained impassive and their eyes stared through him.

Well, they didn't know how fucking tough it was, he thought. Or they just didn't give a shit. They probably figured his rank and an occasional bottle of whiskey made up for it. Or they were too damn ignorant—he looked resentfully at the new corporal, Schmitzer, and at Trankic and the kids in the section, Laurel and Farrel, he didn't even know the names of the others, just that they were still babies with damn little use for the razor blades they'd been issued . . . Still and all, he wanted their approval, and needed to anesthetize a curious irritation at the way Docker had handled whatever

it was between Haskell and Larkin. So he proceeded to
announce to the section what he hadn't intended to tell
them, what in fact had been told him in total confidence
only that morning by Captain Grant and the battalion
commander, Lieutenant Colonel Leary.

"Now I don't want you men to be spreading this
around, but you're not rag-ass rookies, you got a
right—hell, you *earned* a right—to know what's going
on." Whitter rubbed his mittened hands together
briskly. "Every report we've had for the last ten days
tells us the same thing: we got the enemy in a goddamn
meat grinder. They're nothing but kraut sausage and
kraut hamburger now. With any luck at all, we could be
startin' home by Christmas . . ."

"Come here, Little Sicily, I want to talk to you."

Corporal Haskell took Carmine Spinelli by the arm
and led him down the hill a dozen yards from the cannon, where he stopped and poked Spinelli in the chest
with a finger the size of a gnarled sausage.

Spinelli tried to pull away, but Haskell grinned and
tightened his grip.

"Little Sicily, when Larkin was being a fucking wise
guy, I had an idea you were laughing at me."

"No, I wasn't. Why would I do a dumb thing like
that?"

"Little Sicily, I hear you guys still got some of that
black booze Trankic made in Normandy."

"What's this 'Little Sicily' shit? I got nothing against
you."

"No offense, Little Sicily." Haskell continued to
smile, his cheeks bunching and creasing the flaking skin
under his whiskers. When he prodded him again, Spinelli gasped with pain.

"What you want with me?"

"You're not listening. I told you. I want some of that
black whiskey."

"What whiskey?"

"Now don't fuck with me, ginzo," Haskell said

quietly. "The stuff Trankic made from the alcohol he stole at Utah Beach."

"Utah Beach?" Spinelli was recovering some of his confidence; he was safe enough here, so close to the rest of the section that he could almost enjoy the anger darkening Haskell's muddy eyes. "What you talking about?"

Haskell glanced around; no one was watching them. "I told you once, don't fuck with me, you little wop cocksucker."

"Go shit in your hat and punch it."

Haskell smiled. "Know something, ginzo? I'm gonna say you called me a mother-fucker. Which I don't take from anybody. So they'll understand I had to slap them words back down your throat."

"Aw, c'mon," Spinelli said, "I didn't mean nothing. It was just a joke."

He started to back away, but Haskell spun him around as effortlessly as he would a small child. Holding him by the lapels of his jacket, Haskell drew back his hand, abruptly lowered it when Docker said from behind him, "All right, knock it off, Haskell."

"This ain't any of your business," Haskell said. "Unless you want to make it."

"Let me tell you something. Everything that goes on in this gun section is my business. Take your hands off Spinelli."

Haskell stood perfectly still for a moment. Then he nodded slowly. He put his hands on his hips and looked off at the mountains, vague, insubstantial shapes in the rolling fogs. Then: "Okay, Docker, I'll see you around one of these days. Maybe someplace where we can forget them sergeant's stripes of yours."

"Kiss off, Haskell," Docker said, and walked back to the guns with Spinelli.

Lieutenant Whitter took a small ledger and pencil from an inner pocket of his overcoat and made notes of his final orders to Sergeant Docker.

"You head out due east toward a Belgian town called Werpen, it's on your grid maps. It's ten, fifteen miles from here but I don't know how in hell them mountain roads are, so be ready for some shoveling. Like I told your men, there ain't a kraut left between here and the Rhine, but just in case you run into anything you can't handle, you got a fall-back position, a town called Lepont on the Salm, which is about eight or ten miles northwest of here. If you don't have to fall back, keep heading east after you get to Werpen." Whitter studied his notes, nodded and tucked the ledger into his pocket. "I know something's bothering you, Docker. So talk or shake a bush. It's a democratic army, too goddamn democratic if you ask me—so go ahead and spit it out."

"Just a suggestion that we tone down this talk about starting home by Christmas."

"You didn't say anything about that," Whitter said. "I'm the one said it. And I'm about to say something else." Whitter patted the silver bar on his shoulder. "That little piece of brass says I can say anything I want to your gun section."

"I think I understand what Docker's getting at," Longworth said.

Whitter stared at him. "I wasn't talking to you, was I, lieutenant?"

"No, you weren't," Longworth said, and climbed into the rear of the jeep.

Lieutenant Whitter grinned and eased himself in beside the driver, Haskell. "Okay, maybe I was wrong," he said. "However, that's one of the privileges of being an officer, Docker. Screwin' up. It's what Ah, Aich, Ah, Pee is all about. Just don't you screw up, sergeant, 'cause that ain't one of your privileges. You keep everybody on the ball."

The jeep rolled down the hill, disappearing into the fogs, and soon the throb of its motor faded and the silence settled again through the valleys of the Ardennes.

Chapter Five

The command car traveled at speed through country
roads and into the blacked-out environs of the city of
Koblenz. The skies were heavily overcast with smoke
and fogs. General Heinrich Kroll took a sealed envelope
from his pocket and gave it to Karl Jaeger.

"Don't open it just yet," he said.

Heinrich Kroll was slender, with narrow features and
gray eyes enlarged in rather startling fashion by steel-
rimmed high-correction glasses. The general's manner
was elegant, his uniform neat, and in street clothes he
would have blended easily with a gathering of lawyers,
engineers or civil servants.

Deep blue illumination from the headlights and dashboard surrounded the command car in a cocoon of hazy
reflections that splintered softly on Kroll's slightly bared
teeth and thick eyeglasses.

"Remember what I'm about to tell you," the general
said. "Armies gain glory in victory but they achieve immortal character in defeat. From this moment on, Jaeger, you must think and speak and act as if you are
under surveillance by generations of unborn Germans.
What you think will be known, what you speak will be
heard, what you do will be *seen*. Always keep that fore-
most in your mind."

48

General Kroll had history on his mind, Jaeger realized. Appropriate for an historic mission . . . Operation Christrose, he explained, would be launched at three minutes past seven on the morning of December 16th. It would begin with infantry attacks, supported by long-range artillery, to be followed by the assault of three Panzer armies on an eighty-mile front from Monschau south to the border of Luxembourg. The units to be committed were: The Fifth Panzer Army, General Hasso von Manteuffel commanding—four Panzer, three infantry divisions. The Sixth Waffen SS Panzer Army, General Josef "Sepp" Dietrich commanding—four Panzer and five infantry divisions. The Seventh Army, General Eric Brandenberger commanding—six infantry and one Panzer division. In reserve, to be used at the discretion of Field Marshal von Rundstedt, was a force of four Panzer and four infantry divisions. One of the spearhead units to break first from the Christrose start-line would be Kampfgruppe "Peiper," under the command of SS Colonel Joachim Peiper, whose mission would be to strike toward Vielsalm and Werbomont on its drive toward France. These elements would be supported by paratroopers, and by Colonel Skorzeny's Operation Greif commandos, wearing American uniforms and driving captured American vehicles.

"And most importantly," the general continued, "the Messerschmitt-262s are fully functional. A revolutionary power source, rocket jets, replacing the conventional engines. Those planes are flying now, Jaeger, the logical successor to the V-1 and V-2s. I had serious misgivings about these sorties—but Goering would have his way. He insisted the 262s, or V-4s as Der Führer prefers to call them, needed additional testings at low altitudes. His pilots are instructed not to engage the enemy, but can you trust hot-blooded young men with so much power in their hands?"

General Kroll turned and smiled at Jaeger. "In power dives the 262s are breaking through Mach One. They

will make the American Flying Fortresses look like
flying cows."

Jaeger remembered the Messerschmitt test pilot who
had first flown the Luftwaffe's M-262 jet in July of
1942—Fritz Wendel. Jaeger had been sent with a group
of artillery officers to observe a demonstration at a field
near Peenemünde and could remember how it looked, a
streak of silver burning through the white skies. After
the flight they had drunk a toast to Fritz Wendel, a slim
young civilian who had been eager to explain the design
and principle of the revolutionary new plane. They were
not much older than Jaeger himself, these men of rockets and Peenemünde, but they had had a special look in
their eyes. Almost obsessed, he had thought.

"The Führer trusts his instincts on Christrose and so
do I," Kroll was saying. "The operation has the four
essential elements: secrecy, surprise, a massive concentration of strength against weakness and last but far
from least, it has the element of terror in it. Yes, I trust
Hitler in this area. Can you recognize his inspiration?"

The answer seemed obvious. "Vom Krieg?" Jaeger
said.

"Yes, of course," General Kroll nodded emphatically. "They can't get away from him."

Jaeger's thoughts were again flooded with memories
of Rudi Geldman.

General Kroll was saying, "I'm now fifty-seven, Jaeger. My father, Heinrich, was born in 1846. He married
late. And my grandfather, Reinhard, was born in 1783.
When he was of age, he attended the Berlin Military
Academy with—" The general smiled. "You know this,
of course, but my grandfather was a classmate of von
Clausewitz . . ."

Christmas in Dresden and Rudi singing the old
hymns with the Jaeger family, his smile mischievous at
his own apostasy, and around them the candles and the
animals at the manger and the smell of the roast goose
his mother always made with chestnuts and apple pancakes . . .

"It is one of the small but justifiable conceits of our family that Grandfather Reinhard mav have contributed in some small fashion to Vom Krieg when he and Clausewitz were at the Academy . . ."

They had hiked through the woods beyond Dresden, Hedy with them, and they had swum in cold lakes ringed with green trees . . .

"I'd planned like Rundstedt to be retired long before this. I would like to have a home in the country, close to a city with a good library . . ."

What a great, scholarly classroom a defeated Germany would be, Jaeger thought with a spasm of painful humor. Everyone at blackboards with leather patches on the elbows of old jackets. Smoking pipes, painting seascapes. "Der Henker" thoughtfully rehearsing the plays of Lorca and Lope de Vega, illuminating them with personal insights from Guernica. And General Kroll peddling his bicycle toward the local library, a white-haired figure in rough tweeds, to read about Bismarck and Frederick the Great and Hamilcar Barca . . .

"It gives me satisfaction, Jaeger, to know that my ancestors served with Clausewitz against Napoleon. In my grandfather's time there were only professional armies. Military service was a career, like the law or the church. There was no talk of dying to the last man, less of God or king or country. Hopeless battles were not fought. The commanders with inferior forces simply withdrew from the field.

"Napoleon put an end to this tradition by raising an army of patriots. Imagine how this must have struck the professionals . . . to expect peasants, who knew only their meager farms and villages, to fight and die for the concept of a *nation*, an idea which could have had no more reality to them than distant stars, they thought. But Napoleon proved that such patriots would follow their flags into the mouths of cannons. And with them he burned to cinders all the known maps of Europe. And Napoleon said—and think, Jaeger, how many divisions this would be worth in the field today—'The boundaries of a nation's greatness are marked only by the graves of her soldiers and heroes.' "

They drove in silence for several minutes through winding streets toward the center of the city.

Then General Kroll said quietly, "This is our last fling of the dice."

Jaeger's head felt heavy; blood pounded in his ears. He could hardly hear General Kroll now and his thoughts were becoming disturbingly erratic. The songs of Christmas and the blue sheen of lakes in summer, the cheese and coarse bread and young wine on the banks soft and shiny with moss and pine needles. A strange and lovely road to take to the camp at Weimar—

"How long since you've had leave, Jaeger?"

"Nineteen months, sir."

"Not even a day with Hedy and the girls?"

"No, sir."

The general was smiling. "Open your orders now."

Karl Jaeger peeled back the flap of the sealed envelope and, when he recognized the priority orders for rail transport from Koblenz to Dresden, his tightly reined emotions almost betrayed him; he felt a sting of tears in his eyes.

"Twenty-four hours, Jaeger. It was all I could manage."

Jaeger didn't trust himself to speak, but he did allow himself a forbidden luxury. In the darkness of the speeding command car, with bitter winds in his face, he closed his eyes and permitted himself to think of his wife and children.

Chapter Six

December 13, 1944. Lepont, Belgium.
Wednesday, 1400 Hours.

In the gloom of an afternoon laced with snow, a boy named Alain ran along the cobblestone streets that twisted through the village of Lepont, a cluster of old stone houses on the banks of the River Salm.

The boy was fourteen but dwarflike in appearance; five years of wartime privation had checked his growth and pinched his features and the lack of fats in his diet had given him the lusterless skin and hair of an old man. As he hurried through the square, past the Church of the Holy Spirit, the clatter of his wooden shoes was almost lost in the sweep of wind off the river. At the edge of the town, where the village merged with the fields, he stopped at a house and knocked insistently on the schoolteacher's door.

When Denise Francoeur opened it Alain gave her the message from his brother, Jocko. She nodded and turned quickly to collect her heavy cloak from a hall tree. The young woman and the boy then hurried toward the village square to Jacques Berthier's café. Wind coming across the Salm filled her cloak like a sail and she almost lost her balance on the slick stones. She was breathing raggedly, hating the sick, familiar fear she had lived with for so many years. When the German garrison had pulled out of Lepont three months earlier her fears had gradually retreated with them, but now the terrors were alive again.

Denise Francoeur would be twenty-five on her next birthday. Four years before, her husband, Etienne, along with most of the young and able-bodied men of Lepont, had been sent off to slave labor camps in Germany. She had not heard from him in twenty-six months. The last letter had come from East Prussia . . .

Jocko Berthier waited for them in the shadows of the church. He was short and thick, with stocky legs, but with a back so crippled that his body was bent almost parallel to the ground and his neck was perpetually cramped from looking up to meet the eyes of everyone but the children of the village.

When his brother and the schoolteacher came into the square, Jocko led them to his café, where the name—La Chance—was spelled out in cracked gilt letters on veined glass windows shrouded with blackout curtains.

The café was bitterly cold and the only illumination came from a squat candle on a table near the window. Five or six women of the village huddled near the cold stove, pinched, worn faces framed in rough shawls, and they began talking noisily when Denise Francoeur and the Berthiers entered, accusing voices directed at two people who stood apart from them, an old man and a child with a red scarf covering most of her face.

Jocko silenced them with a gesture of his crippled arm, but it was Denise Francoeur who calmed them with a teacher's skill. "Please go home and take care of your own families. Forget that you've been here. Don't talk about it, not even to Father Juneau. That way you won't be involved. If anyone asks, you can honestly say you don't know anything. Do you understand that?"

"We're sick of it all. We've had enough martyrs, Denise," a woman named Madame Homais said.

"Then go home," the schoolteacher said.

When Madame Homais turned to the door, she was

followed in a rush by the others, and soon they were all
sweeping off like dusty bats down the dark streets and
Denise Francoeur was saying to Alain, "Take Margret
to my home now."

When the children had left, Jocko went to the bar
and poured a glass of schnapps for the old man.

"Some of those old witches are cousins of mine,"
Claude Girard said, after downing the drink and smack-
ing his lips. "Such Flemish dung."

"Why did you bring Margret here?" Jocko said.

The old man's story was confused and wandering, his
estimates of time and dates blurred by his fears, but
Jocko and the teacher listened to him quietly and pa-
tiently because they knew the same fears themselves.

Some farmers, Claude Girard told them, and people
working in the woods east and north of Verviers, had
seen German trucks and German soldiers. The rumors
had spread through the villages. German soldiers were
thick as the trees in the Ardennes, hidden by heavy fog.

"But did you see any of them?" Jocko said.

"No, but I heard people talking."

"Are you a crazy old bastard running from shadows
and rumors?"

"They aren't shadows." Claude Girard pounded the
bar with his hand. "I know about these things. I was at
the Marne when the soldiers came to the trenches in
taxicabs."

"To hell with the *merde* Marne and the *merde* taxicabs," Jocko said. "You listened to rumors and you
took the girl and brought her here. Is that all it is?"

"No, there was more."

Some farmers had seen German soldiers with SS insignia, Girard told them. They saw this, Claude Girard
said, and wet his fingertip and drew the outline of a
shield in the dust on top of Jocko's bar. Licking his finger again, the old man carefully drew three vertical lines
inside the shield.

"And they saw that," he said.

The emblem he had drawn so crudely meant nothing

to Denise. She glanced at Jocko, who studied it without expression and dismissed it with a shrug.

"I was frightened, I didn't wait, I took Margret away with me," the old man said. "We followed the river staying on old paths. I had brandy with me and we found potatoes and turnips on the way. On the second day, when it was almost dark, we met Americans, four soldiers. They asked me about Germans. I gave them vegetables. They gave me a hundred francs and chocolate for Margret."

"Where did you meet the Americans?" Jocko said.

"Twenty or thirty kilometers from Werpen. I brought her here because I didn't know where else to take her . . . If you've got a place I can sleep, I'll go back to Verviers in the morning. Without the girl, I'm just an old farmer walking in his fields."

Jocko told him there was an extra bed in Alain's room, and when the old man shuffled through a door to the rear of the house, Jocko looked at the teacher and said, "A drink?"

"No, I'll go home." But she changed her mind. "Yes. Do you think they're coming back?"

"Yes, they'll be back."

"Why are you so sure? You treated Claude like a foolish old woman."

"Because I didn't want him babbling like a foolish old woman. Look." He pointed to the shield Claude Girard had drawn on the bar. "You see what it is? The crusader's shield of Das Reich."

"Oradour," she said.

"And if Das Reich is on the line . . ." Jocko's voice was suddenly weary. The others would be there with them, he told her, the Leibstandarte, the Totenkopf, the Horst Wessel. . . .

Jocko poured two drinks and the moving candlelight sent the shadows of his crippled arms leaping across the walls and ceiling.

"Still, Denise, Coutreau told me that he and his son

have seen only Americans between St. Vith and Malmédy for weeks."

She crossed herself and said, "Will you come by and fix a place for Margret?"

"Yes, I can do that." He sipped his drink and looked at her. "You're the only one in the village who cares to remember me as I used to be."

"It will end, Jocko," Denise said, touching his hand and placing her empty glass down firmly on Das Reich's crusader shield.

She drew the heavy cloak about her shoulders and went out. A faint sound was rising on the air, the rush of night winds circling the church steeple in the square of the village.

Chapter Seven

December 13, 1944. Werpen, Eastern
Belgium. Wednesday, 1630 Hours.

Docker's jeep was parked in the main square of Werpen, a small village of red brick homes above a narrow
tributary of the Our River. Section Eight's guns were
positioned at both ends of the main street, pointing in
opposite directions to give the weapons clear fields of
fire over the farmlands stretching out from the town.

It was a cold and overcast afternoon with snow and
sleet sweeping over the square and battering the old
church and shops around it.

According to the map Docker was studying with
Schmitzer, Werpen was roughly between the big towns
of Malmédy and St. Vith but a good deal closer than
either to the borders of Germany.

The town was empty except for prowling cats and a
few barking dogs tied up in gardens. Fires smoldered in
some of the small homes, and in many of them half-
eaten meals were still set out on tables and stoves. But
the people of Werpen had apparently fled east with the
retreating German troops. There wasn't a cart or bicycle
or baby carriage left in the village. Cowsheds and
chicken coops were empty, as was the tabernacle in the
cold church, its tiny golden door standing open.

Docker had sent out two details to make house-to-
house sweeps. Corporal Larkin, with Spinelli, Pierce

and Gruber, had taken one side of the main street, while Kohler and Sonny Laurel, with Trankic, were checking the other, rifles off safe as they went slowly through the silent dwellings.

Dormund and Gelnick had set up a gasoline stove in the lee of the town's fountain and were opening K-rations and brewing coffee. The fountain was dry, its bottom covered with a solid mixture of mud and leaves. A fluted marble column rose a dozen feet above the basin, and on this pedestal stood the slender marble figure of a huntsman, frozen by its creator in the act of drawing an arrow from a quiver slanted across its ice-slick shoulders.

Fog hung low over the town and the snow flew in blinding currents around the soldiers moving in and out of the empty shops and homes. Heavy sleet fell with tiny hissing explosions into the hot coffee Dormund poured into canteen cups, flakes working their way down the collar of Docker's heavy jacket.

Corporal Schmitzer looked at the silent snow-curtained streets. "Empty towns like this spook me, sarge. We seen 'em in Tunisia."

"I know, you figure somebody's got a bad conscience." Docker folded the map and tucked it under the dashboard of the jeep. "Keep an eye on things. I'm going to inspect the guns."

"Sarge, the motor of your jeep is running rough. Want me to check it? I won't strip it down. Just tune it. We got to snap shit out of here, we can haul ass."

Docker decided then that he could depend on Schmitzer, which gave him Trankic, Solvis and a few of the others. "Okay, check it," he said.

Schmitzer poured gasoline from a jerry can into a bucket and collected rags from the rear of the jeep, then stood watching Docker's tall figure swinging into the sleet toward the machine guns.

The jeep's motor was the only sound in the deserted town as snow fell on the engine block and evaporated in a series of sputtering eruptions.

Gelnick was eating from a can of K-rations with his fingers; cheese and bacon bits rimmed his brush mustache with yellow flecks.

Schmitzer said to him, "Gelnick, why don't you heat some water in your helmet and give yourself a bath?"

A smile appeared on Gelnick's lips. "Sarge told me to help Chet with the chow."

"Then why in hell aren't you?"

"I was taking a break." Gelnick's smile was obsequious, practiced, but he was thinking, Fuck you, you monkey clown, shit on you, it would end and he would have Doris and his family instead of this rotten war which was just another fucking game loaded against him. Sergeant Korbick had tried to kill him back in that stinking Camp Stewart, but he couldn't break him, no one could, not even Docker with his goy's guilt, and so he'd make it, he thought, all the way back to Doris and home—

"So snap some ass," Schmitzer said.

"Sure thing, you just watch me." Gelnick smiled again and gave the corporal a big sweeping salute.

Schmitzer cleaned the spark plugs of Docker's jeep. The engine sounded better then, not perfect, but he couldn't do much more without stripping it. (Suddenly his thoughts burned again with a need for Sonny Laurel.)

To distract himself, Schmitzer emptied the bucket of gasoline, folded the rags and walked aimlessly around the fountain, staring at the stone archer and forcing himself to imagine what his Uncle Ernie would have said about it. He'd probably have shouted that it was put up by working stiffs so rich people could walk by it on fine nights with their ladies while a fat priest bowed to them from the church. Yeah, that's what Uncle Ernie would say. He'd say the workers would get nothing but a cup of gruel and a shafting for using their stupid backs to make a statue that was just for rich people to smile at. Yes, he'd have said things like that if they hadn't broken his crazy head in prison in Barcelona

. . . . Schmitzer's mother and father hadn't known for a long time that Ernie was in prison. They'd just stopped hearing from him. He had written from Madrid, letters full of excitement and bullshit about meeting writers and reporters. No way to know whether it was true or not, because Ernie was always half-crazy anyway, joining weird groups, picketing plants he'd never punched a time clock in . . . Uncle Ernie was like a dog in heat to get to Spain. Then they'd got a handwritten Christmas card from him in Spanish, and that's when they knew he was in jail. He must have got someone to write it for him, and bribed a guard to get it out.

> Jamas iran al olvido—
> Aquellas pascuas pasadas—
> Inolvidables han sido—
> Las familiares veladas—

Schmitzer took it to a high school teacher who had liked him and she had translated it for him. But it was Schmitzer's father who figured out what the poem really meant because he saw that the first letter of each line, in Spanish and in English, spelled out the word J-A-I-L.

> Just remember, I'll never forget—
> All those Christmas days gone by—
> Ineradicably stamped in my head—
> Lovely memories are held high—

The little poem told them what had happened to Uncle Ernie—and what a wild story he would have made about how he had suckered the Spanish jailers with that message, except they'd split his head and killed him before he had a chance to tell everybody how smart he was. But what the hell was he doing off in Spain with a lot of other crazy Americans, anyway, what the fuck business was it of theirs . . . ?

Schmitzer checked the jeep again; it sounded fine,

but he couldn't concentrate on the rhythmic thrust of
the pistons, the smooth hum of the motor, or even what
was around him, Dormund pumping the stoves and Gelnick still feeding his face with the cheese and bacon.
The snow and sleet that cut his cheeks and the backs of
his wrists, he tried to think about that, tried consciously
to *feel* it, but he couldn't, not any more than he could
keep his mind on the statue of the archer and his crazy
Uncle Ernie dead in Barcelona or even the other deaths
that were always present in his mind, his father with the
gun in his hand at the empty coal bin and the portholes
welded shut on the *Lex*. They had all become shadows
through which the face of Sonny Laurel stared at him,
lips soft and curved in laughter, eyes clear and fresh
and gay . . . Schmitzer had tried to convince himself
over the past few days that his pleasure in the boy was
only natural, the way he'd probably feel about anything
that pleased him . . . like a freshly ironed shirt, a hot
meal at a table, a shower he didn't have to share with a
dozen other guys . . . it was normal enough, wasn't it,
for a veteran noncom to look after a raw recruit, help
him on the guns, answer his questions? The effort it
took to justify this had made Schmitzer sullen, resentful;
his feelings were so close to the surface that he had begun to imagine that some of the men in the section were
watching him. Screw them, he had nothing to apologize
for. Hell, the proof of it was a talk he'd had with Laurel
a day or so ago . . . They were together in the cab of
the truck and Sonny had said he'd been afraid the war
would be over before he had a chance to get into it.
And because Schmitzer believed he knew certain things
about life, he'd taken that opportunity to explain them
to the boy. Was there anything the hell wrong with that?
Anything strange or funny about helping out a younger
guy? He'd said, "Look, you're nineteen, I'm twenty-six.
So *listen* to me . . . you didn't have to worry about
getting into the war because they were killing people all
over the world to make room for you." He'd paused to
search for words, picking at skeins of thought as clum-

sily as if he were sorting them with mittened fingers
. . . "So here's the thing to remember, don't make
room for nobody else here. We stay alive. This section's
like a factory with all the jobs filled. No vacancies, no
fucking help wanted. Keep that in your head and
you'll be all right . . ."

Maybe the way he felt about death, he was thinking,
glancing with instinctive caution down the empty streets
of Werpen, maybe that feeling explained his attraction
to Sonny Laurel, a powerful, almost painful response to
someone so *alive*. He welcomed a sudden distracting
sound, relief from the tensions of his thoughts . . . a
vehicle laboring up through the woods to the town, the
motor's echo flat and muffled under the heavy fog. He
picked up his rifle, which he had propped against the
jeep, and as he snapped a round into the chamber saw
Docker running back into the square, his head turned
toward the sound of the laboring engine.

The sergeant climbed onto the rim of the fountain,
tracking the valley with his binoculars until he picked
up a command car traveling through dark stands of
trees. Stepping down, he said to Gelnick, "You better
get lost for a while. Go on into the church and light a
candle or something."

"Hey, I'm a nice Jewish boy," Gelnick said. "What's
this church crap? You want my mother to drop dead,
she finds out?"

"It's Lieutenant Longworth and your buddy Korbick's with him," Docker said. "Let's pay the two dollars, okay?"

"You want me to go hide? Dig a hole or something?"

"Look, Gelnick, Korbick's got you in his sights for
some reason and he'd love to have you back at Battery
headquarters where he could work you over. So don't
let's make it easy for him."

"Sure, I'll go hide. I don't want to spoil his day,"
Gelnick said easily, but his head felt like it might explode; he was afraid his thoughts would goad him into
something reckless, so he managed a wide smile by flat-

tening his lips and squinting his eyes, and that smile
was fixed and steady on his face as he ran through the
square and into the church.

The battery command car with First Sergeant Miles
Korbick at the wheel stopped in the square between the
church and the statue of the archer. Second Lieutenant
Longworth, short and compact with a weathered face
and careful eyes, climbed from the jeep and casually
returned Docker's salute. He had a bottle in his hand
and he tossed it to him, saying, "Think fast, sergeant.
Live bottle of bourbon, courtesy of Captain Grant.
Merry Christmas." . . .

At about this time Carmine Spinelli and Tubby
Gruber were searching the bedrooms of a two-storied
house at the opposite end of the village, accompanied
by Private Leo Pierce, a thin, solemn youngster with
patches of raw acne flaming on his cheeks.

Corporal Larkin shouted at them from the street to
report for mail call and then started toward the square,
where he saw Lieutenant Longworth standing with
Docker, and distributing the section's mail and packages.

Larkin had no letters, he seldom did, but there was
an oblong package for him that he knew contained a
quart-size Mazola oil can. An identical package arrived
every month or so, sent to him by a cousin, the oil carefully rinsed out and replaced with thirty-two ounces of
rye whiskey.

Docker had letters from Dave Hamlin and his father,
who wrote in his cool style of politics and the German
shepherd pups which he had (so long ago, it seemed to
Docker) named after American towns—Wheeling, Chicago, Detroit, Kennett, Rye—"Rye's temperament is
constant, I fear. Violent, that is, particularly in regard
to felines."

Docker's father published and edited two small
weekly newspapers in southwestern Pennsylvania. Of
politics, he wrote: "FDR will bring the country to ruin

and damnation, which we may or may not deserve. I long for the passion if not the principles of Father Coughlin. The voice from Royal Oak is authentic, at least. I distrust people who see all sides of the question. They see none, in fact. Remember, he warned us of 'the prostituted panderings of a purchased press'? I say this with distress, for there is hardly a newspaper in this country I trust anymore."

Docker disagreed completely with his father's politics, but there had never been a way to establish a dialogue in those areas. Even when he was in high school it had seemed to him his father's views were lacking in substantial conviction. He had begun to wonder how deliberate this was on his father's part, because those political views had become a wall between them over the years, sounds without any particular sense or significance, as meaningless as the extensive reports he sent him on the antics of his German shepherds.

Docker next read bits of Hamlin's letter . . . "Yes, only the Swiss and the dead are neutral in this war . . . On campus there is an almost fearful anticipation of the end. The war has animated us and given us a sense of importance. We are growing fat and tough and confident on it . . . Everyone is working again and there is more overtime than the workers can handle. But no sense of guilt—take this with a raised eyebrow if you will—because the civilians feel they are pulling their weight too."

Docker put the letters away in his map case.

First Sergeant Korbick toured Werpen in the HQ command car, stopping only long enough at the machine gun mount to chew out Tex Farrel for not having properly buckled the chin strap of his helmet. Gunning the vehicle, the first sergeant zigzagged through the narrow streets until he came out again on the square. He patted his forehead with a handkerchief and called to Dormund to bring him coffee.

Sergeant Korbick was thirty-one, stout and thick, with very little fat on him. His complexion was dark, his eyes were liquid and brown. His head was large and his black, close-cut hair stuck up and away from a clean white scalp like porcupine quills.

The sergeant had a particular distaste for dirt and foul odors that was near-pathological; his duffel bag was packed with deodorants and foot powders, salves, ointments and balms, stiff brushes and strong laundry soaps. Each night in his tent the first sergeant ritualistically scrubbed himself in a tub the battery's technical sergeant had converted from an oil drum for that specific purpose.

When Dormund brought the steaming coffee, Korbick moistened his handkerchief and carefully wiped the rim of the canteen cup. Glancing around the square, he saw Guido Linari and Laurel scuffling in the snow with a large mongrel dog, and Docker and Trankic talking to the lieutenant. When Longworth and the corporal went off toward the guns, Korbick yelled to Docker, "Hey, Bull! You got more fuck-ups in your section than the whole battery put together."

Docker walked over to him. "What's your problem, Miles?"

"Don't worry about my problem. I just had to raise hell with that Texas hotshot you got on the machine guns. He was sitting there with his helmet strap hanging down like a second cock. I got to do your work, Docker, the least you could do is remember me on payday."

"Sure," Docker said. "What would you like—a couple more bars of soap?"

"That's real fucking funny, Docker, really fucking funny." Korbick grinned at him, looking relaxed and comfortable in his warm sweater and spotless fatigues and field jacket, but a flush of color in his face betrayed his anger. Looking around again, he said, "I don't see my favorite fuck-up. Where's the Jew-boy, Docker?"

"I suspect it's a waste of time to mention this, but he doesn't like being called that."

"Don't give me that shit. He's a Jew, ain't he? And he

sure as hell ain't a man in my book. So what does that make him?"

"It's a tough war without you making it tougher, Korbick."

"What the hell's it to you anyway? This morning you got on Haskell about Spinelli. Now it's Gelnick. Hell, I'm just trying to make soldiers out of these fuck-ups."

"Gelnick doesn't need you pounding on him."

Korbick sipped his coffee, then grinned at Docker. "What is it with you, Docker? You got something going with the Jew-boy?"

Let it ride, Docker thought, but he'd forgotten his own capacity for anger and when he realized he couldn't rein it in, he decided the practical thing would be to get this over fast.

"You shitheads never turn it around, do you?"

"What's this shitheads crap, Docker?"

"I heard you're a Catholic. Is that right?"

"Sure, what about it?"

"Then you've heard the rumor that the Pope's a queer, I suppose."

"Don't put your filthy mouth on me, Docker. We aren't talking about religion."

"Oh, sure we are. You started it and it's interesting. Is that why all those cardinals in Rome wear red? Because that's the color of pansies, Korbick?"

"Good talk, real good college-boy talk." Korbick's hands trembled and coffee splashed on the front of his field jacket. "I'll remember this, Docker, you can bet on it."

"Float a duck for me tonight," Docker said, but his anger was almost gone and the residue of it left him disgusted with himself and what he had said. "Forget it, Korbick, just forget it," he said.

Private Irving "Tubby" Gruber had been conditioned by his mother to believe that comic antics and clownish behavior were specifics against most problems in life. Sarah Gruber had told her son, "If you can make peo-

ple laugh, they don't expect so much." Gruber could
deflect her own infrequent exasperation by making
crazy faces, or wailing and collapsing on the floor, and
this dissolved her frowns into helpless giggles which she
tried to smother behind her small hands.

Now in a freezing bedroom in a house on the outskirts of the village of Werpen, Tubby Gruber was
goading Spinelli to similar laughter by prancing about
with a pink and ruffled corset laced tightly about his
stout waist, batting his eyes in a sexual travesty. The
corset had been constructed for an ample lady; the
lower metal stays were slack at Gruber's hips and even
his fleshy chest was more than comfortable in the huge
cups of the garment.

Spinelli was laughing so hard that the sound of it
seemed to bounce in demented splinters about the icy
room. Private Pierce rubbed a windowpane and looked
into the street, worried now because it had been fifteen
or twenty minutes since Larkin had shouted at them to
get back to the square.

"Hey, we better get going," he said.

"Yeah, I guess so," Spinelli said. "It's time for
chow."

"Well, as long as I'm wearing"—Gruber paused and
said with a giggling lisp—"the *skirts* in this house, I'm
serving chow-chow right here."

"Damn it, cut it out, Tubby," Pierce said. "We're
gonna get our ass in a sling."

Gruber wriggled his hips, which sent Spinelli into another spasm of laughter.

"You guys are asking for it," Pierce said.

"Don't argue with mother," Gruber said, and with
mincing steps started down the stairs to the kitchen.

Docker and Lieutenant Longworth stood together
under the statue of the archer and studied the gray fog
they could see rolling across the open fields and forming clusters like chill cotton candy around orchards of
black fruit trees.

"It's the town," Docker said, in answer to the lieutenant's question. "The look of it bothers me."

He pointed to the empty streets, which stretched out from the square like the spokes of a wheel. "You begin to worry when you don't see girls leaning out windows waving petticoats and American flags. Or the priest blessing the tanks and trucks. The food these people left behind gives me a pretty scary timetable."

"Like what, sergeant?"

"About an hour or so. Some of the meals are only half-eaten and the ashes in the fireplaces are still warm. It could be that German troops aren't far east of here."

The lieutenant stared at the gray, storming horizons. "I'm wide open for suggestions."

"I'd like permission to pull back a few thousand yards west of here, then send a patrol out to look around."

Longworth dropped his cigarette on the ground and put it out with the tip of his boot. He nodded slowly. "All right, Docker. That makes sense. I'll countermand Whitter's orders. You get your section out of Werpen." . . .

Ten minutes later, Docker watched the HQ command car go down the hill and disappear into the gray weather in the valley. He felt an acute loneliness, a peculiar diminishment of spirit he suspected was compounded of the fog and snow and his concern about their position, plus a worrisome notion that he didn't belong on this hill in Belgium any more than he really belonged anywhere else in the world right now. And he wondered, as he had on other occasions, whether invisible parts of him might have been left behind in Tunisia and Sicily, or at Utah, or Avranches.

He knew other soldiers who were haunted by this feeling that something of themselves would always remain in the places the war had taken them, the towns and rivers and fields they would never see again. . . .

Docker was familiar with these emotional swings because they usually came when the jeeps and trucks brought mail from home . . . "Kennett, the tan bitch, seems to regard my study as the ideal place to commit her . . ." And Hamlin . . . "Brutal as it may sound (from the uninvolved) I say hit the beaches of the sacred isles of Nippon with every damn soldier we've got . . . Ran into Amy at a party last week, says she hasn't heard from you but—"

Trankic suddenly began shouting at him. "Bull, for Christ's sake, ten o'clock behind the church."

Everyone in the square turned to where Trankic was pointing, and they all saw them clearly for several seconds, glowing spheres of red light streaking across the horizon accompanied by a faint hissing sound that faded into silence when the lights disappeared behind the long hills and forests sloping off toward the German borders. Docker had seen that it was some kind of aircraft with rockets under the wings, but he couldn't even guess at its power source because he had seen no conventional motors or propellers.

"That's just what I saw before," Sonny Laurel said.

Unexpectedly, Dormund now said, "I saw it, too."

"Then why the hell didn't you say so?" Docker said.

"Well . . ." Dormund's lopsided features twisted in confusion. "I ain't no wretched volunteer."

Docker told Trankic, "Try to get Longworth on the radio, or the battery commander," then turned to Larkin. "Where's the rest of your detail?"

Larkin was drinking whiskey from the Mazola can, which he lowered, then wiped his lips with the back of his hand. "I told them to get back here. Same as I tell them to button their flies or blow their noses. I can't do everything for them, Bull."

"All right, go get them," Docker said. "But snap it, Larkin. We're moving out."

Larkin put his Mazola can into the jeep and went off down the street, his figure lost quickly in the slanting snow and settling darkness.

Still wearing the pink-ruffled corset, Tubby Gruber hammed it up, swishing around the kitchen of the Belgian home, opening drawers and cupboards until he found a crock of applesauce behind the mesh screen of a window icebox.

When Pierce and Spinelli returned from a hasty search of the root cellar and cowshed, they found Gruber seated on a table spooning thick gobs of the cold applesauce into his mouth with his fingers.

Spinelli said, "Hey, you out of your mind, Tubby?"

"Damn it, Docker told us not to touch anything," Pierce added.

Gruber, however, was in too exuberant a mood to pay attention. He loved clowning like this, it reminded him of home and his mother and the smell of food in the kitchen. When he was little and didn't want to eat his cereal or vegetables he could always get around his mother's laments by crawling about on his hands and knees and pretending to gobble up the designs of cabbage roses on the linoleum.

His sister, Hilary, who was seven years older, wailed to her parents that she couldn't bring friends home if Irving didn't stop acting so crazy, but as long as Gruber could control his mother's smiles he was able to control everyone else in the family.

And Gruber felt almost as if he were at home now, making comical faces and gulping down the sweet applesauce, flattered by Pierce and Spinelli's anxious attention . . . "So we'll start chow with some soup, all right?" he said. "Everybody likes soup, just give 'em a fork and let 'em go. Then we'll have some lox and bagels and some blinny-tin-tins. You guys got any idea what blinny-tin-tins are?"

Pierce knew this was all wrong. Worse, it was dangerous horsing around like this in somebody's home, with crucifixes and pictures of people in wedding clothes on the mantel and kids' toys piled in a corner of the room—animals carved from wood with ears and tails made from tufts of braided rope. "I'm getting the hell out of here," he said.

"Hey, don't you want to know what blinny-tin-tins are? They're pancakes with hotdogs in 'em, like rinny-tin-tin." As he laughed at his own wit, Tubby was thinking about the kitchen at home when it was set with chicken soup and egg bread for supper and the way his father always washed his hands in the sink when he came home from his work as a barber at a chair rented from a cousin in a shop in the Williamsburg district of Brooklyn. It was understood that he loved his only son, Irving, but it was also understood that since he worked nights as well as days—Hyman Gruber sold funeral insurance door-to-door at night—he was too tired to spend much time with Irving . . . as much as he'd like to, anyway.

Yet with all this mutual forbearance and understanding, Irving Gruber had not understood what his father told him outside the draft board in Brooklyn on that bitterly cold morning when he had been inducted into the United States Army . . . "Irvy, you're getting into something serious, so I'll tell you what it is. It's life you're getting into, so please don't screw around. All right, Irving?" Hyman Gruber had dabbed at his leaking nose with a handkerchief. "Listen to me, Irvy. This is your father. So listen, please. Here's the thing about life. The guy who screws around is the guy who screws up. Don't laugh and make faces at me. This ain't your bubala mama talking to you. Think about what your father is telling you. Don't screw around . . ."

From somewhere down the street, they heard Larkin yelling for them.

"Damn it! Let's go!" Pierce said.

They crowded into the living room, where Gruber, after a series of grunts and tugs, managed to strip off the big pink corset which he threw on a sofa under a tinted photograph of the Chancellor of the Third Reich.

"*Achtung!*" Gruber shouted, raising his arm in a stiff salute to the picture of Adolf Hitler. Then he made one of the rubbery faces that had always delighted his mother and in a lisping voice said, "I think Adolfums would make a real cute souvenir, don't you, guys?"

"No, goddamn it, *no*," Pierce screamed at him.

But the warning came too late. In the dim, fading light, their young faces were suddenly gray and they stood as if frozen to the old wooden floor.

Because when Tubby Gruber climbed on the sofa and jerked the picture from the wall, they all saw for one paralyzing instant the gleaming metal wires running down the faded wallpaper and into the basement.

The rush of air from the explosion demolished the house and the three men in it; then struck Larkin with massive, buffeting blows, knocking him sprawling backward over snowdrifts into the street. His body rolled along the slick cobblestones, arms and legs spinning in helpless cartwheels, the rising wind pounding his ears and stinging his face with showers of sleet and ice.

A second explosion blasted out two more homes and released pillars of smoke and flame that turned the falling snow into scarlet steam and ripped open the black skies above Werpen like angry knives of lightning.

And then the settling silence marked the end of the war for the young private soldiers Gruber, Pierce and Spinelli.

Chapter Eight

December 15, 1944. Dresden, Germany.
Friday, 1500 Hours.

Karl Jaeger picked up his leather field case and slung it over his shoulder. His greatcoat and visored cap were in the hall but he still hesitated, glancing about the bedroom, remembering the soft impression of his wife's head on the pillow and studying framed pictures of their children, Hannah and Rosa, and bending to look closer at a silver cup he had won in a cadet shooting contest a dozen years ago.

He'd put away the clothes he had worn on this precious leave, flannel trousers and fleece-lined house boots, a chamois hunting shirt and the cable-knit sweater that reminded him of ski slopes and hiking trips with British friends in Devon and Cornwall.

Hedy had taken the girls to visit a neighbor. It was as he wanted it. No tearful good-byes. He would be gone when they came back.

Jaeger poured himself a glass of schnapps from the decanter on a night table and sipped slowly, composing himself for what might well be the last meeting in his life with his father.

Hedy had spent the night in his arms, and he remembered especially now the strong beat of her heart. Hannah and Rosa joined them early in the morning, their round, blond heads bright against the muslin pillows, and their heartbeats had mingled with Hedy's and his own, and the sound seemed lonely and courageous in the little bedroom, and in his fancy he had imagined the

heartbeat of his father in his room off the kitchen, and
around all of them the heartbeat of Germany, to mark
this moment in their lives . . .

Jaeger went into the living room, where the windows
faced a small roof garden with plantings protected by
screens of isinglass. The wooden troughs his father had
tended were empty now except for some carrot tops
dark with frost and a few heads of stunted cabbage.

Stretching beyond was the fairy-tale beauty of Dresden, the rich expanse of spires and cupolas embraced
by the great curve of the Elbe River flowing smoothly
in thin winter light under the city's arched bridges. It
was a great comfort and solace for Karl Jaeger to have
his family safe in Dresden. The old city had been
bombed only once during the war and that was judged
to have been a mistake, a result of faulty flight instructions.

It was widely known that an agreement had been
reached by German and British leaders, guaranteeing
that if this historic city were spared, then the Luftwaffe
would in turn spare the university town of Oxford—an
arrangement that had been made as Hitler and Neville
Chamberlain spoke of "peace in our time" at Munich.

Jaeger placed his field case on his desk, unbuckled its
flap and began to pack away the maps and reports of
Operation Christrose, which he had checked and
double-checked once again last night.

The start-line of Das Reich was on a north-south
front east of the Losheim Gap. From there the division
would strike west at dawn on December 16th with its
infantry and tanks moving at maximum speed to smash
the thin American line loosely held between the towns
of St. Vith and Houffalize. Once behind the American
lines, their columns would swing north to trap the enemy divisions caught between them and the Kampfgruppe commanded by Colonel Joachim Peiper.

Troops and supplies had been funneled to the twenty-
three attacking divisions from Norway, Poland, East
Prussia and Austria. The forests of the Ardennes con-

cealed more than a thousand tanks and hundreds of
battalions of artillery and assault troops. Steel ramps
had been constructed across strategic sections of the
Siegfried Line to give the armor faster access from their
defensive positions into the valleys of the Ardennes.
The onslaught would be masked and ferocious; V-1s
flying toward Liège and Antwerp and London would
create blankets of sound to smother the noise of motors
and tank treads.

Jaeger had memorized the names and features of
dozens of towns on his line of march—Roqueblanc, Lepont, Spa and Werbomont—and was familiar with their
roads, bridges, rivers, as well as their distances from Allied supplies and gasoline depots.

He had been working on these maps and notes yesterday when Rosa and Hannah ran in from school.
They were shy with him at first but broke into giggles
and laughter when he sang their favorite song to them,
"Der Jaeger aus Kurpfalz," which they had always
thought had been written especially for them:

"A hunter of Kurpfalz is riding through the green
    woods—
He shoots the wild game, just the way he likes best.
Trara, trara
Gar lustig ist die Jaegerei
Allhier auf gruener Heid'."

He had bounced them lightly on his knees as if they
were on horseback, and the motion made their blond
hair swing and catch sparks of sun coming over the
church steeples and through the tall windows. Yet the
silly, jolly old song had sadly caused the only time of
friction between Jaeger and his wife.

"It's a waste of time to give them memories from the
past," Hedy had said. "It's not what other people will
remember about us."

Jaeger felt an anger impossible to control. "So they
won't let us forget our past? And just whom do you

mean by *they*? The rootless Americans with their idiot
culture of chewing gum and cowboys? Or the English
whose passion for freedom never extended to the conti-
nents they enslaved? Or are you perhaps speaking of
the French, Hedy, who collaborated with us in their
own disgrace? Is that the they you mean? Or the Poles
whose brains would shame oxen, or those blockheaded
Dutchmen? . . ."

Their enemies knew nothing of Germany's struggle
against intellectual decadence, Jaeger thought as he now
buckled his field case, perversions flourishing in the
name of freedom, standards proclaiming that right and
wrong existed only as concepts to frighten children.
Who were *they* in their insolence to damn Germany?
His country had been gutted and its ashes ground into
mud and slime. But the world knew only enemy propa-
ganda, the beer hall rowdies, the smashed windows, the
yellow stars . . .

He paced in front of the dead winter garden, hands
clenching and unclenching as he attempted to control
his erratic thoughts . . . The so-called avant-garde
artists and architects weren't welcome in Germany because they represented a sickness and distortion that
drained the strength of a healthy people. Hitler himself
had been shocked by the spectacle of Expressionist
paintings in this very city of Dresden and had ordered
the gallery closed. Nudity was banned and the American Negress, Josephine Baker, expelled from Berlin, not
for her songs or because she was black but because she
had had the audacity to perform naked . . . And with
her had gone the gypsies and homosexuals and beggars.
And the so-called artists and whores. But what of the
Jews? Hadn't they flourished here? Only an imbecile
would deny it. Who had destroyed this? The Germans,
or the intellectuals, or the Jews? Kurt Tucholsky with
his taunts at humiliated veterans, attacking whatever
shreds of patriotism the German people had been left
with. And George Grosz' cartoons as savage as a knife
thrust, caricaturing his German hosts as thick-necked

brutes with bulging eyes and nostrils like snouts fit only
to be lowered into gutters or foaming steins of beer.
What in God's name had they expected? Tucholsky had
proudly proclaimed, "There is no secret of the German
Army I would not readily hand over to a foreign
power." Was that sentiment to be taken lightly by a nation on its knees from a brutal war and an even more
brutal peace? No, he thought—he turned back and
forth in front of the frosted windows, his boots matching the furious rhythm of his heart—after Versailles the
pacifism of the intellectuals was the highest treason. Yet
it was these same aesthetes, tireless and clever with their
talk, Germans as well as Jews, a cutting edge of self-
styled advanced thought that proposed a mingling of
German and Jewish bloods, arguing that the Hebraic
strain would provide a healthy correction to the dullness
and heaviness of the German character. An infusion of
agile Jewish genetic stimuli to turn Germany into a
more lively place, a nation of sly humors, and shrewder
heads and hands.

He tried to calm himself, standing quite still and
breathing slowly and deeply. Why should it concern
him? They were all gone now, the artists, the intellectuals, the gypsies, the homosexuals, the whores. But
again he thought of the Jews. Was anti-Semitism some
peculiar miasma rising only from Germany? He had
read in a newspaper . . . What is the fastest thing in
the world? A kike on a bike in the Reich. But not in a
German newspaper, no, an *American* newspaper.

His thoughts swung with pendulum force in an opposite direction, and his heart began to pound so hard that
the sound frightened him. He tried to dam up a flood of
agonizing memories, to obliterate the shadows forming
in his mind. Taking the briar pipe from his pocket, he
drove the stem with all his strength into the back of his
hand, but the pain didn't distract him and the inside of
his head felt hot, his thoughts revealed to him in pitiless
clarity . . . Armies were marching against him, he
could hear them clearly, and the effect was so vivid,

dismaying that he put a hand against his desk for support. But it wasn't boots sounding with the crash of war or trumpets leading a charge, it was a dance of sound and music and in the ranks of that army there were the accusing eyes of those whose homes and shops stood empty now in cities and hamlets across the German fatherland. They looked at him as Rudi Geldman once had, and Jaeger knew where they had gone, even though a part of his mind still shouted that he did not.

They all knew those names, the names of Dachau and Belsen and Buchenwald at Weimar, where Goethe wrote *Faust*, and Chelmo, Sobibor and Treblinka, Belsec and Auschwitz. . . . His strange faintness left him when he heard a voice from his father's room, the old man coughing or calling out weakly for him, but Jaeger resisted the plea and continued to stare through the windows at the thin sunlight on the spires of the city.

Albrecht Jaeger sat alone in the small bedroom off the kitchen. In the daytime his view was of church steeples and a shining curve of the Elbe, but Hedy had drawn the blackout curtains earlier and now the only light in the room came from a gooseneck lamp on his night table. A breakfront, its glass doors removed, bulged with books and correspondence.

He had suffered a stroke three years ago, almost a month to the day after his fifty-sixth birthday. He knew he looked much older than his age; without exercise, his once powerful body had collapsed in on itself, leaving him frail and weary in the grip of his wheelchair. His left eye was covered with a black patch, a vivid contrast to his thin white hair. Since his stroke, that eye had become painfully sensitive to the light but his good eye glowed brightly, almost fiercely, in his ravaged face and he was grateful that he had no difficulty in reading with it. He wore the same dark and simple suit that he had worn in his classrooms for many years. Across his knees was a gray woolen shawl that Hedy had knitted for him, and on top of it his pale and heavily veined hands were locked together to prevent them from trembling.

He called out again, a contorted sound, but his son didn't answer him; the silence in the small flat remained heavy and oppressive.

The worst effect of his stroke was that it had deprived him of coherent speech. He could recall words and form them into linked sentences in his mind, but the massive temblor in his brain had destroyed his mnemonic sensors so that it was literally one chance in millions that the words he uttered would have any connection with what he was trying to say.

He knew that Karl had been home all day. Now that it was night, he knew his son would be coming to say good-bye to him. It was a dreadful penance, to sit mute and helpless, unable to utter a word to save him. Unable to force truth on him . . . Yet what even now did Albrecht Jaeger know of his country's history? Was there, actually, any final truth?

Oh, yes, he had tried to answer the lies, but with sarcasm, humor, an eyebrow raised ironically to suggest disapproval, nothing that would stop a blow or a bullet. Yet, when he had been ready to speak out with force, the stroke had darkened his mind and scattered his words.

Still the most dreadful truth of all was that the truth itself was not, had never been, in hiding. Everyone knew it well. The talk of the relative merits of carbon monoxide and prussic acid as killing agents . . . The failure of the diesels at a camp (Belsec, he wondered?) had ultimately resolved that issue.

Everyone knew. Professor Jaeger had seen the large *J* stamped in the Jewish passports. He knew the law that required all Jews to use Israel as the middle name on official documents. And Jewesses the name Sarah. Confiscation of Jewish property was known . . . and the system of markings in the camps, colored patches on each prisoner's uniform, red for political prisoners, black for anti-socials, pink for homosexuals, green for criminals,

and for Jews, two yellow triangles sewn to form the hex-
agonal Star of David.

In his own classroom he had suffered the myth of
Horst Wessel created by the Nazis, and in tolerating it
had abetted it. Horst Wessel was a pimp who lived off
his mistress, a whore named Erna Jaenecke he had stolen from another party member, Ali Hoehler. Hoehler
shot Wessel through the mouth, and within weeks the
whore's landlady and Hoehler and the whore herself
were all dead from mysterious causes and Horst Wessel
was officially declared a Nazi hero . . . "fallen in the
cause of justice, killed by the Communists."

But what if everyone knew of such things? Did the
universality of knowledge somehow make it all meaningless? Old Isaac Levy, Rudi's uncle, believed that, believed the convulsions inside Germany were nothing less
than a national aberration ". . . they know not what
they do." He could write that even as he sent the stories
and pictures about Rudi from Buchenwald, pasting
them inside leases and court forms. But could old Isaac
Levy say from where this national aberration came?

The stars above, the moral law within . . . Imman-
uel Kant's insistence that man was forever unknowable
and unaccountable—was that where it came from?

The professor looked down at his heavily veined
hands clenched together on the gray shawl over his
knees. It was *he* who had told Rudi Geldman he must
leave his school: that was the new law. Rudi hadn't understood at first. They were friends and he hadn't expected this, not in the Jaegers' home, where he had frequently spent holidays and where he had argued with
Karl about the *Cornet Rilke*, gentle and good-humored
in the beginning, harsher and more accusing as the political climate darkened with the clouds of the coming
war. They had studied this work of love, this famous
poem by the great German artist, Rainer Maria Rilke,
in the old halls of Albrecht Jaeger's gymnasium, and
they had learned it by heart and knew that this romantic
invention of tender and ardent patriotism had been car-

ried in the knapsacks of thousands and thousands of
soldiers in the Great War, as treasured as their packets
of letters from home:

> "He thinks: I have no rose, none.
> Then he sings. And it is an old
> sad song that at home the girls in
> the fields sing, in the fall, when
> the harvests are coming to an end.

> "Then the Marquis strips off his
> great right glove. He fetches out
> the little rose, takes a petal from
> it. As one would break a host.

> " 'That will safeguard you. Farewell.'

> "Von Langenau is surprised. Then he
> shoves the foreign petal under his
> tunic. And it rises and falls on
> the waves of his heart. Bugle-call.

> "My good mother,
> be proud, I carry the flag.
> Be free of care; I carry the flag.
> Love me; I carry the flag."

"Where is the evil in love and patriotism?" Karl had
demanded.

"The evil done in their names," Rudi Geldman had
replied.

And who was right? One answer to that question was
in the pictures of Rudi Geldman and old Isaac Levy's
letter, both on a shelf of the breakfront within reach of
Professor Jaeger's trembling hands.

Isaac Levy, like his nephew Rudi, an inmate at Buchenwald, had been forced to transfer his shares in an optical shop to his partner, Herr Munder. When the papers
came to Munder—lease arrangements, inventory list-

ings, a variety of legal forms—he had discovered that
old Levy had sent a letter and pictures of Rudi Geldman along with them, pasting them cleverly inside the
thick bundle of documents. Herr Munder's daughter
had brought the letter and pictures to Albrecht Jaeger.
She had come to him late one evening, a plain, serious
young woman, her leg heavy with the brace she'd worn
since a childhood illness. A few years before, she was
one of the brightest students in the same class as his son
and Rudi Geldman. And she had defied her own father
to bring him the information from Levy.

And what if the stars *were* above, symbols of God's
glory? Where was the moral law within man?

Old Levy might have an answer. In one part of his
letter to Herr Munder, he had written:

"Try to understand. Punishment in the camps isn't
related in any logical way to unruly behavior or infrac-
tions of the rules. It isn't designed to correct bad habits.
Nor to insure obedience and discipline. Its function is to
degrade and shame a human being to the point that he
becomes convinced of his own vileness, becomes an ac-
complice in this brutalizing process of degradation and
shame.

"Random victimization is the ultimate terror. The
lash has no personal preferences, knows no favorites.
Punishment is administered often on a wooden rack to
which the young and old, sick or well, men or women,
are trussed face down to expose their naked buttocks.

"Rudi's mistake was to insist that there was no degradation in survival. By any means. His liaison with Captain Sturmer was not degrading to Rudi. It couldn't
touch him so long as he owned the dignity bestowed on
him by the will to *endure*. And so long as the relationship made Rudi seem less than a man, it was not only
agreeable but stimulating to the captain. When he realized this wasn't the case, that Rudi would still talk of
philosophies and moral rights, that Rudi was indeed the
stronger man, he turned Rudi over to the guards.

"They didn't care about Rudi one way or the other,

he was just another random victim wearing a yellow star. So remember, what they did to Rudi Geldman was done without any *particular* malice.

"In tears, I say there was nothing personal in it. This same torment was frequently used, I have been told, by soldiers in the old ghettos of Eastern Europe to punish the leaders of uprisings. Some of the guards at Buchenwald must have learned of it down through their great-grandfathers.

"They stretched Rudi's naked body across a bale of hay in a horse stall and shackled his wrists and ankles to iron stanchions. They spread a thick mixture of salt and flour over his thighs and genitals and the soles of his feet. When this hardened they turned two goats into the stall to lick away the concoction with tongues as ridged and abrasive as metal files. In the ancient punishment, the chest of the victim was cinched tightly with leather straps to restrict breathing. Spasmodic and uncontrollable laughter, the helpless response to such a violation of nerve endings, exhausted the oxygen rapidly and the victim died of asphyxiation within half an hour. Rudi's chest was unfettered; his convulsive laughter and screams sounded through much of that night and subsided only when his nervous system collapsed in violent shock. Captain Sturmer ordered the pictures taken." . . .

The door opened and his son entered the room, put his leather field case on the floor and inclined his head to his father in a gesture of respect.

"I've come to say good-bye," he said. "I think you'll be comfortable here until it's over. Herr Moeller assures me there's enough coal to last until the days are milder . . ."

His son was so tall, Professor Jaeger thought, his strength seemed to fill the room. And with the thought, the father's mood became suddenly wild with anger and frustration. He wanted so desperately to tell his son now that nothing could be created in hatred, that hatred consumed rather than nourished, and while it gave an angry glare to eyes, it could never help one to see.

When the words sounded, the noise was meaningless to Jaeger, and looking into his father's naked eye was like staring into the flame of an open furnace.

The professor wheeled his chair toward the breakfront. Breathing heavily with the effort, he pulled down a leather yearbook and opened it to a page of photographs, his hands fluttering on the dry pages with a sound like leaves skittering over winter fields. When he found the photograph he was searching for, he put a finger on it and raised the book with trembling hands to his son.

Jaeger looked at the solemn and unformed features of young Rudi Geldman, the black hair brushed back neatly and only the hint of a smile to suggest his amusement at the absurd solemnity surrounding the taking of class pictures. There was something so graceful and charged with potential in his expression. Karl felt a spasm of pain at the waste of it.

But his father had more to show him, smudged pictures he was removing from an envelope with trembling fingers, and Karl had a fleeting glimpse of a slim, naked body shackled to iron posts, but he looked away quickly and with a swing of his hand knocked the photographs to the floor.

His father cried out something to him and the words the son heard were, "Water is green and love! And cry it forever."

Turning as if on parade, Jaeger strode into the kitchen and filled a glass with water at the sink. He was trembling now with an anger that matched his father's. Where did the old man's moral superiority come from? To dare to weaken him, take the heart from him when within hours their tanks and soldiers would be smashing into the Ardennes . . . and was it not his own father, Professor Albrecht Jaeger, who had expelled Rudi from school? Of course, it was the law. But had he even *tried* to defy it? And what about the fat geese given loyal Germans by Nazi block and cell leaders? Those plump birds decorated with mushrooms and truffles had graced the table of Professor Jaeger when heads were bowed in grateful prayer and the evils of the times forgotten in the steaming aroma of roast fowl and the fragrance of good German wines that accompanied it.

Karl returned to his father's room and put the glass within reach of the old man. "Let me tell you something, father," he said. "After Crystal Night I offered to drive Rudi across the border to Switzerland. But no, he believed *this* was his country, and he sacrificed his life—he threw it away—and to prove what? That in his deepest heart he believed in the Cornet Rilke?"

Karl slung his field case over his shoulder. He had to leave now; his car was waiting. But he couldn't live with the memory of his father's terrible eye glaring up at him . . . "I hope you'll pray for me, father. Pray for Hedy and the children and all our people. And pray for yourself too, father. Because you are the river that flowed into my life."

He turned and walked from the room and the heels of his boots rang hard through the apartment, an impersonal counterpoint to the incoherent words his father cried after him.

Chapter Nine

December 15, 1944. Lepont, Belgium.
Friday, 1700 Hours.

Snow continued to fall heavily over the Ardennes. The sky stayed dark and overcast and the clouds were weighted with moisture. Sleeting storms developed with erratic violence across the terrain held by the American VIII Corps.

Snow packed the chinks of sandbagged revetments, froze the breechblocks of cannons, numbed the faces of soldiers and caused gale warnings to fly along the Channel ports from Ostend to Zeebrugge and down the canal systems of Europe into the tributaries of the Rhine.

The bitter weather swept across lakes and woodlands of the Ardennes, driving what was left of the livestock to cover, forcing starving goats and sheep to huddle together for warmth behind foothills covered with bracken that was as hard and cold as iron. Root crops had been scarce that year. Beets and potatoes were frozen in the fields, the woods thinned by the occupying troops. Great stands of maples and oaks were gone; without these windbreaks the countryside was nakedly exposed to winter gales.

The labor force had been conscripted by the German Army, the diamond and glass and flax industries no longer functioned, and the bulk of food for human consumption came from painstakingly nurtured garden plots, chiefly sustained by human manure, a commodity also in dangerously short supply.

On the banks of the Salm near Lepont the ground had been beaten flat and hard. Across this frozen earth, once thick with silver birch and wild fruit orchards, the winds raced unchecked through the streets of the village. It shook the old panes of Denise Francoeur's brick home, where Jocko Berthier had camouflaged the entrance to the stone cellar, a vaulted enclosure directly below the parlor.

Working by candlelight with the blackout curtains drawn tightly, Jocko had removed the locks and hinges of the cellar door, filling the screw holes with putty and whitewashing the door panels to match the color and texture of the parlor walls. He'd then wedged the door back into place, fitting it closely and snugly with strips of felt.

From a poster of his own ancient bed, Jocko had sawed a wooden angel's head and attached it by a bolt and screw to a cross panel in the cellar door. The illusion of a smooth, unbroken white wall, relieved only by the shining angel's head, was completed when Denise placed a table in front of the whitewashed door and decorated it with a lace cloth and pewter candlesticks. The gracefully carved angel's head was painted blue and white with delicately ridged blond hair and a small pink mouth formed in gentle curves. The eyes of the angel were blank and round, and firelight touched them with a suggestion of sightless innocence.

Later that same afternoon a V-1 in a formation heading toward Liège developed a misfunction and tipped to earth short of its target, exploding in the woods above Lepont and missing by a few dozen yards the gatehouse of a castle that had been occupied until recently by German officers.

From her parlor Denise had watched the robot bomb flash across the skies and curve down into the woods above the village. She went quickly into the bedroom, where Margret, her dark hair fanned out against the pillow, her breathing deep and uneven, was sleeping. There was a look of pain on the child's small, cramped features, and tears had started beneath her eyelids and glistened on her cheeks even while she slept.

Denise woke her niece gently and led her down to the cellar, where there was a cot, candles, a jar of water and some writing paper and crayons.

"If anyone knocks, you won't come up?"

The child shook her head.

"Promise me."

The little girl nodded and her aunt left her, collected her cloak and went into the village.

When she located Jocko Berthier he grumbled, as she'd known he would, but at last pulled on his sheepskin coat and started with her up the winding road, flanked on one side by black trees and on the other by a sheer drop into the valley. Above them, arches and turrets dark against the dull afternoon, they could see Castle Rêve standing on one of twin peaks; the second promontory, slightly higher than the castle hill, was known as Mont Reynard.

At the top of the road they sighted the castle gatehouse, smoke drifting from its chimneys. A crater a dozen yards wide had been torn in the frozen earth above it; small fires still crackled in the underbrush.

Paul Bonnard stood with his back to his stone house, facing the flames with an ax in his hands. His wife, Trude, was collecting shards of glass from the ground and placing them in a reed basket. The flesh of her right cheekbone lay open and a thin stream of blood ran unevenly down to her mouth.

"She was at the window when it fell," Bonnard said. "But it wasn't the glass that cut her. It was the clock. The blast knocked it off the shelf into her face."

The Bonnards were close to shock, Denise saw, Trude's gestures clumsy and reflexive and Bonnard gripping his ax and watching the flames as if they were animals that might suddenly turn and attack his home.

Denise and Jocko helped Madame Bonnard into the gatehouse and to a chair at the fireplace. They told Felice Bonnard, who was sixteen, to bring warm water and some clean cloths.

Later, when Felice took her mother upstairs, Paul Bonnard motioned to Jocko and Denise to follow him outside, where he proceeded up a cart trail that curved into the woods above the crater made by the V-1. He stopped in a glade, pointing into the crown of a tree where a body was suspended by the straps of a tangled parachute, the head twisted at a sharp angle, the legs turning slowly with the winds.

They thought at first the dead man was an American soldier—the helmet was a gray-green, the overcoat brown—but when the wind moved the body, they could see under the open overcoat the field-gray color of a German uniform and the shine of SS insignia.

"Have you see others?" Jocko asked.

"No, only this man. We heard planes sometime in the night—"

"We'd better bury him," Jocko said.

Bonnard brought the ax and a shovel from the gatehouse and he and Jocko hacked out a grave. Denise put the soldier's automatic handgun and wallet in the pocket of her cloak and, after Jocko marked the grave with stones, they started back to the village, the shadows of the castle and Mont Reynard mingling with their own on the road down to the silver edge of the river.

"Can you send a signal?" she said.

Jocko shook his head. "I worked on the transmitter yesterday but Father Juneau came up to the choir loft. I wasn't expecting him."

"What do you think he knows?"

"Everything he can get his hands on, you can be sure of that."

Denise Francoeur made the sign of the cross on her forehead and slipped her cold hands into the folds of her cloak.

Chapter Ten

December 15, 1944. Eastern Belgium.
Friday, 1900 Hours.

___

On the night of December 15th, Sergeant Docker stood in a tent at Dog Battery headquarters checking the personal effects of Privates Gruber, Pierce and Spinelli with a soldier from a Graves Registration Unit, Private First Class Edgar Nessel.

The gear of the dead soldiers was spread out on army cots, revealed in bright detail by an overhead light bulb and the glow from a potbellied stove.

"We'll make up a nice package of their personal things." Nessel was a thin and nervous young man with slightly bulging eyes. "Clean uniforms and all their mail and postcards, of course. We don't want any loose ends. Tidy is a comfort, I always say."

The bodies of Spinelli, Gruber and Pierce, or what was left of them, had been wrapped in mattress covers and tarpaulins and trucked the previous day to a holding cemetery behind the lines.

Nessel checked a quartermaster form and Docker stared at what the soldiers had left behind them.

In Spinelli's effects were pinups of Betty Grable and Rita Hayworth, a pair of dice, unopened chewing gum from his K-rations, a shaving kit, black oxford shoes, V-mail letters.

Pierce had a similar collection. And a slingshot,

Docker noted with some interest, because he'd never seen him use it. There was also an ivory-handled knife tucked into a pair of Pierce's neatly rolled GI socks. The knife belonged to Shorty Kohler and had disappeared a few weeks earlier. No point in making anything out of it now . . . ship it home, let it end up on somebody's mantelpiece as a souvenir of the fallen warrior.

Gruber had apparently kept every letter from home since he'd been in the Army.

"Something's missing, sergeant," Nessel said. "Private Spinelli was issued a rubber poncho with a detachable hood. You happen to know where they are?"

"No."

"I don't like these loose ends." Nessel made a pencil check on his list. "Means a statement of charges. But we won't bother the families. Battalion will send the charges to Battery and they'll deduct it from whatever wages are due the soldier."

The tent flap was pushed open by Lieutenant Whitter, who came in and crowded close to the stove, pounding his hands against his upper arms and shoulders.

"Sergeant, you got us up to our ass in paperwork tonight," he said, but it seemed his irritation was mixed with a measure of satisfaction. "Didn't you tell those guys of yours not to fuck around collecting souvenirs?"

"Yes, I told them."

"They're like babies crawling around sticking their fingers in light sockets. You got to watch 'em all the time. Who in hell was in charge?"

"I was," Docker said.

"Well, we'll go into that later." Whitter took a sheaf of typewritten pages from his overcoat and handed them to Docker. "Right now, I want you to check the statement you gave Captain Grant's clerk and see if you got anything to add to it."

Docker read the four typewritten pages. "No, sir, that's it."

"You don't say for sure whether it's a fighter plane, a rocket, or anything."

Private Nessel gave Whitter a quick salute and slipped out of the tent. Whitter took the pages from Docker. "Your report and some others are going to First Army at Spa and up to Corps at Bastogne. I'll tell you something else, Docker. It's going from there to SHAEF and London. So I hope for your ass that you and your section weren't drunk on some of the black whiskey you stole from Utah." He pushed his way out into the night.

Docker stood alone in the tent that smelled of coal and wool and looked at the personal gear of the dead soldiers. The slingshot bothered him, the childish look of it. And Gruber's letters and Spinelli's pinups of Rita Hayworth and Betty Grable. Clean socks, clean uniforms, theater ribbons and Purple Hearts, a last tidy package courtesy of Graves Registration.

Dog Battery's headquarters was in the fields of an abandoned farm about a dozen miles behind its line of guns, south and west of Salmchateau, a rural complex with stone barns and outbuildings chipped and broken by rifle and artillery fire. Pyramidal tents had been erected among the trees to provide quarters for Captain Grant and the officers and noncoms who maintained the battery's support systems—Supply, Mess, Communications, Medical and Administration. Guards were posted at both ends of the battery "street," a muddy passage running between the tents. Other guards stood duty at the gasoline and ammo dumps and the lean-tos that sheltered food and medical supplies.

The motor pool was quartered in the rear courtyard of the old stone farmhouse, separated from other battery installations by a broad meadow and a stand of fruit trees.

Nessel was waiting for Docker in the battery street. "Sorry to bother you again sergeant, but there's one more little thing."

"What?"

"These men, did they owe anybody any money?"

"I'm not sure, probably not. They didn't gamble much—what else would they need it for?" He glanced along the dark battery street. Several soldiers were in line at the mess tent. Another group stood around the rough bulletin board nailed to a post near First Sergeant Korbick's tent. But he saw neither Larkin nor Shorty Kohler, who had driven here with him.

"We like the families of the deceased to know they didn't owe any money," Nessel said. "Con men in the States check the local papers for obituaries, then write the family and claim the dead GI was in debt to them."

Docker saw Kohler coming up the battery street from the direction of the motor pool.

"They usually make a sad story out of it, like they lent the dead guy money for a girl in trouble or to catch a bus so they wouldn't be AWOL."

Kohler splashed into a mud puddle and was cursing when he stopped beside Docker.

"Sarge, Larkin went over to the motor pool for a crap game and that son of a bitch Haskell grabbed him."

"If possible, we like to assure the next of kin that the deceased have no obligations of any kind to—"

"They didn't owe anybody a fucking dime. Put it in writing, I'll sign it." Docker looked at Kohler. "Was he drinking?"

"Shit, yes. I told him Haskell would bust his balls but you know how he is on that black skull-pop. I tried to get in there, but they got a truck rammed against the gate on the inside."

"How long ago?"

"Twenty minutes, maybe a half hour. We better get goin' or there ain't gonna be much left of him."

"You get the jeep, Shorty," Docker said. "Bring it around to the other side of the battery."

"Where the hell you going?"

"Just get the goddamn jeep."

"You better not go over there alone."

"Goddamn it, do what I tell you, Shorty."

"Well, you're gonna get your fucking head bent in," Kohler said.

Docker ran through the meadows to the courtyard behind the farmhouse, which was enclosed by eight-foot stone walls topped with ragged growths of winter ivy and honeysuckle. He heard voices and laughter behind the walls and through cracks in the gate could see strong lights, but the gates didn't budge when he slammed his shoulder into them. Following a flagged walk to the front of the farmhouse, he kicked in a rotted wooden door. Inside, the rooms were cold and dark and smelled of sour mattresses and moldering wallpaper. A mechanic named Tony Perkovitch stood at the kitchen sink opening a bottle of beet cognac in the glow of a kerosene lamp that spread yellow light on the frosted windows. The soldier turned at the sound of footsteps and blinked when he saw Docker standing in the doorway.

Private First Class Perkovitch was a youngster with heavy shoulders and permanently grease-stained hands. He shrugged and said, "Haskell told me to get him some booze, sarge."

"Maybe he's had enough," Docker said.

"I wouldn't know anything about that. He just told me to bring him a bottle."

"I'm here to get Larkin."

"I didn't have no part in it, sarge."

"Then you better stay inside, Tony. I'll take Haskell his bottle."

"I guess it's okay, if you say so."

Docker nodded and took the bottle from him and walked out onto a rear porch that opened directly onto the courtyard.

The headlights of four GI trucks cut the darkness and formed a lighted ring in the middle of the big yard. Inside this expanse of light, Larkin staggered about drunkenly, blood streaming from his nose and mouth.

Haskell stood watching him. At the edge of that light several of his mechanics, bulky men in soiled fatigues, raised their bottles and drank. Haskell moved forward, grinned and slapped Larkin across the face with enough force so that the corporal turned in a full wobbling circle before tripping and falling to the ground.

Blinking against the glare of the headlights, Larkin worked himself up to his hands and knees, lowered his head and shook it slowly. The lights gleamed on the blood dripping from his mouth into the snow.

Haskell said, "You're not hurt, Larkin. If I used my fists, you would be. So on your feet. We got the whole night to teach you to watch that mouth of yours."

Larkin tried to laugh. He rubbed at his lips. "Haskell, you're the only good fucking argument I know for abortion."

One of Haskell's mechanics, an older man named Lenny Rado, noticed a movement in the shadows. He looked off and saw Docker walking across the courtyard, the low beams of the headlights catching the flash of the bottle in his swinging hand. "We got company," he said to Haskell.

Haskell turned slowly, his big boots sucking against the snow and mud, and grinned at Docker, the tense smile bunching his rubbery cheeks.

Docker looked at Larkin. "Get up, we're going back to the guns."

Haskell drew a breath, causing the roll of muscle around his stomach to bulge over his broad leather belt. "You leaving right now, sarge?"

"That's right."

"But I still got some business with Corporal Larkin."

"No, that business is all over."

"Kind of depends. He comes here with his filthy mouth, gets on me and my guys, it's only fair to give him what he's asking for."

Docker looked down at the blood on the dirty snow. "I think you've done that, Haskell. I told you, it's over."

"Only thing is, part of the country where I'm from,

third parties don't make that decision. Not for fair fights, Docker. And nobody touched this Irish shit-heel but me."

"Sure," Docker said. "Larkin's so drunk he couldn't hit the ground with his hat and you've got fifty pounds on him."

"You said it about your gun section, Docker . . . said everything there was your business. Well, it works the same way here."

"Get up," Docker said to Larkin.

"I been begging him to do that little thing," Haskell said, "so I can slap his silly face into the mud again."

Docker stared at the mechanics standing behind Haskell, remembering their names—Dolan, Granowski, Lenny Rado, but nothing else about them because now they were only ugly reflections of Haskell to him, and for the waste and stupidity they represented he felt an anger that was different from what had gripped him when he had looked at the personal effects of his dead soldiers. This anger had no loneliness or pain or compassion mixed in it . . . it was pure, a destructive feeling that denied Haskell and his men even contempt or bitterness. "You're not listening," he said. "It's over now." There were touches of color high in his face, and behind the masked alertness in his eyes an evidence of something so violent that when Haskell recognized it his smile changed and he rubbed a heavy hand over his lips.

"I didn't go out of my way for this, Docker. Larkin came looking for it."

Docker pointed to the bright headlights. "You're violating blackout security, Haskell. I know you're a goddamn meathead, but I'm surprised at Dolan and Granowski and Rado here."

The sound of their names seemed to startle the mechanics; they shifted restlessly and nervously, like oxen stung on their blind sides by whips.

"Keep this between you and me, Docker. Just leave them—"

"Shut up, damn you."

Haskell sucked in another breath, puffing himself up like a frog, but his voice was unaccountably higher when he said, "You want a piece of me, Docker, I'm right here, I'm not going anywhere."

"We'll get to that," Docker said, and stared at the mechanics. "You're playing in the snow like a bunch of goddamn kids, but if a thermal cut a hole in this weather a German fighter could fly a strafing pattern right down your stupid throats."

Larkin began laughing, the blood dripping from his chin onto the muddy front of his overcoat. "You tell 'em, Bull," he said, coughing and gasping for breath. "Rip their asses off. You didn't go to college for nothing. Not by a shit sight."

Docker drew his .45 and flipped the safe lever to the off position.

Haskell grinned tightly. "Hold it, there's no call . . ."

Docker turned to the mechanics. "Now get those lights out. If you're not moving when I take care of the first truck you'll spend Christmas in a stockade."

Docker steadied the gun in both hands and squeezed off two rounds that smashed out the headlights of the truck nearest him. Before the flat reports had time to echo on the frosty air Haskell's mechanics were running toward the other trucks.

Darkness now plunged over the courtyard, an almost weighable blackness relieved only by the spinning snow-flakes and the yellow glow from the kerosese lamp in the farmhouse. Docker put the .45 away and twisted the metal clip to lock the holster strap, then looked at Haskell. "Just how far do you want to take this?"

"Any fucking place you like, Docker."

"We'll see just how far." He tossed the bottle of beet brandy to Rado, carefully smoothed his gloves across the backs of his knuckles. "Let's go, you sorry meathead."

"Fifty bucks on Docker," Larkin said, his voice shaded with laughter. "Come on, you fuckers, let's see some cash on your meathead. Another fifty says he don't last three minutes."

Docker dropped his helmet on the ground and walked toward Haskell.

"Just hear me first," Haskell said, raising his open hands. "I'm goin' for regular Army, Docker, I can't afford to lose these stripes." An uneasy frown clouded his heavy, stubbled features. "They don't mean all that much to you college guys, you don't have to—"

"Haskell, if you want to get dumped on your ass with your hands at your sides, that's up to you."

Haskell studied the deliberate anger in Docker's eyes, then moved backward and squatted on the ground, picking up a handfull of snow and letting the melting flakes sift slowly through his fingers. He frowned at the thin spill of snow, watching the starry particles melt into the crusted ground.

"I don't want to keep it going," he said without lifting his eyes to Docker's.

"Well, be damned sure, Haskell."

Haskell took the bottle from Rado but didn't drink from it. He looked up at Docker then, his face sullen. "You and me know, sarge, this ain't the right time for it."

"You and I know something else, don't we, Haskell?" Docker said.

"What's that supposed to mean?"

Larkin spoke up, "It means you're a revolving shit-heel, Haskell, a shit-heel from any direction, a mothering, gutless shit-heel coward, that's what it means—"

"Shut up, Larkin." Docker picked up his helmet, put it on him and adjusted the chin strap. "Let's go."

"What Docker means, there'll never be a right time for you, Haskell."

"Goddamn it, at ease, Matt."

"Hup-tup-thrup-four, boss. Movin' out."

They headed for the jeep through the grove of trees that flanked the battery street. "Okay, get the goddamn sermon over with," Larkin said.

"You're turning into a pain in the ass and a fuck-up."
Docker's tone was casual but there was an edge of anger under it. "You probably can't help the first, but
you're not going to foul up in my section anymore."

"That's the best kind of sermon, Bull, nice and short,
then, bless the flock and cut 'em loose for a drink.
That's the best part of mass for us poor micks."

"Listen, I don't give one damn that your uncles got
drunk and tore up their money on payday, or that land-
lords periodically kicked your Irish asses out into the
snow."

Larkin's smile flashed through the smudge of dirt
and beard on his face. "That's pretty good, Bull. You
got a real pair of brass knucks on your tongue when
you want——" He was seized by a coughing fit, stopped
walking and braced his hands on his knees, almost
strangling in his effort to ease and soothe the hot ache
in his lungs. Finally, breathing slowly and carefully, he
straightened and brushed at the spittle and blood on his
lips with a dirty handkerchief. Holding his sides against
a contraction of pain, he hurried to catch up with
Docker.

"You tell Whitter I was in charge of that detail?"

"No, but I'll tell you something. I don't care where
you guys came from or what the hell you're going back
to . . . Trankic's woman runs a boardinghouse in Chicago, that's what he's fighting for, to get back and help
her. Schmitzer's brother went down on the *Lexington*
and he wants to make it home to keep his mother out of
the poorhouse. Okay, that's his trip to the chaplain. My
business, as you may or may not have heard, is running
this gun section."

"You're real sharp, got all of us tucked in pigeon-
holes," Larkin said. "So what's the morning line on Gelnick? You got him figured out?"

Docker shook his head.

Larkin daubed again at his swollen lip. "All right,
pay attention to your Uncle Matt. Gelnick took a shafting from Korbick from day one of basic. But I'll say this

for Gelnick, he took it like a sponge. KP every night
after a full day on the firing range, scrubbing down
grease tubs in the mess hall, his fatigues so dirty they
stank. On weekends Korbick had him digging four-by-
four holes in that red shit they call sand in Georgia,
then filling them up again in sun that took the paint off
the barracks. But the Hogman never broke, never
slammed a shovel into the back of Korbick's head, just
took it and stayed out of the stockade." He uncapped
his canteen and took a short swig of whiskey, gagging at
its raw heat, the black liquor running in icy trickles
down his chin and throat. "You want a belt?"

"Put that away, you've had enough."

"Okay, okay. So then it's time for three-day passes
after sixteen weeks at Camp Stewart, and damned if
Gelnick didn't jolt the bejesus out of everybody by
scrubbing himself to the bone and then pulling a package from under his bunk and dumping out a new uniform, a tailor-made job he'd ordered from a military
supply shop in Athens. So after more than three months
of looking like somebody who slept in a slit trench, Gelnick comes up roses . . . And that had to be one of
Korbick's worst moments, Bull, watching a man whose
guts he hated, a man he'd put the blocks to for months,
marching off the post as smart as a fucking West Point
cadet . . . He told everybody—Kohler, Solvis, Trank
—that he was going to Atlanta but he didn't. He
went to Waycross. I know, because I was there. His
wife was waiting for him, that's right, his *wife*. A Jewish
girl, Doris, I think her name was. Not your all-
American cheerleader type with big tits, but little, almost thin, you could say, but great legs and great black
hair. And brown eyes that made you think she could be
Spanish or something. I met her when I walked into a
bar and saw her sitting with Gelnick. He was so
shocked, he damned near shit himself. He came up to
my room that night, begged me not to tell any of the
guys at camp about his wife. So I promised, but I asked
him why didn't he shape up and get off Korbick's shit

list. And he told me something I thought a lot about. Because it's the way some Irish people think, my uncles anyway. They didn't mind that the drunk wagon was called the paddy wagon. I mean, they pretended they didn't mind, made jokes about it. That's Gelnick for you. He knew he was going to get flak from Korbick no matter what he did. So he stayed sane by making sure he deserved what Korbick was handing out. He knew he was getting it because he was a Jew and there wasn't a goddamn thing he could do about it. But he knew he couldn't stand it if anybody started riding him about his wife. So you know what he did when he got back to camp? Made a bundle of his smart new gear and the next morning dumped it all in the trash fire behind the mess hall, and then he went straight back to being Korbick's favorite fuck-up."

"So what do you want from me? A medal for keeping Gelnick's little secret?"

"Jesus, you don't give a guy anything, Bull."

Shorty Kohler was waiting for them at the jeep, and with Docker at the wheel they started up the hairpin turns toward their guns, with snow and sleet around them and the distant noise of V-1 rockets making a drumming noise inside their helmets.

Suddenly the front wheels smashed into a crusted pothole, and Kohler sprawled forward against Larkin. When Docker got the wheel under control, Larkin sniffed and looked closely at a stain on the sleeve of his overcoat. "What the hell did you smear on me?"

"I slipped on the road," Kohler said. "I stepped in something."

"You stepped in something with your *hands*, you silly bastard?"

"Go fuck yourself," Kohler said, but he was laughing, his breath fusing in white bursts with the cold air. "I had to do something, know what I mean? Some of the guys told me Korbick was getting all fixed up, you know, soaking in that big tub of his, a clean uniform all laid out, just so he could go over to the motor pool and have a ringside seat to watch the other shithead, Haskell, working over Larkin. So I got to thinking, what the fuck? Who we supposed to be fighting? So I went to the supply tent and got me a helmet and filled it with crap from a slit trench behind the barn. That's how I got it on my hands, it was sloppin' over. I took it back to Korbick's tent, he was sitting there in a big tub of water, scrubbing his back. I dumped the helmet over his head. right down to his ears, and was gone before he even started yelling. I tell you guys, he screamed like he had his balls caught in an eggbeater."

Docker braked the jeep and pulled over to the side of the road. "Get out and scrub your hands, Shorty," he said.

"Jesus." Larkin slapped the dashboard. "Perfect."

"Let's forget it," Docker said.

"But you got to admit—"

"I told you, forget it."

"All right." Larkin's voice was quiet, empty. He took a handkerchief from his overcoat and began moistening the blood hardening on his lips. "I know what you're thinking about."

Kohler climbed back into the jeep and Docker gunned the motor. After another hour's drive he made the last winding turn high in the hills, where they saw the smudge of smoke from Dormund's fire and the section's guns against the curtains of snow.

In the rear of a truck Private Solvis sat cross-legged with a blanket pulled around his shoulders. Using a flashlight and a stubby pencil, Solvis brought his diary up-to-date:

"Early chow tonight. Present position north and west of Werpen. We pulled back yesterday to a hill that was covered by fog in this endless damn snowstorm. I've mentioned Spinelli, Pierce and Gruber. Docker and Larkin and Kohler took their personal things down to Battery HQ tonight. Now the big dog (Laurel named him Radar) is barking and I just heard the jeep. So they're back.

"I'm seldom really exasperated with Pitko but I dislike his ideas about religion. He sees the Hand of God in the deaths of these young men. Thinks it's retribution against the section. Because we're ungodly or something. I'm not sure what this means either but he seems to have (not in so many words) a bad feeling about the new corporal.

"Awfully noisy this last twenty-four hours. V-1 rockets sounding above us like a thunderstorm. Must get to sleep. Tomorrow is December 16th. Only nine more shopping days till Christmas. Ha-ha!"

Corporal Schmitzer stood on the loading platform of the cannon and studied the valley mists through his binoculars. Linari and Tex Farrel were huddled in the iron seats on either side of the breechblock, gloved hands resting on cranks that moved the gun barrel through its tracking patterns.

Schmitzer thought about the wet snow creeping under the cuffs of his gloves and the coffee Dormund was making and of Spinelli's face ("Live coconut, corporal!"); sure, it was funny if you thought about it, but some part of his mind strayed helplessly in the direction of Sonny Laurel, who was curled up in a sleeping bag near the trucks . . .

"You got it all wrong," Guido Linari was telling Farrel. "Italians don't like being called wops."

The lanky Texan had merely asked Linari if he'd been born in an Italian neighborhood in New York, but Linari's mental processes frequently produced responses of confused and worrisome irrelevance. "See, Tex, at a ball game when I was a kid a guy called Frankie Crosetti a wop. Crosetti went into the stands and beat hell out of him. So you can't say *he* liked being called a wop."

"Which don't really answer my question," Farrel

said, without interrupting his careful scrutiny of the valley below him. . . .

Schmitzer knew that if he focused his binoculars on Laurel he would see the delicate blond eyelashes feathering his cheeks, the lips slightly parted and traced with melting snowflakes . . . Like a skilled campaigner these past days, Schmitzer had plotted his hours to be near the boy, working beside him on the guns, sitting as inconspicuously close to him as possible at chow breaks, but always furiously aware and hating the reality of it, that this tantalizing proximity would never be enough to satisfy the need he could feel building inside him.

Schmitzer forced himself to look away from the boy and think about his father and brother and uncle, deliberately raising those dark shapes to obscure visions of a sleeping young man and blond hair turned frosted by the cold wind. . . .

The mark on the wall in the basement in Detroit, that was all that was left of the old man, the footprint he'd made near the ceiling, Christ, what a young bull he'd been, laughing and running up the wall like it was a flight of stairs with him and his brother tight in his arms. That faded footprint was just above the empty coal bin where they'd found him one morning with the gun in his hand. And crazy Uncle Ernie dead in a jail where they didn't even talk his language. . . .

Schmitzer knew that private Joe Pitko was staring at him from where he sat near Dormund's covered fire, his eyes bright and watchful under the rim of his helmet, his stubby forefinger, as if with a will of its own, moving slowly across the open Bible on his knee. The bald old bastard had his eye on him all right; every time he was near Sonny Laurel he was damn sure to find Pitko staring solemnly, accusingly at him. Somehow it was all part of the shit of this war . . . Pitko's staring, vindictive eyes, and the awful explosions that tore open the hull of the *Lexington* . . . all the same damn thing . . . all of it could kill you . . .

In Barcelona, one of Uncle Ernie's cell mates had given him a copy of a poem written by a writer named Ernest Hemingway. Uncle Ernie claimed it was written by Hemingway, but the poem had been typed on a piece of ruled paper and wasn't signed so it could have been written by anybody. That's what Schmitzer thought, and the only thing he knew about that Hemingway writer was a fishing piece in a sports magazine. But whoever wrote the poem, it was so goddamn true about war it made him almost weak with anger. It had been shipped back to Detroit with some of his uncle's stuff, old uniforms, a few books and a picture of a girl the family didn't know anything about, a smiling, dark-haired girl who held a leather bottle of wine up to whoever was taking the picture.

Schmitzer had memorized the last lines of the poem:

"The age demanded that we dance—
And jammed us into iron pants.
And in the end, the age was handed—
The kind of shit that it demanded."

That Hemingway, or whoever it was, knew what it was all about, he sure as hell knew the score, Corporal Schmitzer thought as he studied the white expanse of the valley and the hazy outline of the trails leading down and through the rocky gorges and fir trees.

Chapter Eleven

December 16, 1944. The Ardennes.
Saturday, 0530 Hours.

In the first half of December, 1944, a number of intelligence summaries and statements were distributed to appropriate units in the American and British and German sectors of the Ardennes.

United States Army Intelligence, on December 10th, 1944, submitted its daily report to Eisenhower headquarters at SHAEF (Supreme Headquarters Allied Expeditionary Forces), Versailles, France. The report conceded that "beyond vague rumors, there is no further news of General Josef 'Sepp' Dietrich's Sixth SS Panzer Army."

The daily Allied Intelligence report for December 12th, 1944, concluded: "It is now certain that attrition is sapping the strength of German forces on the western front. The crust of defenses is thinner, more brittle and more vulnerable than it appears to our troops on the line. A German collapse may develop suddenly and without warning."

December 16th, 1944: At an early morning staff meeting of Allied general officers at Twenty-first Army Group headquarters, British Field Marshal Bernard

Montgomery summed up enemy options and capabilities in these words: "The enemy is at present fighting a defensive campaign on all fronts. His situation is such that he cannot stage major offensive operations. Furthermore, at all costs, he has to prevent the war from entering on a mobile phase; he has not the transport or the petrol that would be necessary for mobile operations, nor could his tanks compete with ours in the mobile phase."

At midnight on December 15th, 1944, this message from Field Marshal Gerd von Rundstedt was read to all commands of German Army Group B: "Soldiers of the western front. Your great hour has come. We gamble everything. You carry with you the supreme obligation to give all to achieve the ultimate objectives for our Fatherland and our Führer."

Operation Christrose was launched on December 16th, 1944, approximately three hours after the following United States Army Intelligence summary was released at General Eisenhower's headquarters, SHAEF. It was a one-line report which read:

"There is nothing to report on the Ardennes front."

Chapter Twelve

December 16, 1944. Six kilometers from
Werpen. Saturday, 0630 Hours.

On a slope above the hill where Section Eight's guns
faced east, the mongrel dog was barking at something
he heard or smelled in the darkness. To the north and
east there was the heavy, curiously human sound of artillery, noises like distant coughings and mutterings accompanied by gleaming streaks of rockets and tracers
through black cloud masses. Trankic was shouting
something at the men on the cannon and machine guns.

A censor deep in Docker's mind tried to screen out
the sound of that worried voice. He'd been in his bedroll in a drifted lee of the wind only an hour or so,
shaved and washed, carbine beside him, his boots
drying out beside Dormund's fire.

He began to wake then, hearing Trankic calling to
the men and remembering parts of his fragmented
dreams. On his last shift, he had monitored the radio
and looked at the mail picked up at Battery, and there
was an uneasy residue of all that with him now . . .
Bandleader Glenn Miller, Captain Glenn Miller, eight
hours overdue on a London-to-Paris flight. That had
been on the Armed Forces network, and a stateside
wrap-up of Roosevelt's first month of an unprecedented
fourth term as President. And coincidentally, a letter
from his father had said: "The people is a beast. I don't

know who said that first but it's on the mark and FDR
knows it. He's bought the people of this country the
way you buy a dog's loyalty—through the stomach,
through handouts and giveaways. But since I'd rather
write of real dogs than FDR, I must tell you the big
male, Sheboygan, has shown scant regard for . . ." He
blinked his eyes to focus on the canteen of steaming
coffee that Trankic was forcing into his hands.

"You better take a look, Bull. This sure as hell ain't
our artillery."

"Go get my boots, Trank."

Walking to the guns, his boots hot and stiff, Docker
looked at the horizon. In the east there were bright
flashes at ground level. Above them vivid parabolas of
tracers and rockets showed against the sky. The artillery
shells sounded like freight trains rumbling over their
heads. Docker tightened his cartridge belt and buckled
his helmet strap. "Schmitzer, get everybody out of their
sacks. Trankic, try to raise Battery or Battalion . . ."

The sergeant looked toward the horizon through his
binoculars and saw what looked like tiny balls of fire
spurting up behind the mountains. Then he felt rather
than heard a deeper sound, a jarring noise that seemed
to come up from the ground and through his boots, the
sound of tanks. He told Farrel, "Pick up a bazooka,
Tex, and get the jeep over here." Larkin and Schmitzer
were ordered to load the food, ammunition and gasoline
and warm up the engines of the trucks. "I want to move
out fast if we have to. If we get separated, our fall-back
position is Lepont on the Salm, two kilometers south-
east of grid coordinates A-7 on our large-scale map."

He took the wheel of the jeep and with Trankic beside him and Farrel in the rear, drove down the trail
toward the valley. Ahead of them snow glistened in the
blackout beams of their headlights.

Farrel, holding two bazooka projectiles notched carefully in the fingers of his left hand, was watching the
road with steady eyes. Docker stopped the jeep fifty
yards below the crest of the next hill and the men

scrambled the rest of the way on foot, crawling through frozen underbrush to a hedge of gnarled trees.

Rocket bombs flashed methodically through the skies, hanging along the horizon like flaming lanterns. Several thousand yards off they saw barrage lights rising from the next ridge of hills, coating the underside of the low clouds, the reflections brilliantly illuminating the white ground.

Docker's glasses picked up movement in the distant woods and then he could see German soldiers in long winter-camouflage coats, rifles a dark slash across their chests, the splintered reflections from the barrage lights shining on their helmets.

He lowered his glasses because now he could see the German troops with his naked eye and, not more than a thousand yards away, a white skirmish line moving relentlessly through sparse stands of beech and fir trees. They were still like toy soldiers at this distance, black boots moving up and down as rhythmically as pistons, their long white uniforms and black helmets blurred by flurries of snow. However, when the winds changed abruptly, blowing harder toward Docker and his men, the illusion of miniature soldiers disappeared, the changing gales bringing the sound of their singing to the Americans, a heavy rumble of song that stiffened the fine hairs on Docker's neck.

"Jesus Christ, Bull," Trankic whispered, "there's thousands of them."

The effect of the reflected barrage lights was magical; the ranks of soldiers seemed to merge with the leaping shadows, disappearing and materializing again in the gleaming mists rising from the hoar-white fields and forests.

Trankic grabbed Docker's arm and pointed beyond the soldiers to the distant silhouettes of German tanks grinding through the snow. Docker gave his orders with gestures, and the men scrambled to their feet and ran down the hill to the jeep.

The guns were hooked to the trucks, with Larkin and Schmitzer in the cabs. Docker swung the jeep in front of the lead truck and pumped his fist up and down in the air.

"March order," he shouted, and both trucks rolled out after him, double-clutching for speed and traction against the mud and sleet. In the valley below them Docker saw three German tanks emerging from a black growth of trees, their tracks churning up a storm of snow, Panzer IIIs or Panzer IVs, heavily armored with 75-millimeter cannons.

The tanks sighted the truck convoy, and the first projectiles smashed into the mountainside fifty yards behind the Americans, shattering trees and rocks and sending whistling fragments tearing at the sides of the jeep and trucks. But before the German gunners could make corrections, the three vehicles had swung around a turn that put the bulk of the mountain between them and the tanks. Seconds later they were gathering speed recklessly down a treacherous roadway toward another range of hills. . . .

Dog Battery's Section Eight spent the rest of December 16th bivouacked in a narrow rocky gorge above a tributary of the Our River.

They knew from fragmentary radio reports that the Germans were attacking on a broad front, and from the sound of heavy transport and tanks echoing for miles around them in the frosted air they knew they had been overrun on both flanks by columns of mechanized enemy troops. Eating cold rations and maintaining a full guard mount, they pulled out at dawn the following morning and headed west toward Lepont on the Salm.

Their only ally was the weather; heavy fog and zero visibility reduced the risk of detection by German aircraft and armor and provided Section Eight cover for the tortuous passage through the mountains.

Later that afternoon, as the darkness gave them another degree of safety, the section's last truck was

waved down by a soldier in an American uniform who
stumbled from the underbrush and ran alongside the
cannon, his boots slipping and sliding in the mud.

Radar barked loudly but Laurel whacked the dog
and he and Kohler braced themselves and reached for
the desperate hands of the young soldier, touching his
fingers, then his wrists and finally hauling him over the
tailgate into the truck.

The youngster's face was drawn and white with fatigue, eyes wide and staring above his roughly chapped
cheeks. His boots were clogged with mud, frozen in
ridged crusts along the soles, and he fell into a sitting
position with his knees drawn up to his chest, his red
and swollen hands locked under his arms. The collar of
his jacket and shirt was open and Solvis saw a pulse
pounding rapidly at the base of his throat.

In response to Laurel's first questions, the young soldier said his name was Jackson Baird, that he'd been in
a line company with the 106th Division. Kohler wanted
to know what the Germans had hit them with, tanks or
infantry or both, but Baird was so close to shock from
exposure that it was obvious he had no clear idea what
had happened to him or his outfit.

"He needs to rest, let him alone now," Solvis said,
and taking a blanket from his bedroll he slung it over
Baird's shoulders, tucking the ends around the boy's
chapped wrists and hands. Solvis also noticed then that
Baird had no rifle and that there was no sign of dog
tags behind the open collar of his woolen shirt.

"You want a cigarette?" When the youngster shook
his head, Solvis said, "Then how about a drink? We've
got some whiskey. Might do you good, kind of thaw you
out."

The soldier shook his head again, with no expression
at all in his white face and glazed eyes. He seemed to
withdraw into himself then, trembling slightly and hugging himself for warmth, his body swaying with the motion of the truck.

Chapter Thirteen

December 17, 1944. The environs of
Lepont, Belgium. Sunday, 1500 Hours.

In the afternoon of the day that would be known as
Bloody Sunday, Dog Battery's Section Eight took cover
in a grove of fir trees, protected from wind and observa-
tion by heavy green limbs weighted almost to the ground
with layers of ice and snow.

The men were exhausted, but Docker had ordered
the stop only for cold K-rations. From his maps, he estimated they were about five or six miles from Lepont.
Above the village was a promontory identified as Mont
Reynard, and he knew if they could get the trucks to
the top they could control the river and bridges below
with their guns.

Trankic had been checking Battery and Battalion
headquarters every hour since the first German attacks
but so far had raised neither unit.

Dormund and the Hogman were opening K-rations
and spooning the contents into mess kits. Private Joseph
Pitko had cleared snow from the base of a tree and sat
cross-legged reading his Bible, a short and powerfully
built man with a totally bald head and brown eyes that
seemed to darken with the intensity of his emotions, a
state he achieved effortlessly when temporal distractions
were not besetting him and he was able to pursue and
savor a complete union with his God. Pitko had no need

to look at his Bible in order to read from pages fly-specked with dirt and faded and stained from exposure to weather; he knew the Word of the Lord by heart. Now he stared at the white fir trees, his body motionless, a carven figure of Old Testament fervor and purpose, relevant in a mythical fashion to storms and sleet and the sound of artillery on the horizons, but detached and unrelated to the men of the section who were preparing food and checking the guns and maps.

Pitko did not believe Almighty God had been speaking in metaphors when He called the human body a temple for His presence. The religious conviction that had seized and permeated him since earliest memory was a natural, elemental force he had no interest in trying to explain or share; he did not believe in the rationale of those who became converted to the Lord on reaching the age of reason. Or at any other age. The Hand of God was offered to each man and woman at birth and he who refused it was either blind or foolish, and Pitko had no tolerance for those who would not see and believe, who needed to be "converted" to the truth.

Dormund brought a mess kit of food to Pitko and shifted his weight uncertainly from one foot to the other, scratching his neck and searching for words, because while he wasn't afraid of Pitko, he was awed and puzzled by him.

"Joe, it's kind of wretched stuff, but Sarge says no fire."

Pitko's fingers continued to move across the page of his Bible but his eyes remained fixed on the trees. "Compose your mind to the indignation of the Lord," he said in his quiet, resonant voice. And then, "He hath said: 'The mountains shall be thrown down, and the hedges shall fall and every wall shall fall to the ground. And I shall judge him with pestilence, and with blood, and with violent rain and hailstones. And I shall be magnified and they shall know that I am the Lord.' "

Pitko pointed at the fog-shrouded mountains where

the sound of artillery was like an avalanche rolling
down the hills.

"Reflect on what He has spoken, Dormund, and
what He is now bringing forth, because He said, 'For I
will rain fire and brimstone upon him and upon his
army, and upon the many nations that are with him.' "

Pitko stared at Dormund, his eyes almost black now
in the pallor of his lined and angry face. His finger had
stopped under the word "Lord."

"There will be fire soon for all of us, Dormund," he
said. "You may trust the Lord."

There were times when Dormund thought Pitko was
crazy, because Pitko believed everything in the Bible
and that made Dormund uncomfortable since he wasn't
sure about anything he read, even in comic books.
Maybe somebody just made it all up. Even the Bible.
He thought of making a joke about that with Pitko, but
knew it wouldn't work, that it would come out wrong.
So he backed away and took the rations over to Farrel
and Sonny Laurel, who were playing with the big dog.

Trankic called to Docker. "Hey, Bull, I'm getting
something."

Docker walked to the jeep, but by then only static
was sputtering from the speaker.

"What was it?"

"It was some English but mostly German," Trankic
said. "Maybe it's a lot of bullshit. They say they got
Bastogne surrounded. The Twenty-eighth Division is
knocked off the line, the One-hundred-sixth is kaput.
They say nine thousand men captured, ammo, gasoline,
the works."

Shorty Kohler said: "That's the outfit the guy we
picked up is from, the One-hundred-sixth. They got a
lion on their shoulder patch, the Golden Lions, that's
what they're called. Golden fuck-ups, you ask me. All
fucking POWs now."

Jackson Baird was seated on the tailgate of a truck, his helmet beside him. He had a mess kit of K-rations in his hands but wasn't eating; he was watching the dog playing with Farrel and Sonny Laurel and his food had whitened with a powder of snow.

He looked strong and wiry, Docker thought, of medium height but on the thin side, with sandy brown hair, and what Docker's father would have called a "good" jaw—hard and firm, a hint of stubbornness in its bony strength.

Docker had not yet had a chance to talk with him, so he joined Baird and said, "I'm Sergeant Docker. I'm going to tell you something just once now. Put your helmet on and keep it on."

In a scramble, Baird put his mess kit aside, slid off the tailgate and crammed his helmet onto his head, buckling the chin strap with shaking fingers. "I'm—I'm sorry, sergeant. I was brushing snow from under my collar and I forgot that I took it off."

"Okay," Docker said. "Remember to keep it on. Where's your rifle?"

"My rifle? I don't know, sergeant, in all that firing, with the shells landing, it got knocked out of my hands."

"Let me have a look at your dog tags."

"Well, I lost them, too. I fell down the side of a hill and they got snagged on a bush or something."

"You have a wallet, letters from home? Any ID at all?"

"All that stuff's in my musette bag. It was with my bedroll and I didn't have a chance to get it."

Docker said, "Start at the beginning, Baird. How did you get separated from your outfit?"

"Well, our company was on the left flank of the division somewhere near the Losheim Gap. The Fourteenth Armored was on the line north of us, I think."

Shorty Kohler and Farrel and several others had gathered in a loose semicircle behind Docker.

"Yesterday morning—I guess it was around six o'clock—we heard artillery and saw a lot of rockets to the east of us. Then while it was still dark, the German tanks and troops came across the fields. It was like a nightmare after that, everybody running and shooting. There was so much noise we couldn't even hear what the noncoms were telling us."

Baird looked uneasily at the men standing behind Docker, his eyes shifting away from Kohler and Linari and Matt Larkin. "Nobody knew what was going on." Moistening his chapped lips he pushed a strand of hair back under his helmet. "It was like, I don't know—like we were caught in a tornado or something."

"Who's your commanding general?"

"Major General Jones. Major General Alan Jones."

"And your company officers?"

"The company commander is Captain George Dilworth, sergeant. The lieutenant in charge of my squad was Lieutenant Rick Russo. Our sergeant was Floyd Greene."

"Were you on guard when the Germans attacked?"

Baird nodded quickly. "Another private and me, Tommy Guthrie, we were posted about two hundred yards from company headquarters."

"Did you sound an alarm?"

Baird moistened his lips again. "Sure, sergeant. I mean, we yelled and fired our rifles."

"Did an officer or noncom tell you to fall back from your guard position?"

"I don't know who gave the orders, sergeant." Baird's eyes were blinking more rapidly now. "But somebody yelled at us to get out of there. It might have been Lieutenant Russo or Sergeant Greene."

Docker said, "Baird, you'd better try to remember your last orders. And who gave them to you. Because you're at least a dozen miles behind your division now. Do you understand what I'm telling you?"

"I'm not sure, sergeant."

Without any particular emphasis, Kohler said,

"You're a fucking deserter, that's what the sarge is telling you."

"At ease, goddamn it," Docker said. "Baird, what happened to the other soldier on guard with you?"

"Tommy Guthrie? I don't know, sergeant. After I fell down the hill, I didn't see any of them again."

"Where you from in the States, Baird?"

"Well, I was born in Chicago but we moved a lot. We've been living in New York State for the last ten years or so, in Peekskill—"

Trankic's call to Docker interrupted. "Hey, Bull, you better get over here."

Most of the men followed Docker to the radio, but Sonny Laurel stayed behind and looked at Baird, who was picking listlessly at his food. Tex Farrel stood nearby, holding Radar on the leash they'd made from strips of knotted tarpaulin. "I wish Kohler would keep his big mouth shut," he said.

Baird saw them watching him and managed a narrow smile. He whistled to the dog. "Looks like he's half Alsatian."

"His name's Radar," Sonny Laurel said. "It's what we call him anyway. We requisitioned him from Werpen."

Farrel pulled the lunging dog over to the truck and gave the lead to Baird. "Hold him," he said. "There's foxes around here and he'd like to go AWOL."

Sonny and Farrel slogged through the snow to the jeep, where the rest of the section stood with Trankic and Docker, listening to a miniature, static-threaded, voice.

". . . a First Army unit, I'm sure, shoulder patches of the Seventh Armored . . ." The voice was British, exhausted but charged with tension. "This is Tail Gunner Euan Perlough in a farmhouse about a mile from the village called Baugnies. I have a bad leg since bailing out over Cologne. Made it this far on plain luck. There's been a frightful massacre here . . . a hundred or more Yanks herded into a field and gunned down

. . . cut down in their tracks with their hands in the air. Seventh Armored chaps, most of them . . ." The British gunner's voice rose in a burst of emotion. "Command Group Peiper, it was his outfit . . . the Yanks had their hands in the air, thought they were being taken prisoner, some of them even laughing. More than a hundred in all, never a chance . . . at Malmédy . . ."

Silence then, broken only by humming threads of static. A few seconds later they heard, "I'd better make a try—" and then there was a final click and the set went silent.

Docker gave his orders, the sharpness in his voice discouraging discussion or reflection. "We're pulling out. Nobody inside the trucks, everybody on the gun mounts, rifles off safe. Jackets open so you can reach grenades. No goddamn talking. Pitko, you ride shotgun in the first truck with Schmitzer. Shorty, take the cab with Trankic. Larkin, you and me in the jeep. Now let's haul ass."

When everyone was in position, the huge dog tied to the stake of the lead truck, Docker climbed into the jeep and pumped his fist twice and the two trucks followed him out of the clearing, their motors making a rasping sound against the heavy silence of the hills.

In the truck behind the jeep, Corporal Schmitzer slowly and carefully applied the brakes as they started down a slick grade. At his side, Pitko lightly stroked the pages of his Bible with his fingertips. Schmitzer peered out the open window and saw nothing but fogs and falling snow. Anxiety had created a cold twist of tension in his stomach; you couldn't see the enemy, couldn't fire at him, you couldn't even run from him . . . His mood was agitated, bitter; he had seen the warmth between the three youngsters in the section—Sonny Laurel, Farrel and the straggler they'd picked up, that Jackson Baird. Their youth and excitement seemed to draw a circle around them, shutting everybody else out . . . He felt a sudden exasperation for Pitko and his Bible, which were both about as useless as the Hogman, if you got down to it . . . "Look, I don't mind you reading your Bible, that's your business, but keep an eye out your side of the truck, okay?"

Pitko's face was reflected in the windshield, eyes shining darkly in the frosted glass.

"A man doesn't read the Bible," he said. "The Bible reads the man. A man doesn't choose the Word of the Lord. It chooses him."

"You mean it's like a Ouija board?" Schmitzer's attempt at a light tone failed; the intensity of Pitko's manner tightened the already painful knots in his stomach.

"Listen to what I'm reading," Pitko said. "Listen to the Word of God." Without glancing at his Bible, he intoned quietly, "The sun was risen upon the earth, and Lot entered into Segor."

To Schmitzer, it seemed as if the sound of artillery had begun to rise on all the horizons . . . Well, he tried to reassure himself, Pitko couldn't know . . . he'd hardly spoken to the boy in the last week . . . except he now remembered what had happened the night Docker had gone back to Battery headquarters with Larkin and Kohler, and the guilty thoughts created a furtive riot in his blood, the heat of it flaming his cheeks and starting a pulse of guilty pleasure throbbing in his spine . . . Schmitzer had no way to analyze his emotions, no guide to lead him from his shameful needs. He had grown up despising queers, fairies, fags, whatever you called them, encouraged by the priests to dump them on their soft asses if they ever tried anything funny. But there had been no money for dates and taking girls to the movies or anything like that, and the one time he had been to a whorehouse he had gotten drunk first and the big black woman had laughed at him and poked his limp sex organ with her finger and said in her soft, chortling voice, "Maybe it'll grow up when you do, honey." . . .

It had been a gray afternoon, the light diffused by the fogs, when Dormund and Linari had got into a noisy, good-humored wrestling match with Sonny Laurel, trying to pin him to the ground in the snowdrifts piled up between the section's trucks.

Suddenly the playful mood of the game had changed and Laurel began squirming and shouting in genuine anger, his voice breaking in an adolescent tremor, because Linari had trapped his arms with a scissors hold and Dormund had pulled his trousers down and was stuffing lumps of snow into his underwear.

Schmitzer had come around the side of the truck at that moment, staring at the writhing figures on the ground, moved so strangely by the sight of Sonny Laurel's exposed flesh that he was powerless to move or act or speak. Laurel's skin, bare from his chest to his groin, seemed white and translucent as silk, his slim muscles trembling in spasmodic contractions against the melting snow. And below the boy's thrusting hips, Schmitzer could see the arch of a golden crest, soft curls of fine hair glinting like a spray of new wheat.

It was an interval of emotion attenuated by a willing conspiracy of all his senses; he had stood motionless for how long he would never know, his nerves bared to pleasure that was like a sweet agony, and it wasn't until he felt the shocking weight of desire, a shuddering contraction at the very center of himself, that the terrible awareness broke the instant of physical bondage and he had shouted hoarsely at them, "Goddamn it, cut it out . . . you don't have work to do, I'll find you some." . . .

He gripped the steering wheel now as if he would splinter it in his powerful hands. "Why did you read that stuff to me?"

"I told you, a man does not choose the Word of the Lord." Pitko began reading again, his voice running deeply under the sounds of battle. "And the Lord rained on Sodom and Gomorrah brimstone and fire from the Lord out of Heaven."

Feeling threatened in ways Pitko couldn't really

know—could he?—Schmitzer said between his teeth, "Fuck the damn Bible."

"That defileth his neighbor's wife, that grieveth the needy, that lifteth up his eyes to idols, that committeth abomination—"

"Stop it, for Christ's sake," Schmitzer said, a sound inside matching the swell of artillery in the mountains.

"Seeing he had done all these detestable things, he shall surely die, his blood shall be upon him."

Schmitzer thought helplessly of the *Lexington* and his father's footprint on the wall near the ceiling.

"Listen, listen for grace," Pitko went on. "For the Lord asketh: 'Is it My will that a sinner should die,' saith the Lord God, 'and not that he should be converted from his ways, and live?' "

And from the depths of his anguish, Schmitzer heard himself ask . . . "How did you know?"

"I have seen you look on the boy," Pitko said, like a judgment. "From the tribe of Levi, the truth of Leviticus, I know the punishments for unlawful lusts. For if anyone lies with a man as with a woman, both have committed an abomination and their blood shall be upon them . . ."

Docker saw it the same instant as Larkin, an ME-109 crossing the valley on a flanking course with the section's jeep and trucks. When it streaked away and disappeared into a bank of fog, Docker hit the brakes in pumping motions and stopped on the shoulder of the road. Sounding his horn twice, he listened tensely as the trucks braked and skidded on the slick ice behind him.

They couldn't use the cannon or machine guns in this position; the ricochet of their own fire from the trees could be as dangerous as an attacking aircraft. The sergeant told Larkin and Trankic to spread the men on both sides of the road, where they could use their rifles. Most of them had long since filed the sears off their M-1s, making the weapons fully automatic—without

sears to lock the operating rod spring after each shot,
one trigger pull emptied the clip in a burst. But in spite
of their deployment the plane flared around the mountainside and was over and past them before they could
fire. And with its passage came the whistling roar of its
props and crescendoing bursts of gunfire, the bullets
stitching their way up the frozen ground of the white
hills.

Above the noise Docker heard someone shouting,
"Pitko, get up!" He ran along the road to the first truck
and saw that its windshield had been smashed out by
bullets. Shards of glass hung from its metal frame, trembling like cobwebs in the sweeping winds. Other bullet
holes gaped in the canvas body of the truck.

Somebody shouted, "Christ, look at him!"

Pitko was lying on the ground beside the open door
on the passenger side of the truck. A single bullet had
pierced the front of his helmet and had come out the
back, furrowing the surface of the road and leaving
flecks of metal and bone and blood on the glistening
white snow.

Docker's hands were shaking; he tightened them on
his rifle and looked around at the men. "Schmitzer, you
and Laurel get a tarp and take him into the woods. You
know what to do with his dog tag?"

Schmitzer barely nodded, a man walking in a daze.

Docker then told Dormund and Gelnick to remove
the splinters of glass from the frame of the windshield
and ordered the others to get back on the guns. He
picked up Pitko's rifle, pushed back the operating handle until it caught, tilted the rifle, put his thumb in the
breech and looked down the barrel. His thumbnail
gleamed in a faint light reflected from the falling snow.
The lands and grooves were clean and shining; Pitko
had taken good care of it. Docker let the bolt fly home,
the sound a dry *crack* in the silence, then threw the rifle
hard at Jackson Baird. To his surprise, Baird caught it
competently, one hand above the balance, the other

on the stock. "You got yourself a rifle now," Docker
said.

He walked to the jeep, feeling less that they had lost
something than that they had wasted it.

The big dog was barking exuberantly, its head looming above the tailgate of the truck. Larkin offered
Docker his canteen. Docker took a short pull of the
black whiskey, then yelled to Tex Farrel to make the
damned dog shut up.

The forest was quiet, the artillery distant. The snow
fell through the willow and poplar trees and settled in
layers on growth of heather and lichens and honeysuckle. Schmitzer and Sonny Laurel laid Pitko's body in a
natural hollow between two towering silver fir trees.
Schmitzer wrapped the tarpaulin tightly about the body,
securing the corners with the straps and eyelets spaced
along the edges of the water-repellent fabric. When he
slipped a fold of the tarpaulin under Pitko's head,
Sonny Laurel knelt and took off his helmet and thought
that this wasn't at all the way he'd imagined it would be
back there on a green lawn in his hometown of Chicago
when a neighbor's beautiful wife read him those stirring
letters from her husband in the Pacific . . .

Schmitzer opened a button of Pitko's field jacket,
found his dog tag chain and broke it with a twist of his
wrist. He put one dog tag in his wallet. Sonny Laurel
watched with wide, shocked eyes as Schmitzer forced
open Pitko's mouth and dropped the other dog tag into
it. With the heel of his hand, Schmitzer forced the dead
man's jaw shut, letting several inches of the chain hang
from the stiffening lips.

"Something happens to us, there's a chance somebody'll find the other tag on him," Schmitzer said.

"Shouldn't we say a prayer?"

"I guess so."

"What would be right?"

"I don't know. He was the expert on that."

Schmitzer looked at the snowflakes melting in Laurel's blond hair and coating the shoulders of his overcoat. Standing above and behind him, he could see the curve of the boy's cheek and the smooth, soft arch of his throat. He looked quickly away, before Laurel might turn and see what was revealed in his eyes and on his face.

Pitko had seen it, a mark, an abomination. And Pitko was dead. He had warned him, though. To save the boy. Maybe to save them both . . .

Schmitzer remembered the words in the Spanish poem his uncle had sent them from the jail in Barcelona. Maybe it wasn't just right, he thought, but what the hell, and in a low and earnest voice he said, "Just remember, I'll never forget. All those Christmas days gone by. Ineradicably"—he stumbled on the word—"stamped in my head. Lovely memories are held high."

"Lovely memories are held high," Laurel said. "That's nice."

His skin looked soft, pale against the rosy color in his cheeks, but as he secured the tarpaulin over Pitko's face, Schmitzer made himself think of the other deaths hounding his life, a defiant uncle, his father at an empty coal bin with the gun, his brother on the *Lex* when the planes tore her hull apart—he forced himself to think of them and he vowed, he *vowed* bitterly in the cathedral silence that his abomination of feeling would never contaminate anyone but himself, that it would die here and forever under the trees with Joe Pitko.

"Now listen to me good, Sonny," he said. "It's part my fault Pitko got hit. He got talking about something that had nothing the fuck to do with staying alive. Like I told you, we gotta make sure nobody takes our place over here. Pitko forgot that, he forgot what he was here for, and it's my fault because I let him." Schmitzer drew a deep breath. "So get this. I ever say anything to you, *anything*, that isn't about our job, you take that rifle and ram the butt into my face, understand? Goddamn it, you understand?"

Laurel was startled, almost frightened by his intensity. He nodded quickly. "Sure, I understand." Except, of course, he didn't.

They looked for a moment at Pitko in the canvas shroud already layered with snow and then turned and went down a trail to the trucks. "Lovely memories are held high . . ." Shit, Schmitzer thought. The wind was cold and strong in his face and he was glad because it froze the tears in his eyes. The other guy knew more about it . . . "The age demanded that we dance, and jammed us into iron pants . . ."

When they swung themselves up into the trucks, Docker shouted, "March order," and within the hour they were cresting a hill that sloped down toward the Salm River and the village of Lepont.

Chapter Fourteen

December 19, 1944. The Ardennes.
Tuesday, 1500 Hours.

On the fourth day of the German offensive, intelligence officers at First Army and VIII Corps prepared the following reconstructions and summaries for Supreme Allied Headquarters at Versailles.

Operation Christrose had been launched on a ninety-mile front from Monschau in the north to Echternach in the south, a striking force of more than twenty-seven full-strength Panzer and infantry divisions with a reserve estimated at seven divisions.

On the northern shoulder of the German line, General Sepp Dietrich's Sixth SS Panzer Army had smashed through the Losheim Gap into the forward positions of the Americans' 14th Armored Division. In the center, General Manteuffel's Fifth Panzer Army had broken the same division's left flank and bypassed it to open approaches into the deep valley of the Our River.

On the southern flank, General Brandenberger's Seventh Army was driving a wedge below at the rail center at Bastogne, its objective the Meuse River and its tributary, the Semois.

These spearheads were savaging the American 4th Infantry Division and positioning their armor to provide a shield against the expected counterattacks from the south by General Patton's Third Army.

At dawn on December 19th, the 106th Infantry Division (the Golden Lions) had been surrounded on the Schnee Eiffel by a pincer movement of the Fifth and Sixth German Panzer armies; nine thousand troops of the division were captured with their supplies intact, gasoline, medical stores and ammunition.

Fragmentary reports reaching Intelligence from the broken American lines indicated that elements of the American V Corps were barely holding their position on the Elsenborn Ridge.

The 9th Armored and the 28th Infantry Division had been badly mauled in the first stages of Christrose. Kampfgruppe Peiper had broken cleanly through the American front, its columns driving toward the Salm River and Trois-Ponts.

Strategically important towns captured or invested by the enemy as of this date were Malmédy, Stavelot, Vielsalm, St. Vith, Houffalize, Longvilly and Wiltz.

Bastogne was known to be surrounded, the 101st Airborne Division trapped inside a ring of German armor.

Intelligence summaries created this picture: American forces were retreating by the thousands to an illusion of safety in rear-echelon areas, discarding weapons and even overcoats and food supplies in a flight through streets clogged with the wreckage of tanks and trucks and rotting with decomposed bodies.

To contain the great breach in the Allied eastern lines, General Eisenhower had placed certain units of General Omar Bradley's Twelfth Army Group under the command of British Field Marshal Bernard Montgomery.

Patton's famous Third, the Lucky Forward, was marching north to relieve Bastogne. Various other divisions—the 1st, the 30th, the 7th Armored and the 82nd Airborne—were given new orders and committed to the Battle of the Bulge.

First intelligence reports also included brief sketches and descriptions of two German officers and their operations, as well as information suggesting that these missions were crucial to the success of Christrose.

Colonel Friedrich August Heydte: the commander of a brigade of paratroopers who were being dropped into Belgium and France from heavy transports (JU-52s) as far as the outskirts of Paris. The numerical strength of the brigade was estimated at two thousand officers and men.

Colonel Heydte was in his middle forties, five feet nine, narrow features, high cheekbones, dark hair and eyes, scars on left side of forehead. Fluent in English, a member of the German nobility (a baron), Knight's Cross with Oak Leaves with Swords, one of his country's most feared and audacious commanders. (To this someone added a notation: Heydte once received a Carnegie Fellowship in International Law to teach at an Ivy League university in the United States. Start of hostilities precluded this.)

Colonel Otto Skorzeny: born June 12, 1908, Vienna. A physical giant, six feet six, weighing 275 pounds. Dueling scars at left temple, left cheek, left side of jaw. His unit's mission: to infiltrate American lines in the Ardennes in United States army uniforms. Mission is code-named: Greif (the Griffon).

Skorzeny's troops were fluent in English, briefed on American politics, sports, movie stars, popular music, and so forth. "It is imperative," the report continued, "that American troops regard with suspicion all soldiers in American uniform *not known to them personally*. ID and dog tags to be inspected. Suspects, regardless of rank, to be interrogated. Intelligence officers will provide suitable questions for such encounters and distribute to all units. Senior American commanders will travel with armed escorts. The number of German soldiers assigned to Colonel Skorzeny's Operation Greif unit is unknown at this time."

Above the valley of the Ourthe and Amblève rivers, two American military trucks traveled west toward the town of La Roche-en-Ardennes. The trucks were loaded with soldiers, several with arms in splints, some with bandages stark white against grimy faces. A half-dozen soldiers were clinging to the hoods and fenders of each truck, and more were packed on the lowered tailgates. As the trucks turned off a winding road toward a bridge spanning the Ourthe, both were waved on urgently by Americans wearing MP brassards on the sleeves of their overcoats. A U.S. command car was parked off the road, VIII Corps insignia on its hood and door panels.

An MP corporal shouted at the driver of the lead truck, "Move your ass, Mac. Snap shit."

"Where the hell's the fire?"

"You heard me—move it. On the double!"

When the trucks rolled onto the bridge, tires making a sucking sound, lumbering black shapes almost lost in the freezing mists, the corporal waved to a sergeant standing near the command car.

The sergeant raised a gloved hand, then walked behind the car and leaned his weight on the plunger of a concealed detonating device.

The charges under the bridge exploded in a series of heavy, linked blasts. Smoke and flames rushed toward the swollen sky. The bridge broke into jagged sections, beams and girders splintering as if struck by giant hammers. The trucks were rent into nightmarish shapes by the upward surge of the explosion, jackknifing and falling in fragments into the icy currents below them.

The screams of the dying soldiers were faint but clear in the rolling echoes created by the detonations.

The soldiers in American uniforms climbed rapidly into the command car marked with the numeral viii on a blue field surrounded by blue and white hexagons. The vehicle was lost in the haze of the Amblève valley even before the sounds of the explosions were carried away by scattering winds.

On the same afternoon, Lieutenant Donald Longworth and his driver, Private Lenny Rado, were waved down by an American officer standing beside a recon car on the road above the Amblève, several kilometers east of the Belgian town of Stoumont. Lenny Rado waited for a nod from Longworth before braking their jeep and pulling off the road.

The American officer, a captain, walked toward them, his body bent against the freezing winds.

Longworth stepped from the jeep, a hand close to the open holster of his .45 automatic. The captain wore an VIII Corps shoulder patch and an overcoat buttoned to his throat. Twin silver bars were pinned to his epaulets. Two white stripes shone on his helmet.

"The name's Madden." The captain's face was lined with fatigue but there was a look of energy and vitality in his sharp, blue eyes. "Where the hell you guys lost, strayed or stolen from?"

"Lieutenant Longworth, sir, Two Sixty-ninth Automatic Weapons Battalion."

"And you, soldier?"

"Private Lenny Rado, same outfit, sir."

At the wheel of Madden's recon car a sergeant watched Longworth and Rado.

"Lieutenant, you're a damned fool to volunteer information," the captain said. "Maybe you haven't heard, but there's a brigade of Germans in the Ardennes wearing our uniforms. So let's see your dog tags. You, too, soldier."

Longworth and Lenny Rado opened their overcoats and flipped out their ID tags.

Madden checked them. "Where you from in the States, lieutenant?"

"San Diego."

"You, soldier?"

"Wisconsin, sir."

"What kind of fishing you got there?"

"Pike, bass, muskies if you're lucky, sir."

"I could use a mess of 'em right now," the captain

said. "Lieutenant, what's that big hotel on the island off San Diego?"

"The Del Coronado, sir."

"You guys go to the head of the class. Let's get back to this goddamn war. I been looking for some sign of the Eighty-second Airborne. We heard it's heading toward Werbomont. You meet any of their units?"

"Captain, let's take a look at *your* dog tags," Longworth said.

"I was wondering what the fuck you were using for brains," the captain said, and pulled out his dog tags.

Longworth checked them, then said, "Where you from in the States, sir?"

"Chicago, the Windy City."

His sergeant stepped casually from the recon car, a hand near his gun.

"Tell me about Chicago," Longworth said.

"Sure. The Palmer House, the Drake, the Cubs and White Sox, Chicago University, and more polacks than you'll find in Warsaw." He grinned at them. "I'll tell you something else. There's a great little tattoo parlor on South State Street. Take a look."

The captain pushed back the sleeve of his overcoat and tunic, revealing a blue-and-gold tattoo on his wrist, the slender figure of a nude woman holding two feathered fans. Underneath the tiny posturing dancer were the words: "Chicago World's Fair. Miss Sally Rand."

"She's a comfort on a cold night." The captain tensed the muscles in his forearm, causing a ripple to tremble up and down the dancer's body.

Longworth smiled. "Looks like we're on the same side, sir, including Miss Rand. No, we haven't seen anything of the Eighty-second. But according to German transmitters, the Hundred-and-first is in trouble at Bastogne."

"Well, you can't believe those fucking kraut-heads." His sergeant laughed and the captain said, "What'd you say your battalion was?"

"The Two sixty-ninth, sir."

"We ran into some of your headquarters people about half an hour ago. Straight down this hill, first fork on the left."

Rado put in, "First left on this road, sir?"

"That's right. The turn is about twelve or fourteen hundred meters from here." The captain smiled at them, his eyes amused and cheerful. "Here's a tip if you run into anybody else you're not sure about. Ask 'em what's on the flip side of Bing Crosby's 'White Christmas.'"

"They could bluff me out of the pot," Longworth said. "I haven't a clue."

The captain thought about it, frowning and rubbing his jaw, then laughed. "It beats the shit out of me, too, lieutenant. We better check it with Der Bingle next time we see him."

Longworth gave a casual salute at the captain, who returned it smartly, the blue-and-gold tattoo twinkling softly through the gathering sleet-flecked darkness.

Climbing into the jeep, they drove slowly down the hill, Rado staying as close as possible to the side of the mountain. Longworth looked across at the fog drifting above the drop into the valley.

"What's bothering you, sir?" Rado said.

"I can't put my finger on it."

"How far he say that turn was?"

"That's one of the things."

"Twelve hundred meters. That struck me kind of funny too," Rado said. "Should of been yards."

"Everything about Chicago checked out," Longworth said. "So why that last stupid question about the record?"

Rado saw the left fork in the road through the fog and eased the jeep into it, the vehicle picking up speed rapidly as it started down the slick grade into the valley.

"We'd better have another talk with the captain," Longworth said. "Turn around the first chance you get, Lenny. Maybe I'm just—"

The lieutenant never completed the sentence, for neither he nor Lenny Rado had seen the taut steel wire stretched across the road four feet above its frozen surface. And had they seen it, there was nothing they could have done because there was no time to stop, no way to check their swift acceleration . . . The quarter-inch cable tore away the metal posts of the windshield, shattering the glass into sparkling fragments, cutting off the screams rising in the throats of Rado and Lieutenant Longworth.

The jeep itself swung about in a wild lashing circle, then went over the side of the road, taking the bodies of the lieutenant and his driver into the depths of a gorge studded with jagged rocks and the stumps of spruce and pine trees. . . .

A half mile away, Waffen SS Captain Walter Brecht stood beside his recon car and studied the road below him through U.S. Army binoculars, watching smoke and flames curling up from the wreckage of the American jeep, spreading through the trees and underbrush, creating dull yellow reflections against the cover of haze and mists, and the sight reminded him of Guernica, and standing braced against the wind on foreign soil once again, Brecht thought suddenly and resentfully of Karl Jaeger, knowing that it was not possible to apply Jaeger's fine distinctions on how one killed his country's enemies. The soldiers in the burning jeep below him were as dead as if he had eliminated them in a punctilious duel, or as if they had fought each other to the death with lances on the backs of chargers. It was an indulgence close to outright treason to prefer to destroy your enemy by honorable means—the word stood out in his mind in brackets—in "honorable" cavalry charges or behind an "honorable" flash of bayonets. This wasn't a chivalric war; the very phrase was an absurdity.

Jaeger's division, Das Reich, was on schedule, Brecht knew, spearheading elements of General Dietrich's Sixth SS Army across the Salm Valley. His tanks were smashing through all resistance, "honorably" destroying bridges and villages and farms, spreading "honorable" terror over hundreds of square miles in the Ardennes, and these bloody pursuits were considered "honorable" simply because Jaeger and his men wore field-gray uniforms with silver SS runes on their tunics. With their Knight's, Crosses and polished boots they had convenient memories. No one boasted of Das Reich at Oradour-sur-Glane, with the locked church jammed with women and children and put to the torch . . . No, that name would never be celebrated in drinking songs or emblazoned on Das Reich's battle standards.

Brecht was proud to be known as "Der Henker" and needed no excuse for his role in Operation Christrose. Whenever you killed your country's enemies was the right time for it. However you did it was a good way to do it. It didn't matter that it might earn one only a crude tarpaulin, the wooden arrow pointing to the sky above a grave, to the mournful strains of *"Ich hatt' einen Kameraden."*

Brecht recalled then—memory was a strange and illusive comrade itself, he decided—the name of the song on the opposite side of the Bing Crosby recording of "White Christmas." It had been an awkward moment when he'd forgotten, but the Americans had been too careless to notice. *"Stille Nacht,"* yes, "Silent Night," and it seemed an appropriate and fortuitous thought with Christmas and the memories of silver bells so close at hand.

Chapter Fifteen

December 20, 1944. Le Pont, Belgium.
Wednesday, 0600 Hours.

Section Eight had been dug in for three days on the crest of Mont Reynard. From that height they had a view of the Salm Valley and the village far below them on the curve of the river. Opposite their gun positions, a thousand yards away, were the gatehouse of the Bonnards and the dark castle (which they had learned was called Castle, or Château, Rêve).

The top of Mont Reynard was the size of a football field, an expanse of slate and rock broken only by sparse clusters of spruce and oak and rime-whitened growths of bracken and wild berry bushes.

The men worked two days and nights using dynamite and shovels to blast and shape protective revetments for their weapons and ammunition. The M-51 machine-gun mount (with quadruple fifties) was emplaced at the fork of the narrow road that led up to the gatehouse. On the other side of the hill, rising above the Salm Valley, the cannon was secure in a deep enclosure of frozen rocks. Under the frost line they had found a gritty soil, laced with splintered shale, and with it had filled dozens of sandbags to line the top of the low barricades.

In smaller revetments behind the cannon were the section's power motor and fire-control apparatus, a metal-encased unit supported by a tripod and fitted

137

with a range wheel and telescopic sights. These fed elec-
tronic data directly to the cannon and automatically
controlled its tracking patterns. When linked to the director, the cannon could fire one hundred and twenty
rounds per minute, each point-detonating projectile
containing sixteen ounces of trinitrocellulose. The syn-
chronized machine guns were capable of firing bursts of
three thousand rounds per minute and these weapons,
plus rifles, carbines, bazookas and grenades, gave the
section lethal firepower.

Near the cannon revetment, the men had widened an
opening in an escarpment of rock, clearing away loose
shale and underbrush, and covering the narrow entrance with a tarp to make a shelter from snow and
winds. When the position was secure, with frozen tree
limbs and bushes camouflaging the circular outlines of
the revetments, Docker split the section into two units,
assigning one to the guns and sending Larkin and four
of the younger soldiers across the hill to the Bonnards'
to get some sleep. He then walked to the edge of the
precipice and studied the valley through his binoculars.
Only the faintest dawn light touched the village and the
spires of the squat little church. Nothing was moving
except a fox or a dog digging among the weeds at the
river's edge.

As long as they could hold the hill, Docker planned
to relieve the men in shifts, giving each a chance to
scrub and change into dry clothes, the only way to prevent rashes and the crippling effect of trench foot in this
wet, freezing weather. There was plenty of windfallen
firewood on the hill and food for at least ten days—
canned turkey, salt pork, powdered milk and eggs, flour
and K-rations. In the trench they'd dug for ammo were
two hundred and eight 40-millimeter projectiles and
several thousand rounds of .50-caliber shells. Secure in
a smaller revetment, topped by fresh-cut logs, were two
insulated boxes of dynamite, firing plungers, detonating
caps and loops of fusing wire obtained by Trankic from
a British sappers' unit on their hot and dusty march to

Avranches; with Docker's permission, the corporal had traded-off five gallons of black whiskey for these extra explosives and hardware.

Docker had known for the last two days that his section was cut off behind the German lines, isolated on this mountain under a low bowl of sky. As the light spread, the wind died. In this vacuum, the cold and silence were intensified to a harrowing pitch; every sound trembled on the frozen winds, the scurrying of small animals in the trees, the distant rumble of artillery on the horizons.

Trankic walked across the hill from the jeep and joined Docker. "I just picked up something kind of funny." The big corporal's cheeks were so swollen with the winds and sleet that his eyes looked like pinpoints of light under his helmet. Docker knew he hadn't slept more than a few hours since they'd brought the trucks up the twisting road to Mont Reynard. "It was a transmitter in a town called La Roach-something-or-other, but the guy sending was an American. Claimed he was in a truck that got blown up on a bridge there with a lot of other GIs. He says the guys who blew the bridge were American soldiers. And he wasn't off the air more than a minute before I got another signal, this time from our own network in Brussels saying there're all sorts of Germans behind the lines in our uniforms. So you know what I'm thinking."

Docker nodded. "Frigging A."

"He certainly looks like an all-American kid."

"Let's be certain."

"But him not having ID is kind of in his favor."

"Sure. If he were a German, he'd damned well be fixed up with dog tags and snapshots of his girl back in the States."

"I'll go get him," Trankic said.

Samuel Gelnick stamped through the snow with an armload of firewood and went into the gatehouse. Trude Bonnard stood at the kitchen stove adding vege-

tables to a thick turkey stew, potatoes and green winter
cabbage. Chet Dormund sat at a table cutting up a slab
of salt pork with a heavy knife. Madame Bonnard
talked incessantly as she worked, telling them how difficult life had been with Germans living at the castle and
rocket bombs smashing around their heads, but since
her complaints were delivered in rapid-fire French Dormund had only the vaguest idea of what she was saying.
His confusion was deepened by the fact that she called
him Richard—she assumed that was his name since every other word he used—"wretched"—sounded like
"Richard" to her ears.

"How come the old lady calls me Richard?" Dormund asked Gelnick.

"Maybe it's because she thinks you've got a big
dick," Gelnick said. "Like a fungo bat."

Dormund said nervously, "You shouldn't talk like
that, not in a place like this."

The sight of the castle against the sky with its suggestion of privilege had made Gelnick feel small and vulnerable. He said now, "Look, instead of Trankic making you a new head, Richard, how about if he makes
you a new joy-stick. You never use the one you got for
anything but to piss with, so maybe there's something
wrong with it."

"I ain't no Richard," Dormund said. "And you better
cut out that wretched dirty talk in here."

Outside, the change from night to day had been almost imperceptible. Grayness spread slowly above the
eastern hills revealing at intervals the white lawns between the gatehouse and Castle Rêve, bringing details
into slow relief, marble statuary of nymphs and archers
and mythical deities, the classic figures emerging like
frozen specters from darker backgrounds of formal gardens bordered with tall clusters of topiary figures over-
grown and misshapen from wartime neglect . . . the
giant rabbit had gained a paunch over seasons of inattention, and a hedge of rearing ponies now looked like

draft horses with tendrils of shaggy vines hanging from their hooves.

Castle Rêve's leaded front windows and terraces commanded serene views of the Salm Valley. The castle's twin towers were ornamental; rising only a dozen feet above an arched roof, the pinnacles had been constructed without windows and perched for effect on slate tilings like a pair of large stone spools.

Tex Farrel and Jackson Baird stood outside the gatehouse waiting to help Dormund and Gelnick haul hot food up to the men on the guns.

Sonny Laurel sat on a wrought-iron bench a dozen yards from them, watching Monsieur Bonnard walking up the road toward the castle, a stout figure in black clothes, smoke trailing from his pipe.

Later Sonny saw Larkin heading in the same direction, but Laurel wasn't thinking about Larkin or Felice's father, he was thinking about what had happened to him last night, still barely able to believe it, even with the memory of her blond hair against his face. . . .

Monsieur Bonnard had made sleeping arrangements for the Americans, sending Laurel up to a loft on the second floor of the gatehouse, a room with low, beamed ceilings and walls partially enclosed by the chimney stones connected to the fireplaces downstairs. He had crawled into the bed, scrubbed clean for the first time in weeks, and so dog-tired his muscles were trembling with fatigue. He knew that Tex Farrel and Dormund were outside on guard, he could hear Larkin and Bonnard downstairs in the parlor drinking and talking, and he had been thinking sleepily of his home on the north side of Chicago and of Tom and Betsy Blacker, who lived close to them in a big white house that belonged to Tom's parents . . . When Tom Blacker was killed in the Solomons and the Purple Heart and personal effects were shipped back to that big house on the tree-lined *Saturday Evening Post* street, something seemed to die in the tall, leggy girl-wife who made lemonade for the neighborhood boys and read them parts of her husband's letters about aerial warfare over straits and islands whose names she could hardly pronounce. Sonny Laurel had just wanted badly to go off and fight what had killed the light in Betsy Blacker's eyes . . .

His thoughts had become so languorous that when the door creaked open and Felice Bonnard sat on the side of the mattress he felt he was dreaming. She wore a white flannel nightgown with red and blue flowers hemstitched along the collar, and her eyes were big and solemn in her still face.

Laurel heard a door close softly below, and realized that Monsieur Bonnard knew his daughter was upstairs, and that dry and final click of the door latch had been a ritual sound of approval.

Felice slipped beneath the eiderdown and he felt her body cold and shivering, and he still couldn't believe it, not until there was a dawn light in the room and a sound of branches against the window and she was sleeping close to him, her pale face gleaming on the pillow beside him.

Tex Farrel held his rifle in the crook of his arm and studied the ground and trees with a hunter's eyes. At early dawn he'd seen tracks of fox and deer in the snow and scrambles of rabbit prints under wild berry bushes.

He glanced at Jackson Baird, noting that they were about the same age and wondering why it was he felt so much older than this boy with the blinking eyes and face screwed tight. The men in the section had given the stranger clean clothes but everything was about two sizes too large, and the baggy fatigues and overcoat gave him the look of an orphan.

"Listen to me, Baird," Farrel said. "You're worried, I can tell. But if there were any Germans right around here, I'd probably of heard or seen them. So if that's what you're worried about, forget it."

"That's not what's bothering me."

"Then what is? You worried about Docker?"

"That's part of it. I don't think he likes me."

"That's bullshit. Docker don't waste time liking or disliking guys. You want my advice, try looking more like a soldier. Snap shit when he tells you to."

Baird nodded and said, "I'll try." Then, as if sensing this wasn't emphatic enough, he added, "I'll try like hell."

They turned at the sound of a motor and saw the jeep with Trankic at the wheel coming up the road toward the gatehouse.

Larkin stood on the terrace of the castle sweeping the meadows with his binoculars. He focused them on Trankic beckoning to Jackson Baird, watching as the youngster climbed in beside the corporal, who then turned the jeep and drove back up the hill toward Mont Reynard.

Larkin began to cough, trying to swallow the brackish bile in his throat and breathing through his gloved hands to warm the air searing his lungs. His cheeks felt raw and peeled. He had shaved at the Bonnards', a damn fool mistake, and now the wind and sleet were like rough salt on his skin. He uncapped his canteen and took a swallow of black whiskey, and though it almost gagged him the corporal was grateful for the heat moving like sluggish fire through his body.

Larkin turned and went into the castle and walked through several big cold rooms and down a flight of stairs. Paul Bonnard was waiting in the cellar, and Larkin followed him into a kitchen that smelled of mold and stale food. In an adjoining storeroom, Bonnard lit a kerosene lamp and played the light across shelves and bins stocked with food and wine and spirits.

Larkin inspected various jars, casks and crates, knowing then that what Bonnard had told him last night was literally true, that this liquor and food was damn near worth its weight in gold. There were cans of boned ham from Holland and Westphalia, tins of paté, bottles of herring, stacks of fruitcake in waxed linen wrappers, jars of brandied fruits, rabbits packed in lard, French mustards, and wines from France, Italy and Germany, liqueurs from Holland, Denmark, and even a half-dozen cases of Cutty Sark whiskey. On the floor stood several casks of olive oil, sacks of charcoal, massive wheels of cheese and three canisters of Swiss chocolate.

Bonnard watched him with an appraising smile. "Well? Satisfied?"

"Why didn't the Germans take this loot with them?"

"The trucks coming from Brussels were hit by one of their own rocket bombs. They were like chickens with their heads off. Major Hunsicker's staff took what they could in the single car that was left."

At the end of the storeroom Larkin saw two chairs and a table with a stump of candle on it. He picked up a bottle of Cutty Sark and opened it. "Get some glasses," he said.

Bonnard's confident smile slipped. "I'll have to bicycle a dozen kilometers to take word to Gervais. There's no time."

"We better make time," Larkin said.

Bonnard hesitated, but there was something sullen and obstinate in the corporal's expression, so he shrugged and turned into the kitchen. Larkin sat down and lit the candle.

He realized bitterly that he was intimidated by these elegant delicacies, potted meats and vintage wines and labeled names he couldn't even pronounce, like Slivovitz and Kirschwasser and Armagnac. Jars of truffles and fish paste and goose liver paté were as off-limits to him as an officers' hotel in Paris, or for that matter, the St. Regis or the Stork Club in New York.

The bottle of Cutty Sark paradoxically brought back a pair of sustaining memories, a night when he and Agnes had gone to the Richelieu on Fifty-second Street and had a good time drinking scotch and dancing and listening to a comedian, and another time at Christmas when he'd been working Penn Station and a group of Hollywood people traveling with the actor Lee Bowman had lost their luggage waiting to board the Broadway

Limited for Chicago. Larkin found the suitcases, six of
them in matched pigskin, and some guy in the party
gave him a double sawbuck and a bottle of Cutty Sark
for his trouble. And that night in the Railway Express
baggage rooms, Larkin and his pals got a nice buzz on
drinking and listening to the Christmas carols pouring
in from the loudspeakers in the main waiting room.
Their boss, old "Killjoy" Kranston, had tried to put a
stop to it, but they were in no mood for his bitching and
they laughed at him and told him where to ram it. That
was some night, he thought, as Bonnard came back
from the kitchen and set down a pair of wine glasses.
Larkin poured drinks, and sipped slowly, a weariness
settling over him.

It had seemed so easy last night, sitting by the fire
and drinking the familiar black whiskey with Bonnard.
Just borrow a truck, haul this food and booze over to
Liège, a few hours from here. Bonnard knew a black
market dealer, a Belgian named Gervais, who would
sell the loot and they'd split the money three ways. Now
Larkin was having second thoughts. Common sense told
him he should take maybe a case of whiskey and a few
cans of ham for the section and tell Bonnard to fuck
off. It was too rich a deal for an Irisher from the lower
East Side who, as his uncles had frequently told him,
would be scratching a poor man's ass all his life.

"There's no danger, no risk for you or me," Bonnard
was saying.

"And that's the way you like it," Larkin said. "No
chance of getting your ass caught in the wringer. Let
somebody else take the flak."

"What are you talking about?"

"I'm talking about your daughter, Bonnard."

Bonnard looked startled. "What has Felice got to do
with this?"

"Look, don't shit me. I was there when you set it
up."

"Wait. You don't understand—"

"I understand the whole deal, Bonnard. You put her

on the block like a pig at a farm sale. Sure, your ass is never in the wringer. But while you're standing on the sidelines, your daughter's screwing Sonny Laurel and I'm driving a truck through country crawling with Germans."

Bonnard sipped his drink and sighed, then said, "What I did was best for Felice."

"That's bullshit. You should of shot anybody trying to get to her."

Actually the anger he heard in his voice disgusted him, as hypocritical as righteous old biddies gossiping at clotheslines behind East Side tenements, speculating with relish and indignation about who was drinking himself to death, who was waiting for pawnshops to open, and who had up and got married with no notice at all. Larkin found it difficult to find anyone to feel superior to. And his tirade at Bonnard, he realized, was only an attempt to convince himself that a father pimping for his daughter had to be a few shitty rungs below a thief working the black market.

Bonnard sighed again, but when he spoke his voice was brisk, a businessman explaining the details of his shop to an apprentice. "Look. When the Germans came here, Felice was ten years old. Major Hunsicker treated her like a pet. He liked her to bring his breakfast coffee. Our family is hated by the village, but we survived the Germans. We'll be here when they are gone and you are gone. What's the good of fighting when you have nothing to fight with?"

The Belgian put an imaginary pistol to his forehead and closed his index finger with a decisive gesture. "Edmond Francoeur, the brother of the schoolteacher, recruited some idiots and blew up the baggage train from Liège. Francoeur and nine hostages were shot in front of the church in Lepont. Did that teach the stupid patriots a lesson? No. Jocko Berthier, who walks like a broken crab, placed a radio transmitter in the church. And the schoolteacher—"

"Hold it," Larkin said. "Is the transmitter working?"

"No, not for months."

"What about the schoolteacher?"

"Her brother married a Jewish girl in Germany. There was a child, Margret. And the schoolteacher is keeping the child in her home. How many hostages will die if the Germans come back and find that Jew? How many lives is that useless transmitter worth?" Bonnard shook his head emphatically. "Staying alive, that's what matters." He drew a handkerchief from an inside pocket of his overcoat and blew his nose. His eyes had become moist and red. "So, in my place, corporal, what man would you choose?" He tapped his forehead. ". . . the childish one, your cook? The one who is so frightened? Who would *you* choose, corporal? I know the sort of man your Laurel is. He won't hurt Felice. And she'll forget him before the snows run down to the river in the spring."

Larkin smiled bitterly. "You picked Sonny Laurel for lover-boy. And me for the thief. Is that what I look like?"

Bonnard shrugged, and Larkin thought maybe this one time his uncles might be wrong, maybe he wouldn't have to scratch a poor man's ass the rest of his life.

"Anybody else know about this loot?"

"No. Not even the priest, not even Trude."

"Let's keep it that way." Larkin put the bottle of Cutty Sark in his pocket and went up the stairs and out the front doors of the castle. His chest felt better, the whiskey had eased the pain, but the winds stung his raw cheeks and the change in temperature made him feel almost drunk. He knew he'd better work that off before he talked to Docker.

The sergeant and Trankic and Jackson Baird stood together at the edge of the hill, the bulk of the cannon revetment behind them, their figures blurred and indistinct in the mists.

"I worked on a construction job one summer in Peekskill," Trankic said. "Where'd you live, kid?"

"Near First and South Division Street."

"What's the name of the big public park?"

"It's Depew Park, named after Chauncey Depew."

"On the north side, right?"

"No, the south side."

"You know where the old hospital is?"

"On the bluff just above the railroad."

Docker: "You ever visit West Point?"

"Yes, our scoutmaster took us there a couple of times."

"How'd he get permission?"

Baird told him that the troop secretary wrote to the provost marshal's office listing the date they preferred and an alternate choice. They received pass cards by mail usually within about a week . . . Baird was able to smile tentatively now as some of his confidence seemed to return and touches of color showed on his sharp white cheekbones. He went on to mention other features of the Point, parades in the Central Area and snapshots he'd taken of changing colors in the trees along Lee and Jefferson Roads, talking with increasing assurance until Docker held up a hand. "Okay, that's fine. Let's talk about your rifle and dog tags. Your rifle first. How'd you lose it?"

"Just like I told you, sergeant."

"Tell me again, Baird."

The abrupt switch in subjects obviously jarred the young soldier; an expression of remembered panic pinched his wind-raw face.

"I—I got knocked down by a shell that exploded near me and when I got up I couldn't find my rifle."

"You sure you looked for it?"

"Yes, I crawled around but I couldn't find it."

"And your dog tags?"

"It's just like I said. I tripped and rolled down the side of a hill. That's when I lost them, they must have got hooked on a branch or something. . . ."

Trankic studied him. "You have your overcoat and shirt open?"

"I'm not sure, I don't remember."

"Well, unless you were running around bare-ass like Tarzan, there's no way a tree branch could rip off your dog tags."

"That's what Shorty Kohler thinks," Baird said flatly. "He thinks I'm a deserter."

"You're the only one knows the truth," Docker said.

"It's not that simple. It's possible I could be a deserter and not even know it."

"How do you figure that?"

Baird wet his chapped lips. "Well, I read about a witchcraft trial in New England once. They were trying an old lady. Some kids said she gave them stomach-aches, nightmares, things like that. And a farmer said the old lady had put a hex on his cow and made her lose a calf. So the judge decided she was a witch and sentenced her to be burned to death. He asked her if she had anything to say . . . and this is what I mean, sergeant . . . the old woman didn't disagree with him, just asked him if it was possible that she could be a witch and not even know about it."

"So what did the judge tell her?" Docker said.

"He told her sure, and that's why they were going to burn her at the stake."

Docker took out his canteen and uncapped it. "You want a drink, Baird?"

"No, no thanks."

Docker drank and tucked the canteen back into the pouch on his cartridge belt.

"Baird, my guess is that thousands of GIs got cut off from their outfits the last few days. A lot of them may have dumped their weapons. If they're Jews, they got rid of their dog tags too. They'd be idiots to risk being captured with that *H* for Hebrew 'round their necks. I think you're smart enough to know all this. So what's bothering you?"

"It's just . . ." Baird looked down at the river and its cover of fog, and Docker saw that his lips were trembling. "It's just that my family is strict about things. I mean if there was *any* talk about my being a deserter, they couldn't live with it."

"Listen to me," Docker said. "Forget about that old lady they burned for a witch, and forget about being a deserter and not knowing it. Just don't fuck up around here and you'll be all right."

When Baird had trudged off through the snow to the cannon, Trankic shook his head and said, "He's still not leveling with us, Bull. Is that something we got to worry about?"

"Well, we're worrying about everything else," Docker said. "Why make any exceptions?"

"Merry Christmas," Larkin said, and took the bottle of Cutty Sark from his overcoat pocket and handed it to Docker.

Docker opened it and sniffed it. "Goddamn it, Matt, it's *scotch*."

They were seated in the cave near the cannon revetment, the tarpaulin tight across the entrance. The canvas had iced over and occasionally the winds made it crack like pistol shots. The blasts stirred the fire and started shadows running like quicksilver across the walls.

"Your professor pal, Hamlin, fascinates me," Larkin said. "Remember the letter he wrote about therapy sessions for returning GIs?"

In the firelight, Docker saw that Larkin's eyes were hot with more than whiskey, and his resentment was obviously deep because that letter from Hamlin had arrived at least three months ago.

Dave had written: "With the usual disclaimers, consider the source and all that crap, I think we need something like a decompression chamber for GIs honorably home from the wars. It's a pragmatic thing . . . it's not their fault, and it's not ours. They've seen the ugliness, we haven't. That's all there is to it. It would be reasonable to expect more forbearance on our part, but in all honesty we don't know what exactly we should be forbearing *about*.

"Here's an example: Tim Ryan was invalided home from the Pacific. The following sequence is arguably not entirely his fault, but please consider the details and specifications of the charges: 1) Tim got in two brawls with guys in bars. The first was a 4-F like your humble servant, deferred for a perforated testicle, I imagine. The other chap happened to be a Marine with a pair of Purple Hearts. 2) Tim's account of a strafing raid on Guadalcanal caused three young children (remember the Hansens?) to go screaming for cover under the dining room table. 3) He has had a total breakdown in communications with his parents and also with the man he used to work for, a branch manager at Sears, Roebuck . . ."

Dave Hamlin had an idea that returning combat veterans should be put through a process roughly the *opposite* of basic training. Instead of close order drill and the manual of arms, they would be given counsel by psychiatrists and clergymen and business leaders to help them to merge smoothly into the flow of life in their communities.

"They could have a great course for amputees," Larkin said. "How to handle a teacup with hooks on your wrist. But maybe your pal Hamlin should turn his idea around. A training camp for civilians is what we need, for 4-Fs and football and baseball players who haven't missed a game the last four years. For a lot of guys with doctors who gave them a wink past the draft board."

"All right, let's have it," Docker said.

Larkin sipped whiskey, and said quietly, "There's millions of guys who paid no more attention to this fucking war than if it was a Rotary parade going by in the next county. I'm twenty-nine. I got drafted when I was twenty-six. I spent seven years before that at Railway Express, and nineteen months before that looking for a job. I've got an apartment at Thirty-second Street and

Third Avenue that costs sixty-five a month, living
room, a bedroom, a kitchen. And I got Agnes and a
three-year-old daughter. Those years at Railway Express are just seven times Christmas and seven times
Thanksgiving for me. I worked those holidays, every
fucking one of them at the Grand or the Penn watching
college boys come home and whooping it up waiting for
their parents or whoever the shit was meeting them.
And you know something, Bull? I wrote my boss at
Railway Express six months ago to see about my job
and he took about four months to answer me, and I got
his letter the same day that prick, Hamlin, wrote to you
about decompression chambers for GIs. My boss told
me some neighborhood news and he told me who Connie Mack had picked for his all-time all-star baseball
team, and then he got to the point of saying they'd hired
some older guys and some deferred guys and they were
cutting the mustard real good, and while he wanted to
be fair to everybody he couldn't promise me I could go
back to work."

"You've got me hooked, Larkin," Docker said.

"What the fuck you mean?"

"Who the hell did Connie Mack pick?"

"Shit. Let's see. George Sisler at first, Eddie Collins
at second, Honus Wagner at shortstop, Tris Speaker in
center field, the Babe in right—"

"Okay, okay, get to the point."

"Up at the castle, there's thousands of dollars worth
of food and liquor, Bull, which is where I got this Cutty
Sark." The words were coming faster and the leaping
fire highlighted the strain in Larkin's eyes. "Bonnard
knows where we can unload it, Bull. All he wants is for
me to use a truck for a few hours. All I need is that
truck. That stuff's got to be worth eight or nine thousand dollars."

"Forget it," Docker said. "You're not going into the
black market, Matt, and neither is anybody else in this
section."

"What the hell good is that food and booze doing anybody in that castle?"

"That's not the point, so forget it."

"You want to turn it over to the brass? So it will wind up in some officers' mess in Paris or London?" Larkin took another sip of whiskey. "Bull, I don't think you heard a goddamn word I said. It's a three-way split between me and Bonnard and this character, Gervais. I'll cut you in for half of mine, and if I can clear around two thousand it means I got ten or twelve months' breathing space to find a job when I get out." His voice rose angrily. "Don't you understand, for Christ's sake? I'm talking about the rest of my whole fucking life."

"Goddamn it, no," Docker said.

Larkin lit a cigarette and flipped the match into the fire. He admired Docker, but distrusted him because he always expected too much of people. Which was another way of saying he wanted them to disappoint him. If you insisted everybody had to be perfect, like the priests did, naturally you'd have a world full of sinners to forgive. Larkin shrugged and was pouring himself another drink when the tarpaulin was pulled back by Solvis, who stuck his head and shoulders into the cave.

"You better come quick, sarge. Shorty Kohler just pissed all over the new kid's chow."

Docker could hear Kohler's angry voice, clear on the frozen air, as he and Larkin ran toward the men who formed a tableau against the snow and fog streaming through the valley.

"Fucking-A, I'll tell you why I did it. I did it because you're a mother-fucking deserter. Is that straight enough for you, Baird?"

Gelnick, Farrel and Dormund stood by the wheelbarrow they had used to bring up the hot food from the Bonnards'. They were all staring solemnly at Baird's mess kit, which was tipped on the ground, the turkey stew and vegetables soaking in a yellow urine that had soaked the snow around them.

"You shouldn't have done that." Baird's lips were trembling; he looked close to tears.

"Okay, I shouldn't have done it," Shorty Kohler said. "So what the fuck *you* gonna do about it?"

"Shorty, knock it off," Docker said in a tone he seldom needed to use. He took Baird's arm and pulled the boy around to face him. "Now listen to me, goddamn it. You don't have to take this kind of crap from anybody. You understand? From *anybody*."

"I don't want to fight him—"

From the revetment Trankic shouted, "Bull, for Christ's sake, get over here!" Docker turned and saw the big corporal waving urgently to him from the loading platform of the cannon.

"I'll settle this later, Kohler," he said, and ran across the crest of the hill to Trankic. "What the hell is it?"

"I ain't sure, Bull. Some kind of crazy light behind those mountains, something like we saw at Werpen."

Docker unslung his binoculars and walked to the edge of the cliff, listening to the winds sweeping around him as he scanned the valley.

Tex Farrel stared down at the congealed lumps of food in Baird's mess kit. "You know something?" he said conversationally. "We shouldn't wait for Docker to settle every little thing that goes on around here. Seems to me the sarge's got enough on his mind . . ."

"What the fuck you mean?" Kohler said.

"What I guess I really mean, Shorty, is that you are full of shit," Farrel said, spacing the last few words slowly and deliberately.

Kohler looked around at the other men and then back at Farrel, his smile puzzled, tentative. "What the fuck is this, Tex?"

"I just told you. You're so dumb you can't figure it out? Baird's part of this section now. Besides, you're a professional, at least that's what you tell people, and he's just a kid."

"Hey, wait a minute. I got no beef with you."

Tex Farrel took off his helmet and put it on the ground. He removed his field jacket and handed it to Solvis. "Shorty, where I come from no white man would be low enough to piss on a hungry man's food."

"You better watch that loud mouth of yours, Tex."

"Just put your hands up, short pants, and start worrying about your own mouth."

"All right, you Texas meathead." Kohler moved in fast and slugged Farrel with a left hook to the body that sounded as if he had swung his fist against a taut drum.

Farrel grunted and backed away, but when his boots were planted firmly he said, "Shit, I thought you did this for a living," and snapped a hard left into Kohler's face.

Shorty pulled his jaw down under his shoulder and crowded Farrel, stinging him with a flurry of blows, rocking him with hooks to the body and trying to measure him for straight rights. But the frozen ground hampered him, he couldn't hook off his jabs, and most of his punches lacked precision and power.

Watching, Gelnick thought that they were just as rotten to one another as they were to everybody else, pissing on good food like that. He filled his own mess kit with food from the wheelbarrow and took it to Baird, but the dumb nebbish didn't want it, staring at Tex Farrel fighting, not believing anybody could stick up for him, which Gelnick could understand, like he understood all those *goyim* wanted to be Christ on a cross, naked in the wind with everybody feeling sorry for them. So screw them all, he thought, and hunkered down with his mess kit to watch the fight.

Kohler was breathing hard now, feinting with his head and shoulders to set Farrel up for combination shots. Farrel slipped his left lead and threw a punch over it, a powerful right that caught Kohler on the jaw and put him flat on his back.

At the edge of the hill the big dog had begun barking. Inside the revetment, Trankic suddenly called to Docker. "Goddamn it, Bull! *Look*. We got mail coming in!"

Docker turned and saw twin globes of what looked like fire materializing dully from behind the curtain of snow and fog above the river.

"On the guns!" he shouted, and ran to the revetment wall and climbed onto the loading platform of the cannon. Within a few seconds the other men were at their posts, Larkin behind the director, Sonny Laurel and Farrel on the tracking scopes.

Trankic engaged the lever connecting the cannon to the fire-control system, and when Laurel and Farrel found the target, the barrel elevated and swung hard right to track the lights glittering in the fog.

Docker noted that Gelnick was missing and that Baird was still standing outside the walls of the revetment. "Get your ass in here," he said. "Give Dormund and Kohler a hand. Grab a clip of ammo and be ready if I yell for it. Don't make me turn to look for it."

Docker checked the foot-long cartridges visible above the breech, the brass casings wet with the falling snow. From the opposite side of the hill, Schmitzer, on the machine guns, waved to him and Docker knew he had spotted the blazing spheres coming through the valley.

Everyone watched the lights, and when a series of thermals tore the fog apart, they saw an aircraft with a steel-ribbed bubble over the cockpit and a triangular tail with black swastikas painted above the tapered ailerons. Under the plane's single wing a pair of slim nacelles were mounted tight against the fuselage, and from them flames streamed behind the tail assembly, crimson against the spuming snow. A low whine trembled through the air as the plane streaked by their position.

The barrel of the cannon swung so rapidly that Docker nearly lost his balance. Steadying himself against the curved columns of the loading chute, he slammed his foot down on the firing pedal. Three tracer shells exploded from the gun barrel, arching toward the plane and cutting parabolic slashes of white light in the sky.

The projectiles trailed far behind their target, curving futilely in the wake of the aircraft, which banked and disappeared into the mists. After the staccato firing, the silence was so complete they could hear the hiss of snowflakes on the hot barrel of the gun.

"Ammo," Docker said, and without turning reached behind and felt the cold shells against his bare hands. "And where the hell is Gelnick?"

"He ducked into the wretched cave," Dormund said. "Can't get on me for that, sarge."

"Christ!" Docker said, realizing that the tarpaulin wouldn't provide any protection against machine-gun fire or shrapnel, that the only safe place in a strafing attack was inside the revetment. "Go get the dumb bastard," he told Solvis. "On the double."

Solvis squeezed through the narrow opening in the revetment wall and ran for the cave, bending down into the winds.

Docker felt cold drops of sweat gathering on his ribs and running down his side. Their tracer fire had pinpointed the gun position; the German pilot could now choose the time and direction of the next attack.

Radar began to circle the floor of the revetment, whining with excitement. Stiff fur stood up on his neck as he began to bark in the direction of the castle.

Docker waved to Gelnick and Solvis, who were coming over the crest of the hill. "Move it, you guys!"

The men on the cannon heard humming tremors rising over the valley, but it was impossible to determine their exact source; the damp air was moving in gentle vibrations and the low, rhythmic sounds trembled all around them.

Docker hoped they'd get a few precious seconds to zero in on the German plane, time enough to establish the pattern of their tracers.

But they didn't get those precious seconds, they got no warning at all. One instant they were straining to pick up the source of the singing vibrations, the next the plane was flashing at them from behind the castle, its ammo blazing and clawing at the slopes of the mountain.

The barrel of the cannon swung hard right, and Docker pounded his foot on the firing pedal.

The rockets from the attacking aircraft ripped open the frozen earth and sent splinters of rock over the revetment like grenade fragments.

Solvis ran clumsily through the slush and snow, arms and legs churning, throwing himself down against the wall of sandbags, but Gelnick, crying out in surprise, dropped to the open ground, jerking his knees up to his chin and covering his helmet with his arms.

Docker screamed at him to get up, a pointless warning because no voice could have made itself heard above the whistling boom of the plane's passage and the explosion of its rockets against the frozen mountain.

The cannon was off target but so was the aircraft, its ammo gouging tracks twenty yards from the revetment before it vanished into the fogs.

The impact of the explosions had knocked Gelnick's body a dozen feet down the slope of the mountain. His arms and legs were bent at distorted angles, his blood stained the snow, and he looked just like the other casualties Docker had seen in this war, suddenly and touchingly small in clothes that always seemed too large after the first bullets destroyed the quickness of life.

"He was running right beside me," Solvis was chattering. "He could have made it. He was right with me. Why should he do a thing like that?" Solvis walked toward Gelnick's body but continued to look over his shoulder at the men on the cannon. "Can you tell me why he did that?" he said, in a loud, oddly querulous voice. "I made it all right. Why didn't he have the brains to follow me?"

"Solvis, get back in here!" Docker said.

Solvis made no move to return. His face was white, eyes out of focus. "I don't understand." He wasn't shouting now, his voice was like a worried child's, soft and anxious. "You guys understand it? Any of you guys?"

Jackson Baird squeezed through the narrow corridor of sandbags and ran through the snow. Taking Solvis by the arm, Baird led him back to the revetment, hurrying the stunned soldier along with awkward, stumbling strides.

Within minutes they heard again the delicate, trembling vibrations of the plane. When it emerged from the hills behind the castle it was aimed at their revetment like a powerfully thrown dart. They saw muzzle flashes from the rockets, then tracks of projectiles striking the mountain and climbing toward their position like a ladder pounded into the hillside by invisible hammers.

Docker hit the firing pedal and the cannon bucked beneath him, the massive breech slamming back under almost twenty tons of recoil, and he saw that their tracers were directly on target, flight patterns transformed into an optical illusion by the plane's speed. From where Docker stood above the smoking breech, the line of glowing projectiles seemed to bend like a stream of water from a hose as it curved smoothly into the tapered nose of the aircraft.

There were two explosions then, flashes of searing light followed instantly by eruptions of black smoke, and the front of the plane's fuselage was thrust up and back as if it had flown into a mountainside.

Docker realized the pilot was trying for altitude in the last seconds of his life. The aircraft soared up and over their revetment, twisting and buckling, and the men below ducked instinctively from the heat of the flames rushing down from the wings and cockpit.

But it was a directionless mass of iron by then, its graceful union with the air forever destroyed, hurtling into the mountains hundreds of yards above and behind them and taking down dozens of giant firs before it finally exploded in bursts of rupturing metals and leaping orange fires.

The echoes of the crash returned like distant thunder through the reaches of the valley, the reverberations replaced at last by the sounds of winds and the snap of delicate ice in the trees, and then there was nothing left of the plane and its passage but a black scar in the frozen mountainside and flames reflected in sullen colors against the stormbound skies.

Chapter Sixteen

December 21, 1944. Salmchâteau-sur-
Amblève. Thursday, 1030 Hours.

They were traveling at a labored pace through columns of military traffic over roads churned into pools of mud and ice. Visibility was poor; their driver was leaning over the steering wheel, rubbing the windshield with a gloved hand and gesturing helplessly at the lines of stalled trucks that made the twisting roads of the Ardennes forests nearly impassable.

General Kroll swore softly, and as he did Karl Jaeger understood his impatience and anger. The 2nd SS Panzer Division was almost thirty-six hours behind the timetable assigned it by Operation Christrose. But of greater immediate significance was the fact that an ME-262 had been shot down by an American gun section and Kroll, whose units were closest to where the V-4 disappeared, had been ordered by OKW-Berlin to locate and destroy it.

On December 16th Das Reich had moved out at dawn from a start-line east of the Losheim Gap, but after the first hours of triumph and exultation, with glowing cables of congratulations from the Führer himself, tanks and infantry had been stalled by snarled skeins of their own tanks and truck traffic backed up on the narrow mountain roads.

In contrast, von Manteuffel's Fifth Panzer Army had

161

captured one American division intact, the 106th Infantry, and savagely mauled two others, the 9th Armored and the 28th Infantry. From that point, two of Manteuffel's crack units, the Panzer Lehr and the 26th People's Grenadier, had smashed across the Clerve River, capturing Noville and Wiltz and laying siege to the great Allied rail network at Bastogne. Other elements of Manteuffel's army had bypassed the trapped town and were now charging toward Namur on the Meuse.

Jaeger looked out at fields covered with snow and black trees with ice ridged along their limbs. The first phase of Christrose had been therapy for him; he had been grateful for the narcotic effect of the action, which distracted him from his leave in Dresden and thoughts of his wife and daughters and his father, the single eye blazing at him with intensity.

"The reading of history is never enough," Kroll said, speaking rapidly and chopping the air with a hand for emphasis. "Squeezing the truth from the past is a waste of time unless you understand and act on it."

Jaeger took his pipe from his pocket and tried to keep his mind on what Kroll was saying, but a sudden dizziness was eroding his selective faculties.

"We are buying time, Jaeger, to launch a political attack. Certain of our leaders have sympathetic friends in the highest councils of Great Britain and the United States. Thus, we have the means to appeal for an honorable peace and concentrate our mutual energies on those mongrel hordes out of Russia who, mark this, will be at the throat of the world when the German shield is broken . . . Jaeger, what is it? You've cut your hand with that pipe . . ."

"It's nothing, sir, a scratch." Jaeger folded his arms so that his hands were covered by the sleeves of his greatcoat.

General Kroll looked at him, obviously concerned by his behavior, but he accepted Jaeger's explanation and returned to his original subject. "Bastogne will fall in twenty-four hours. Even Patton can't prevent it. His army is moving north, a quarter of a million men and more than one hundred thousand vehicles, but he can't bring it off. Not even Rommel achieved anything like that in Africa, or von Rundstedt on the way to Dunkirk."

Yet something, Jaeger knew, was hardening the spines of the Americans. They had regrouped after the first shattering attacks and were fighting savagely for every crossroads and village on the route of the Panzers. Perhaps it was the knowledge that Patton and his Third Army were on the way, or possibly because this kind of terrain and warfare was ideally suited to the descendants of plainsmen and Indian fighters. In intelligence reports he had seen lists of American soldiers receiving honors and decorations, information culled from papers in the States, and he had been impressed by the numbers of the solid old yeoman names—Thompsons, Jacksons, Hayworths, Boyds, Reeds, Stoners, Smiths— he could imagine men like that in the hills and trails of America, scouts and trappers living off the country and through the winters with sacks of salt and flintlock rifles. He envisioned their grandsons, descendants of the men he'd read about in Harte and Cooper and Jack London, fighting the Tiger tanks at Bastogne and St. Vith and Trois-Ponts. And now Patton in the van of his tanks with the arrogant scarf and ivory-handled revolvers . . . there were copies of the general's speeches clipped to division bulletin boards all over Germany . . . "I don't want to hear of any man in my command being captured unless he is hit. Even if you are hit, you can still fight and that's no bullshit." And the frenzy of profanities and gestures . . . "Men, if you're men, you won't leave the fucking to the cowards back home. They'll breed us nothing but litters of cowards." The stars of his rank gleaming openly and defiantly on his helmet and tunic . . . "Sure, we all want to go home, but just remember this: The quickest way home is straight through Berlin." . . .

The command car drove past sentries into the court-

yard of the farmhouse serving as Kroll's headquarters
near Salmchâteau. Staff vehicles, hospital vans and supply trucks were parked on the muddy driveways in front
of the house.

In the parlor, officers monitored situation maps and
radio operators manned field transmitters and telephones. Orderlies were distributing barley soup in mugs
and platters of coarse bread heaped with ground sausage and mashed potatoes.

While Kroll listened to reports from his senior officers, Jaeger told a sergeant he wanted a telephone line
to the executive officer of his battalion, Major Bok. In
an adjoining dining room, Kroll then introduced Jaeger
to Captain Hans Schenk of Luftwaffe Intelligence. The
tables and sideboard were heaped with military gear—
rifles, duffel bags, helmets and greatcoats. On the walls
were pictures of children in Holy Communion costumes
and an old-fashioned wooden clock with Gothic numerals and a silent, motionless pendulum. Captain Schenk
indicated a tripod and map rack on which were spread
several large photographs of the terrain above Lepont.

"The peak in the foreground is called Mont Reynard," Schenk said. "On the opposite peak"—he indicated a small stone house with the tip of a pencil—"is a
gatehouse and above it a castle. The ME-262"—he
pointed to an elevation behind Mont Reynard—
"crashed here and slid down into a narrow ravine about
a thousand meters above the American gun position,
which is"—the pencil moved again—"there, colonel, at
the edge of the precipice."

"You have a magnifying glass?"

"Yes, colonel."

Jaeger took the glass and studied the photographs,
scanning the details of the castle, the gatehouse and the
narrow roads twisting up to the American gun position.
The road between the castle and Mont Reynard, Jaeger
decided, was too narrow and winding for a tank to ma-
neuver, which left him one obvious alternative: a fron-

tal attack up the steep mountain face at the 40-millimeter cannon emplaced behind the military crest of the hill.

General Kroll had already given Jaeger the strategic parameters of his mission: to demolish and burn the wreckage of the ME-262 and to eliminate any persons who could conceivably identify it for what it was—a revolutionary jet-propelled aircraft, potentially the most sophisticated and powerful weapon to be developed in all the years of this war.

The V-4s represented the second phase of Christrose. They would support the hammer blows of the tri-pronged operation on the ground, the capture of the Belgian port city of Antwerp, the destruction of all supplies and communications between American and British forces and the eventual seizure of open plains all across France into Paris.

"When did you take these photographs?"

"Just before dawn, colonel. The pilot of the ME-262 managed a signal before he crashed yesterday, but it took us most of the night to triangulate his position."

"Was the enemy aware that you took these photographs?"

"No, colonel. We used film and lens developed for high-altitude night missions."

Jaeger turned to General Kroll. "I have no other questions, sir."

When the captain saluted and withdrew, General Kroll indicated one of the photographs and traced a line with his finger up the steep slope Mont Reynard to the American gun position. "You see the problem, Karl?"

"Yes, general. With respect, you seem to forget I'm also a graduate of the Berlin Military Academy."

The remark put Kroll in a better humor. "Yes, and I shouldn't imagine any of the Americans on that hill have similar credentials." Abruptly his mood changed; he sighed and looked at Jaeger. "This isn't the time for exhortations. The banners, the torchlight parades, the voice from Berlin sounding from the loudspeakers, that's all over for now. But we're depending on you, Karl. The terrain is so difficult we couldn't risk paratroops or infantry without compromising security. Your mission is truly vital. The Luftwaffe has eighteen hundred fully operational ME-262s, and with Christrose, they represent the last hope for our future. If we lose the element of surprise, this final throw of the dice will come to nothing. So remember what I told you when we left Adlerhorst, Karl. My command car is available when you need it."

When Kroll left the room, Jaeger studied a large-scale map of the Ardennes, making careful estimates of the distance and terrain between Salmchâteau and the peaks of Mont Reynard. It was a straight run to Vielsalm, from where he could travel north to Stavelot, swinging west into the Salm Valley and the village of Lepont.

When a lance corporal advised him he had raised Battalion, Jaeger spoke into the headset. "Major Bok, Jaeger here. Please record. You will detach the lead tank from Third Sturm and Sergeant Trakl's crew from our reserve." Trakl had been with Jaeger in Russia at Kursk, as had the sergeant's crew—corporals Elbert, Henze, Wesse and Gratz. Jaeger told Bok where he wanted the tank to rendezvous, a crossroads near Salmchâteau, and then ordered a vehicle for his own use with extra supplies of petrol and ammunition.

At Adlerhorst Kroll had said to him . . . "Think and speak and act as if you were under surveillance by generations of unborn Germans . . . what you speak will be heard, what you do will be seen . . ." And with the memory Jaeger was suddenly aware that confusion was once again maddeningly reducing his convictions to impotence . . . Broken, as in the death of Cornet Rilke, the rose broken as one would break a host, the foreign petal under his tunic, rising and falling on the waves of his heart . . . be proud, I carry the flag . . .

When he received the confirmation of his orders

from Bok, Jaeger took a deep breath, buttoned the lapels of his greatcoat and strode out into the sleet of the courtyard, where a driver waited for him at General Kroll's command car.

Chapter Seventeen

December 21, 1944. Lepont, Belgium.
Thursday, 1630 Hours.

Darkness came early to the towns on the Salm and Amblève. By midafternoon gray stone bridges were merging with the heavy cover of snow and clouds. Docker turned on headlights when he and Trankic drove down the narrow road from Mont Reynard, twisting through stands of trees and underbrush, following the river into the village.

Stopping at the square in front of the church, chains noisy on the cobblestones, Trankic went into Jocko Berthier's café and Docker got out of the jeep to check the darkness and listen to the wind in the trees. Blackout curtains of the houses on the square were drawn. Nothing moved in the narrow streets but occasional flurries of snow.

Docker had left Schmitzer in charge of the section, no longer feeling he could trust Larkin; something seemed to have gone dead inside the Irishman. It was more than the dark whiskey, it was some kind of insidious anger eating at his sense and energies. Larkin had, though, told him what he'd learned from Paul Bonnard. About the schoolteacher, a Jewish child and Berthier's transmitter . . . he had a theory that people confided in Larkin because the pain in his eyes convinced them they had at least that in common . . .

After the gun section shot down the German plane, Docker had sent Trankic with a detail into the peaks above their position to find it. The men had climbed to a point where they could see the plane in a ravine packed with snow and ice. By then only a few streamers of black smoke drifted from the wreckage. The sides of the gorge had been too steep to risk a closer inspection, but even at that distance Trankic had seen that the aircraft was constructed without conventional motors and propellers, only long jets under each wing, rent and battered now by the crash.

Docker had sent out a signal on the X-42, with a description of the plane and the grid coordinates of the crash site, but after twenty-four hours without acknowledgment, he and Trankic had decided to check out the Lepont transmitter.

When the corporal returned from the café, his cheeks were flushed with something more than the cold wind and his breath smelled of brandy.

"She lives just a couple of hundred yards from here," he said. "You make a left turn at the river, it's the last house."

"What about the radio?"

"They got one all right, but it's dead as Kelsey's nuts."

"Can you fix it?"

"I don't know. Jocko says the wires are broken on the lead to . . ." Trankic shrugged. "It's the audio rectifier or the transformer, near as I can figure this Walloon talk."

"Will he help you?"

"He's crippled as hell, Bull. It happened when the Heinies were sending guys from here to Poland. Some drunken Krauts didn't want to lose their bartender so they busted him up one night. He fought back, and they put the boots to him. So to answer your question, fucking-A he'll help."

At a junction of secondary roads between Trois-Ponts and Stavelot, Colonel Karl Jaeger braked his command car and signaled to Sergeant Trakl, who was traveling directly behind him, standing high in the turret of a Panzerkampfwagen Mark VI.

Jaeger turned his vehicle into a logging trail between a row of fir trees. Glancing at the map clipped to his dashboard, he saw that there were still three more hills between them and the valley leading to the slopes of Mont Reynard.

He had stopped because in the light of his blackout beams he had seen a small boy walking near the woods on the side of the trail, bundled up against the weather in a wool jacket and ragged leggings. Trailing from one of his hands was a pair of small-game snares made of polished sticks and thin leather straps. The boy, who was about ten or eleven, smiled tentatively, his teeth white in the subdued beams from Jaeger's car, then scrambled over a ridge of snow and ran into the trees.

Jaeger signaled to Sergeant Trakl and pointed after the running boy, whose small figure was already indistinct in the snow-spin of the forests.

Followed by two corporals, Trakl ran into the woods after the boy, and within minutes they had collared and marched him back to Jaeger's command car.

"We're not going to hurt you, stop struggling," Jaeger said.

"You'll get me in trouble." The youngster spoke in French. "My mother expects me home for supper."

"Do you have a father or brothers?"

"No, sir, just my mother."

The boy's face was pinched with the cold, his cheeks chapped and raw, but he didn't seem frightened; there was a lively curiosity in his bright eyes as he stared up at the huge tank.

"Do you know who we are?" Jaeger asked him.

"Yes. You're Germans."

"What's your name?"

"It's Simon Coutreau, sir."

Jaeger wondered if it had been only his own nerves that had alerted him. No, there was the business of the snares and the darkness . . .

He took the briar pipe from his pocket and put it between his teeth. He smiled at the boy and said, "Are you afraid of us, Simon?"

The boy shook his head. "I've done nothing to be afraid of, sir."

"Did someone tell you to watch for us? You might as well tell us the truth."

"No, I came to the woods to set snares. I come every day. There are rabbits here."

"You must be a fine hunter, Simon, to find their tracks in the dark."

"But it was light when I started, sir. I'm on my way home now."

"Yet you've set no snares."

"Because I found no tracks, sir."

Jaeger looked at the road ahead, the snow shining in the light of his blackout beams, and then studied the white fields and dark woods on either side of him.

"Let him go, Sergeant Trakl," he said.

"Let him go, sir? He might be lying."

"You heard me, sergeant. We're not at war with children."

The boy ran off toward the woods, and Jaeger turned his command car back onto the road to Lepont.

Chapter Eighteen

December 21, 1944. Lepont-sur-Salm.
Thursday, 1700 Hours.

When the knock sounded, Denise Francoeur hastily collected the picture books from the floor and gave them to the child, who held them tightly as the schoolteacher pulled back the partition concealing the cellar stairway.

When Margret had disappeared into the dusk of the cellar, Denise smoothed her skirt and opened the front door to a tall American soldier whose face was shadowed by his helmet.

"Sorry to disturb you," he said. "My name is Docker, Sergeant Docker."

"Can I help you?"

"Monsieur Bonnard told us you buried a German paratrooper a couple of nights ago and that you have his ID." She looked puzzled. "His papers. I'd like to see them. I can speak some French if it would help."

"No, please come in. My English is quite well." She closed the door quickly against the winds. "Only . . . it's rusty, there was no one to . . ." She paused again. ". . . to practice with for some time."

"I'm sure your German is better," he said.

Her sense of irony and other subtleties had been blunted by five years of war; she did not know whether the American was being rude or simply stating a fact. He noticed her reaction and said, "Bonnard told me you were the schoolteacher so I assumed you'd know languages."

"I'll get the papers," she said. "He also had a gun. Would you want that, too?"

"Yes," Docker said, glancing at the worn rug with its design of vines and peacocks, at straight-backed chairs near the fireplace, a sewing basket on the floor with a darning egg resting on a frayed blouse.

One wall had been constructed oddly, he thought, in three jointed sections, the middle one decorated with a carved and brightly painted angel's head.

A small log fire burned in the grate. On the mantelpiece stood a cut-glass bowl heaped with pinecones. Docker looked at himself in a clouded mirror above the mantel, surprised at the gray in his temples, silver now in the candlelight, and surprised too by the lines of weary tension in his features. He was listening to artillery fire from the direction of St. Vith when she came back with a wallet and a holstered handgun, which she gave to him.

"Would you like some coffee? We make it from roasted barley but it's hot."

"Don't go to any trouble."

"No, it's on the stove."

In the dining room adjoining the parlor, Docker sat at a pine table, bare except for a jar holding dry oak leaves.

The gun was a .25-caliber automatic with ivory handgrips and small diamond-shaped decorations framing black swastikas. There was a round of ammunition in the chamber and seven more in the cartridge clip. Docker ejected the bullet and put the gun on safe. Papers from the cracked black leather wallet gave him the name and rank and age of the dead German paratrooper: Willi Bremer, Feldwebel, twenty-three. There were several pictures of girls, a pay book, a scapular medal in tissue paper and newspaper clippings of soccer matches in the Stadtswald in Frankfurt am Main. None of these fragments told Docker what he had hoped to find out, which was whether the dead German in a GI uniform had been part of a strike force infiltrating the area or simply a lone flier who happened to bail out of a damaged aircraft above Mont Reynard.

"We took these from his uniform." She handed him a pair of lapel insignia shaped like tiny silver lightning bolts, the jagged SS of the Schutzstaffel.

"Is his the only body you've found? Or that you've heard about?"

"The only one, sergeant."

"Are there any strangers in the village, people you don't know or haven't seen before?"

"No."

Docker fingered the silver SS runes and watched the candlelight glinting on them.

"I'll get the coffee," she said.

Docker put his canteen and cigarettes on the table, watching her as she poured coffee into pewter mugs. She was thin and pale with long black hair held back at her temples with tortoiseshell combs. When she brought him coffee, he put a splash of whiskey in it.

"Would you like some? It's homemade but not bad."

She nodded and Docker added whiskey to her mug. She looked at the backs of her hands and moved her fingertips slowly over the planks of the old table.

"Did Monsieur Bonnard tell you about my brother?"

"Only that he'd been shot, ma'am, with other hostages."

"I'd like to tell you something else about him." She pushed a strand of hair from her forehead and looked about her, a puzzled frown on her face, as if for a moment she'd forgot where she was. "When you call me 'ma'am,' it makes me feel quite formal, like I'm in the classroom. I'm twenty-six. You may call me Denise, if you wish. I haven't talked to anyone for such a long time. My husband was taken almost four years ago and since the hostages were shot, there's not even my brother."

"What did you want to tell me about him?"

"Everything," she said . . . "How he let me watch him shave when I was young. How we sang together at the holidays—No, I don't mean that. I wanted to tell you that the Germans shot them right here, in the square in front of the church, you can see where the bullets broke the stones below the little statue of the Virgin . . . Did Bonnard tell you my brother had a daughter?"

"He said your brother married a Jewish girl and they had a daughter named Margret," Docker said, and sipped the coffee, bitter with Trankic's whiskey.

"My brother, Edmond, got Margret out of Cologne after Crystal Night. He crossed the border through the forest. When he was able to return, his wife and her family were gone. They had been taken away. Edmond left Margret with relatives in Verviers, a large family where she could go unnoticed."

Docker lit a cigarette and watched the smoke in the candlelight. "And is that what you wanted to tell me, ma'am?"

Docker saw that her hands had tightened into small fists, the knuckles white against the table's dark pine boards.

"Did you know about Crystal Night in America?"

"I imagine some people did." Docker thought of Gelnick, his mouth straining wide, bleating in surprise as he dropped to the ground, crying out when rockets and shrapnel tore open his body. Why was he surprised? Why in hell was Gelnick *surprised*?

"Did you, sergeant?"

"What's that, ma'am?"

"Did you read about Crystal Night?"

"Yes, it was in November, I think. Five or six years ago. A German official was killed in Paris by a young Jew. There were reprisals in Germany."

"Yes, you have it right. It was a night of looting and burning. Synagogues and Jewish shops and homes were broken into and burned to the ground. They smashed windows all over Germany and so the announcers on the German radio called it *Kristallnacht*."

She watched him as he poured another splash of whiskey into his coffee. His bland expression made her angry. "As you surmised, I speak quite good German."

"If they come back, that should be useful," he said.

He heard her intake of breath. "They will come back?"

"I don't think you've got anything to worry about."

"Why do you say that?"

"I don't know if you're telling the truth and I wouldn't blame you if you weren't," he said. "Either way, it's none of my business. But it's the usual civilian story when the enemy troops leave. Everybody hated them, everybody fought in the underground. Nobody ever drank with them or slept with them. They blew up trains, and prayed to the Virgin for the Yanks to arrive with chewing gum and chocolate to play Santa Claus."

Docker picked up the silver SS runes, juggled them in the palm of his hand, then put them back on the table. "You buried young Willi Bremer, kept his wallet and the pictures of his girlfriends, even saved his gun and goddamn SS insignia. If the Germans come back, you've got a nice story for them, and a well-tended grave of one of their finest."

"Yes, we need a story like that," she said. "We have nothing else."

"And you've got another story for the Yanks, the resistance movement, reprisals, even a little Jewish refugee."

Again he heard her soft intake of breath. "Bonnard told you . . . that Margret is in this house?"

"Yes, he told us that, ma'am. Would you like another drink?"

"No, thank you, I've had enough. Probably more than enough." She looked at him, a deep weariness in her face. "At first I didn't understand, when you said you thought I would be fluent in German," she said. "But you thought I'd slept with so many I learned the language thoroughly, even all those impossible verbs."

"I told you, it's not my business."

"I can't tell you I didn't have anything to do with Germans . . . after all, I was raped twice. But rape, I found out, is subject to interpretation. And Father Juneau didn't agree with my interpretation. He wouldn't give me absolution because he said it was my duty as a Catholic woman to struggle until I was unconscious, until I could no longer know or feel what was being done to me. To submit while conscious is a willingness, a mortal sin. The first time they were common soldiers and when I fought they put my head in a rain barrel until I choked. The second man was a captain. He was older and had been in the cavalry and his legs were so strong that when he clamped his knees around me I felt my back would break—"

"There's no reason to tell me this," he said.

She shook her head and lit one of his cigarettes. "It's quite easy, it's not difficult at all. Those men I had never seen before, I have learned to face what they thought of me. But if my husband comes back, can I expect him to think me unchanged? Will he want to know why I didn't let them drown me? Or why I'm not a cripple like Jocko with my back broken?"

Docker heard a sound behind him and turned quickly. A child stood in the doorway, and he realized he had seen her once before, only then she'd been bundled up in sweaters and a red scarf so that only her dark eyes were visible. Now she wore a blue cotton dress, black woolen stockings and a small white bow in her hair. She came slowly into the dining room and laid a coloring book on the table beside the dried oak leaves, then moved closer to the schoolteacher, putting her dark head against her skirt. In his careful French, Docker asked if she remembered him, but the girl shook her head.

"Not even the chocolate?" Docker said.

"You must think chocolate is the greatest luxury in the world," Denise Francoeur said. "It's the second time

you've talked about it. But the true luxury is anger, sergeant, and maybe that's what the people who have lied
to you can't afford."

The child picked up Docker's mug of coffee, but he
took it from her before she could drink from it. She
looked anxiously at her aunt when he lifted her onto his
knee, but after a moment she opened her book and
pointed to a page where she had drawn pictures of small
birds in flight, each wing made with a single curving
stroke of a crayon.

The room was warm and quiet, silence broken only
by the click of sleet on the windows and distant artillery
fire. The child soon lost interest in the pictures and put
her head against Docker's shoulder. In a moment or so
her faint breathing joined with the sounds of weather
and the crack of logs in the fireplace.

"I'll take her downstairs," Denise Francoeur said.

"She sleeps there all night?"

"Yes, she has a cot with blankets. I go down often to
see that she's all right." She took the child from him
and went into the parlor where she turned and said,
"Good night, sergeant."

Docker pulled back a blackout curtain and stared out
across a field that was dark except where the winds had
swept snow into white banks against a hedge of thorn
bushes, then watched the filmy texture of the fogs
breaking close against the windowpanes.

He poured an inch of Trankic's whiskey into his coffee mug and sipped it slowly. Was she right about anger? His father savored an anger, choleric in intensity,
at the present political administration in the United
States. But was that a luxury? Or high frustration? Dave
Hamlin's anger *was* pretty goddamn luxurious, to be
able to stay out of a war and still feel qualified to criticize the manners of those caught up in it. But was Gelnick's anger a luxury, or simply a burden that got him
killed . . .

He turned and saw Denise Francoeur watching him
from the doorway.

"Why did you stay?"

"I'm not sure." He finished the coffee and put the mug down beside the German automatic. "Well, I unloaded this gun and I thought I'd better show you how to reload it." He picked up the gun and pulled the receiver back to its maximum extension. When he released it, the receiver snapped forward and drove a round into the chamber. He pointed to the safe-fire lever. "When you move that to the red dot beside the trigger guard, the gun's ready to fire."

"And that's why you stayed? To explain about the gun?"

"No, I stayed because I'm sorry about what I said. I was angry and I wanted to get rid of it."

"There's no reason to—"

"No, listen. A man in my section was killed yesterday. His name was Gelnick. He got the same survival kit the army gives everybody—stay alert, keep your rifle clean, don't get trench foot, don't get clapped-up, get behind something when they're firing at you . . . but he didn't pay attention. Maybe he didn't want to, or just couldn't." Docker took a sip of Trankic's whiskey. "You understand any of that?"

"No," she said. "You're talking too fast."

"Well, it's not important. But I was angry at what happened."

"And I must say something too. It isn't what my husband may think that frightens me, it's what I think of myself." The words came in a rush and there was a sudden, warm color in her cheeks. "I want to say this but I can't if you look at me. Do you understand? Please sit down. But look at your coffee or the floor, please."

Docker stared down at the candlelight glinting on the rim of the coffee mug. "What is it?"

"I hated those Germans, not just with my feelings, but with my body. I don't want to bring that hatred to my husband. Ever since it happened, I don't like looking at myself. I can't help hating what they hated. And they must have hated me to hurt me so terribly. I

thought if I could be with someone who didn't force me
or hurt me . . ." She swallowed, and the sound of it
was dry in the warm room. "I watched you with Margret . . . I was happy for her, and I envied her. She
seemed comfortable with you. Do you have children?"

"No, I'm not married."

"This is very selfish, and very difficult. I thought I
could say these things to a stranger quickly and without
feeling anything. I'm not speaking of love or kindness,
just to be with someone without contempt and pain . . .
then it might be different for me . . ."

He looked up and saw tears.

"It might be enough," she said.

But it wouldn't be enough, Docker knew. The
warmth of impersonal flesh wasn't enough, even though
that was the kind of ersatz caring the war had taught
them . . . His arms felt empty without the child, but
war gave them all substitutes. His father had his dogs,
Schmitzer an ache for the dead, Larkin oblivion in a
bottle, and Gelnick the final kind . . . She hoped to
exorcise the memory of rape with the therapy of flesh
that was, at best, not angry or cruel or hateful. He knew
his own needs weren't quite that simple . . . the
warmth of the child in his arms had been a rebuke to
the loss of caring he regretted but had no defense
against. It was the signature of their times perhaps, and
it was Count Ciano, Mussolini's own son-in-law, who
had added a flourish to this cynical indifference by describing the children blown to death in an Ethiopian
landscape as putting him in mind of flowers, providing
improbable but brilliant colors in the smoke and flames
of destruction.

But the plus was . . . if there was ever a plus to
war . . . it could at least make you feel there was
something worth risking yourself for. In some way the
trust of it brought you closer to strangers than to people
you'd spent a lifetime with. Here he could feel closer
and more important to this sad young woman and her
dead brother Edmond than to names and faces he could

remember from a campus in America, and the broken stones of her church were somehow more significant to him now than the skyline of his native city.

"You're a Catholic," he said. "Isn't that important?"

"Yes, but I'm not sure how much. Father Juneau wants to survive. In fairness, he wants us all to survive. He says we're helpless, there's no valor in fighting, only foolishness. Even if that's true, I can't say my brother was foolish. We'll all be dead someday. If we don't take the chance now, we never will. Isn't that true?"

"Yes, I think it is."

"Then this is true. I believe it can be different for me. If we have hope, it's only logical to have faith. Margret fell asleep because you were holding her, and whether it was an illusion or not, whether you cared or not didn't matter because she believed you did."

"All right," he said. "But don't tell me anything about him. Not a word, not even his name—"

"It's Etienne," she said softly.

Docker waited in the dining room until she called him, then put out his cigarette and went into her small, cold bedroom, where a fragrance of dried flowers mingled on the air with the smoke from a snuffed-out candle.

Entering the church choir loft by a narrow, spiral staircase, Jocko and Corporal Trankic removed panels from the back of the organ and Trankic, on his hands and knees, with Jocko training a flashlight over his shoulder, worked almost two hours locating and repairing the transmitter's malfunctions. After re-soldering the wires to their connections, he and Jocko spent another half hour fine-tuning the equipment. They sent signals in French and English from the La Chance transmitter, but as Trankic began to repeat the grid coordinates of the German plane's position, he was interrupted by an incoming message.

Jocko held up his hand and leaned closer to the speaker, hearing over an eruption of static Paul Cou-

treau calling La Chance from Stavelot. Coutreau repeated his warning twice, telling them what his son Simon had seen in the woods near Lepont, his voice low
and tense, a straining metallic whisper in the cold silence of the church.

Chapter Nineteen

December 21, 1944. Mont Reynard-
Castle Rêve. Thursday, 2100 Hours.

"My shop's in a street called Rue de Bas," Henri Gervais said, examining a case of brandied cherries, the
necks of the bottles gleaming with silver foil. "I haven't
seen this item since 'itler turned off the bloody lights in
Paris. It's right opposite the railway station, Yank, a bar
and 'orehouse beside a packing plant."

Larkin and Bonnard and the black-market dealer
stood in the storeroom of Castle Rêve, Bonnard holding a lamp above his head, the light flaring across
shelves stocked with foodstuffs and spirits. Gervais
made an inventory on a note pad, occasionally stopping
to admire the delicacies. He was small and compactly
built, probably in his mid-forties, Larkin thought, wearing a black overcoat and a black fedora decorated with
a spray of Alpine feathers. A smile flickered constantly
below his narrow dark mustache.

Bonnard had explained that Gervais traveled with
two sets of papers, one identifying him as a civilian em-
ployee of the German Army, the other as a technician
assigned to a U.S. Army hospital unit. Gervais had
come over from Liège on an ancient motorcycle, a
thirty-odd-mile trip that took him more than four hours
because, as he'd told them in his accented English,
many stretches of road were under artillery fire.

Larkin tried to push away a morose conviction that he was getting in too deep, that his Irish ass would indeed be in a sling if Docker found out what he was up to. But he was as worried about this alley-smart Belgian prick as he was about his sergeant. He knew Gervais was out to shaft him, yet he still felt a need to please the man and earn his approval. And that confused and embittered him because in the cold storeroom surrounded by cases of foodstuffs whose names he couldn't even pronounce, Larkin had gained an unwanted insight into the nature of class warfare, which wasn't a war, he realized, wasn't even a goddamn armistice, just a plain fucking surrender before a shot was fired by some slob scratching his poor man's ass and hoping for a break from the shitty Gervaises of the world . . . He twisted the top off a bottle of Cutty Sark, and took a short pull from it, then said, "I haven't heard any goddamn talk about money yet."

"Wouldn't be fair now, would it? I ask you, would it be fair, Yank, before I get the count on all these lovelies you're selling?"

"Well, let's snap a little shit."

"Ah, there's the soldier talking." Gervais gave him an approving smile. "No wonder 'itler's on the run with blokes like you nipping at his bloody heels."

Larkin felt better then, warmed as much by Gervais' conciliatory response as by the heat of the whiskey spreading through his body. . . .

Bonnard went into the kitchen adjoining the storeroom to boil water for powdered coffee, and Gervais spent the next thirty minutes making a list of the merchandise. Then, after nodding thoughtfully at the totals, he squinted through cigarette smoke at Larkin.

"I might have missed the odd tin or two, but that could be in your favor as well as mine. Anyway, it's the brandy and whiskey brings us home and dry."

"Sure, in Paris a bottle of whiskey goes for thirty or forty dollars," Larkin said.

"But we're a long way from the Tour Eiffel and Pig

Alley, aren't we, Yank?" Gervais rubbed his fingertips together. "Payoffs every foot of the way. So, for the brandy and whiskey, for everything in the lot, I make it six thousand dollars. And that's a fair price, take my word for it."

"Why don't you take a flying fuck at a rolling doughnut?"

"I get your drift. Yes, I do, Yank. Shall we put it up to Bonnard?"

"No, I'm running this show."

"But if the Heinies come back, who'll be running it then? Dicey business, eh, Yank? I mean, who really owns this loot now? So I'll tell you what. I'll add a hundred to each of the three shares, makin' it sixty-three hundred for the lot. Nothing could be fairer, Yank."

It was probably a royal screwing, Larkin thought, but he said, "Then it's half down now and half on delivery."

"Sorry, Yank, I pay *only* on delivery. There's a war on, don't you see . . ."

"Yeah, that slipped my mind. But not a thing goes off my truck until I got my share of that cash in my hand, every fucking simoleon of it."

Bonnard pulled open the door connecting to the kitchen, and Larkin immediately noted the tension in his face. "There's a truck and jeep pulling up the drive, it's your people, the sergeant and the big corporal—"

"Anybody with them?"

"I couldn't see anyone."

Larkin had *known* something like this would happen, a banana peel waiting for him to take a pratfall on. "You guys stay down here," he said, and stuffed the bottle of Cutty Sark into his overcoat pocket. "Turn off the lamp and lock the door when I leave." He ran through the kitchen and up the stairs to the big drawing room, and by the time he'd crossed the foyer and pulled open the doors facing the driveway and park Docker was climbing from the jeep, a small, dark-haired girl in his arms.

"What the hell's going on?" Larkin asked him.

Trankic stood beside the truck, a hand on the open door. Docker put the child in the cab, tucked a blanket around her knees, then crossed the driveway to Larkin.

"Schmitzer told me you were up here," he said.

"Yeah, I took a break to pick up a jug." Larkin pulled the bottle of Cutty Sark from his pocket. "You want a belt?"

"Put it away, Matt."

"What the fuck's eating you?"

"Trankic and the Belgian, Jocko, picked up a report on the Lepont transmitter. There's a German tank and recon car headed this way. It was spotted near Stavelot a couple of hours ago. The little girl is Jewish. The schoolteacher told us there's a convent outside Lepont, the Sacred Heart, where she'll be all right. I can't spare the jeep. I need the radio at the guns."

"Which leaves me and the truck and the Jewish kid, is that the deal?"

"It's not an order, Matt."

Larkin sipped the cold whiskey. "But you're sure as hell asking for volunteers."

"Right. You're the best wheel man in the section, if you'd put that bottle down."

"Jesus, you don't have to lie to me, Bull . . . Women and children first, right?"

"Yes or no," Docker said.

It would be yes, of course, Larkin thought. Had to be. But wasn't this just what he wanted? A truck, handed to him like a gift from heaven? With Bonnard's help, he could load up, drop the Jewish kid wherever he was supposed to, then head for Gervais' warehouse in Liège. It was like fate or something, and he was just one little cog being pushed around by whatever you wanted to call it, the stars or just dumb luck. So why not grab it and thank God for it? But he couldn't take it like that, because he knew there had to be a catch in the deal somewhere, an ace up somebody's sleeve; he'd been a loser so long he didn't believe that things would

ever fall in place for him . . . So this had to be just
another little joke. Docker was offering him everything
he'd wanted on a silver platter, a stake for the future, an
opportunity to walk the streets of his old neighborhood
without forever scratching a poor man's ass. But
Docker had added a catch to the deal, maybe without
even knowing it, but it was there, a price tag that somehow would break him . . . Docker and Trankic, he
noted, were clean-shaven in spite of the freezing
weather, first-class field soldiers, helmet straps tight under their jaws, cartridge belts with grenades hooked to
the webbing, rifles slung across their shoulders. They
were soldiers with jobs to do and he wanted to be with
them on the hill with the guns. That was the price he
would pay for being a thief, the certain knowledge that
he wasn't good enough to be there with them . . .
Docker had picked the most useless man in his section
to chauffeur this Jewish kid to some godforsaken convent. And it wouldn't have taken him longer than a
fingersnap to make that decision. Linari and Dormund,
dumb shits with IQs that wouldn't break a hundred put
together, they couldn't be spared. Or Shorty Kohler, or
Tex Farrel, or Solvis. Christ, no. And don't even think
about Schmitzer or Trankic. So naturally, that left Larkin. And could you blame Docker? Larkin with the
drunken uncles, the cough of a boozer, the week-old
beard and a bottle of whiskey in the pocket of a dirty
overcoat. Would you pick him for a soldier's job that
took brains and guts? Or put him in the lifeboat with
the women and kids?

"All right, Bull," he said. "All right."

"Okay, go down the hill to Lepont, make a right at
the river and head out about nine miles. Look for gray
stone walls, an iron gate on the right side of the road
past a pair of oak trees. It's the Sacred Heart Convent,
Sacré-Coeur. The mother superior is Sister Gabrielle.
You got that now?"

"For Christ's sake, you think I'm some kind of
dummy? What's the kid's name?"

"Margret. She's the little girl we met the night we were heading for Werpen."

"With the old guy we bought vegetables from?" And when Docker nodded, Larkin went on quickly, "Sure, I remember . . . he wanted Belgian francs, he didn't want the Invasion currency, and he had some carrots and beets and I was thinking about making some kind of sauce if I could find some fresh eggs. And the same night . . ."

Larkin's voice trailed off, and he realized he'd hardly been aware of what he was saying, but like a child trying desperately to keep an adult's attention he had been talking because he didn't want Docker to go, or Trankic either, didn't want them to leave him alone here at the castle in the snow and dark.

"You guys better take off," he said.

Trankic tossed him the truck keys. "Take care of yourself."

They climbed into the jeep. Docker looked at him. "Be careful, Matt," he said.

Larkin laughed. "Sure, I'll be careful. I want to get home as much as the next guy. In fact . . ." He started to laugh again. " . . . maybe a little more than the next guy, Bull."

Docker nodded. "Sure you do, Matt."

When the jeep turned out of the driveway and started down the road to the gatehouse, Larkin said a Hail Mary for all of them, for himself and the soldiers on the guns and the little girl he could see staring at him from the cab of the truck, but he couldn't hear the words because they were blown away by the winds coming across the wide gardens of the castle.

Chapter Twenty

The first light of dawn was reflected flatly in the freezing waters of the Salm. Fog had moved across the valley during the night, surrounding Section Eight's position with currents of opaque white haze.

The isolation was so complete, seamless, that Docker was startled when a flock of rooks flew overhead, dark forms and faint cawing sounds fading swiftly away into banks of gray clouds.

On the precipice of the hill the huge dog began barking at something in the valley below the cannon revetment. Trankic and Docker unslung their rifles and walked out to the level crop of rock where Radar was growling at the mists coming up the mountains.

"Maybe it's a rabbit or something," Trankic said.

Farrel, who had joined them, said, "If it was, Radar'd go after him."

"Let's tone it down," Docker said.

Winds gusted through the fog and cracked the ice on the limbs of the trees, but these were the only sounds they could hear over the barking.

"At ease, goddamn it." Trankic clamped the dog's jaws shut with his gloved hands. "You heard the sergeant."

Docker said then, "Tex, get over to the ammo dump

189

and pick up a few grenades. Collect a pair of bazookas and bring them back here."

Trankic released the dog, who snarled again at the mists, and bounded after Farrel.

"Where do you think Larkin is? The way he's belting that booze, he could be passed out somewhere. You think of that?"

"Surprisingly enough, that occurred to me," Docker said.

He could now see the white curve of the river and smoke curling from houses in the village, and thought of the schoolteacher, and the priest who had told her that if she could have resisted one more minute, one more second . . .

Lowering his binoculars, Docker let them hang free around his neck.

"That tank they saw, maybe it was hit," Trankic said. "Pulled into the valley to make repairs. Or maybe it was heading for the action near St. Vith or Bastogne. Hell, it might be miles from here by now."

"Well, we'd better stop guessing about it."

"Sure. You want me to ask for volunteers?"

"No, take Farrel and Kohler. Stay close to each other and go slow. Use hand signals. If you find the mother, don't try to be heroes. I just want to know where that tank is and what shape it's in."

Larkin had decided not to risk driving down the mountain at night. Instead, after loading the truck with Bonnard's help he had coasted only a mile or so, the wet grind of the big tires the only sound in the darkness. With the child huddled beside him, he had then slept for a few hours off the road, scrubbed his face with snow and started out again at dawn, driving with careful concentration, taking the looping turns under controlled power, double-clutching on the grades and not relaxing until they were out of the mountains and on the level road beside the river. Visibility was good for several hundred feet then, and he could mark the sentinel

beeches along the banks, dappled trunks blurred with
the sleeting snow. Larkin settled himself more comfortably behind the wheel, trying not to disturb the little girl
who was asleep or resting now, lying quietly beside him.

"Excuse me, darlin'." He moved her just enough to
let him pull the bottle from his pocket, then let her
snuggle up to him again and took a drink without taking
his eyes from the road. He put the Cutty Sark on the
dashboard, wedging it against the windshield with a
grease rag.

He could feel the whiskey exploding in his stomach,
and some of it ran coldly along the chinstrap of his helmet. About nine miles, Docker had said, stone walls
and a gate past some oak trees. Sacred Heart Convent,
Sister Gabrielle. Even though the little girl seemed
asleep, Larkin started talking to her because his
thoughts felt warmed and honest with the whiskey . . .
"It's gonna be all right, you'll see," he said. "It's gonna
be all right, Matt Larkin says so . . ."

He saw the reflection of his smile in the windshield,
teeth starkly white against his black beard. "You got it
rough, I'll admit that. Being a Jewish kid without a
home on a night that would freeze the balls off a brass
monkey. But if you think I had it good when I was your
age, you got another think coming . . ." He drank
more whiskey, grateful for the heat flowing from his
loins down his legs and into his feet, which had felt wet
and frozen for weeks. He was sorry he'd started talking
about what it was like when he was a kid, but it was
something he couldn't help . . . "How's it at the syn-
agogue? They give you that Lamb of God crap?" His
voice was harsher, demanding answers from his reflection in the windshield . . . "Ark of the Covenant,
Gate of Heaven and that old Lamb of God, which is
funny if you think about it, like the Lamb was the way
He got his gun off. I guess we stole it all from you anyway. Tower of David, House of Gold, Refuge of Sinners. Maybe that's what drove my uncles into such
crazy drunks, sitting in church with their hangovers and

the priest telling them to say their prayers to all those
Jews in Jerusalem. But I'll tell you one damned thing
that's for real . . . it's what made the Virgin Mary
bedtime story go down smooth and easy, because if
those priests ever tried to tell them holy mackerels that
Joe the carpenter was really screwing Mary, they'd have
got their churches burned down . . ." He glanced at
the child. "Look, I'm sorry. Don't pay no attention to
me." He was embarrassed by the language he'd been
using. She was just a little girl, after all . . . "It's gonna be okay, we got these Heinies on the run, and things
are gonna be okay for you. Maybe you'll grow up and
get married and have some kids. You might even get to
the States someday. This is a night we could talk about,
even though you won't probably remember it. We could
have a steak or something and maybe some drinks at
a place I hang out at called the Green Castle. It's on
Lexington, right at Forty-ninth Street . . ."

Larkin felt a spasm of disgust for himself and the
sentiments spilling from his mouth. It would bring a
tear to his mother's eyes, it would make his uncles pour
sloppy drinks all around the kitchen table. The priests
would cream themselves over it, stuffing the Lamb of
God down your throat with beauty and peace and love
and sending you home to get your ass kicked or your
nose broken by a brutal, brutalized parent or cousin or
uncle who'd heard you were necking with one of the
Moran girls on the roofs of those rotten brownstones
that stretched up from the city streets to contaminate
the stars . . . Ahead on his right, Larkin saw an im-
mense pair of oak trees and beyond them a gray stone
wall set back from the road. Parking the truck in front
of the convent's iron gates, he climbed down from the
cab and rang a bell suspended above a cairn of stones.

Within a few minutes, candles appeared at the foot of
a graveled driveway leading through a grove of fir trees.
The two nuns who unlocked the heavy gate wore rough
wool habits and had the faces of weathered, aging peasants.

Larkin explained the situation to them in English, speaking loudly in an effort to stir a gleam of understanding in their watchful eyes.

When he switched in frustration to the few phrases of French he'd picked up, one of them walked to the truck while the other smiled tentatively and pointed to a wooden alms box on a post outside the gates.

"Sure, sure." He took out his wallet and stuffed a half dozen Belgian notes into the poor box.

One of the nuns lifted the child from the truck. The little girl stared at Larkin, her eyes wide and dark above the edge of the coarse brown blanket. There was nothing more he could do for her but he felt guilty just standing there and looking at her. He waved but wasn't sure whether she tried to wave back because her hands were tucked underneath the blanket.

"I tell you, it's gonna be all right," he called to her as the nuns closed and locked the tall iron gates.

Waving again, he watched the nuns and the little child and the twin lights from the candles disappear on the graveled path through the fir trees, then feeling lonely as hell, swung himself into the cab of the truck, gunned the motor and pulled back onto the road that would take him into Liège and Gervais' warehouse.

Chapter Twenty-One

December 22, 1944. Mont
Reynard/Lepont. Friday, 1230 Hours.

The sun was pressing through heavy cloud cover when
Radar began barking again at something that had
alerted him in the valley. Corporal Trankic's detail had
been back several hours, finding no sign of the German
tank in a reconnaissance that had taken them from the
base of Mont Reynard to a network of logging trails
around the village.

Docker stood at the edge of the precipice where the
overhang was topped and spiked with bracken and
frozen thornbushes. He swept the valley with his binoculars, holding the scopes on an area where fir trees
swayed and bent underneath layers of fog. Lowering the
glasses, he listened to distant grinding sounds that shook
the ground beneath him. Trankic and Tex Farrel came
running to join him, and the men in the revetment
climbed onto the cannon's loading platform for a better
view of the snow-shrouded valley.

Something massive and powerful broke through a
screen of trees a quarter of a mile from them, and
Docker said, "Jesus Christ!" as he saw the dark shape
of a tank driving toward the base of Mont Reynard with
mist floating like tendrils around its turret. The tank
clawed through the frozen timber toward the slopes,
stopping in a grove of trees glittering with hoarfrost and

ice. Directly behind the tank a German command car turned into the cover of a hedge of white junipers. The engines of the tank and command car cut out simultaneously, and a deep silence settled over the valley. A few moments later they saw a German soldier in a greatcoat and visored cap walk from the row of firs and disappear behind the tank.

Chet Dormund, his face twisting with excitement, said, "Sarge, you see that wretched, fucking thing down there?"

Jackson Baird used his hands to shield his eyes against the stinging sleet as he studied the tank.

"What is it, Bull?" Trankic said.

"I'm not sure." His binoculars couldn't bring the tank into a sharp focus through the trees. "Probably a Panzer IV."

Baird glanced nervously at him. "Sergeant, maybe you should take another look. I don't think it's a Mark IV. It's got a glacis plate and machine-gun ports that are different—"

Docker cut him off with a gesture, waved everyone but Trankic back from the edge of the hill and trained his binoculars on the German soldier, who was partially concealed and protected behind the tank's chest-high treads. The German seemed to be giving orders to his crew, and Docker had a passing impression of angular features and darkly hollowed eyes. After glancing casually up the slopes of Mont Reynard, the officer moved out of view behind the tank.

Docker lowered the glasses, not knowing whether or not the Germans suspected an American gun section was positioned above them on the hill.

"So what do we do now, Bull?" Trankic said.

"Get the truck and hook up the cannon."

"We're pulling out?"

Docker nodded. "At least to where we've got better cover and can make a break for it."

They backed from the cliff and ran to the revetment,

where the men—except Schmitzer and Linari—were
waiting for them.

Baird said anxiously, "Sergeant, I've got to talk to
you. It's important, please believe me."

"Make it fast then."

"We can't run for it. There's no way we can—"

"Baird, this isn't a goddamn debating club. Trankic,
on the double."

"You got to listen to me, sergeant. You've *got to*."

"For Christ's sake, what *is* it?"

"That's not a Panzer IV down there, sergeant. It's a
Tiger Mark II."

"How the hell would you know?"

"I've seen them, that's how. I know what they look
like."

Trankic put in, "Where'd you see them, kid? In some
fucking comic strip?"

"What difference does it make where I saw them?
That's what's down in the valley. It weighs almost
eighty tons and its turret armor can take direct hits from
our Grants."

"Hold it a minute," Docker said to Trankic, and returned to the cliff's edge. He trained his binoculars into
the valley until the details of the tank sharpened in the
scopes, and he saw that Baird was right, it was not a
Panzer IV down there in the sleet-laden trees, it was the
most dangerous ground weapon in the German arsenal—a King Tiger Mark II. The sergeant had seen a
column of them in North Africa, but today—in heavy
weather—he had not picked out the Tiger's distinctive
features. Now he could identify the massive turret with
its black cross, the high profile of the glacis plate, the
commander's periscope and the huge 88-millimeter cannon . . . The Mark II was an awesome sight under
any circumstances, and the way it seemed to be hiding
in the cover of the mist and trees charged it with an
additional, an almost unnatural menace, as if it were
more than a great engine of war but rather some species
of intelligent, invincible beast, crouching, waiting with

infinite patience for the betraying panic of whatever it
fed on.

Docker walked back to the revetment. "Trankic, get
the truck."

"You don't *understand*," Baird said, an edge of des-
peration in his voice.

"I understand who gives the orders here," Docker
told him.

"But you'll lose whatever edge we've got—"

"Goddamn it, Baird, I won't tell you again to shut
up," Docker said, and gave his binoculars to Farrel and
told him to keep the scopes on the Mark II.

The wind had picked up suddenly, gusting around
the revetment, sweeping the snow up in blinding eddies,
whining through the trees that studded the crest of the
hill.

"You're wrong, you don't know what you're doing!"
Baird screamed the words at them. "You guys are going
to get yourselves killed!"

"Jesus, take a break . . . didn't you hear Docker?"
Trankic said, and started for the trees, where the single
truck was parked.

He had not taken two steps when Baird said, "Hold
it, corporal," his voice unsteady, and backed quickly
away from the group and unslung his rifle.

Trankic said very quietly, "Don't point that thing at
me, you crazy, fucking kid."

"Baird, put it down," Docker said.

"Not until you listen to me, sergeant."

The youngster's face was whiter than the snow driving across the hill, his breath was coming so fast that it
made a small keening sound. There was a comic look to
his outsized uniform and trailing overcoat, but nothing
funny in the way he held his rifle, sweeping its muzzle
steadily across the men behind Docker and Trankic.

Sonny Laurel smiled uncertainly and walked toward
him. "Maybe this is a joke, but it's no time for it. Come
on, give me that rifle. Hey, this is crazy!"

"No, stay away from me—"

"You wanted to talk, so let's talk." Docker spoke quietly, almost casually. If Baird started firing—even if he didn't hit anybody—those shots would betray their position to the Germans.

Trankic said, "Sure, why not speak up, kid?" Shifting his weight casually, he moved closer to Baird, thumbs hooked carelessly over his cartridge belt. "What's on your mind?"

"I know the T.O. for a Mark II, sergeant," Baird said. "It calls for five men—a tank commander, two corporals, an ammo leader and a driver." He backed off another few steps. "Maybe I did learn all this from books and training manuals. It doesn't matter. I can tell you what else is down there with that Tiger II. A German officer wearing SS insignia and three braids on his collar tabs. Same rank as a lieutenant colonel in our army." He moistened his lips. "Just listen to the rest of it, sergeant—then you can have this damned rifle."

Trankic was almost within arm's reach of him now. Docker said easily, "Sure, Baird, let's hear all of it."

Baird let out his breath slowly. "If we pull this cannon and try to make a run for it, we're dead. They won't attack until they know what's up here, what kind of firepower we've got. With a field-grade officer in charge, they won't make any mistakes in tactics. But if they hear us leaving, they'll know they can take this hill. And then it's just a matter of arithmetic. A Tiger Mark II makes thirty miles an hour on flat ground, maybe half that coming up the mountain, and when it gets here it's equipped with a Porsche turret that can traverse three hundred and sixty degrees in less than twenty seconds. We won't be halfway to the river before their eighty-eight opens up on us . . . but they won't take the chance unless we give them the high ground . . ." He pointed to the mist-shrouded peaks above their position. "What they want is—"

Trankic closed on him now with a rush and tore the rifle from his hands. He tossed it to Farrel and struck Baird once in the body and again in the face, the second blow spinning Baird around and dropping him to the ground. Trankic flipped him onto his stomach, dug a knee into the small of his back and used Baird's own belt to tie his wrists behind him, securing the knots with a pair of tight hitches.

The blood from Baird's lips stained the trampled snow. Docker hated the look of it. It reminded him of Larkin and Haskell and he was sick of his feelings, of his fears and responsibilities he couldn't admit to or avoid. Baird's eyes were closed, his breathing ragged.

Laurel took out a handkerchief and knelt beside him. "You didn't have to bust him up like that, Trank."

"Just try minding your own business, Sonny. Crazy punk could have blown the shit out of all of us." Trankic turned to Docker. "Unless Larkin gets back before we haul out of here, we gotta leave the machine guns. You want me to pick up Schmitzer and Linari when I get the truck?"

"No, Trank." Docker shook his head slowly. "We're not leaving."

"What the fuck you mean?"

"I mean he's right."

Trankic stared at Docker. "Mind spelling it out for me?"

"They've got to come up this hill while we're traveling at least three miles down to the river. For six, or eight minutes, we'll be in their sights. That damn eighty-eight won't miss at that range."

Trankic studied the narrow road curving down the hill from Mont Reynard and Castle Rêve, tracking its misted length through the meadows and trees to the river. He massaged his nose with the back of his hand. "Yeah, I guess our little Napoleon called it at that." His voice was empty, quiet. "They got us in a fucking trap—"

Suddenly Tex Farrel was waving to Docker from the edge of the hill. "Sarge, they're zeroing in."

Concealed by the hedge of frozen underbrush, Docker stared into the valley and saw the turret of the massive tank revolving slowly, the long, gleaming cannon rising toward the crest of the hill.

He realized that his first hope had been simply a reflex of wishful thinking; the Germans in that tank damn well knew there was an enemy position on Mont Reynard. How they knew and what they were after were irrelevant now . . .

"Get back," he said to Farrel, and ran toward the revetment, calling to the others to hit the ground before throwing himself full-length onto the frozen earth.

The tank's cannon sounded with a roar and the first projectile struck the rim of the cliff, showering the hill with shards of rock, the fragments whining around them like bullets. The next three blasts came at rapid fire, and Docker locked his arms over his helmet as the projectiles rushed high above them toward the timberline of distant mountain ridges.

Then there was silence again, broken only by the shifting winds and the noise of rock flows rattling down the sides of the hills. A painful ringing sounded in Docker's head, and warm blood streamed from his nostrils.

Laurel had thrown himself across Baird, protecting him with his outflung arms and legs. "He's all right, sarge," he called out.

"How about you?"

"I'm okay," but his eyes were bright with shock.

The sleeve of Trankic's jacket had been ripped open, and blood ran down the back of his grimy hand. Sitting up, he picked tiny pieces of rock from his thick forearm, wincing as patches of skin came free with them. Dormund had blood coming from one of his ears and complained of a killer headache. Solvis was limping; he'd been knocked flat, cracking his knee against splintered rocks. Docker told Dormund and Laurel to untie Baird and put sulfa on his face cuts. Then taking his field glasses from Farrel, he crawled back to the edge of the cliff.

The Mark II had not changed positions, its gray bulk

looming through the frosted grove, the cannon covering the overhang of Mont Reynard. He saw now that the small-arms ports were open, revealing the snoutlike muzzles of the 7.9-millimeter machine guns. There was no way that he could see—no reasonably safe way—to get close enough to the tank to destroy its treads, and thereby its mobility, with grenades. He remembered what young Baird had said and knew he was right: With a field grade officer, there'd be no mistakes in tactics. The tank was positioned so that its machine guns covered the open terrain around it, and the thick grove of trees gave the crew the option to leave the tank and double as riflemen.

Docker heard an engine revving up somewhere below him, but his ears were aching from the cannon barrage and he couldn't immediately locate the source of the staccato sounds. Until he saw the German command car race out from behind the tank, drive into a logging trail and shoot out of sight among the trees before he could so much as raise his carbine at the colonel who was at the wheel, a visored cap shading his features. . . .

Chapter Twenty-Two

December 22, 1944. Environs of Liège,
Belgium. Friday, 1400 Hours.

After leaving the girl with the nuns, Larkin drove back
into the mountains, where he surmised there would be
less chance of running into either American or German
troops.

Heading north and west for Liège, the cab warm and
snug, he relaxed comfortably as the big truck powered
its way up the grades in low gear, clawing through the
slick, dangerous turns, dropping from heights into
gorges and parting the thick fog and snow with the battering force of its wide grille and fenders.

He'd put the half empty bottle of whiskey on the seat
beside him. He felt alert and confident and intended to
stay that way. And he also wanted to save something to
celebrate with, a couple of fingers of Cutty Sark when
he collected his loot from Gervais. Driving fast but
carefully, he leaned forward to peer through the flying
veils of snow, then relishing the pressure against his
back when he swept down the hills, the solid weight that
came from dozens of crates of food and wine and whiskey . . . He thought cheerfully about the money he
would collect in Liège and remembered with a good,
warm feeling what he'd told Gervais, that nothing left
the truck for the warehouse until he had his share in his
hands, every damned one of those twenty-one hundred

simoleons. He thought about Killjoy Kranston and that made him feel like singing, so he hummed a verse of "Molly Malone," beating out the rhythm with his fingers on the steering wheel.

With his share of the loot, Larkin figured he wouldn't have to kiss the Killjoy's behind for a job when he got home. He could take a year off, let Agnes buy some furniture, and maybe even go back and finish that last year of high school. There wasn't much mystery about getting ahead in the world. It wasn't brains that made the difference, it was the breaks. And it wasn't what you knew but *who* you knew. Except that made him remember something that dampened his spirits. He'd said that once in a bar in the Bronx and some smart-ass prick had corrected him, saying no, Larkin, you got it wrong, you dumb mick . . . it's not who you know, but *whom*.

Well, fuck him, he thought, and Killjoy Kranston . . . and throw Docker in for good measure . . . Larkin knew he'd need a story when he got back to the section, Docker wouldn't buy a con job about a flat or engine trouble or getting lost in the storm. Maybe the nuns would be his best bet . . . say he had to take the Jewish kid to her room, light a fire for her, then the nuns had asked him to bring in more wood for their cookstove . . . That would work okay, he could say he'd had a meal with them, something like that. . . .

Braking his way into a hairpin turn, Larkin found himself wishing it had happened that way, that he'd in fact made sure the kid was safe in bed and maybe had some coffee or something with the nuns in the kitchen. He was sorry about how he talked to the little girl because even when you were being as honest as you could, talking about the priests and why you were afraid had a way of sounding dirty . . . Poor old Gelnick knew all about being afraid, so maybe it wasn't the priests but a fear everybody had because they weren't sure what would happen next, or whether there even was any next . . . what was her name? Doris, that was it.

Maybe he and Agnes could take Gelnick's wife to dinner when he got home, up to Frank's in Harlem or
somewhere on the Island or downtown to Neptune's for
their fish platter. They might even arrange to hook up
with Docker and get him to come along. . . .

Near big towns, Larkin knew, the traffic would be
too heavy for the MPs to check everything on wheels,
so he swung the truck into a downgrade and started
back toward the valley and the river, figuring it was
safe now for the final run into Liège. But when he
came off the hill he saw a group of American soldiers
standing near a recon car at the junction of the Salm
River road. He told himself he didn't have anything to
worry about, the stuff he and Bonnard had packed into
the truck was concealed by tarpaulins lashed from the
top of the truck right down to the tailgate. Still, he felt a
coldness in his stomach when one of the soldiers, an
officer, stepped into the road and waved him down with
a flashlight. He was sixty or seventy yards from them,
so he braked the truck to a crawl to give himself time to
think . . . Play it nice and easy now, real businesslike.
On a tight schedule, hooking up with an outfit in Liège.
Meeting a supply train. Something like that was always
good. Or say they told me to pick up a general. General
who? How the fuck do I know? They just said he's
wearing two stars, waiting at the railroad station, move
your ass, corporal . . .

Larkin rolled the window down and saluted an
American captain.

"What's your name and outfit, soldier?"

"Corporal Matt Larkin, sir. The Two hundred sixty-
ninth Automatic Weapons Battalion."

"Where you heading?"

"Liège, sir."

"Let's have a look at your orders."

"Well, I don't have any, captain. Not written ones,
anyway. We been out of touch for a week. This morning one of our officers told me to get over to Liège and
pick up some other guys from the battery."

"What the hell they doing in Liège?"

"It's mostly the Headquarters clerks." The inventions flowed easily and smoothly. "They got knocked out of their position the first day of the attack and hitched a ride with some medics over there."

"What're your officers' names, corporal?"

"Lieutenant Bart Whitter and Lieutenant Longworth, sir. The B.C. is Captain Joe Grant."

Several of the other soldiers came and stood behind the captain. One of them walked to the rear of the truck, inspecting the stake and lashings with his flashlight. They all wore MP brassards and VIII Corps shoulder patches on their overcoats and field jackets.

"We're checking out everybody, corporal. The Germans have dropped troops around here in GI uniforms."

"Yeah, we heard about that, sir."

"Where you from in the States?"

"Lower East Side of Manhattan, sir."

"Which way is Wall Street? Uptown or downtown?"

"About as far downtown as you can get, sir."

"What's the tallest building?"

"Empire State, sir."

"What do they plant in Madison Square Garden?"

Larkin grinned and said, "Cauliflowers, sir."

The captain looked a bit puzzled and his men shifted their weight and stared at Larkin. "I'm not sure I understand," the captain said slowly.

Larkin felt a dryness in his throat. Stop the dumb jokes. Stop being a wise guy . . . play it straight . . .

"Cauliflowers, like in cauliflower ears, sir. The way the fighters get banged up, their ears get lumpy."

"Yes, sure."

And then, because Larkin felt he was practically home free, he grinned and said, "Maybe I better check you out, too, captain. Where *you* from in the States?"

"That's smart, corporal. No point taking chances. I'm from Chicago."

"What're the names of your baseball clubs?"

"Cubs and White Sox. Wrigley Field and Comiskey Park, Hack Wilson, Kiki Cuyler, Ted Lyons. Want some batting averages?"

"Frankly, I'd just like to haul ass, sir."

"Well, if you're ever in Chicago, stop and give a big hello to the little lady."

While Larkin was wondering what that meant, the captain pulled back the sleeve of his overcoat and showed Larkin the blue and gold figure of a fan dancer tattooed on his wrist. "Sally Rand brings you greetings, and hopes her memory will send you speeding off to the whorehouses in Liège."

Larkin smiled appreciatively, and he and the captain exchanged salutes.

One of the MPs waved him on, shouting, "Okay, buddy, move it, move it! Get the lead in!"

"An Italian salute to your mother, too," Larkin yelled back at him, and cranked up the window, accelerating rapidly as he turned onto the empty road flanking the river.

He was still grinning and could see the flash of his teeth in the windshield, gleaming against his dark unshaven face. His spirits were exuberant. That business had gone off pretty damn good, and Larkin decided he'd earned himself a drink. So it's not who you know but *whom*, was it? Fuck him, fuck everybody, he thought, and took a short sip of whiskey . . .

And then he remembered what the MP had shouted at him, and suddenly he felt the blood draining from his face. The whiskey couldn't touch a dreadful coldness spreading down his legs and paralyzing his loins. The muscles in his stomach contracted abruptly and violently, the pain so agonizing it made his eyes water. He began coughing, his body wracked by convulsive spasms.

"Get the lead *in*!" Not *out*. Jesus, the guy had said get the lead *in*. And the captain didn't know about cauliflower ears . . .

Corporal Matthew Larkin thought of the twenty-one

hundred dollars and Agnes and a bartender named
Tony at a steak house he liked in the Bronx, a place
called Jackson's on Fordham Road with sawdust on the
floor, or maybe it was Dolbey's where the Yankee ball-
players liked to eat after the games. Docker would
probably know . . . but there was no time to think of
anything else, because the dynamite charges on the
frozen road exploded under the truck then and hurled
the motor into his chest and a thousand fragments of
glass into his already sightless eyes.

Chapter Twenty-Three

December 22, 1944. Mont Reynard-sur-
Lepont. Friday, 1800 Hours.

Winds swept the dark Salm Valley, making keening
sounds as they battered the mountainside. In the thick-
ening dusk, Docker could no longer see the Tiger Mark
II but he knew it was still there in the stand of fir trees;
if it had changed positions, they would have heard the
noise of its engine and tracks. However, he wasn't sure
whether the officer had returned; the wind at times had
been strong enough to muffle the sound of any motor-
car.

The men of the section were deployed in defensive
positions on the perimeter of the hill, Kohler, Linari
and Dormund with grenades and bazookas while the
others manned the cannon and machine guns. Docker
had nothing in reserve and no way to relieve the soldiers who had been at their posts for hours. With Baird
under technical arrest and Farrel detailed to guard him,
the section's already slender strength was cut by almost
twenty percent. In addition, Docker decided as he pa-
trolled the cliff's edge, Larkin had probably stopped
somewhere, curled up with a bottle for the night, so
they couldn't expect any help from him until the morning.

Trankic joined him to report they were still out of
radio contact with Battery and Battalion. "But I got a

couple of signals from First Army and some Kraut outfits at St. Vith and Bastogne. Christ, Bull, the whole
fucking front's falling apart. Bastogne ain't gonna last
the night, they're throwing heavy stuff in there from
three hundred and sixty degrees. So we got the Fifth,
the Tenth Armored and the Twenty-sixth on the way,
and up north the First and Second and Ninth are on the
line, but what about now . . . ?"

Farrel came around the revetment and said, "Sarge,
maybe you better take a look at Baird, okay?"

"What's wrong with him?"

"Well, I don't know." Farrel shrugged. "I tried talking to him but he's kind of mixed up, like he's got a
fever or something."

"All right, get back to your post, Farrel. I'll see him
when I can."

"Right, sarge."

Baird sat on the cold floor of the cave and stared at
the small wood fire, hardly conscious of the icy wind
forcing its way around the sagging tarpaulin. His skin
felt hot to his hand and the occasional eddies of sleet
stung the cuts and bruises on his face. He moistened his
cracked lips and tried to think of the farm in Middleburg, Virginia, but his memories were so confused and
erratic that he found it difficult to keep them in a con-
secutive line.

Section Eight was more a home than the big farm
had been, where he was alone most of the time except
for the housekeeper and the old black groom, Mr. Skipper, who slept in the tack room and took care of the
horses. There was only one room in the house he felt
comfortable in, and he thought about it now, the library
with the gun cases and the hunting ledgers and maps.
He liked to go there after school when the late sun was
coming in the windows facing the pond.

There was a silence in that house you could almost
listen to, even when the rooms were filled with his father's friends, tall rangy men who knew everything there

was to know about hunting and guns and horses, even when they argued or laughed over their drinks, still there was the silence you could hear if you listened for it, and somehow this had always saddened him, because it was a tantalizing but deceptive conduit that led almost, but never quite, to his father's attention . . .

He blinked and looked down at his combat boots. They were stiff with mud, the cross-laced thongs frozen hard and gleaming with flecks of ice, stiff and brittle as pieces of straw, and he thought of the library with the sun turning everything into warm colors—the shining old campaign desk, the animal skins and deep suede chairs, the round, leather game table and the framed portraits of soldiers in their uniforms from the wars against Germany and Spain and England and the Civil War in America.

He remembered holidays on the farm and family dinners and his father and his brother and other men shooting skeet in the high meadows beyond the pond, with Mr. Skipper releasing clay birds when they shouted, "Pull!" and the sound of shotguns with silver trim on their stocks booming through the brilliant fall countryside, and he remembered, too, the feeling of pride and terror his father's guns evoked in him when he was small, and Baird almost began to cry then, the heat of the wood fire stinging the cuts on his face, because he was thinking of the German soldiers in the woods and the sound of their artillery and rifles that had sent him stumbling in panic toward the shelter of the woods . . .

He was so sick, so depressed and so near delirium that he didn't hear the tarpaulin pulled back from the entrance to the cave—

"What the hell's wrong with you, Baird?"

He looked up then, rubbing nervously at the tears that finally had appeared on his cheeks. Docker was crouched by the fire, watching him.

"I'm all right."

Docker unstoppered his canteen and handed it to him. "Take a drink of this."

He shook his head, but Docker said impatiently, "Goddamn it, it'll do you good."

He took a small sip of black whiskey, and began coughing.

Docker looked at the boy's wet boots and at the bruises on his face. "Use some more sulfa powder, then I want you to rig this tarp to keep the wind out and take off those boots and dry them at the fire. And don't sit on that frozen ground, get some blankets under you."

"I'm all right," Baird said again. "Really, sergeant, I'm fine."

"Yeah, you look great." He took a short drink of the cold whiskey. "Baird, you've been lying ever since you hooked up with this section. So now how about leveling for a change."

In the shifting light, Baird's eyes were empty. "I wanted to tell the truth," he said, his voice so low the words were almost lost in the wind rustling through the cave.

"But you sure as hell didn't. You want another drink?"

"No, but I think it helped."

"Good." Docker put the canteen away. "Okay then. Let's have it."

"Just turn everything around one hundred and eighty degrees and you've got the truth. Shorty was right all along. I'm a deserter. That's why I lied about everything." Baird's voice had begun to break and there was an unnatural brightness in his eyes. "I just ran when I heard the artillery and saw those German soldiers."

"And threw away your rifle?"

"That happened later. I tripped in the woods and fell. I dropped my rifle and didn't look for it. I just got up and kept on running."

"What about your dog tags?"

In a listless voice Baird said, "I threw them away."

"Is Baird your real name?"

The boy laughed softly, but there was no humor in it. "Sure, that's my real name. But I wanted to get rid of my Army serial number, I didn't want anybody checking it out. I was too scared to think straight." He looked away and wet his lips. "If I had guts, I'd be in a German stockade with the other guys. I disobeyed a direct order from you, I pulled a gun on everybody in the section. What do the dog tags matter? What more do you need?"

"Damn it, Baird, this isn't a court-martial . . . But you're still holding out on me. You know a helluva lot about weapons, and you know a lot about West Point. You mentioned taking snapshots on Lee and Jefferson Roads—that's where the superintendent of the academy lives, an area about as restricted as Ike's privy at Versailles."

"Trankic didn't believe me either, I guess."

"He'd sure as hell like to," Docker said. "You handled yourself fine when Gelnick got hit."

It was obvious to him that Baird wasn't listening now. His voice was tired, threaded with pain when he said, "They usually had drinks in my father's library before dinner. That's where the family portraits are . . ." Baird smiled at the fire. "My family called it the Hall of Gentlemen. On holidays the ranking officer would propose a toast. It was always the same: 'To absent friends.'"

"Who is your father, Baird?"

"I lived at the Point for eight years when he taught there. He was a full colonel then. Now he's a major general on MacArthur's staff at Port Moresby in New Guinea, the last I heard. Major General Jonathan Baird. My brother, he's twelve years older than I am, he's a major with the Eighty-eighth Infantry in Italy."

Docker heard someone outside the cave calling his name, the words blown into grotesque rhythms by the wind.

"When they both went overseas, I stayed at our farm in Middleburg. My mother died years ago, there was nobody there but a cook and the groom. I knew if I missed this war I'd never have anything to talk to my father about. It would just be"—he made a helpless gesture with his hands—"it would just be all over, my whole life, like I'd never been born. So I enlisted. I was going to surprise him so that when we all got together again . . . " With an obvious effort, Baird raised his head and looked at Docker. "Now do you understand about those dog tags? Can't you see how it was?"

Docker didn't, probably no one else would either. He'd learned that much in the olive groves and deserts, had matured with the sound of gunfire, and at least knew that it was pointless and ultimately presumptuous to try to "understand" how another person might react when he was fired on.

"Does your father know you're over here?"

"He does now. I wrote him from basic training, and when the One hundred sixth shipped out."

Docker heard heavy footsteps outside the cave. The tarp was pulled back by Schmitzer, whose impassive face was tight with excitement. He handed a white scarf to Docker. "You better come over to the machine gun, sarge. The Bonnard kid just brought this up. She's talking French so I ain't sure what she's saying. All I can make out is that the German officer is at the castle and wants to talk to you."

The scarf was made of heavy silk, the initials *KJ* at one of the fringed ends, the letters embroidered in a Gothic style with black and yellow threads.

"Let's go," Docker said, and went outside and told Farrel to find Sonny Laurel and send him over to the machine guns.

Corporal Schmitzer leaned against the multiple gun mount and looked at Laurel, who was staring after the lights of Docker's jeep, the spinning snow lightly touching his lips and eyelashes.

Docker had first wanted to know from Felice how the German officer had got to the castle past their ma-

chine guns. With Laurel helping to translate, she had
explained that the village priest, Father Juneau, had
guided the German up a logging trail from the other
side of the village . . . Schmitzer's thoughts were as
bitter as the winds around them as he watched Laurel
looking down the road where the blackout taillights of
Docker's jeep were turning toward the iron gates of
Castle Rêve. He'd got the little Belgian girl, Schmitzer
knew; maybe that's why they'd stopped calling him
Goldilocks. It was no secret, but even if he hadn't
known, it was there in the way they looked at each
other, the way he watched her eyes and her lips, solemn and breathless, as she told Docker about the German and the priest.

Docker was stalling for time, but there was no hope
for any of them now and the sergeant must damn well
know it. Some of Schmitzer's frustration and anger dissolved with that knowledge because he could almost
welcome what was coming, if it didn't take too long
. . . Now he watched as Laurel turned without looking
at him and walked to the crest of the hill, where the
wind was bending the scrub trees almost flat to the
ground and the sleet made dry, clicking sounds on the
outcroppings of rock and shale. Schmitzer stood alone,
under the barrels of the machine guns, and watched
Laurel go from him.

Docker left Felice Bonnard at the gatehouse, parked
the jeep and walked up the winding drive to Castle
Rêve looming high against a sky of driven snow and
heavy clouds. The German officer's command car was
parked near the stone steps at the entrance of the castle.

Docker stood motionless until his eyes adjusted to the
darkness and shifting shadows, then checked the area
around the car, scanning the formal gardens, the over-
grown clusters of topiary, and listening to the sound of
the wind in the crowns of the big trees.

He went through the gardens and up to the wide flag-
stone terrace that overlooked the river and the valley.

Standing at the railing with his back to Docker was a German officer in a greatcoat and visored garrison cap.

"*Herr Oberst.*"

Karl Jaeger turned and looked thoughtfully at the American sergeant. "*Ah, 'n Abend, Feldwebel. Sprechen Sie Deutsch?*"

Docker nodded, "*Ja, ein wenig.*"

They exchanged names. The German officer was almost as tall as Docker. The name of his division, Das Reich, was stitched on the cuffs of his coat, the letters in yellow against a field of black.

Docker handed him the silk scarf and Jaeger accepted it with a faint smile.

He said, "*Schön. Sie sind wohl Deutsch-Amerikaner?*"

"*Ja, aber—*" Docker began, then, in English: "Let's get to the point, colonel."

"*Von mir aus. Bin ich allzu optimistisch, aus Ihrer Gegenwart hier zu entnehmen, dass Sie die Lage begreifen?*"

Docker's German was not that proficient. He said, "Sorry, *Oberst. Ich nicht ganz verstehen.*"

Karl Jaeger unbuttoned his coat and looped the white scarf about his throat.

"*So? Und da glaub' ich nun Sie verstehen die Sprache unserer Vorfahren, die Sprache Goethes und Schillers, Uhlands und Mörikes.*"

The German's condescension was as puzzling to Docker as it was irritating. "Sir, let's save all this for the next literary tea party," he said. "What did you want to talk to me about?"

The sergeant was intelligent, Jaeger realized, obviously cultivated, but seasoned and hardened by this war. A good soldier, probably a good man, and Jaeger found this gratifying because leniency toward a respected enemy was not a weakness. "Your guns are no match for the firepower of a Tiger tank," he said. "I think I've demonstrated that. But if I am forced to attack your position again, sergeant, I'll destroy it. With

the war coming to an end, what would be the point of
sacrificing yourself and your men?"

"What do you have in mind?"

"That you immediately surrender your men and
weapons to my command." Jaeger took a briar pipe
from his pocket and cupped it in the palm of his hand.
"Unconditionally, but honorably, sergeant. You will
drive alone to the square in Lepont, bring all rifles,
handguns, grenades and so forth. The rest of your men,
unarmed, will then come down the hill in groups of
three at fifteen-minute intervals."

"You seem convinced we've got no alternative."

"Not a practical one. Your presence tells me that.
You wouldn't be here unless you hoped something
would be gained from it."

"Doesn't the same apply to you, *Oberst*?"

"Of course not. And you will regret it, sergeant, if
you force me to prove that you are wrong. Your men
will be allowed to keep their personal effects, letters,
diaries, toilet articles, cigarettes and rations. We'll re-
quire only names, ranks and Army serial numbers."
Jaeger tapped the stem of the pipe against the back of
his hand. "What do you say?"

Something didn't hang together here, Docker
thought; like a picture taken slightly off focus, the situation had a blurred, disturbing look to it. Why bother
asking the section to surrender? Why all this Geneva
convention bullshit about toilet articles, cigarettes and
rations? The German tank could destroy their position
in seconds. If these had been war games in training
areas with military umpires and judges vetting the action, Section Eight would already have been checked off
as a destroyed target with eighty to ninety percent casualties. Why was the officer avoiding a firefight? Why
did he prefer surrender? He could be concerned about
his own casualties but there was more to it than that,
Docker was suddenly convinced. Not knowing the German's purpose, Docker decided he'd better play for
time.

"I don't have the authority to surrender under these circumstances. It's a decision I can't make."

"What about the authority of plain common sense?"

The wind had picked up and the flying snow was like a porous wall between Docker and the German officer.

"I can't surrender or retreat until my present orders are countermanded and I'm given new ones," Docker said smoothly, and untruthfully. "My section receives two radio signals every twenty-four hours from Battery headquarters. Their transmitter sends at four in the afternoon and four in the morning, and shuts down between those signals. I'll present your proposals to the battery commander when and if we're in contact tomorrow morning. Then I'll follow his orders."

"You're obviously a very dedicated soldier," Jaeger said. "But you're also damned stupid if you think there's anything heroic about being slaughtered for no good reason." Jaeger paced the terrace, his boots grinding through the crust of ice on the flagstones. "I'm a serious man," he said. "You'd be wise to keep that in mind. If you are lying to me, I should tell you something: I received a report only an hour ago from our weather station in Frankfurt. The present weather front will hold for at least another three days and nights. So don't put your trust in the Eighth Air Force." Jaeger was trying to control an expanding frustration; there was something unbending about the American sergeant that infuriated him. "You think you have some God-given right to defend that hill?" His voice had suddenly become hard with tension. "Some sacred duty, some moral responsibility to travel thousands of miles from your own innocent country and drop bombs on hospitals and schools and streets filled with women and children?" Somehow his words, with their evocation of his little daughters Rosa and Hannah, calmed and steadied him. "Let me tell you something," he said quietly now. "In every country whose borders we've crossed, thousands of volunteers have joined our colors. There are Waffen SS units made up of Danes and Frenchmen and

Norwegians, commanded by their own officers. The Eleventh Nordland Division was raised from Scandinavian volunteers only last year. From the earliest days of the conflict, sergeant, the German armed forces accepted recruits from Holland and Finland and Belgium . . . yes, from this very ground we're standing on came some of our finest combat units. And from Hungary and Romania and Bulgaria there were dozens of divisions fighting at our side against the Russians."

Jaeger's voice became harder. "Have you ever asked yourself what you—an American—are fighting for on this old soil of Europe? For *what*, sergeant? To save England's empire? Or to help Bolshevik tyrants? Is that what you're here for? If so I ask you to remember this: no cannons are firing across the borders of America, no bombs have smashed your cities into rubble and not one, not *one* American man, woman or child has yet to be killed by German bombs on your homeland."

Jaeger put the briar pipe in his pocket and walked across the terrace to the flight of steps. Stopping there, he looked at Docker, his features blurred by the shifting snow and fog.

"I'll hold my attack until first light, sergeant, which will be in approximately six hours. No, make that five hours and forty-five minutes. My little history lesson was on your time, not mine."

"If I'd known, I might have paid more attention," Docker said.

Jaeger nodded slightly. "Your inattention probably does you credit, since most history is shaped by the communiqués of victorious generals. Still, I urge you to be realistic when you talk to your superior officers. I have no wish to kill you and your men, sergeant."

Jaeger went down the steps into the garden. When the sound of his command car faded on the air, Docker walked slowly back to his jeep through the shadows of topiary and weathered white statues.

Chapter Twenty-Four

December 23, 1944. Mont Reynard-sur-
Lepont. Saturday, 0100 Hours.

Private Edward Solvis sat hunched in the front seat of
Docker's jeep, protected from the winds by a blanket
and a tarpaulin pulled around his shoulders.

He warmed his gloved hands around a canteen cup of
coffee, and when he felt heat and life in his fingers,
took a notebook from his pocket and began to bring his
diary up to date.

His life as a soldier had been a time of profound
change for Solvis and from the date of his induction, he
had resolved to keep a complete written record of it.
The weeks of training and range firing in the sweltering
humidity of a Georgia summer, he had put that down.
And shipping out from Boston at night in an atmosphere charged with secrecy and tension, all that was in
his notebooks, as was the invasion and the sound of
guns on Beach Red and Beach Tare . . . all fully recorded in his neat, precise handwriting, because Solvis
realized with a sure intuition that these adventures
would become the literal peaks of his existence, and
that if he survived the war the rest of his life would
serve only as a vantage point from which to look back
on these dangerous and uniquely alive years . . .

Now he wrote: "It's after midnight, about one
o'clock. The usual snow and wind. Docker told us about

219

meeting with the German officer, Colonel Jaeger. We know they've shot and killed hundreds of unarmed prisoners at Malmédy, so surrendering (this is Docker's point) would be pretty goddamn stupid. But something isn't kosher here and Docker knows it. There's no way we can stand off a Tiger tank. So what are they waiting for?

"We could fire point blank at that tank with our .40 and not even dent it. Maybe time's working for them. Could be Bastogne is gone and the Germans are on their way to Paris. That colonel won't risk casualties because he doesn't have to. Kind of ironic to risk your life in a mopping-up operation that doesn't mean anything.

"Docker's got Linari, Trank and Laurel on the edge of the hill with bazookas and grenades. They'll cut loose when and if the tank makes a move, so at least we'll know it's coming. I'm monitoring the X-42, but haven't had a signal for a couple of hours. The last one sounded like an RAF crew down east of Frankfurt, that's all I could get. I took Baird some coffee a while ago. He asked me for something to write with. Maybe he feels this is a last chance for a letter to somebody. A girl or his family. Everybody knows now who his father is."

Solvis heard a whisper of static from the X-42 but as he fine-tuned the frequencies, the sound faded to a windy silence. He tried several times to pick up the elusive signals, then began writing again:

"Thinking about Baird made me decide to put down some thoughts of my own. But I don't really have any 'last thoughts,' about the bank or Davenport. Which is kind of strange. I worked and lived there seven years but the things I remember could just as well have happened to another person. This seems to be the only important time of my life. Not heroic or anything, that's not it, but it means something. I know I'll never forget Gelnick and the others. His body is wrapped in a tarp pinned down with rocks on high ground in the woods.

What I keep thinking about is why he couldn't save himself, why he just froze like that . . ."

Solvis glanced over what he had written and saw that some of the words were already blurred by the melting snow.

Tex Farrel and Jackson Baird walked across the crown of Mont Reynard through the darkness, stumbling, trying to avoid the stretches of bare earth polished and frozen slick by the winds.

Farrel told Baird to wait at the revetment and went out to the edge of the precipice, where Docker was studying the dark valley.

"Sarge, Baird wants to talk to you. You want to blame somebody, blame me. He asked me if it'd be okay and I said sure."

"What made *you* so sure?"

"Because I know what he's thinking and I figure you'd want to hear it."

After another sweep of the slopes, Docker gave the binoculars to Farrel and walked to the revetment, where Baird was waiting for him.

He noticed that despite the raw weather and driving winds, Baird was pale, the bruises on his cheeks standing out darkly. The youngster handed him several sheets of ruled notepaper, an uneasy smile on his damaged lips.

"Will you just look at them, sergeant?"

"First, let me ask you something. Before Trank unloaded on you, you started to say something. What was it?"

"Well, I wanted to tell you I didn't think the tank is after this gun position. There's too much firepower and rank down there. So it has to be that experimental aircraft we shot down. That colonel is here to retrieve it or destroy it."

"If that's true, then why in hell doesn't he get on with it? Why not just knock us off and complete his mission?"

"If you'll look at those notes, sergeant, maybe you'll see what I mean."

Docker nodded and snapped on his pocket flashlight and in its slender column of illumination saw that the sheets were covered with diagrams and penciled notations in Baird's cramped, precise handwriting. After reading them twice and studying them for another moment or so in silence, he looked at Baird. "Where'd you get the specifications on the Mark II?"

"Some I knew from before, some I remembered from ID manuals in basic training. They could be off a fraction of an inch, but not enough to make a real difference."

Docker spread the pages on top of the revetment wall and secured them against the tugging winds with his helmet and leather gloves.

"It could work, sergeant. I know it."

Docker rubbed a hand over his head and felt the snowflakes melting in his hair.

"Maybe it could, Baird." Still, Docker felt little conviction about making the decision facing him, and worse, he wasn't sure he even had the right to make it. A battle plan that could cost them their lives and this hill, that's what Baird was proposing—Private Jackson Baird, a distraught eighteen-year-old whose knowledge of warfare had come almost completely from books and pictures . . . With his plans they would be facing a Tiger Mark II commanded by a field-grade officer who had probably been leading tanks and men for a decade or more . . . Docker hadn't been deceived by the German colonel's talk of linguistic priorities and Goethe and Schiller. Another reality was represented in the gold clasp Jaeger wore on the left breast of his tunic, the Nahkampfspange with its oak leaves and swastikas, the close-combat decoration awarded only to soldiers who had survived fifty hand-to-hand encounters with the enemy. He had seen that clasp when Jaeger looped the silk scarf about his neck, and he had seen only one

before—on the torn jacket of a dead commander in the
Afrika Korps . . .

Docker now used a pencil to trace the diagrams on
the pages, checking the distance Baird had estimated
between various points to their position. And watching
the sergeant, it seemed to Baird that the inside of his
head was as white as the snow spinning around them, a
billowing expanse streaked and colored with names and
memories. It was a remembered childhood sensation,
the springs inside his body coiling painfully with anxious thoughts of examinations and grades, muscles
tightening at the prospect of not making the cut on ath-
letic squads or failing to hold fire when hen birds were
walked up in the meadow by his father's gunning parties, dreading the fear of hearing his shotgun go off
without a single cock bird in the sky above them, scarlet
against the clouds. His constant effort to measure up to
somebody else's standards had always trapped him between what was expected of him and what he could ac-
complish on his own, suspending him between equally
demanding, and impossible, alternatives . . . He recalled now regiments and flags and medals and battles
he had studied as a child in his dormer room on the
third floor of their home in Virginia, turning pages of
spidery maps and brilliant pictures until he fell asleep,
and always knowing that the morning would be gloomy
or sunny depending on how accurately and rapidly he
answered his father's questions at breakfast about those
yellowing manuscripts and engravings—

"Couple of things I'm not sure about," Docker said,
and Baird felt his heart pounding in tense anticipation,
as it might have when Jonathan Baird turned from the
sideboard, shoulders and silvery head silhouetted
against the frosted windows to say, "What you seem to
forget about Grant, son, is what he learned at . . ."
or "The element of surprise on the battlefield means
very little unless it creates chaos. Don't confuse surprise
with the merely unexpected . . ."

"There are just too damned many assumptions here," Docker was saying.

"But they're all logical, aren't they?"

Baird's theory was that the reluctance of the German commander to attack was based on two factors: One, by what he *did* know about the strength of their gun position. And two, by what he *didn't* know. According to Baird, it had to be assumed that the German tank crew knew there was an antiaircraft cannon on the top of Mont Reynard. Nonetheless, they couldn't risk a frontal attack because of a structural weakness in their tank's armor, a weakness noted in specifications Baird had remembered from United States Army manuals.

He had written out these specs on one of Solvis' ruled sheets of notepaper. They read: "Panzerkampfwagen VIB, Tiger Mark II with Porsche turret; *Weight*: 80 tons; *Crew*: 5. *Height*: 10 feet, 6 inches; *Width*: 12 feet, 5 3/4 inches (with wide tracks) and 10 feet, 8 3/4 inches (with narrow tracks). *Length*: 36 feet, 8 inches. *Engine*: one Maybach HL 230 P .30 inline, 600 hp; *Speed*: 30 mph on roads and 12 mph cross-country; *Range*: 106 miles on roads and 75 miles cross-country; *Armament*: one 8.8cm KwK43L/71 gun (88-mm cannon) with 80 rounds, and three 7.92-mm machine guns with 5,850 rounds; *Armor*: hull front 150-mm (6 inches), turret armor, 200-mm (8 inches), decking, sides and rear armor: 100-mm (4 inches)."

Baird had underlined the final specification with double pencil strokes.

"BELLY ARMOR: 40 MM. (1-3/4 INCHES)."

"If he comes straight up the hill at us, he's got to risk—"

"Yes, goddamn it, I can see that much."

"Then the rest of it makes sense. The German officer doesn't know what else we've got up here. Wellington said all warfare was just finding out what's over the next hill. You can see his problem. He can't attack our center, not with real confidence, and he won't risk attacking our flanks because he doesn't know what we've got in reserve. That's why he's trying to con us into surrendering. My father told me once—"

"Baird, will you forget about Wellington who's been dead a few hundred years? And your father who's a million miles away in the Pacific?" Docker tried to light a cigarette but the tobacco was soggy and wouldn't burn. He threw it aside and said quietly, "Okay, what did your father tell you?"

"He said he could look at the order of battle on a map and guess the grade of the officers who'd planned it. The higher the rank, the stronger the reserve—that's what my father told me. Generals, he said, always keep a lot of strength close to their headquarters. So if we show that German commander everything we've got, flank the cannon with our machine guns, he'll think we're committing all our resources to defend the edge of the precipice. That kind of recklessness is what a field-grade officer would expect from a gun section with noncoms in charge."

"Incompetent fuck-ups."

"I didn't say that."

"No, I did. Okay, we make him think we're throwing our whole reserve onto the line. Which gives him the option of attacking our machine guns, which are no real threat to him. That about it?"

Baird let out his breath slowly. "With the dynamite, that's about it, sergeant."

"Yes, let's not forget that little item."

Docker studied the pages spread on top of the revetment and realized he was almost hoping to find a flaw in Baird's proposals. They were dangerous, of course. God-*damn,* they were dangerous, but the longer he analyzed them, the more it seemed they were so simple and logical that they had at least a prayer of working. Still he hesitated, feeling the wet snow on his bare head and wishing to Christ he'd had enough sense to put his cigarettes in an inside pocket where they wouldn't have got soaked in this weather . . . Finally he said, "I'm not sure we've got enough dynamite."

"We do, sergeant."

"How do you know that?"

"Tex asked Laurel to check the ammo dump before we came over here."

Docker nodded and looked at his watch. "I'm not sure we've got enough time left, but there's only one fucking way to find out."

He waved to Farrel, and when the Texan came running toward him, shouted over the wind, "Get the rest of the guys up here. Tell them to snap ass."

Docker braced himself against the sleeting blasts and looked at the faces of the men in Section Eight who, except for Dormund and Linari, stood in a loose formation in front of the revetment. Linari and Dormund were on the firing seats of the cannon, leaning forward over the cranking handles to hear what Docker was saying.

"Our only chance is to immobilize that tank," he said. "If we can stop it, we've got enough firepower to handle the crew when they come out of the turret. Baird has an idea how to do it. I'll spell it out for you, then we'll talk."

When he finished, Trankic said, "Are we cutting it too fine, Bull?"

"If they hit us at first light, that still gives us about three and a half hours."

Trankic rubbed his jaw, his hand making an abrasive sound against his whiskers. "We cut the machine guns with blowtorches and hacksaws, maybe we can make it. No problem setting them up on this side of the hill. But without tripods, wedged into rocks, they ain't gonna have a three-sixty field of fire."

"What about detonating caps and fusing wire?"

"We're talking about maybe forty yards on each flank, we got plenty."

Schmitzer said bluntly, "You guys are acting like it's all settled. Don't I get something to say about this deal?"

Docker looked at him. "All right, Schmitzer. Make it fast."

There was a deliberate challenge in Schmitzer's eyes, and anger in his voice. "You say make it fast, that's what bothers me, Docker. What's the point of going a mile a minute when you're talking about something that could get everybody killed?"

"Say what's on your mind."

"Maybe I should ask the Boy Scout here." Schmitzer stared at Baird. "Tell us, kid—what happened the last time you saw German soldiers."

"Shit! We don't need this," Farrel said.

"Listen, goddamn it! I ain't trying to make anybody look bad. I know how few heroes there are, how many guys shit their pants when a shell goes over."

"Then get to the point," Docker said.

"I'm saying we're up here with a popgun for a cannon, and some rifles and grenades that couldn't stop a snowball fight. And we're going up against a Kraut officer and the biggest goddamn tank the Nazis got, and we're using battle plans figured out by"—Schmitzer swung a long arm around at Baird—"by an eighteen-year-old kid whose only experience comes from playing with lead soldiers and reading a lot of shit about war in his playpen."

"If I'm right, does it matter where I learned it? I'll bet you that—"

"You'll bet *what*?" Schmitzer said. "Next month's pay? A three-day pass to Paris? You're betting our lives." Schmitzer turned to Docker. "Here's another goddamn thing you haven't mentioned. We don't *have* to surrender to them Krauts. And we don't *have* to stand here and let 'em blow hell out of us either. We can walk, Docker, we can get the fuck off this hill. Take our rifles and fade into the woods till they get what they want and get the hell out of here. That way nobody's a hero, nobody's a coward, but everybody's alive."

"I don't care how close it is to Christmas," Docker said, "we're not giving them that kind of present."

"Why the fuck not? It's just another goddamn hill and you know it. Who cares now about those hills in Africa and Sicily you and me got our ass shot up taking? There's nothing there now but rag-head Arabs and old ginneys walking up the trails through donkey shit. There comes a time when there's enough of them hills. And that's where I've got to."

Docker thought fleetingly of jokes he'd heard before they went to war, when most Americans wanted no part of it, and comics in nightclubs made elaborate routines out of nothing but place names, demanding to know who in hell wanted to die for places called Minsk and Linsk and Pinsk and Cracow and Gdynia. Names you not only couldn't spell but couldn't pronounce, couldn't even find on maps, full of people with beards who drank sour milk out of leather gourds and slept with goats and wouldn't know what to do with an American toilet except maybe wash potatoes in it . . .

"It's our hill now," Docker said. "That's what makes it different, Schmitzer."

"Yeah, and for my old lady a couple of thousand square miles of the Pacific Ocean are different," Schmitzer said. "That's where my brother bought it on the *Lexington*. She's got a telegram on the wall, and under it she wrote the latitude and longitude where the *Lex* went down, the Coral Sea, twenty-five thousand feet. Latitude fifteen degrees and twelve minutes south; longitude one hundred fifty-five degrees and twenty-seven minutes east. They welded steel plates over portholes to protect blackout. My brother got it when an explosion ripped one of those plates out and took the top off his head. There's no grave markers there. Nobody's ever going out there in a fucking rowboat and blow taps over him." He looked hard at Baird. "I'm not trading my life for your cowboys and Indians."

"We can handle this job with just five men, Schmitzer." Docker looked at the group near him and beyond to Linari and Dormund. "I want four volunteers. Sound off."

Dormund shouted, "I'm with Docker, and don't you wretched bastards ever forget it." Solvis and Tex Farrel moved away from the revetment to stand with the sergeant.

"Come on, Bull," Trankic said. "What's this volunteer shit? Like you always said, we ain't a goddamned debating club."

"Okay, pick yourself a detail and get to work."

"Count me in," Laurel said, and hurried to join Trankic.

Baird looked expectantly at Docker, who said, "Sure. What did you think?" Schmitzer stood alone, not moving.

"Schmitzer, you can take off if you want to," Docker said. Then without any particular emphasis, he added, "But I think you've got a stake here, too, and it's more than a few yards of rocky real estate."

Schmitzer felt the words like blows. He forced himself not to look at Sonny Laurel, who was saying something to Farrel and Baird, his voice threaded with laughter and excitement. And Schmitzer wondered with a sharp fear how much Docker had guessed, because he did have a stake here, just as much as the other guys. If all the shit you read in the papers was true, they were fighting for what they loved and believed in. And they were proud of it. Well, so was he . . . Schmitzer allowed himself to look steadily at the boy for a last time, studying the lively eyes and full lips brushed with fleeting snowflakes, knowing that what he wanted so badly he could never have beyond his own fantasies. And yet—the thought was painful and bitter—if what he felt never contaminated anyone else, there might be for him the thing the priests were always talking about, even the rummy priest who told them about his brother—the condition of forgiveness and the state of Grace . . . He held on to the instant until he saw that Docker was frowning at him. He silently whispered good-bye to the boy and said, "I might as well volunteer, too, sarge.

Make it fucking unanimous. I'll get the ammo belts off them machine guns, Trank."

Swinging his rifle across his shoulders, he walked from the revetment toward the crest of the hill, and within seconds his hulking shape was lost in the darkness and mists.

Chapter Twenty-Five

December 23, 1944. Lepont, Belgium.
Saturday, 0600 Hours.

Colonel Jaeger stood in the square of Lepont and watched the first early light breaking above the stone bridges, coating the frozen surface of the river the color of steel. He looked at his wristwatch and then at the passageway beside the café, La Chance, where he could see two of his corporals, the faint light breaking on their MP-40 machine guns.

The Americans and their sergeant had fifteen minutes left. . . .

Jaeger began pacing, his strides smooth and rhythmic. Nothing in his bearing revealed his awareness of the eyes watching him from the houses facing on the square. The silent vacuum he moved in was disturbed only by the winds against the church and the crunch of his boots on the snow-encrusted cobblestones.

A knot of anxiety was winding tight in his chest. Anger suddenly made him light-headed.

He had arranged with the priest to use the church cellar as a guardhouse for the Americans until they could be trucked to a camp behind the German lines. His corporals were present only to carry out these details. After that, his crew would conclude their primary mission, finding and eliminating any trace of the ME-

262 before the weather broke and Allied planes on reconnaissance flights might spot it.

Except Sergeant Ebert had reported by radio that the
American soldiers gave no evidence of surrendering; instead they were strengthening their line along the sheer
edge of the cliff, emplacing machine guns on both
flanks of their cannon revetment. They had test-fired
these guns within the last hour, and Jaeger had listened
to the flat, whistling echoes and had seen the faraway
streams of tracer ammunition arching through the darkness high above the valley. Showing off like stupid children . . .

His orders had been to destroy the Americans, not to
take them prisoner, and he couldn't conceive, *wouldn't*
conceive, that the sergeant was refusing to accept the
almost comradely terms he'd proposed on his own authority and for which he undoubtedly would have to accept serious consequences . . . To distract himself
Jaeger thought of his family in Dresden: Hedy and his
daughters, forcing himself to recall the exact texture of
spring days when he walked with them through parks
and along the banks of the river. He remembered shops
where they bought chocolate and hot spice cakes and
the way the birds hopped about, and blue and white
horses that Hannah and Rosa loved to ride on the
merry-go-round, their fair hair blown about their faces,
rosy in the fresh winds which—when he was a child—
his father had told him were broken and gentled by the
Aeolian spires of Dresden's old cathedrals . . . He
thought of those carefree days when the war was only a
promise of future vindication, when he and Rudi Geldman explored the silent woods and swam in clear lakes
and read together at the fireplace in his father's apartment . . .

He looked at his watch and saw the Americans' time
was running out, and he knew that his corporals were
watching him and the people of the village were watching him.

But those generations of unborn Germans that General Kroll fancied as the moral custodians of some distant future, they were not watching him, he was alone as he tried to decide who would live and who would die near a frozen village on the banks of the Salm River. Morality existed on the cracked edge of the present, not in the past or future. What he and the sergeant decided to do today was what was—or wasn't—moral; what unborn generations might think about it would be history.

Jaeger's anger had grown so that he felt helpless to deflect or control it, but it also seemed a cleansing emotion . . . Rudi had said that when reason slept, the beast in the blood awakened, and Rudi had believed, with deep sorrow, that reason had gone to sleep in Germany . . . Jaeger looked at his watch one last time, but there was no mistake, no optical illusion, he had not misread the hands or the numerals—the sergeant had declined his offer of a moral solution to their problem, a humane surrender.

Alerting his men, he told them to return immediately to the tank position, but as he swung himself behind the wheel of his command car he was seized by a sensation that intensified so powerfully he felt it might break his mind into pieces . . . his thoughts searing and painful . . . of Rudi and a child the priest had told him about . . . the accusing eye that glared at him from his father's ravaged face . . . Almost with a will of its own his hand moved to the seat beside him and touched the cold metal clasps of his leather field case. They had expected him somehow to right the wrongs of the world, wrongs they couldn't even give a clear name to. The American soldiers on the hill didn't deserve to die, and neither had Rudi Geldman, but if he could never make amends for any of this, if in truth he had not been allowed to, then he didn't deserve—as a soldier and father—the burden his own father had willed him, the letter and pictures the old man had placed in his field case on their last meeting in the tiny bedroom in Dresden, the last pictures taken of Rudi Geldman at Buchenwald . . . In his heart Jaeger couldn't believe he deserved a guilt and remorse that was beyond human responsibility, that sublimated all action to an acceptance of forces outside a man's control—the Will of God, or Fate, or whatever that possessive, malevolent thing was in the ancient stars.

Drawing a deep breath of the chill air to clear his head, Jaeger took the letter and pictures from his field case and studied them with deliberate attention under the faint yellow cone of his dashboard light.

Chapter Twenty-Six

December 23, 1944. Mont Reynard-sur-
Lepont. Saturday, 0530 Hours.

Section Eight had worked steadily through the early
morning darkness. Trankic and Schmitzer with acety-
lene torches and hacksaws had cut the four machine
guns from their yokes in the mobile mount and with
assistance from Farrel and Solvis had carried the heavy
weapons across the windswept crown of Mont Reynard,
boots slipping on the frozen rocks, the cold metal tearing at their fingertips.

Under Docker's direction they set up the .50s at natural strongpoints on the precipice, wedging them into
forked outcroppings of shale approximately fifty yards
on either side of the dug-in and reveted cannon. The
muzzles of the machine guns and the ammo drums were
concealed with underbrush, and the firepower of both
these strongpoints was supplemented by bazookas and
grenades.

As the faint morning light came over the valley,
Docker knew they were running short of time. They had
eaten nothing, not even breaking for coffee, but they
still had not planted the dynamite charges, and Docker
checked the rising sun as he carried a blasting machine
out to the right flank, where Sonny Laurel and Kohler
were cutting fusing wire into hundred-foot lengths.

At the revetment, Trankic prepared the dynamite for

235

the insertion of electric caps, his muscular hand and wrist twisting a wooden punch into the brittle end of the sticks, driving the pin deeply into the hard-packed explosive. When three were ready, he lashed them together with heavy black friction tape and handed them to Docker, who attached an end of fusing wire to electrical detonator caps, inserted one into each of the holes Trankic had drilled into the dynamite, clipped the unattached ends of wire to the blasting machine and checked the hand plunger, the test-pilot light and the charging switch. Then, carrying the taped bundle of explosives under his arm and the coils of wire over his shoulder, he waved to Trankic, who was now standing at the opposite flank, a small figure in the hazy mists.

When he saw Trankic settle to his knees and go over the side of the hill, Docker started down the slope himself, crouching to take advantage of natural cover, clusters of iron-hard bracken and frozen clumps of bushes still bright with pips and berries. He crawled and slid headfirst a dozen yards, then stopped to rest, his chest and stomach numb with snow that had soaked through his woolen shirt. When his breathing slowed, he studied the area where he intended to place the charges, a level bed of rock about thirty yards below him. Raising himself on his elbows, he studied the floor of the valley which was quilted with white clouds, the tips of fir trees studding this screen like big green spools.

The Tiger Mark II was almost completely submerged in these ground mists, only the massive turret and cannon visible through the white layers.

In Baird's theory, the Tiger II would attack either of the machine gun positions, and it was Docker's job on this flank—and Trankic's on the other—to anticipate its route up the mountain. He looked at the machine guns above him and moved eight or ten yards to his left, traveling like a crab on his knees and elbows to place himself at last on a direct line between the tank and the guns.

He saw Laurel and Kohler watching him from the

crest of the hill, their helmeted faces framed by the machine gun barrels, and for an instant he was shocked by their ravaged appearance, until he realized they all must look like that now, dirt and fear and exhaustion a common mask.

Docker started down to his target area, a rough ledge of rock that would give the tank treads a solid grip for the final thrust up and over the top of the hill. Stretched at full length, he worked carefully toward it, freezing motionless whenever his body created a betraying spill of snow and shale. When he reached the flat shelf, he planted the lashed bundle of dynamite behind a small outcrop of rock and covered it with snow and matted brown grass. He then rested for a moment, feeling his sodden shirt begin to stiffen against his body.

After making a last check of the detonator caps, he started back up the mountain, rapidly playing out the fusing wire and aware now of the growing daylight and the black muzzle of the big cannon covering the steep slopes of Mont Reynard.

Chapter Twenty-Seven

December 23, 1944. Lepont-sur-Salm.
Saturday, 0600 Hours.

She heard the car stop, the sound of the motor mingling briefly with the sleet and wind against her window-panes. She knew it was not from Lepont. The only vehicle left in the village was an ancient Citroën used by the pharmacist to visit the sick on snowbound farms, but even those trips had halted in the last few months when petrol supplies had run out.

A knock sounded. Denise Francoeur opened the door, wind sweeping around her in chilling blasts. She stepped back instinctively and put a hand to her throat.

"You do that nicely," Karl Jaeger said. He came into the room and swung the door shut behind him. "It's an attractive gesture, suggesting graceful repugnance for the Hun, a defense of virginal treasures. You're alone here, mademoiselle?"

He spoke in French and smiled at her, but she was frightened by the tension in his bright, unfocused eyes.

"Yes, I'm alone, colonel."

"You recognize my rank? Good." Jaeger spoke in German now. "Can I assume from that you've been friendly with my comrades-in-arms, fräulein?"

"There were times when I had no choice."

"So if you were friendly, it wasn't a matter of

choice." He glanced about the room. "You're the
schoolteacher here?"

"Did someone tell you that?"

"What is there to be evasive about, fräulein? You
speak French and German, the look of your hands
hardly indicates you spend much time in the barnyard."

"I didn't mean to be evasive. I was surprised."

He smiled as if accepting an apology and walked
about the room, glancing at the mirror over the mantelpiece, then at a sewing basket on the floor. Stopping, he
removed his gloves and studied the solid wall, the central panel decorated with a brightly painted angel's
head.

He looked at the schoolteacher, the smile leaving his
face. "In my case, fräulein, I've never been a teacher.
A student, of course, and not too bad, some of my in-
structors were kind enough to tell me. But perhaps they
were just trying to get rid of me, give me good marks so
they could pass me on to someone else."

He removed the briar pipe from his overcoat and
stared at it with a puzzled frown, wondering what he
had planned to do with it. His words made no sense to
him. ". . . but perhaps they were just trying to get rid
of me . . ." What did that mean, they wanted to get
rid of Rudi, not Karl Jaeger . . . ?

"At the Berlin Academy I studied fortifications,
fräulein," he said. "This involved mathematics, engi-
neering, that sort of thing." With one hand, he made a
gesture of dismissal. "Of course, I couldn't build a cathedral or a château, I wasn't trained as an architect,
but I think I could put up a little house like this . . .
yes, I'm quite sure of it . . ."

He rapped the wall above the gaily decorated angel's
head and glanced at the schoolteacher, found he was
unable to bring her pale features into focus. He blinked
his eyes, but failed to clear away the strange veil between them . . . her dark hair continued to float like a
cloud about her face . . . He rapped again on the wall
and began to pound the middle panel heavily and

rhythmically with his fist. "But if I built a house, I wouldn't make the mistake of blocking off a stair-way—"

"It was done to save heat."

"How do you get down to the cellar?"

"There's no need to, colonel."

"What about storage? What about vegetables and firewood?"

"There's nothing left to store. The firewood is in a shed in the garden."

"You sound as if you've memorized those answers, fräulein. Which you probably have. I know you're lying." Jaeger pounded his fist for emphasis against the wall. "I've talked to the priest here, Father Juneau. He's been very helpful. He's the one who told me that you're the schoolteacher here, and that you have a Jewish child living with you."

The alarm that drummed on her nerves sent an involuntary shudder through her body.

"No, that's not true."

"Why would the priest lie to me?"

"I don't know."

"You don't know why he's lying, which amounts to saying that he *is* lying. Correct, fräulein?"

"Perhaps he thought it was the truth. Or the truth as he knows it."

Denise was beginning to realize, and with a sense of exquisite relief, that she had nothing to fear from this German officer. Her first shock of panic had been like a racial memory of terror, a nervous spasm that had made her forget for an instant that Margret was safe with the nuns. Now there was only herself, and while this man might hurt her or even kill her, she felt that if he did, he would be damaging something renewed and valuable.

"Colonel, Father Juneau's truth has a way of changing, depending on whether he's talking to members of the Resistance or German soldiers."

"Why would he lie when the truth is so easily proven?"

She shrugged. "I don't know. Why would a priest lie when a lie is a sin against God and everything he professes to believe? Didn't you ever discuss such things at your school in Berlin?"

"Those matters have nothing to do with warfare . . . I was taught to use guns and tanks, and to obey orders. But I learned what lies sound like, and I know Father Juneau was telling the truth." He studied the briar pipe, then put it away in a pocket of his greatcoat. "Do you deny there's a Jewish child here?"

"Yes, I do."

"She's your brother's daughter. Was Father Juneau lying when he told me that?"

"As you said, the truth can be easily proven. Why not smash this house down and see for yourself?" She savored the reckless anger in her voice. "And if you find a Jewish child here, will it save your world and your soul to stand her up in front of a firing squad and kill her?"

"You can't say things like that to me." A tightness in the muscles of his throat made it difficult for him to speak. He began to pound his fist against the wall. "You can't pretend you're all saints and angels. Too late for that—"

The panel shattered under his blows. He hammered at the carved angel's head and when the bolts broke free the tiny figure fell to the floor and rolled onto the hearthstone, where it rocked back and forth, its blank eyes glittering in the firelight.

Jaeger was so agitated he felt beads of sweat gathering on his forehead, prickling the backs of his hands . . . "Who betrayed you, fräulein? And the Americans and the Jewish child? It was the priest who wants to be safe and comfortable, with a warm fire on winter nights. Those are his eternal verities, a good meal and a bottle of wine, not the truth of God he pretends to live with.

Yet you accuse *me* of being a monster, of lusting to
execute a helpless child. I have children of my own, did
you know that? Two little daughters in Dresden . . ."
The constriction in his throat worsened; his voice was
high and straining, as if the words were being squeezed
past his corded neck muscles. "I've disobeyed my orders, fräulein. Do you think that's easy for a soldier? I
was told to destroy every member of the American gun
crew on your Mont Reynard. Instead I've offered them
honorable terms of surrender. But will they accept? Will
they trust me? No, because their sergeant is a madman,
too stubborn and stupid to distinguish between reality
and appearance." . . . Jaeger raised a booted foot and
slammed it against the wall, and the boards broke and
fell with a crash into the stairwell leading to the cellar.
Taking a flashlight from his overcoat pocket, he
snapped it on and went quickly down the narrow flight
of stairs.

As he did so Denise ran to the wooden bureau on the
opposite side of the room, jerked open the top drawer
and lifted out the holstered automatic. She tried to open
the holster flap, but her fingers were too cold and stiff
as they tugged clumsily against the leather strap locked
in a metal clasp. She could hear the German in the cellar shouting something she couldn't understand, but the
wildness in his voice intensified her fear. Somehow, the
strap did come free and she pulled the gun from the
holster, trying to remember what the American sergeant
had told her . . . "Move the safety lever toward the
red metal dot." She tried to do that now but the lever
was jammed or broken and would not budge. When she
heard him clattering up the wooden stairs, she put the
gun behind her back and turned quickly to face him.

"Where is she?"

"I told you, I'm alone here."

"That's not what I asked you. She was here, the child
was here." He thrust a sheaf of papers in front of her
and pointed at them with an accusing finger. "Look!
Pictures of birds, a child's drawings. Where is she?"

There was such bewilderment, despair, in his expression that she suddenly realized *she* had the power to hurt *him*.

"We knew you were coming back, we knew the child wasn't safe. The American soldiers have taken her to a place she'll be cared for."

His reaction was not what she'd expected; she had been braced for blows or an angry, defensive outburst but instead he dropped the drawings to the floor and turned slowly from her, almost as if he had forgot her presence, and walked to the fireplace and picked up the splintered angel's head.

The ornament was painted a glossy blue and white, the ringlets of hair blond, the innocent mouth a rosy pink. A crack showed in one of the blank eyes; in the shifting light the small figurehead seemed to be winking at him . . . "You must understand, fräulein, that what was done to many children, to many of the innocent—" He stopped because he couldn't find the words. And then to his relief he realized that the crippling duality no longer seemed to be cracking his mind; he could isolate his thoughts now, examine them clearly.

"What was done," he said, speaking carefully and precisely, "was not done by soldiers. So you see, fräulein"—Jaeger smiled at the blank but strangely intimate eyes of the angel—"your alarm for the Jewish child wasn't necessary. No one would have harmed her. I wouldn't have permitted it. It would have been a simple matter to arrange papers, to provide her with an escort . . ." Yes, he thought, a simple matter indeed to save the child as he tried to save the Americans. Still, he remembered again, with an empty feeling, someone else he had forsaken. And again he found it difficult to speak . . . "I came here to *tell* you the child would be safe. I've assured Father Juneau of that. And I will not violate the cease-fire and terms of surrender I gave the Americans. I am a soldier, I have daughters of my own, I'll show you their pictures if you like . . ."

He turned from the fireplace, saw the slim Belgian

woman was pointing a gun at him, holding it inexpertly
in both hands, but his reflexes took over and he hurled
the angel's head at her face an instant before she pulled
the trigger. As the blast filled the room, the bullet ricocheting from the stone chimney like a furious metallic
wasp—in that finger-snap of time Jaeger struck the gun
from her hand and knocked her sprawling with a back-
handed slap that sounded like a second pistol shot on
the cold air.

The blood on her cheek was as red as the lips of the
angel head lying on the floor beside her. He picked it
up and was relieved to see that it had suffered no further damage. Putting it under his arm, he knelt and collected the drawings of birds and went back down into
the cellar. Someone had drawn more pictures on the
white walls there—a child to judge from the wavering
strokes of the crayon—birds in flight soaring over
sketches of woods and lakes.

Jaeger tore up the papers with the birds on them and
dropped them on the floor. He took the letter and the
photographs of Rudi Geldman from inside his greatcoat
and, after studying them for a moment or so, ripped
them into dozens of pieces which he allowed to fall
slowly and deliberately from his hands, watching them
with frowning attention as they fluttered in circles and
drifted at last to the floor to mingle there with the tat-
tered scraps of childish drawings.

The stir and drift of paper kindled a memory neither
welcome or unwelcome, of the death of Cornet Rilke:
"*Eine lachende Wasserkunst*" . . . "a laughing fountain." It had been Rudi's own fantasy of death. To die
saving one's country's flag . . . "The sixteen curved
sabres that leap upon him, flash on flash, are a festi-
val."

"A laughing fountain."

Jaeger went upstairs and knelt beside the schoolteacher. He felt for her pulse; it was slow but firm. Lifting her slight body, he carried her into a bedroom and
placed her on a bed covered by the same sort of hand-

knitted coverlet he remembered from his grandmother's home in Bavaria.

Next he took two small photographs from his wallet, pictures of Hannah and Rosa taken on the merry-go-round in the park at Dresden, and put them on the pillow beside the schoolteacher's mass of tangled black hair. She would believe and understand what he said about children and soldiers when she saw the pictures of his daughters.

As he ran to his command car, he was thinking that it wasn't so important what your country asked you to live for, but what it asked you to die for, and Colonel Karl Jaeger was determined to show the Americans on the hill, soldiers who had denied him the exercise of compassion, that he clearly understood this important distinction.

When he bent to pull open the door of his car, he realized with surprise that he still held the brilliant little angel's head in the crook of his arm. Why hadn't he left it in the cellar with the pictures and drawings? It didn't matter, the angel's head didn't matter now. He dropped the ornament on the snowy cobblestones and swung himself behind the wheel of his command car.

Chapter Twenty-Eight

December 23, 1944. Mont Reynard-sur-
Salm. Saturday, 0630 Hours.

The big dog began growling and barking. Docker swept
the road and trails to Lepont with his glasses, checking
the open stretches and trees wrapped like cotton candy
with the swirling fogs, but nothing moved down there
and the silence was broken only by the cries of birds
and whining winds forcing a passage through the ice-
laden trees.

Trankic joined him. "What's spooking Radar?"

"Nothing that I can see."

"Look, Bull, Kohler wants to see you."

"About what?"

"I don't know, he says it's important."

"Christ," Docker said, and gave Trankic the glasses.

The dog bounded from the revetment and joined
Docker as he walked through the snow toward the right
flank of their line, where Linari, Kohler and Sonny
Laurel manned the machine guns. Docker had posted
Schmitzer, Tex Farrel and Dormund to the left flank,
leaving Solvis and Jackson Baird at the cannon.

Kohler's battered face was tense with exasperation.
He nodded at Guido Linari. "Sarge, you better make
this rupture-head tell you what's bothering him."

"Shit, I don't need no kind of trouble like that," Linari said.

"What trouble?" Kohler shouted. "That tank comes up here, blows a round up your ass while you're worrying about some piece back home, *that's* trouble."

"She ain't no piece, Shorty."

Sonny Laurel said, "Could I explain it, Guido?" He was trying not to laugh, Docker realized. "That way *you* didn't tell anybody, *I* did."

A dim understanding glinted in Linari's eyes. He shrugged. "You wanna tell Docker about it, that's your business. It don't matter to me."

"Sarge, Guido got engaged on his last leave in New York. Now he's worried because he never told Captain Grant or Lieutenant Whitter about it."

"Why should he? It's none of their business."

Kohler punched Linari on the arm. "That's what we been trying to tell this ginney bastard."

Linari said, "Well, I thought . . . I mean, everything we do is supposed to be written down. Like fuckin' short-arm inspection. Like you got to put your initial and serial number on your clothes, even a jockstrap if they gave you one. Insurance, your pay, your ma and pa's names and where they live. It's all written down, Korbick's got it all somewhere—so I got worrying about it 'cause I never told anybody. With that tank down there, I figure somebody should know about it."

"You have a picture of her?" Docker said.

The dog was circling them, whining and yelping, then standing still to bugle across the valley, the echoes coming back mournfully from distant fog-banked peaks. Docker looked over to the revetment where Trankic stood with the binoculars to his eyes.

"She's in the middle, sarge. That's her mother next to her."

Docker took the wallet from Linari and glanced at the photograph tucked behind a celluloid shield, a festive group in tuxedos and long dresses and flowers, the smiles stiff but blurred because the camera was out of focus.

"Her name's Josefina, Josie Carducci. I known her

all my life." Linari was so pleased to have Docker look at his girl, with Sonny smiling and Kohler pretending to be mad, that he thought of telling them about when he was little and his mother called him "pretty star-baby," mixing up the words so they came out "Guido bambini, Linari stellini," and how his father had once explained that he could never be in the second half of the class because their initial *L* was number twelve in the alphabet, so he would always be in the first half when the teacher called out names. But it was too late now, the sergeant wasn't looking at Josie anymore, he was watching Trankic.

"I hope it works out great," Docker said, and started for the revetment, Radar bounding ahead of him and Laurel following him for a few paces.

"You took a load off his mind."

Docker stopped and looked at the young soldier. "You got any last requests?"

Laurel smiled and pushed his helmet back. The wind and sleet stirred his blond hair. "Sure, sarge. I'm the only guy in the section who's never had a taste of our famous black whiskey."

"Well, we can fix that." Docker uncapped his canteen. "Good health."

Sonny took a sip of whiskey and almost immediately began to cough. When he could speak, he said hoarsely, "Wow, it's even worse than Baird said."

Trankic suddenly waved to them and pointed into the valley, where they now heard a car, the laboring strokes of its motor muffled by the inversion of heavy fog.

Docker ran back to the rocky shelf in front of the revetment. Taking the glasses, he picked up the dark line of the logging road where it cut through the woods and across open fields, tracking it until he focused on the gray shape of the German command car driving at speed toward Mont Reynard. Without lowering his binoculars he said, "If the tank moves out, cover whichever flank it heads for. Make damn sure no one hits the plungers too soon."

A rising wind swept down the valley, driving patches of fog ahead of it like huge tumbleweeds. Docker lowered his glasses and saw the German officer climbing from his command car and running the last dozen yards toward the great tank.

One of the Tiger II's treads ground powerfully into the frozen ground, turning the tank and cannon to face the upper slopes of Mont Reynard.

"I say we open up now, Bull. I say it's about fucking time."

"Not quite," Docker said.

Earlier he and Trankic had used local maps and the heights of trees to make rough, visual triangulations, from which they had estimated the distance from their positions down to the floor of the valley as approximately a quarter of a mile—somewhere between four hundred and five hundred yards.

Using Baird's stats on the tank, they figured the tank's uphill speed at between ten and fifteen miles an hour. They had calculated that—unless it were stopped by the charges of dynamite—the Tiger II would reach the machine guns on the left or right flank of their position in about sixty seconds. One minute.

The tank was moving forward now in low gear, its laboring engine shattering the silence and its tracks digging deep into the frozen rock, sending trails of sparks spinning through the early morning curtain of mist.

"Christ, don't cut it too fucking fine, Bull!"

Docker looked to his right where Kohler and Linari and Sonny Laurel were crouched behind the machine guns, hands on the firing grips. To his left Schmitzer and Farrel were on the other guns, Dormund behind them with shiny belts of ammunition. All the men had turned to watch Trankic and Docker.

"All right, hit it!" Docker said.

Trankic pumped a fist high in the air and the machine guns tore the silence apart, the bullets ricocheting instants later with shrill drawn-out whines against the thick armor of the tank. Echoes of the bursts streaked

through the valley, and the tracer ammunition formed
brilliant looping arcs above the hill, fiery guidelines for
the moving tank.

The Tiger II was accelerating rapidly now, gathering
momentum for its charge at the mountainside. The
sound of its engine and the grind of its tracks shook the
ground; Docker felt the tremors through his boots and
could see miniature avalanches starting on the hillside,
streams of rock and shale and ice hurtling down to the
floor of the valley. He also saw the Tiger II's huge cannon tracking swiftly toward the machine guns on their
right flank. As he yelled at the men there to take cover,
the ground and air shook with cannon blasts and the
twenty-five pound projectiles pounded against the overhang of the mountain. A storm of splintered rock and
shale burst around them, one taking an inch-long strip
of flesh from Docker's forehead and so disorienting him
that only the feel of the cold rock against his face made
him realize he had been knocked to the ground.

Crawling to his knees, he saw that the Tiger II was
coming straight up the mountain at their cannon, ignoring the baited flanks, traveling swiftly and safely between the charges of dynamite below the machine guns.
And for an instant he saw the tall German officer and
one of his soldiers running in a crouch behind the tank,
machine pistols in their hands.

The tank's 88-millimeter cannon was now swinging
back toward the center of the hill. Docker ran toward
the revetment, but the Tiger II fired again and the projectiles exploded into the overhang behind him, the concussion striking him in the back and throwing him
against the sandbagged walls around the cannon . . .
The whole world seemed shredded by noise, the staccato bursts of their machine guns, the rupture of frozen
rock under the tank's tracks, the fire from the tank's
big cannon breaking over them like flails. The weight
of it all pressed almost unbearably on Docker, the
churning sounds fragmented and seemingly inflamed by
the blood filming his eyes.

Trankic had run toward the right flank of the hill
when the tank's cannon turned in that direction. By the
time he saw—as Docker had—that the tank was heading toward the center of their position, the first shells
were already smashing into the mountainside, the impact stunning and driving him to his knees . . . When
his head cleared, he could smell the stench of powder in
the air, its smoky taste mingling with the wet snow and
smell of fresh earth churned up by the cannon blasts.
When he stared around, instinctively tightening his grip
on his rifle, he saw Docker on the ground, and Baird
climbing over the revetment wall above him . . .
Kohler and Linari were firing down the hill at the tank.
Laurel was lying beside them, an arm over his helmet.
The tank was not heading for the machine guns and the
dynamite, Trankic knew then, it was coming straight at
their cannon. Firing the dynamite was a long shot,
maybe they'd get lucky, Trankic thought, the blast
could take out the Germans behind the tank, a slab of
rock might crack one of the tank treads . . . he
twisted around and slammed a fist down on the plunger
of the detonating machine.

The exploding dynamite ripped the ground open,
clouding the hillside with dust and black smoke, sending
bursts of ice and rock and clods of frozen earth arcing,
wheeling through the smoke-threaded mists, and then as
they lost their thrust and fell spinning back to the
ground they rattled noisily but harmlessly around the
turret and armor of the charging tank. . . .

Shock waves from the first dynamite blast knocked
Schmitzer off his feet. Shouting at Dormund to take his
place at the machine guns, he scuttled across the ground
to fall across the plunger and detonate the charges on
the left flank of the hill. . . .

Docker and Baird crouched a few feet apart outside
the wall of the revetment, ducking instinctively when
fragments from the second blast whined over their
heads.

"You all right, sergeant?"

"I'm okay."

"There's some blood on your face."

Raising his voice, Docker shouted, "Get back on the cannon, Baird. Move it now!"

When Baird had crawled over the sandbagged wall, Docker ran back to the edge of the cliff and saw through screens of smoke that the Tiger II was only a hundred yards below him on a course that would bring it to the top of the hill a dozen yards to the right of the revetment. One of the German tank crew was lying on the ground halfway down the hill, his face dark and wet in the frame of his helmet, but the officer was still on his feet, firing alternately with his machine pistol at the left and right flank of the hill.

The blood from the gash on Docker's forehead streaked his eyes and vision, and in his distorted view the German tank looked like some huge animal trying to tear the mountain open. He shook his head, trying to focus better. Slabs of armor gleamed through smoke made red with his blood, like the scales of a great beast, the ranging cannon suggesting feelers or antennae directed by a frightening intelligence. Only the squared black cross on the steel plates above its treads defined the rampaging object as an engine of war and not, as it appeared in Docker's bloodied vision, some vestigial monster out of memory and time.

He rubbed the haze from his eyes and ran back to the revetment, where, climbing onto the loading platform of the cannon, he gestured urgently to the right. Solvis, his face streaked with smoke, nodded and cranked the gun barrel to the point where the tank would breach the precipice.

Baird was trying to say something to Docker then, shouting to make himself heard, but the words were whipped away in the wind and gunfire. Docker had the impression, though, that there was a new confidence in the boy's face, surely no sign of panic . . . He gripped Baird's shoulder quickly, but there was no more time for talking, no time for deliberation or choice. The Tiger II was suddenly on them, the flaming muzzle of its cannon coming over the edge of the mountain only twenty yards from the front wall of their revetment.

Solvis and Baird made the last corrections in their sightings, and when the tank—its grinding tracks almost vertical, the cannon pointing straight up at the low skies—reached its full extension, its underbelly of thin armor most exposed and vulnerable, Docker slammed his boot down on the firing pedal and their own cannon came to life as it poured round after round of point-detonating ammunition directly into the bottom armor of the climbing tank.

The steel heads of the cartridges smashed into, pierced the Tiger II's belly-plates; the payloads of trinitrocellulose exploded in a series of flashes that caused the tank to quiver for an instant like an animal in torment. When its center of gravity suddenly shifted, the left treads lost their traction and spun out of control, and the right tracks ground into the earth, twisting the tank sideways in erratic convulsions.

Black smoke now began to stream from the rim of the tank's turret. Docker covered his bloody face with his arm and fired three more rounds, the explosions creating storm waves that knocked him from the loading platform back onto the rocky floor of the revetment.

Those final blasts tipped the Tiger II back over the edge of the hill, where its own ammunition began exploding, the interior eruptions causing it to slide down the slope, its descent stopped only by trees and boulders sundered by the blasts of dynamite. At last, when the tank crashed slowly and heavily onto its side, the roar of its cannon spent a final projectile harmlessly into the gray skies above the valley of the Salm.

Trankic took Docker's hands and pressed them around his canteen. "Go ahead, take a drink."

Docker tried to sit up but the effort was too much for him; his head rang and his eardrums throbbed with pain.

Trankic's broad face was swollen, his eyes bloodshot

and angry. "They didn't give it to us on a fucking platter, Bull. The kid here and Sonny."

Docker was sprawled on the rocky ground behind the cannon. He drank a mouthful of black whiskey and gave the canteen back to Trankic. The gash in his forehead ached, and the wind was like sandpaper against it. He put both hands under him and stood up, feeling groggy and sick. The big dog circled him, whining anxiously. On the wet cold wind was the stench of cordite.

Docker looked up at the cannon. "Oh, Jesus!"

Jackson Baird's body hung in the metal seat beside the cannon's breechblock, boots swinging slowly in the wind. The boots were caked with mud, shoelaces white with frost and snow. A piece of shrapnel had pierced the front of Baird's helmet and had come out the back of it.

Docker walked stiffly from the revetment to the rim of the hill, where Solvis and Farrel stood together, dazed with shock.

Schmitzer knelt beside the body of Sonny Laurel, whose face looked clear and tranquil in the thin light. There seemed to be no mark on him, only dark patches of blood on the front of his fatigue jacket.

Docker felt drained. The wound in his forehead throbbed. He could hear it as well as feel it, but in the falling snow everything else was weirdly still . . . until from far below, he heard a distant motor. The pounding in his ears made it impossible to tell, though, whether it was traveling toward or away from them.

On the hillside a dozen yards from the wreckage of the tank, Docker now saw the sprawled body of the German commander, a sheen of snow already gathering on his greatcoat and black boots. And below him was another body in German uniform, a twisted heap on the mountainside.

Docker turned to Solvis. "Where's Linari and Dormund?"

"They went to heat up some water."

Farrel said, "At first Kohler thought Sonny didn't

look so bad. He said some sulfa and hot water was all—" He rubbed his lips. "Then we opened his jacket."

Docker saw that the German officer had raised his head and was staring up at him. He told Farrel to watch for the vehicle he'd heard and started down the hill, arms raised against the backlash of thornbushes, climbing over the heaps of earth and rock churned up by the Tiger II and the dynamite charges.

He stopped near the tank and looked down at Karl Jaeger. A vivid burn was on the left side of the man's face, his lips were flecked with blood. .

"My soldiers . . . " He turned and pointed to the smoldering tank. "In God's name, do what I can't, sergeant . . . do you understand?"

There was no way to open the fused turret of the tank, no way to get the German crew out of it. And if they were still alive, Docker thought, they didn't deserve that final ordeal. No one did. He unholstered his .45 and walked to the tank and fired four spaced rounds through a vision-slit into the interior of the Tiger II. And hearing the bullets ricocheting inside the metal walls of the tank, he remembered with the therapeutic irrelevance of shock a demonstration he had once witnessed at Fort Benning: one round from an M-1 rifle fired into a Sherman had made nine hundred and forty separate gashes against the white paint on the insides of the tank.

Smoke drifted from the tank's turret and flames flickered on the heavy gray armor, the light glowing yellow in the snow. The echoing sound from the bullets had intensified the ache in Docker's ears, but he could still hear a vehicle somewhere in the valley.

Jaeger told him, "You can shoot me if you like. But I'll be dead soon enough."

Docker put the .45 back in its holster.

"I can't repay you." The words were soft, blurred. "I have nothing left—"

"For God's sake, there's nothing I want from you."

Jaeger thought of his wife and daughters, grateful for this instant to think of them before he died. Then another thought forced him to raise himself on one elbow. "But there *is* something I can give you."

"Look, colonel, just go ahead and die"—he thought of Laurel and Baird—"it's what you wanted, goddamn it. You sent your tank straight up at our cannon . . ."

Staring up the hill, he listened to the approaching vehicle, louder as it turned off the road toward their gun position. It was an American jeep, and it stopped now near the revetment, and Docker saw an officer climb out and return Trankic's salute—

"I give you righteousness," Jaeger broke in. "It's very useful. We have had it and I know." His face tightened with pain. "But it is also a very great burden . . ."

The other members of Section Eight had joined the American officer and Trankic on the rock shelf in front of the revetment. The blackout headlights on the jeep cut pale tunnels through the falling snow and transformed the flakes into a froth of radiance.

The men of the section now stood facing an American officer who leaned against the hood of his jeep, a boot hooked on the bumper and a Browning automatic rifle slung over his shoulder . . .

"Sergeant, listen to me," Karl Jaeger was saying.

Docker saw that the German officer's expression had changed; the smile, fixed against what must have been awful pain, had gone, and as he listened to the voices floating on the winds from the revetment, a frown replaced it . . . "Since you are probably the last person I will ever talk to, I want you to know this. I am a husband, the father of two small girls. My home is in Dresden." The words were slurred again but held a sudden intensity. "I haven't lived what you would call a casual or flexible life. Condemn me if you wish, but at least I've lived by the rules." Jaeger shifted his weight to one elbow and looked up the hill. "By my rules, I have been a good soldier. And for these reasons, I would like to make one last request of you."

"What?" Docker said, still staring up at the officer and his men.

"I wish to surrender my sidearm to you. We cannot speak of mercy, we can leave that to diplomats. But it would be merciful of you to accept it."

Docker held out his hand, at the same time trying to isolate and identify the source of his sudden anxiety.

Jaeger barely managed to unsnap the flap of his holster. Play-acting and charades, he thought bitterly; reducing it all to sham and masquerade, destroying whatever dignity battle might have with caperings more fit for a harlequinade than honest war, the trade of kings . . . And he thought of the bedroom in Dresden, not of the eiderdown on the bed or his love for Hedy, but of the trophies on the dresser that he had won in shooting contests as a cadet . . .

The officer on the hill was giving commands. "Okay, let's line up there, men. Forget about Sally Rand freezing her tits out here . . ."

Jaeger drew his Luger from its holster and extended it butt-first to Docker, his eyes never moving from the officer in the American uniform who stood above them bracketed by the jeep's headlights.

Something in the intensity of this dying German officer's expression sounded another warning to Docker—

"That man is out of uniform, sergeant," Jaeger said abruptly.

And as Waffen SS Captain Walter Brecht unslung his automatic rifle, Docker shouted a warning to his men. But before the first echoes of his voice sounded on the sleeting winds, Jaeger had reversed the Luger and fired three shots up the hill—shots, which struck "Der Henker" in the face and formed a pattern there so compact and tidy it could have been covered by the hand of a child.

The two of them died at almost the same instant—Brecht collapsing at Trankic's feet, the BAR slipping from his arms . . . Karl Jaeger alone, finding a unity at last in the darkness that came to him on the slopes of Mont Reynard.

"Sarge, you think I should go down and tell the Bonnards?"

"Tell them what?"

"About Sonny," Farrel said. "It seems to me one of us should tell Felice about it."

"All right, tell Felice. If there's anything of his she'd like, a snapshot—" He let out his breath. "Make it fast, we still got a gun section here."

Corporal Schmitzer had wrapped the bodies of Jackson Baird and Sonny Laurel in tarpaulins and taken them to the high ground in the woods and laid them down alongside Gelnick. They had found no radio in the VIII Corps jeep, only maps of the area, GI binoculars, a thermos of cold coffee, a pack of Camel cigarettes . . . and stenciled under the lining of the driver's seat—WAFFEN SS CAPTAIN WALTER BRECHT.

On Docker's orders Linari parked the jeep behind a stand of shrapnel-torn bushes and joined Solvis and Kohler in repositioning and reloading the guns.

After the bodies of Captain Walter Brecht and Colonel Karl Jaeger had been covered, Trankic and Docker walked to the shelf in front of the revetment and looked out over the valley. Trankic uncapped his canteen and offered it to Docker. "Only thing, Bull, there's nothing fucking much to drink to."

"What about Christmas?"

"Sure," Trankic said. "I forgot about that."

The German officer had said something to Docker before he died, something about war being the trade of kings. Docker wasn't sure he understood that, and anyway, it all depended where you were when the war was going on.

"So Merry Christmas," he said.

The two soldiers drank from their canteen cups, the

cold metal rims burning their lips, and looked down the slopes of Mont Reynard, where the falling snow turned blue on the smoke rising from the wreckage of the German tank.

Chapter Twenty-Nine

February 14, 1945. Liège, Belgium.
Wednesday, 0830 Hours.

Liège, capital of the Belgian province of the same name—on the Meuse in the heart of Walloon country—is an industrial center of several hundred thousand inhabitants.

The city (with Antwerp) had been a top priority target for German V-1 and V-2 rockets during the Battle of the Bulge. When that offensive was finally checked and contained, Liège remained a functioning city, although many of its boulevards and buildings had been shattered by months of rocket and artillery fire.

A number of main streets were blocked off to traffic, and the walls of most hotels and office buildings had been shored up with wooden scaffoldings and stacked rows of sandbags. A nighttime blackout was in effect, but the essential activities of Liège continued to flourish; shops and markets opened at dawn and the city's avenues funneled traffic from the Channel ports toward First Army's supply depots. The Army's administrative offices were now being transferred closer to the increasingly stable front but ranking officers were still quartered in a complex of buildings on the outskirts of the city in an area known as Brabant Park.

On a cold, sunny morning, Buell Docker drove into Liège and parked on a crowded street near the Hotel

Leopold, a massive gray stone building which had been requisitioned by First Army as a billet and mess for transient officers. The hotel straddled an intersection of avenues near the railway station and central flower markets.

At the reception desk an elderly clerk looked at his orders and directed Docker to a room on the third floor, where a wrought-iron balcony crusted with soot-grained snow gave him a view of river bridges and church steeples.

The room was warm, but the water in the bathroom taps was as cold as if it had been piped over open ground from a freezing river. He showered quickly, standing next to a sputtering radiator to towel himself down, then opened his duffel bag to change into a clean uniform and an Eisenhower jacket with the faded outline of his sergeant's stripes on the sleeves. The gold bars on the shoulders had been lent by Captain Grant when Docker was commissioned in the field to replace Lieutenant Longworth. . . .

Gun Section Eight was relieved from its position on Mont Reynard in the last week of December and posted to a temporary staging area west of Namur. In the last six weeks, Docker and Trankic (now sergeant) were occupied writing reports on their losses in personnel and equipment, answering interrogatories from Graves Registration and supervising the instruction of recruits assigned to the section and platoon from redeployment depots.

Each member of Section Eight (except Schmitzer) had been queried by Air Force Intelligence to collate their impressions about the speed, tactics, performance and silhouette patterns of the ME-262 jet aircraft the section had shot down over Mont Reynard on the afternoon of December 20th.

Docker was asked by Captain Joe Grant to prepare a report on the movements of his section (casualties, actions engaged in, exact route of march) during the thirteen days the unit had been out of communication with Battery and Battalion headquarters.

Three weeks later Captain Richard Travolta from First Army's Judge Advocate's staff visited Dog Battery at the staging area west of Namur to take depositions from the section regarding the action and casualties on Mont Reynard, the specific thrust of his inquiry focusing on the deaths of privates Samuel Gelnick and Jackson Baird.

As a result of these interviews and statements—despite them or because of some lack in them, Docker wasn't sure which—Docker had been ordered to report to Liège on this date, February 14th, 1945, to give additional testimony at a board of special inquiry convened by First Army. . . .

A knock sounded now and a woman's voice called something in French that he couldn't make out. He opened the door and a thin maid looked inquiringly at him and made exaggerated gestures of using a scrubbing board. Docker pointed to his duffel bag and told her he'd appreciate it if she'd take care of his laundry.

A male voice hailed him from the end of the corridor. "Lieutenant Docker? We've been expecting you."

An officer with captain's bars on his jacket stood in the open door of the elevator. "I'm Captain Walton. Traffic here's a pain in the ass, so let's get moving."

"Be right with you, sir." Docker picked up his overcoat and joined the captain. They rode to the first floor in silence and walked out to the curving driveway where a PFC waited for them beside a covered jeep.

When they pulled away from the curb, the captain said, "Major Karsh runs a shop so tight your asshole will be squeaking. I hope you had breakfast."

"I'm fine, sir," Docker said.

"Good, real good. You field soldiers never stand short, I guess."

Captain Walton was in his early thirties, slender and tidily put together with a thin, blond mustache that drooped like wilted feathers at the corners of his mouth.

His eyes were round and blue behind steel-rimmed glasses, which lent an old-fashioned look to his narrow, youthful face.

"Hey, isn't it about time for the goddamn spurs and bat?"

Docker glanced at him in surprise but saw that Walton was speaking to his driver, who was leaning on the horn as he maneuvered the jeep through columns of big army trucks.

The driver laughed. "Bat and spurs ain't half of it. I'm giving every damn horse I got his head this morning."

"My driver's a rowdy old boy from Tennessee," Walton said. "Unbroken, uncivilized, un-everything you can think of, but still the best goddamn jeep jockey in the whole First Army . . ." Walton stroked his mustache. "I'm sure, lieutenant, you're curious about these hearings, but Major Karsh will spell that out for you. He runs a tight ship, like I said: Nobody at the wheel but the skipper. You get the idea?"

Docker nodded. He got the idea.

First Army's board of special inquiry convened at ten A.M. on February 14th in the ballroom of the Hotel Empire, whose entrance faced tree-lined boulevards and a brilliant curve of the Meuse River. An MP corporal was posted at double doors that opened from the mezzanine into a ballroom. The corporal wore a class-A uniform and helmet liner and stood at parade rest, rifle canted away from his body, back and shoulders erect against the carved panels of the tall doors.

The MP presented arms when Docker and Captain Walton entered the ballroom. The captain walked to a conference table where two officers were seated, a second lieutenant and a major. Smaller desks flanked this table which was piled with briefcases, manila folders and legal tablets.

On one desk stood an Army field telephone and a tray with coffee makings. A WAC sergeant sat at the other, notebook and jar of pencils in front of her.

Captain Walton joined the major and lieutenant and waved Docker to a chair facing them.

"You've met Captain Walton," the major said. "I'm Major Sydney Karsh. This is Lieutenant Clement Weiffel. We are the presiding officers of this board of inquiry, which has been convened by the Judge Advocate's staff of First Army. Our recording secretary is Sergeant Elspeth Corey." The major removed his heavy, horn-rimmed glasses. "We'll be ready to begin in a few minutes, lieutenant, so meanwhile, make yourself comfortable."

As the major distributed manila-bound files to his aides, Docker looked around the ballroom. Many of the windows had been splintered by bomb blasts and were now crisscrossed with patchwork designs of heavy tape. Wooden scaffoldings stood braced against the beige walls. In some places the heavily damaged plaster was covered with canvas. Decorative crystals had been removed from the three huge chandeliers and naked bulbs cast a glaring light across the gold-leafed ceiling. Clusters of sofas and chairs were draped with white sheets, and a shiny parquet floor was scattered with faded old carpets.

The WAC sergeant would have been attractive, Docker thought, if it weren't for the severity in her expression. She was simply doing a job, a slim, blond secretary in Army uniform, but something in her gathered energies suggested a different image to Docker—perhaps a sleek cat with all of its attention concentrated on a mousehole.

When Major Karsh said, "Lieutenant Docker, I'd like to explain—" she began recording with precise pencil strokes, but Karsh glanced at her and said, "Sergeant Corey, this is an informal preliminary statement, so don't bother taking it down." A smile flared and faded quickly on his face. "When I need a transcript, I'll nod to you." The major's smile came again, as if to underscore the amiability of his instructions. "There'll be a good deal of casual discussion," he said, "and there's no point in burdening you with all of it."

"Yes, Major Karsh." When she shifted her position and lowered the notebook, the overhead light shifted and moved like quicksilver along her slim and neatly muscled legs. Docker wondered how she'd be in the sack, wondered if she'd come to attention and salute and request permission to merge with the infinite or haul her ashes, as Kohler would put it . . . but he also told himself he was being defensive, that he resented these freshly groomed and well-tailored officers with their legal pads and judgmental frowns and gestures.

Major Karsh glanced at Docker, another smile sharpening his features.

"Lieutenant Docker, let's start by fixing the time element. The chronology of events. On what date was Jackson Baird killed?"

"December twenty-third, sir."

"On what date did he join your section?"

"December seventeenth, sir."

"He was with your unit just one week then?"

"Yes, sir. One week."

"So it follows that your knowledge of Jackson Baird and his background, and whatever insights you have of his character and personality and so forth, were gained in that seven-day period from December seventeenth to December twenty-third. Correct, lieutenant?"

"Yes, that's correct."

"Let's go forward a bit. After Private Jackson Baird was fatally wounded, your gun section remained on Mont Reynard until you made contact with your battery headquarters. What date was that, lieutenant?"

"December twenty-eighth. Lieutenant Whitter, our platoon commander, arrived then and gave us orders to withdraw toward Namur."

Karsh said, "And that was when you learned of the deaths of Lieutenant Longworth and Corporal Larkin?"

"Yes, sir."

Major Karsh checked the notes he'd made on his pad. "I think that gives us the chronological bookends, so to speak . . . Young Baird was picked up by your section on the seventeenth, killed by enemy fire on the twenty-third, contact with your battery reestablished on the twenty-eighth."

Karsh glanced at Captain Walton and Lieutenant Weiffel. "Any questions about this so far?"

They both shook their heads.

"Very well." The major looked through the stack of files in front of him, selected one and pushed it across the table toward Docker. Again his quick smile.

"Would you take a look at this, lieutenant?"

Docker opened the manila folder, which contained two files of typewritten pages.

"You recognize those documents, lieutenant?"

"Yes, sir."

Major Karsh nodded to Sergeant Corey, who adjusted her note pad and prepared to take down their exchanges.

"Lieutenant, please tell us in your own words their origin and nature."

"These are two separate reports, one of which I made at the request of our battery commander, Captain Joseph Grant, and the other at the request of an officer from the Judge Advocate's staff of First Army, Captain Travolta."

"What's the date of the first report, lieutenant?"

"December thirtieth, 1944."

"And the second?"

"January twenty-third, 1945."

"Then for the record, we'll call the report written December thirtieth, File A. And the report written the twenty-third of January, File B. Is that clear enough, lieutenant?"

"Yes, it's clear enough."

Major Karsh glanced at the sergeant. "We'll go off the record for a moment. Lieutenant, I want this hearing to proceed as casually and efficiently as possible.

But I also expect you to observe the conventions of military courtesy at all times. In answering, you'll address the members of the board either as 'sir' or by their appropriate ranks. Is that clear, lieutenant?"

"Yes, sir."

"You may proceed. Would you like the sergeant to refresh your memory?"

"I'd appreciate that, sir."

She glanced at her notebook. "Question: 'You recognize these documents, lieutenant?' Answer: 'Yes, sir.' Question: 'Lieutenant, tell us in your own words their origin and nature.' "

She looked at Docker. "Is that sufficient, lieutenant?"

"Yes, that's fine . . . sergeant."

Docker glanced from the files to Major Karsh. "Sir, after our section was ordered to pull back from Mont Reynard, I had a briefing session with Captain Grant at the battery CP outside Namur. He told me then to write a full and detailed report covering the time Section Eight had been cut off from Battery Headquarters."

"Did Captain Grant suggest to you what to include— or *not* include—in that report, lieutenant?"

"No, sir. His instructions were to make it as complete as possible."

"I see. And you followed those instructions?"

"I did my best, sir. The report includes an account of the German plane we shot down—an ME-262, a jet aircraft, a model and design we'd never seen before. And it also includes the fact that a radio signal Corporal Trankic sent from a Resistance transmitter in Lepont had been picked up by Eighth Air Force station near Brussels. File A also covered the section's casualties, and the details of a combat action with a German tank, a Tiger Mark II."

The major looked steadily at Docker. "And File A included, did it not, the report of a conversation between you and Jackson Baird during which, according to your testimony, Baird told you he had deserted his post during an enemy attack on the first day of the Battle of the Bulge?"

"Yes, sir, that was in the report."

"Lieutenant, did you feel under some obligation, honor-bound as it were, to include that conversation in your report?"

"No, sir, I didn't."

"But the fact is, you did include it, lieutenant. Would you explain why?"

"I'll try, sir," Docker said, and wondered whether he could explain it even to himself, let alone the major, whether he could find somewhere words to interpret and support his decision. But his thoughts went back . . . back to the time west of Namur, to Dog Battery's shattered sections bivouacked in tents on a sodden meadow outside the town. Someone had been playing a guitar in a nearby tent, singing along with it, a railroad song about a pine box in a baggage car behind the coal tender, a pale young mother waiting down the line, the sounds rising and falling with the rain and wind beating against Docker's tent and making noisy drafts in the big iron stove.

The battery commander, Captain Grant, slender, with thinning red hair and mild and thoughtful eyes, had pushed his way through the tent flaps, saying, "Well, your report's okay as far as it goes, Docker, but I guess you know it's not complete. You have any of Trankic's juice nearby?"

"Sure thing, sir." Docker had taken a canteen of black whiskey from his footlocker, placing it with two metal cups on the table beside the stove. "Help yourself, captain."

"You look like you could use a belt yourself, Docker. Some rest area, right?" The captain had taken off his wet, shining helmet and damp overcoat, dumping them in the sling of a canvas chair. "Well, let's get on with it, Docker. You know your report in its present state just won't wash."

The captain had taken a sheaf of typed pages from

the pocket of his coat and dropped them on the table. Sitting down, he had stretched his muddy boots toward the stove and poured himself a drink. With the tip of his forefinger he then pushed the typed report toward Docker.

"According to this, you picked up a straggler named Jackson Baird the day after the Germans kicked off their counterattack in the Ardennes. All you add is that he died a week later helping to defend your gun position against an enemy tank."

"Maybe that's all I know for sure, captain."

"I don't think that's good enough, Docker." Captain Grant's eyes were troubled; a shudder had run through his slender frame and he sipped the cold whiskey. "God, I'd rather be in a firefight where things are relatively simple. I'm bone-sick and tired of picking up the pieces afterward. I've heard the latrine rumors. Shorty Kohler took a swing at Baird, didn't he? So let's start there. What was that all about?"

"Christ, it could have been any of a dozen things. Kohler's a good man to have with you in a brawl, but judgment and brains aren't the first things you notice about him."

"No? But Kohler was smart enough to know Baird was picked up about eighteen miles behind his own company. And knew he hadn't got that far just taking a wrong turn in the dark—"

The sound of Elspeth Corey's voice brought Docker back to the present, shattering memories of a mournful song mingling with the wind and rain, and the look of compassion in Captain Grant's eyes.

"Lieutenant Docker, Major Karsh's last two questions were: 'Lieutenant, did you feel an obligation, honor-bound, as it were, to include that conversation in your report?' Answer: 'No, sir. I didn't.' " After pausing to glance across her stenographic pad at Docker, Sergeant Corey continued reading in a light, neutral voice: " 'The fact is, you did include it, lieutenant. Would you explain why?' "

Major Karsh said, "Lieutenant, do you understand what I'm getting at?"

"Yes, sir. I believe I do."

"Then I would appreciate an answer, a full and responsive answer . . ."

They had discussed it for another hour or so that night, Docker and Captain Grant, the canteen catching reflections from the stove as they tipped whiskey into their cups . . . "I've got reports of my own to write," Grant had said, his voice tired. "Johnny Weyl from Section Three, the kid who did magic tricks at camp shows in basic. I'll be writing his family tonight. He's not going home, and neither is Corporal Hooper from Headquarters or Sonny Laurel or Lieutenant Longworth or Lenny Rado. But those men died with their outfits, at their gun positions or following orders."

Captain Grant had stood then, collecting his helmet and overcoat. Picking up Docker's report, he had studied it, shook his head, then dropped it back on the table. "You'd better complete it, lieutenant. Would it help if I made it a direct order?"

"No, sir, it wouldn't."

"I'm not surprised. You want to protect the boy and I can understand that, but I've found that at times like this, nothing does a better job than the truth."

"That's not quite it, sir. I want to protect him, but I'm not sure of the best way to do it. I've been turning over just one question these last three or four hours, which is what in hell *Baird* would want from me."

Grant had checked his watch. "I've got a guard mount to inspect, Docker, I'll be back for your report in about an hour—"

In a mildly exasperated tone Major Karsh was saying, "Lieutenant, I'm trying to be patient but I must insist you answer my question. To repeat it—perhaps unnecessarily—I asked you to explain to me *why* you included a particular conversation between yourself and Jackson Baird in the report you filed with Captain Grant."

"There were two reasons, sir. Captain Grant specifically asked me for a complete account of Section Eight's positions and activities during the period we were out of communication with the battery. Secondly, I felt that Jackson Baird himself would have wanted the facts known."

Karsh's dark eyebrows rose. "Did Baird tell you that in so many words?"

"No, sir."

"Then your opinion is simply a subjective evaluation, right, lieutenant?"

"I guess you could call it that, sir."

"Your subjective evaluation, then, is that Jackson Baird, for some curious reason, wanted to be posthumously indicted as a coward and deserter. Is that about it, lieutenant?"

"Except that it wasn't for what you call a curious reason, major. It was for a damned good reason. It was because Baird respected courage, as only a man who's lost it and got it back can. I put all the facts down because . . . Baird's memory *deserves* it. I also think he'd have wanted his family to know everything he went through."

"I don't mean to be abrupt, lieutenant, but let's confine ourselves to weighable, measurable issues. There's little to be gained in getting mired down in cocktail-party psychoanalysis. Let's move on now to your second report. Would you tell us, again in your own words, the nature and origin of File B?"

"Yes, sir. I wrote that report on January twenty-second at the direction of Captain Travolta. The captain was interested specifically in Jackson Baird. He wanted a detailed account of where and how we picked him up, how he conducted himself in our section. Captain Travolta also took depositions from other members of Section Eight. But since he told us not to discuss the interviews among ourselves, I have no knowledge of any statement but my own."

"Lieutenant, I'm going to proceed as candidly as pos-

sible in this matter," Karsh said. "There'll be no sur-
prises, and hopefully no unexpected developments.
Captain Travolta was assigned to the preliminary stage
of this investigation by the Judge Advocate's section of
First Army. This board has copies of all the statements
the captain received from members of your gun section.
Captain Travolta also sent a list of pertinent questions
to Corporal Schmitzer at the Twenty-third Base Hospital at Orléans, but his doctors decided he wasn't up to
answering them at this time. Something about a nervous
disorder . . ."

Karsh glanced at his notes and said, almost casually,
"I should also advise you we have statements from your
platoon commander, Lieutenant Bart Whitter, and from
personnel at Battery D's headquarters, namely motor
pool corporal Cleve Haskell."

"Then you probably know more about this business
than I do, sir."

"That may well be the case," Karsh said quietly.

Docker could feel a subtle, disturbing change in the
atmosphere of the room, a vibration that sounded under
the smooth surface of the major's legalistic, nicely
turned phrases. It was a sense of incongruity that
alerted him, the same feeling he'd gotten from the
stately but seedy ballroom: a golden ceiling and ornate
moldings trying to harmonize with shattered windows
and cracked plaster, drafts raising spools of dust on fine
old carpets. Something didn't hang together; Docker
was beginning to sense a glinting edge beneath the po-
lite questions and formal manners.

It was a soldier's reaction, a knowledge learned in
fear and pain that had told him (not always in time)
that such-and-such dusty road through the olive grove
was too quiet to be trusted.

And something else. The major's smile, he realized,
wasn't a smile at all, but a reflexive grimace, a rictus
that creased his cheeks and bared his teeth, but never
touched his dark eyes.

Docker studied the other officers at the table and

their ribbons—good conduct medals, marksman's badges, theatre ribbons without battle stars.

Walton, with his defeated mustaches, was, Docker guessed, the back-slapping type who savored the trappings of a war—the masculine patina of uniforms, the spit and polish and music of parade grounds, who wanted the affection of his men more than their respect . . . ("a rowdy old boy from Tennessee, unbroken, un-everything, best goddamn jeep jockey in First Army").

Lieutenant Weiffel was short and bald except for black tufts of hair ringing his soft scalp, and fat, with rolls of flesh bulging over his collar and forming ripples under his tunic when he leaned forward to scribble his notes. Docker had no particular reading on Weiffel, just his tendency toward obesity that was evidence of indulgence, which he noted as he would the weakness in any enemy position.

Major Karsh was the dominant force at the conference table. In his late thirties, Docker judged, with a dark and coarsely grained complexion, thick, black hair, deeply set eyes, coldly watchful under jutting brows, a face like a blunt scimitar with that deceptive rictus occasionally flaring over his sharply cut features.

Docker looked thoughtfully at the three officers, then addressed himself to Karsh. "May I ask a question, sir?"

"Yes, what is it?"

"I'm wondering if the major would tell me the purpose of these hearings."

Karsh said deliberately, "The purpose of these hearings, lieutenant, is to establish the truth about certain events which are presently subject to a variety of interpretations."

"Major, if those certain events relate to Jackson Baird, I've already given two written depositions: one to Captain Grant, the other to Captain Travolta. Frankly, I don't see what more I can contribute."

"Let me clarify something, lieutenant. This isn't a court-martial, it's a board of inquiry. Our function is

to review the matters included in the depositions taken
to date. To inquire into those events and, hopefully, to
shed fresh light on them. When we're through, full tran-
scripts will be returned to the senior officers who have
overview responsibilities for this board, Colonel George
Rankin and Major General Walter Adamson. They'll
determine what further action, if any, is to be taken. Is
that much clear, lieutenant?"

"I'm afraid not, sir. The testimony I've given on two
other occasions is obviously unsatisfactory, for some
reason. I think I've got a right to know who objected to
it and why."

"We'll be getting to that, lieutenant." Major Karsh
picked up a stack of manila folders and looked steadily
at Docker, the rictus smile showing again. "In regard to
the points you've made, let me say this. No one has
found your testimony unsatisfactory. But in all the depositions I have in my hand, you're the only witness who
states categorically that Jackson Baird deserted his post
under enemy fire. Now, you may be right. But considering the grave nature of your testimony, the serious reflection it casts on that young soldier, the distress it will
cause his family and friends, our function here, lieutenant, is to check and double-check all the putative evidence and facts. This board's responsibility is to inquire
into the validity of your general testimony, to determine
whether you might have been unwittingly inaccurate in
your conclusions, or mistaken or forgetful in certain
substantive areas. Is that clear, lieutenant?"

"I'm not exactly sure, sir."

"Then I'll put it this way. The issue before the board,
quite simply, is to determine how reliable a witness you
are, lieutenant."

The major dropped the stack of folders on the table,
and the sound was unexpectedly loud in the faded ele-
gance of the old ballroom.

"We'll recess now for ten minutes." Karsh removed
his heavy glasses and rubbed the bridge of his nose.
"Until eleven hundred hours."

Docker smoked a cigarette in the lobby outside the ballroom and looked through the bay windows at streams of American and British military trucks clogging the boulevards. The river was brilliant in the sunlight as occasional gusting winds rippled the glasslike surface of the water. A river gull, blurred and indistinct against the white skies, arced and settled and became instantly visible on a dark stone piling.

He knew it was pointless to speculate on where Karsh's questioning might take them. Or how much time they would spend (or waste) trying to reconstruct a past whose significant substance, reality, existed in immediate fear and anger and passion and not the approximate truth of remembered emotions and conclusions gleaned from dates and statements neatly clipped together in administrative folders.

When he turned away from the window, Docker saw that Sergeant Elspeth Corey was seated on a leather divan against a brocaded wall of the lobby. She looked up and gave him a brief, tentative smile, but before Docker could react she turned and put out her cigarette with several nervous taps in a sand-filled urn beside the sofa.

"Lieutenant Docker, let's commence with the day your section picked up Private Jackson Baird."

Major Karsh arranged his folders in a tidy formation on the conference table and drew a line under a date on his legal pad. Putting on his glasses, he adjusted them carefully with his fingertips.

"That was December seventeenth, lieutenant."

"Excuse me, major. Shall I take this?"

"I'm sorry, sergeant. Yes, this is for the record. Lieutenant, the seventeenth of December was the second day of the Ardennes offensive. Your section, Section Eight, D Battery, the Two hundred sixty-ninth Automatic Weapons Battalion, was proceeding in the direction of Malmédy." Karsh glanced up at Docker, the quick smile twisting his face. "We've pieced together your route of march and certain other details from the depositions given by you and other members of your section."

The major returned to his notes. "Now, would you tell us, lieutenant, in your own words, of your first encounter and impressions of Private Jackson Baird."

"Yes, sir." Docker's thoughts turned back to those hours of coldness and fear, the German troops materializing in white forests, the section's retreat through the mountains, the bursts of shrapnel spraying the sides of their trucks.

"Baird hooked on to our second truck," he said. "Solvis told me later he looked close to shock. Solvis offered him a cigarette and a drink but Baird didn't want anything."

"Excuse me, major," Captain Walton said.

"Yes?"

"Lieutenant, what kind of drink are you referring to?"

"Whiskey, sir."

"Would that be Section Eight's notorious black whiskey, lieutenant?"

"Yes, sir. Solvis had a canteen of it."

"Did everybody in the section have a supply of it?"

"Some of them didn't care for it, sir."

Walton nodded and glanced at the major. "I have no further questions at this time, sir."

"Very well," Karsh said, seeming, Docker wondered, to be hiding his impatience with Walton? "Go on, lieutenant."

"Later that day, I called a halt to check our bearings and maps. That was the first time I talked to Baird. He'd taken his helmet off, and I told him to put it back on and keep it on. I asked him what happened to his rifle and dog tags. He told me he'd lost them. Said the rifle had been knocked from his hands by an artillery blast and that he'd lost his dog tags when the chain caught and snapped on a tree branch."

"Did he explain why he had left his position?"

"Yes, sir. Baird said he heard someone shouting to fall back."

Karsh made a quick note, obviously waiting for Docker to continue, but when Docker remained silent Karsh removed his glasses and said, "Lieutenant, I've asked you to tell us about this sequence of events in your own words. I'd like to know what you said to him, what his responses were, something about his emotional state and so forth. I'd appreciate those details, if you don't mind."

"Yes, sir. Baird told me that his company was on the left flank of the Hundred and sixth. He'd been on guard a couple of hundred yards from his company headquarters. It was dark when the Germans attacked. Baird said it was like a nightmare. His exact words were that 'it was like being caught in a tornado.'"

"Let's go back a bit. Did he tell you who gave him orders to withdraw?"

"He wasn't sure about that. His company commander was a Captain Dilworth, I believe that's right. His lieutenant was named Russo. He also mentioned his sergeant, whose name, I think, was Greene. But Baird said there was so much wind and artillery fire he couldn't tell whether it was the captain or Lieutenant Russo or the sergeant yelling at them to get out of there."

"And what did Jackson Baird tell you he did after acting on those orders?"

"He told me that he had lost contact with the other men in his company. He headed west then and joined our section the next day."

"You had no reason to question any of the details of his story?" Karsh looked up at Docker. "The missing dog tags and rifle, the unidentified voice ordering retreat, all of this struck you as reasonable at the time?"

"Yes, sir, it did."

"I see." Karsh made a check mark on his legal pad. "And so, after that first conversation with Jackson Baird, you accepted him as a member of your section, assigned him duties and so forth?"

"Yes, sir."

"In fact, you provided him with a rifle, didn't you, lieutenant?"

"Yes, sir."

"Wouldn't you describe that as an act of faith in Jackson Baird's bona fides?"

"Not exactly."

The major looked mildly exasperated. "Then tell me, lieutenant, how would you describe this display of trust and confidence in a youngster who was a total stranger to you?"

"If I trusted anything, sir, I guess it was my own judgment."

"Very well, let's move on to another area. I'd like to discuss"—the major glanced at his notes—"the action in which Private Samuel Gelnick was killed. I'll recap those events, lieutenant, and if I'm in error, please correct me. Private Gelnick was running toward the gun revetment with Private Solvis when the ME-262 attacked your position. Is that correct?"

"Yes, sir."

"Private Solvis made it safely to the revetment and Private Gelnick did not. Correct?"

"Yes, sir. Gelnick hit the ground and froze. He was killed by shrapnel. Solvis took cover against the outer wall of the revetment."

"Immediately after that attack did Private Solvis take cover *inside* the revetment?"

Since Karsh had received depositions from every member of the section, Docker realized he must already know the answers to these questions, but he said, "No, sir. Solvis did nothing to protect himself. He seemed dazed by concussion, and by what happened to Gelnick."

"Lieutenant, would you characterize Solvis' situation at that time as extremely dangerous?"

"Yes, sir, I would."

"Exposed and vulnerable to an attacking enemy aircraft?"

Docker knew what the major wanted, and he had every intention of giving it to him, but he found the theatrical emphasis depressing because it cheapened his memories of that action on the hill, the sleeting winds, the sound of the guns, and waiting for the plane to come back, with nobody able to tell Solvis why it had happened to Gelnick . . . "Yes, he was very vulnerable, sir."

"And then?"

"Baird went and got him, sir, grabbed him by the arm and hauled him inside the revetment."

"Exposing himself to considerable danger in the process?"

"Yes, sir."

"And in the subsequent action—I'm referring to the shooting down of the aircraft—Baird also conducted himself in a soldierly fashion?"

"Yes, he certainly did, sir."

Major Karsh made notes for a moment or so, and then, after carefully reading what he'd written, glanced at the other officers. "Gentlemen?"

Captain Walton said, "I'd like to clarify one point, lieutenant. When Baird went to Solvis' aid, was he acting under your orders?"

"No, sir, he wasn't."

"Was he acting under *anyone's* orders?"

"No, sir. He saw what had to be done and did it without regard to the danger and his own personal safety."

Walton seemed pleased. He glanced at Karsh, eyes bright behind the old-fashioned glasses. "That does it as far as I'm concerned."

Major Karsh nodded and checked the heavy silver watch strapped to his muscular wrist. "I want to make a point for the record before we recess for lunch. I consider it a privilege to include this information in the transcript . . . 'The plane shot down by Lieutenant Docker's gun section on December twentieth was no ordinary aircraft. It was an ME-262, a jet-propulsion plane with defensive and offensive capabilities superior to any aircraft flown in this war. Army engineers recovered that prototype aircraft from the Mont Reynard mountain range. The identification of its potential gave the Allied Air Force valuable lead time to prepare a strategy against the more than two thousand ME-262s which flew missions during the closing stages of the Battle of the Bulge.' " The major's eyes had become intent, serious. "The men of Section Eight, *all* the men of that section, are to be commended for their courage and resourcefulness during that action."

"Hear, hear!" Captain Walton said.

Karsh turned his smile toward the sergeant. "When you've typed up copies of this transcript, remind me that I want this particular section initialed by all three officers of the board."

The MP corporal pulled open the double doors of the ballroom and came to attention as Karsh, briefcase under his arm, strode toward him, his leather heels echoing on the parquet floors.

Walton collected his papers. The sergeant slipped her arms into her overcoat.

"Elspeth?"

She glanced at him. "Sir?"

"Sorry, just curious. About your name, I mean. Is it French, or what?"

"It's British, captain. I was named after a great-aunt in London."

"Cheerio and pip-pip, eh what? Elspeth, our mess is off limits to EMs, but as court secretary, I think we could shoe-horn you in."

"Thank you, captain, but I've already made plans for lunch."

"Well, suit yourself. Docker, if you're tired of GI food, there's a damn good brasserie, Le Chat qui Fum, near the flower market. That means 'the cat who smokes.' "

"Hear, hear," Docker said, and picked up his overcoat and left the ballroom.

"Surly bastard," Lieutenant Weiffel said.

"He may have reason to be." Walton looked at his watch. "Let's chow up. Karsh said two o'clock."

Docker had coffee and a sandwich at a riverside café, where old men in jackets over woolen sweaters stood at a zinc-topped bar drinking beer and brandy. When he returned to the ballroom of the Empire Hotel several minutes before two o'clock, Sergeant Corey was at her desk and the officers were seated at the conference table arranging their files and notes.

As Docker took his chair, Karsh said, "Lieutenant Weiffel? Do you have a question?"

"Yes, sir."

Docker recognized the book opened in front of Weiffel as a U.S. Army Small-Arms Training Manual.

Weiffel said, "Lieutenant, in Private Farrel's deposition, he states that he filed the sear off his M-1 rifle because you told him to. Is that right?"

"It wasn't an order, sir. It was a suggestion."

"Well, did you file the sear off *your* rifle? And if so, would you tell us why?"

"Yes. To convert it to full automatic."

Weiffel leaned forward, a smooth roll of fat rising pinkly above his shirt collar, and put a finger on a paragraph of the Small-Arms Manual. With his other hand the lieutenant began stroking his soft scalp, a habit of his that struck Docker as curious because Weiffel always accompanied the gesture with an expression of surprise and alarm, as if he were freshly conscious of loss each time his hand strayed to his bald head. He said now, "I guess you know, lieutenant, that once you file that sear off, the rifle can't be converted back to normal semiautomatic function?"

"I understand that, lieutenant."

"By stretching of point, you could say that you destroyed government property without proper authority."

"The purpose of making that modification was to get more firepower in the air."

"And is that all that matters? The amount of ammo you can pump off?"

"Well, it sure as hell doesn't do much good on the ground."

"Lieutenant Docker," Karsh said. "Some of these questions may strike you as irrelevant, but keep your answers pertinent and responsive. Is that clear?"

"Yes, major, but the lieutenant's question made that kind of answer very difficult."

Karsh nodded to Sergeant Corey. "Please read the last few exchanges."

"Yes, sir." She flipped back a page of her notebook and found the place with her pencil. "Lieutenant Weiffel's question: 'And is that all that matters? The amount of ammo you can pump off?' Lieutenant Docker's answer: 'Well, it sure as hell doesn't do much good on the ground.'"

"Thank you, sergeant . . . well, lieutenant, you may have a point, the query might be construed as ambiguous, but that wasn't intentional—"

"Then I've got just one more question," Weiffel said. "I'll try to make it real clear. You say you didn't order Private Farrel to file the sear off his rifle. But you suggested he do it. Have I got that straight now?"

"Yes, sir."

"Lieutenant, did anyone order you to file the sear off *your* rifle?"

"No, sir."

"Well, did someone *suggest* to you that you destroy government property?"

"Yes, sir."

"Who, lieutenant? And under what circumstances?"

"After Kasserine, a colonel on the division commander's staff advised us all to file the sears off our rifles. He made it clear he didn't want to be quoted on the subject but I'll identify him if you think it will shed light on these hearings."

"No, that won't be necessary," Weiffel said, and looked uncertainly at the major.

Karsh said, "If the colonel preferred to remain anon-
ymous, so be it. Captain Walton?"

The captain opened a folder and leafed through it.
"I'd like to inquire into a certain issue raised by Lieu-
tenant Bart Whitter." He nodded to Sergeant Corey.
"There's an *h* in that name, sergeant, W-*h*-i-t-t-e-r."
Adjusting his glasses, Walton ran his finger across the
open file. "Lieutenant Whitter states that the then-
Sergeant Docker and other members of his gun section
unlawfully appropriated fifty-five gallons of ethyl alco-
hol from Utah Beach in Normandy—" He stared at
Docker. "That was just after the Allied landing in
France last year. What's your comment on this portion
of Lieutenant Whitter's deposition?"

"It's not true, sir."

"You mean the lieutenant is mistaken? Or that he's
lying?"

"Probably a little of both, sir."

The major stared at him over the frames of his heavy
glasses. "Try to be more specific, lieutenant."

"Yes, sir. In the first place, Lieutenant Whitter
wasn't on Beach Red that day. He was on a reconnaissance inland with Captain Grant, and a check of our battery records will show that. Secondly, we didn't appropriate anything, for the simple reason that it was
impossible to *steal* anything from Utah Beach. There
was only one rule the beachmasters enforced: empty
trucks hit the beach, full trucks leave the beach. We
didn't have a full truck so we added those jerry cans of
alcohol to our load of tents and camouflage nets. The
beachmasters were screaming at us through bullhorns to
clear out by then, which we were glad to do because the
beach was under fire from German fighters and artillery. A stray shot would have turned us into a bonfire. I
submit with respect, sir, that Lieutenant Whitter didn't
know what the hell happened on that day. So someone
must have told him what happened. If he believes it's
true, he's mistaken. If not, he's lying."

There was a reluctant admiration in Karsh's smile.

"You make a good case, lieutenant. But isn't it true that your section never made any attempt to deliver that alcohol to a medical unit, or turn it over to your own supply sergeant?"

"Yes, sir, that's true."

"And isn't it true that Corporal Trankic employed his professional skills to convert that alcohol into a whiskey which your section used exclusively for its own consumption?"

"Yes, sir."

"Then isn't it understandable how you and Lieutenant Whitter could draw opposite conclusions from basically the same set of facts?"

Docker hesitated because he didn't know what Karsh was getting at, but he knew that the black whiskey wasn't the issue here; Karsh had to be laying the groundwork for something else. With no notion of what that could be, Docker shrugged and said, "Yes, I can see how that could happen, sir."

"Ultimately, of course, it might just be a matter of opinion. Would you agree with that, lieutenant?"

"I suppose I'd have to, sir."

"I'm not trying to direct or influence your answers, lieutenant. The very purpose of this board is to examine such differences of opinion, gray areas, so to speak, and to try to establish a consensus of truth."

Karsh removed his glasses and rubbed the bridge of his nose with his thumb and forefinger. "In regard to this black whiskey, lieutenant, you could be excused for thinking we're pounding a very small point into the ground. But there's a reason for it, as you'll see." Replacing his glasses, Karsh adjusted the frames and said, "Let's go back to December fifteenth, the night before the Germans launched their offensive. You were at D Battery's headquarters that night, lieutenant. Correct?"

"Yes, sir."

"Would you tell us why?"

"Three men in my gun section had been killed in a booby-trapped home in the town of Werpen, sir. I was at the battery CP to check their personal effects with a clerk from Graves Registration."

"Not very easy duty, I'm sure," Karsh said. "Now, after that business was taken care of, you went on to the battery's motor pool. Correct?"

"Yes, sir."

"Would you tell us what took place at the motor pool that night?"

Docker sensed a change in the attitude of Karsh and the other officers. They regarded him with a new intensity, a sharpened and more aggressive interest. Until this point, Docker had been unable to make out any pattern in their questions. The dusty olive grove still looked deceptively pleasant and inviting, but he was battle-smart enough to know that the questions about the black whiskey and filing the sears off their rifles had been a smoke screen for what was coming.

"We're waiting, lieutenant." Karsh's voice was quietly insistent.

"One of my men, Corporal Larkin, was there, sir. He'd been drinking and I thought he might be in trouble."

"Was Larkin's behavior normally a source of concern to you?"

"Not usually, sir. But when he was drinking, yes."

"Would you say Larkin had a drinking problem?"

"I don't know, sir."

"Would you describe him as a heavy drinker?"

"I think I'd have to, sir."

"Did you ever report Larkin's drinking to your officers?"

"No, sir."

"I see." Karsh made a note on his pad. "Tell me this, lieutenant: how would you describe your relationship with Corporal Larkin?"

Docker had told himself to keep a grip on his temper, but he realized now that would be difficult because these officers with their legal phrases and uniforms that smelled of soap and starch were inquiring into the lives of sweating, shat-upon men who couldn't defend themselves at hearings like these because they were lying dead in the mud and snow they had been told were fields of honor, *so to speak,* to borrow the major's bullshit phrase . . . He found it hard to channel his thoughts; it was the same feeling of disarray he'd experienced when they'd questioned him about Baird, because his sharpest memories of that youngster were of his outsized overcoat, the muddy boots with frozen laces, and the thin wrists burned raw with wind and sleet. And so what was the truth of Larkin, what did he remember about him . . . the cough you could hear night and day around the guns, the dark smudge of whiskers, the irreverent anger, the way he laughed when he checked and raised? Or was it in his bullying uncles, or the sick worry he felt about his job and his wife Agnes and the daughter he hadn't seen in two years? How could he sum up what else there had been (*"Describe* your relationship, lieutenant . . .") under the impersonal scrutiny of officers in a ballroom designed for string quartets and punch bowls full of wine and strawberries?

"Would you like Sergeant Corey to repeat the question, lieutenant?"

Docker let out his breath slowly. "I don't need my memory refreshed about Larkin, sir. He was a good soldier and a good friend."

"That's a generous answer, lieutenant." Opening a folder, Karsh said, "I will quote now from Corporal Haskell's statement. 'When Docker shot the lights out of that truck, I was scared as hell. There was no way to guess what he'd do next. With that gun and mad as he was, it was like he was out of his frigging head.' "

Karsh marked his place with the tip of a pencil. "Is that an accurate description of how you behaved that night, lieutenant?"

"No, sir, it's not."

"Then I'd be pleased to hear your version."

"Larkin was drunk," Docker said. "Haskell had fifty

pounds on him and was working him over. I told him to stop. I also told Haskell's mechanics to turn off the headlights of their trucks because they were violating blackout security."

"And when they didn't, you shot out those lights?"

"Yes, sir."

"Wouldn't you say that was a rather drastic overreaction?"

"I wouldn't argue the point, sir," Docker said, "but it got the job done."

Karsh looked at him, his fingers drumming on the table. Captain Walton leaned forward to say something, but Karsh checked him. "We won't digress now, captain." He studied the open folder. "I'll quote again from Haskell's statement, lieutenant. 'After he shot out the lights, Docker asked me how far I wanted to push this thing, how far I wanted to take it. I'd busted up Larkin, sure, because he'd called me things no white man would take. I got nothing to apologize for, but I'll admit the way Docker looked scared me. Maybe he wouldn't of used that gun, but plain, frigging common sense told me to back off. I ain't sorry I did just that.' "

Karsh looked inquiringly at Docker. "Would you care to comment on Corporal Haskell's testimony?"

"For the record, sir, I didn't threaten him with a gun. I holstered the forty-five before I asked him how far he wanted to take things."

"And that's your only comment?"

"Except, sir, that for a man with nothing to apologize for, I'd say Haskell's done a pretty damn good job of doing it."

The rictus flared on Karsh's face but no other emotion showed in his expression as he closed Haskell's folder. "We'll recess for ten minutes, gentlemen."

At Karsh's words, the MP corporal came to attention and opened the doors of the ballroom. Sergeant Corey glanced at her watch and recorded the time in her notebook.

"Lieutenant Docker, this information is from the statement Captain Travolta took from a Paul Bonnard." Captain Walton scanned an open file and absently stroked his wilted mustache. "According to Paul Bonnard, Corporal Larkin told you about the cellar full of liquor and foodstuffs at the castle near your gun position. Is that correct?"

"Yes, Larkin mentioned it to me, sir."

Walton settled back in his chair, the bright overhead lights coating his glasses, and Docker saw in his expression then, in the expectant complacency of his smile, the outline of the land mines hidden in those still-quiet olive groves.

"Why, lieutenant? Or more to the point, what did Corporal Larkin have in mind?"

Docker remembered the bitterly cold morning they had talked about it, the two of them close to the fire in the cave on Mont Reynard, the wind pounding the tarpaulin over the entrance and Larkin coughing painfully, his face smudged with dirt and creased with bitterness, jabbing a finger at him for emphasis and talking of his job at Railway Express and Hamlin's modest proposal to build decompression chambers for returning GIs. . . .

Walton was saying, "Did you understand my question, lieutenant?"

"Yes, sir. Larkin wanted to sell those supplies on the black market. He wanted to use one of our trucks to haul them to Liège."

"Let's get this straight . . . Corporal Larkin asked you for permission to use one of Section Eight's trucks. Is that right?"

"Yes, sir."

"And what did you tell him?"

"I told him to forget it, sir."

"Would you be more specific? You told him to forget about asking your permission? Or to forget about selling those supplies on the black market? Or what?"

"I told him to forget the whole business, sir."

"But since he obviously didn't, I'd like to know something else. What did Corporal Larkin offer you in return for the use of that truck?"

Docker saw that Walton's pencil was poised over his notebook, and that Weiffel and Major Karsh were watching him intently. Even Sergeant Corey was looking at him now, frowning slightly.

"What did he offer you, lieutenant?" Walton repeated.

"Larkin offered me half of his share."

"How much would that have amounted to?"

"I don't know, sir. I don't think he did either."

"You'll excuse me, but I find that difficult to believe," Walton said. "Are you telling us that Larkin was prepared to go AWOL from his gun section, prepared to commit a felony without any notion of what kind of money was involved?"

"His guess was the goods would bring something around eight or nine thousand dollars."

"You recall that now. Good. Did you inspect those German supplies, by the way?"

"No, sir."

"Then you can't tell us whether the corporal's figure was realistic or not." Walton studied his notes. "According to Paul Bonnard again, there was a black market operator involved in this deal, a Belgian named Gervais. Did you know him?"

"No, sir."

"So what we have is a three-way split between Larkin, Bonnard and Gervais." Walton looked up at Docker. "And the deal was that you'd get half of Corporal Larkin's share, right?"

"I've already told you—"

"You told us lots of things, lieutenant. Right now just answer my question. You were supposed to split with Corporal Larkin. Right?"

"I've testified he suggested that to me and that I told him to forget it."

Walton continued as if he hadn't heard this. "Let's

see what we're talking about in terms of dollars and cents. We'll accept Larkin's estimate for that purpose, make it an even nine thousand." The captain scratched figures on his legal pad, drew a line under them and jotted down the results of his calculations. A small smile appeared under his mustache. "A three-way split of nine thousand would give Larkin three thousand and you fifteen hundred. You want to check my arithmetic, lieutenant?"

"There's no need, captain. I'm sure you're qualified to divide three into nine."

Major Karsh said sharply, "In your interests, Lieutenant Docker, I will ask the recording secretary to strike that last remark."

Sergeant Corey nodded and drew a line across her notebook and initialed the margins.

Walton bent forward and wrote rapidly on his legal pad, his expression sullen. He didn't look up when he said, "You took no action against Corporal Larkin, lieutenant?"

"No, sir."

"Even though you knew he had entered into a criminal conspiracy with Paul Bonnard and a black market dealer? Even after he had offered you a bribe to take part in that conspiracy?"

"What the hell do you think I should have done, captain?"

Captain Walton's face flushed red and he threw his pencil on the table. "I'm not going to take any more of your insubordination, Docker." His voice was rising. "Under the Articles of War, you had not only the authority but the responsibility to put him under arrest."

"We were in a combat situation, we'd already suffered casualties. I needed every man I had on the guns. I couldn't spare Larkin and another soldier standing guard over him."

Major Karsh said quietly, "I'd like to interrupt for a moment. Lieutenant, when your section reestablished contact with your battery, did you tell Captain Grant about Corporal Larkin's deal with Bonnard and Gervais?"

"Yes, sir."

Karsh removed his glasses and began cleaning them with a handkerchief, obviously taking his time about it, and allowing the commonplace sights and sounds in the old ballroom, the shadows on the brocade walls, the stir of pencils and papers to ease the palpable tension between Docker and Walton.

Then he said, "Tell me, lieutenant, was Corporal Larkin usually involved in the black market?"

"No, sir. But like practically everyone, he traded cigarettes and chocolate for wine or brandy, things like that."

"Yet now he was getting in much deeper." Karsh held up his glasses to catch the light from one of the tall windows. "How do you account for that?"

"I can only make a guess, sir."

"And what would that be?"

"Larkin was worried about a job when he got home. He was married, had a young daughter and wanted a stake any way he could get it."

Karsh replaced his glasses and said casually, "By the way, lieutenant, did you mention to Captain Grant that Larkin offered you some fifteen hundred dollars to come in on this black market deal with him?"

The question caught Docker off guard—he knew from the way the officers were watching him that Karsh had meant it to. It was becoming increasingly apparent to him that nothing in the conduct of these hearings was casual or unpremeditated; the three officers had their lines and cues like actors on a stage, and Docker realized that he and the recording sergeant were the only players on the scene without scripts.

"The question was, did you mention Larkin's offer to your battery commander?"

"No, sir."

"Why not?"

"Because it didn't seem to make any difference, sir.

Larkin was dead and that was the end of it, I thought."

"I can see how you might think so. But as things stand, we have only your word that you were not an active and willing partner in Corporal Larkin's black market plans. Isn't that about the face of it, lieutenant?"

But before Docker could reply, the double doors were pushed open and the MP corporal called out in a parade-ground voice, "Atten-*shut!*"

A two-star general, accompanied by a bird colonel, entered the room, trench coats over their arms, rows of medals and theatre ribbons bright against the olive drab of their Ike jackets.

"At ease, gentlemen," the general said, and with a glance at Sergeant Corey, who was also standing, "you, too, young lady. Major, excuse the interruption. Colonel Rankin and I had a meeting with SHAEF's G-2 people, they're billeted here, so I thought we'd look in and see that everything's moving along smooth and fast. The operative word being 'fast,' major."

"We're making good progress, General Adamson."

"If it's not pressing you unduly, I'd like a firm date."

"We'll be through tomorrow night, I think, sir."

Docker studied General Adamson and Colonel Rankin, remembering that Karsh had said these two officers had the overview responsibility for First Army's board of inquiry. General Adamson was of middle height and years, thin and wiry with a pale complexion and eyes alert with humor and intelligence. Docker had heard colorful stories about Adamson from men who'd served under him: that he drank four inches of whiskey neat each night before bed and that he had once called Patton a fucking idiot to his face and that Patton had laughed and said if he had to be an idiot it was some consolation at least to be a fucking idiot.

Colonel Rankin was in his early forties, a head taller than the general, with the whalebone hips and stomach of a cavalry man, and gray eyes set so wide apart in his weather-rough face that his sweeping glances seemed instantly to embrace the whole room and everyone in it.

While the general conferred with Karsh, Colonel Rankin studied Docker with deliberate appraisal, then said, "I'm Colonel Rankin. I'm just as interested as the general in seeing a transcript."

"Yes, sir."

"Did you know that General Jonathan Baird was an instructor of mine at the Point?"

"I didn't, sir," Docker said.

"General Baird taught a review course in math and artillery." The colonel continued to assess Docker. "I knew the general's older son, the one who's in Italy now. But I never met his youngest boy, Jackson. They're a fine family."

General Adamson turned from Karsh and looked with interest at Docker's campaign ribbons. "You've been around a bit. Were you with my division in North Africa?"

"No, sir, I was with the First."

"Terry Allen, eh?" The general smiled. "Another damn good bunch. George, let's let these people get back to work."

The MP corporal presented arms, and when the senior officers were gone, the doors swinging shut on them, Karsh looked through the windows, where a fresh snowfall streaked the gloomy afternoon shadows.

He took off his glasses and rubbed his eyes. "I think everyone could use a cup of coffee. Shall we take a break for ten minutes?"

When the hearings resumed, Major Karsh settled himself in his chair and turned to Sergeant Corey. "Sergeant, would you please read the last exchanges between me and Lieutenant Docker?"

"Yes, sir." Using the tip of her eraser, the sergeant flipped back a page of the notebook and began reading. "Lieutenant Docker: 'Larkin was dead and that was the end of it, I thought.' Major Karsh: 'I can see how you might think so, but as things stand we have only your word that you were not an active and willing partner in

Corporal Larkin's black market plans. Isn't that about the face of it, lieutenant?' "

"Thank you, sergeant." Karsh looked at Docker. "Well, lieutenant?"

"As you say, sir, you have only my word for it."

"I don't think it's quite that simple." Karsh took another folder from his briefcase and opened it. "There are, unfortunately, these gray areas that tend to blur perspective. Here, for example, is another. In your deposition and Corporal Trankic's there's mention of a child—"

Adjusting his glasses, the major ran his pencil down a typewritten page. "Yes. Margret Gautier. Lieutenant, you took that child from her aunt's home in Lepont and delivered her to nuns at the Convent of the Sacred Heart." Karsh looked over his glasses at Docker. "Why, lieutenant?"

"We had learned that a German tank was heading toward the village. The child is Jewish. It made sense to get her out of there."

"The child's aunt"—Karsh checked his notes again—"Denise Francoeur, she agreed with that decision?"

"Yes, sir."

"Let's see if I've got the sequence right. Corporal Trankic learned from the Lepont transmitter that a German tank was coming your way. And told you that?"

"That's right, sir."

"And you in turn told the child's aunt?"

"Yes, sir."

"Now, this is important. Whose decision was it to take that child away from the village?"

"It was mine, sir."

"Not her aunt's, lieutenant?"

"No, sir."

"You were *that* convinced that the mission of this eighty-ton German tank was to track down and execute one nine-year-old child?"

Docker thought of the slight weight of the little girl in

his arms, an angel's head in a gutter and the jagged streak of cracks in the stone walls of the church.

"I'm not sure what I was convinced of, sir. I knew her father had been shot as a hostage and that her mother was Jewish."

"I'm sorry, lieutenant. I didn't get that," Sergeant Corey said.

Docker was surprised by the intensity in her expression, her eyes dark in her pale face.

"I said that the girl's father had been shot by the Germans and that her mother was Jewish."

"Well, I grant you had reason for concern," Karsh said, "but then you turned the child over to Corporal Larkin, is that right?"

"Yes, sir."

"Why, lieutenant? That is to say—why Corporal Larkin?"

"Because I thought he could handle the job, sir. He was the best driver we had."

Karsh underlined several words on his legal pad. "Lieutenant, what was it you told us Larkin wanted from you?"

Docker could see what was coming now as clearly as the events of a nightmare in slow motion. "He wanted the use of a truck, sir."

"More precisely, he wanted your permission to use a truck, correct?"

"Yes, sir."

"Lieutenant, you may have acted in accordance with your best instincts, but it's also true that you *did* provide Corporal Larkin with the one thing he needed to make his scheme work, the one thing he was prepared to pay dearly for, namely, your permission to use one of your section's trucks."

It seemed to Docker that there would be no point in adding futile words to the silence that stretched away through the cold ballroom, and isolated him in his memories.

"And the Convent of the Sacred Heart is situated on a road to Liège. Is that correct, lieutenant?"

"Yes, sir, that's correct."

Turning up his collar against the wind and snow flurries, Docker walked through the dark flower markets, where old men and women in shawls and bulky jackets stood beside counters that were stocked with assortments of pine boughs and small heaps of wizened tulip and hyacinth bulbs.

The blackout curtains had been pulled into place on the frosted windows of the shops, and the sidewalks were empty except for occasional British and American soldiers. He caught snatches of their talk as they went by him and heard the impatient horns of military trucks clogging the streets.

The hazy darkness of the city and the pinched look of the markets matched Docker's mood perfectly—he couldn't keep his thoughts away from Matt Larkin, nor stop examining the doubts Karsh had raised in his mind. There had been no time to sort them out at the hearings, with the questions coming more and more rapidly and Karsh abruptly turning the thrust of the investigation to his and Trankic's second interrogation ("interrogation" was now the major's word) of Baird, when they'd questioned him about the town of Peekskill and its landmarks and about West Point—where Karsh had interrupted him in mid-sentence saying, "Lieutenant, since you have testified that Baird's *first* account of himself was reasonable and straightforward, why did you decide a *second* interrogation was necessary?" Docker had almost lost the slippery grip on his temper then, trying to explain the fear and chaos created by Operation Greif. It wasn't helped when Walton added to the transcript, "for the record, that recent information indicates that Operation Greif did not exceed the normal scope of a *ruse de guerre*, and that its effect has probably been exaggerated by troops in the field . . ."

"Larkin and Lieutenant Longworth will be very

pleased to hear about that, sir," Docker had said, at
which point Major Karsh, with a pained expression, had
recessed the hearings with the comment that the board,
on reconvening, would examine what he considered to
be "the grayest area in the entire spectrum of these inquiries . . ."

Gray. Docker was beginning to buy that color, at
least as it applied to the after-the-fact issues of right and
wrong, of "morality," and thinking of the winds on the
castle hill, he remembered the German officer demanding his surrender who had said, "Most history is shaped
by the communiqués of victorious generals."

Still, Docker believed there were "facts" that couldn't
be dismissed by cynical distortion or by claiming that all
truths were merely relative, and he needed those facts
now as an anchor in the turbulence the hearings had
stirred up in him.

Fact: thousands of American soldiers had died in the
Ardennes campaign. Another fact: on December 26th
at 1700 hours, the siege of Bastogne had been broken
by General Patton's Fourth Armored Division. And
Sonny Laurel and Jackson Baird and Sam Gelnick had
died on Mont Reynard. Their deaths weren't a matter
of opinion, they didn't make up one of the major's eu-
phemistic little gray areas. And only hours after their
deaths gale-force winds swept the fogs and snows from
the Ardennes and Allied planes were flying from bases
in England and France to fill the skies above Germany
like tiny silver crosses . . .

A youngster came from an alley and ran along beside
him, grinning and pantomiming the action of puffing on
a cigarette. He was raggedly dressed, thin to the point
of emaciation, his teeth stained with neglect, but a survivor's hope flashed in his eyes, a last-chance smile
strained his young-old face.

"Please, GI," he said, panting to keep up with
Docker. "You got smoke for Benny, hey, GI?"

Docker stopped and took a pack of cigarettes from
his overcoat. He had about a dozen left, so he parceled

out six for the boy, who clutched them in a hand like a monkey's paw and ran off into the dark street, laughing and waving the cigarettes in triumph above his head.

And that boy still living and determined to go on living, that was no gray area. It was another fact, by God.

Chapter Thirty

February 14, 1945. Hotel Empire, Liège, Belgium. Wednesday, 1800 Hours.

"We will turn our attention at this time to the matter of Jackson Baird's alleged desertion," Major Karsh said when the hearings were resumed at six o'clock that evening.

"I propose to summarize certain events which occurred in your gun section, Lieutenant Docker, on Friday, December twenty-second from"—Karsh consulted his notes—"from approximately twelve noon, when your men first sighted the German tank, until about ten-thirty that night when, according to your testimony, Baird confessed to you that he had deserted his post under fire on December sixteenth, the first day of the Ardennes offensive."

The major unstrapped his watch and placed it on the table.

"Since we will be at this for some time, I think we might have some coffee. Sergeant, would you mind?"

Elspeth Corey poured coffee into thick china mugs, her movements fluid and economical, but when she glanced at Docker, half-smiling and making a tentative gesture with a cup, he shook his head.

Karsh thanked her and placed his cup on a blotter beside his briefcase. "Lieutenant, we'll start at the time Baird pointed his rifle at you and other members of your section. First. Did you think he was ready to use it?"

"No, sir, I didn't."

"Then you did not feel threatened by his actions?"

Docker hesitated. "No, I didn't think he'd fire. But that was only a guess."

"A guess based on what, lieutenant?"

"For one thing, sir, he never took his rifle off safe."

"Under the circumstances, I'd say that was pretty observant of you. So you obviously thought he was bluffing. Right?"

"Yes, sir."

Karsh picked up a file from the table and looked through it briefly.

"When you became aware of that German tank, the Tiger Mark II, you decided to pull your cannon and make a run for it. Baird told you that would be unwise. In your own deposition, lieutenant, you've explained his reasons very cogently. Since they're part of the record, I won't repeat them unless you want me to."

"There's no need for it, sir."

"But you didn't act on his proposals?"

"Not immediately, sir."

"And that's why Baird pointed his rifle at you? To make you listen to him?"

"I believe so, sir."

"To emphasize that point, I'm going to read a portion of Harlan Farrel's deposition." Karsh took another file from his briefcase and ran his finger down a page until he found the paragraph he was looking for, then said, "I'm quoting Private Harlan Farrel now. 'Baird begged Docker to listen. He said something like—*just let me finish* or *hear me out*—. Whatever it was, he just wanted to explain the problem. And I remember him saying to Docker—*then you can have the damn gun.'* "

Karsh looked at Docker. "Did Baird say that to you, lieutenant?"

"Yes, that's what he said, sir."

"Speculation is speculation, but I'd like to ask you a question, lieutenant. You don't have to answer if you don't care to. But in your judgment, what would have happened if you had ignored Baird's advice?"

"I've no objection to answering," Docker said. "If we'd tried to pull our cannon and get down that hill, the German tank would have had us in its sights in about sixty seconds. Some or all of us would have been killed."

The major nodded and there was something in his expression that puzzled Docker; it was neither complacency nor resignation, but he couldn't come any closer than that to defining it.

"I've no further questions at this time," Karsh said.

Lieutenant Weiffel and Captain Walton did. Walton wanted to know in detail how Trankic had subdued Baird, how often he had struck him, whether the blows had been to the boy's face or body, how much damage they had done. Weiffel, between sips of coffee, asked why it had been necessary to tie Baird's wrists behind him. He opened a folder and read an additional segment of Harlan Farrel's deposition into the record: " 'You can't blame Trankic for hitting Baird, he was mad as hell. But he's a powerhouse, he didn't have to lower the boom that way. Sonny Laurel came right out and said it to him. Sonny told Trankic right on the spot he didn't have to bust him up like that.' "

Captain Walton said, "Tell me this, lieutenant, when that tank fired into the side of the mountain and over your gun position, when shrapnel and rock fragments were exploding around you, was Baird lying helpless on the ground all that time, hands tied behind his back?"

"Yes, sir."

"What action did you take when the firing stopped?"

Fucking civilian, Docker thought, but he said, "I checked to see who was hurt. Then I told Chet Dormund and Sonny Laurel to untie Baird, put some sulfa on his cuts and get him under blankets."

"And didn't you also place him under arrest at that time, lieutenant?"

"Yes, sir."

"And detailed a man to stand guard over him?"

"Yes, sir. Private Farrel."

"Then I'd like to point out a contradiction in your testimony. You told us you couldn't arrest Corporal Larkin because you were short of men. Now you tell us you arrested Baird and in addition assigned a man to stand guard over him. How do you explain the inconsistency?"

Docker thought a moment, then said, "If you'd been there, captain, you wouldn't need an explanation."

"I've warned you once about your insolence, lieutenant."

"It wasn't my intention to be insolent, sir. But your line of questions forces me to be insultingly specific, just as I thought you were when you reminded me that my gun section's actions on Utah Beach took place during the Allied landings at Normandy. You may know that from reading about it in the newspapers, sir. We knew about it because we were there—"

"Now I've had just about as much as I'm going to take—"

Major Karsh broke in, "Lieutenant, you will answer the questions as briefly and responsively as possible."

"All right, I'll try to, sir," Docker said, but saying it realized that there was no way, no goddamn way to make them really see it, because how could he re-create the winds and the sounds of the cannon and the fear and pain around a damn conference table . . . ?

"There wasn't anything inconsistent about arresting Private Baird and not arresting Corporal Larkin," he said. "When I arrested Baird an eighty-ton German tank was sitting a few hundred yards below our gun position. In a firefight against those odds I didn't have the time or energy to worry about how a green, unstable soldier would handle himself. I'd rather be shorthanded than have to depend on anybody I wasn't sure of."

Karsh said, "Captain, I'd like to postpone this line of inquiry for a moment." He turned back to Docker. "Lieutenant, let's go directly now to your conversation with Jackson Baird on the night of December twenty-second. No one else was present at that time. Correct?"

"Yes, sir."

"It was then, according to your deposition, that Baird finally told you the truth. Told you his father was Major General Jonathan Baird and that he'd deserted his post under fire on the first day of the German offensive."

"Yes, that's what he told me, sir."

Karsh looked through several folders, frowning. "You've testified that on December seventeenth, the day Baird joined your section, you questioned him about his unit, how he'd been separated from it, and so forth. Then you and Corporal Trankic queried him again on related subjects on December twentieth. And on both occasions you testified that you believed his answers to be candid and credible. But here—the night of December twenty-second—after the boy had been through a dreadful ordeal, here you are hammering at him again." Karsh looked steadily at Docker. "Why were you so convinced he was lying to you?"

Docker wished that the "truth" of this matter was as tangible, as demonstrable as the broken ring of enemy troops around Bastogne and the squadrons of Allied planes in the skies above the Ardennes. All he could say was, "Because his stories didn't check out, sir."

"I might ask you *what* stories, lieutenant, since you haven't mentioned any so far that don't hang together pretty well. But I won't challenge that answer at this time."

For what seemed the thousandth time to Docker, Major Karsh removed his glasses and rubbed his forehead with the tips of his fingers. This time, though, in the glare of the light from the chandeliers, it seemed to Docker that the major's eyes had lost some of their coldness and intensity.

"According to strict rules of procedure it's not our business to make assumptions," the major said. "But let's assume for the moment that Baird told you the truth the first time you questioned him, lieutenant. And let's assume he told you the truth the *second* time. Now try to imagine that youngster's mental and emotional frame of mind. He had been through a terrible ordeal. He had been knocked unconscious by Corporal Trankic, left helpless and exposed during a bombardment." Karsh hadn't raised his voice, but now its tone had become harder and more insistent . . . "Yet after that harrowing experience, he still had to face a *third* grilling from you, lieutenant. Hasn't it occurred to you that Baird might have been so shaken by all this that he finally reversed his original story and told you the one he was convinced you *wanted* to hear?"

The question was unexpected and jarring in its implication. Docker hesitated, felt a stir of doubt as he thought back to that conversation with Baird, remembering not only the words but the cold wind tearing at the tarpaulin in front of the cave, the caked blood on the boy's lips, the bruises on his face and the anguish and pain in his voice when he talked of his father and those absent friends in the Hall of Gentlemen. And Docker wondered if Karsh had come on the real truth at last, an ultimate "true" truth. Could it possibly be that simple? That Baird had given up hoping to be believed, was so in need of acceptance, which he'd never gotten from his father . . . where he'd needed it most . . . that he'd lied because he thought that was what was *wanted* of him? And if that were the case, it made a joke of his own noble conviction about what Baird would have wanted . . . He remembered with bitter distress his moralistic tone to the major at the beginning of these hearings, tiresome banalities about men respecting courage because they'd lost it, talk from survivors about what the dead would truly want . . . wasn't that just a way of establishing black and white moral categories, damning this, praising the other, all stemming from—what had Karsh's phrase been?—opinions based on subjective evaluations? Had he simply been too goddamn righteous in this whole business, exercising the German colonel's last bequest, the arrogance of total conviction?

Maybe . . . and yet Docker still believed, though not so strongly now, that he had at least tried in these hearings to give Baird a last chance to explain himself to his father . . .

"I won't press you for an answer," Major Karsh said. "But I can assure you I would be most interested in whatever response you might care to make. Specifically, to repeat myself, do you think Baird was simply telling you what he thought you wanted to hear?"

Docker shook his head slowly. "I'm not sure, sir." His voice sounded muted in the drafty ballroom. "I can only give you my opinion, major—"

"Then let's have that."

"I felt the best thing Baird had going for him, the only thing, in fact, was to tell the truth. I thought he did. I still do, but I grant you I can't be absolutely certain—"

When a knock sounded abruptly, the mood in the ballroom was so intense that Sergeant Corey visibly started. The MP corporal swung open the doors, accepted an envelope from an elderly lobby attendant and delivered it to Major Karsh, who opened the envelope and read the note inside it, then strapped on his wristwatch and began collecting his notes and folders and putting them into his briefcase.

"Gentlemen, we will recess until ten o'clock tomorrow morning," he said, but as he closed his briefcase, another thought seemed to occur to him and he looked directly at Docker. "Lieutenant, I said at the start of these hearings that I'd conduct them as openly as possible. Therefore, I will tell you that I have just received a confirmation from Lieutenant Whitter that he will be available to give testimony when the hearings reconvene tomorrow morning."

There was mail at the Hotel Leopold for Docker, two
letters someone had brought to his room and left on the
bedside table. Since he had left Battery headquarters
that morning before mail call, Docker assumed Captain
Grant had sent them over to Liège with the supply
truck.

One of the letters was from Dave Hamlin, dated February 2nd. There was mention of his commission, and
of his father, who in Hamlin's words looked worn and
tired, and something about the German shepherd, Detroit, and coming down with dysentery. The other letter
was from Lepont, his name and address written in ink,
the script ruler-straight and graceful on the coarsely fi-
bered envelope.

He showered in a thin drizzle of water and shaved
before a mirror whose flecked surface reflected the
overhead lighting in erratic patterns. As his face
emerged with the strokes of the razor, he was puzzled
by the bitterness in his expression. Still, it seemed an
appropriate match to his cold eyes and the slivers of
gray at his temples, the gray he still wasn't used to . . .
it had come too soon, he hadn't been gone that long
from the walks through the campus and the talks with
Hamlin, the tubs of beer at beach parties and the noisy
rides to New York in old cars and the long empty Sunday afternoons with his father . . . Putting on a fresh
uniform, he tried to understand his depression. He uncapped his canteen and poured a splash of black whiskey into a glass and stared at his reflection, drinking
slowly, feeling a coldness at first and then small explosions of warmth in his stomach. He touched the gold
bars of his tunic and wondered what kind of soldier he
had really been through all these years, knowing there
would probably never be a "real" answer.

At the same café where he'd lunched, Docker now
settled at a table in the rear, as far as possible from the
GIs along the zinc-topped bar. He ordered a brandy
from a white-haired waiter with a towel draped over his

jacket. A radio tuned to the armed forces network was playing loud country music.

Docker drank the brandy, which tasted faintly of beets and made him think of the old man they had bought vegetables from a long time ago. He opened Denise Francoeur's letter while the brandy warmed him and the music drifted through layers of blue cigarette smoke.

Her note was brief, and Docker could imagine her pale face and black hair as he read it. The village was quiet again, she had written, the soldiers gone. She had walked into the woods on a mild afternoon and collected fresh green fir boughs and bunches of holly to put on the mantel and windowsills. The big dog—she didn't know his name—had run away from the Bonnards. Jocko had seen it at the river one evening and was keeping a watch for it. The boy from his section, Tex Farrel (she had spelled it "Tix"), had come back to Castle Rêve to see Felice Bonnard. The nuns would keep Margret until everything was safe. On sunny afternoons, the snow was melting in the low parts of the hills and the water was collecting in puddles along the river road—

The radio music stopped and the voice of an announcer sounded sharply, silencing the noisy laughter at the bar.

"We interrupt this program to bring you a special bulletin from Paris. In massive attacks over the past twenty-four hours, British and American bombers have dropped thousands of tons of bombs and incendiaries on the German city of Dresden. In one of the heaviest raids ever launched in the European Theatre of Operations, the city has been—according to eyewitness observers—almost completely demolished. Hundreds of fires are raging through the ruins and can be seen from fifty to a hundred miles by the crewmen of approaching aircraft. American Flying Fortresses and British Lancasters have been flying round-the-clock bombing mis-

sions over the ancient city, once called by Germans 'the
Paris of the north' . . ."

The old waiter asked Docker if he wanted another
brandy. Docker nodded, but he was hardly aware of the
noisy talk resuming at the bar, or the heavy cigarette
smoke mingling with the smell of damp boots and sour
wine.

He was thinking of the German, Karl Jaeger, the
thoughts merging with memories of Denise Francoeur.
He had seen her only twice after the clash with Karl
Jaeger's tank, one night in her home and again in the
square before the church where she had stood with
other villagers waving to the trucks and guns of Section
Eight as they wheeled through Lepont on their way west
to the bivouac area at Namur. She had told him of Jaeger's distraught behavior, the angel's head he had
smashed from the camouflaged wall and the photographs of his rosy blond daughters he had put on the
pillows of her bed . . .

"Fire storms have gutted most of the city. Bridges
have collapsed into the Elbe River. The population of
Dresden has swollen recently to more than one million,
every available building crowded by German refugees
from the east and an unknown number of American
and British prisoners of war. And because of these conditions, it is now estimated that the death toll in Dresden may exceed one hundred and fifty thousand persons—"

After an erratic burst of static, the country music
sounded again and the waiter asked Docker if he
wanted something to eat; he was going off duty presently but would be pleased to bring the lieutenant a
sandwich if he wanted it. Docker asked the old man for
another brandy.

He sat in the noisy bar trying to remember what Karl
Jaeger had said to him in the last minutes of his life on
the torn, rocky slope of Mont Reynard . . . "I give
you righteousness. Condemn me if you wish, but at least

I've lived by rules. By my rules, I have been a good soldier."

The village of Lepont and the rooms in her home were places where he had left part of himself, he knew, as he had left something in the other towns of the war, on the roads where there had been faces and weather to remember before they were swept away into the past beyond retrieving.

Still, Denise's letter had created a sense of a remembered permanence . . . the melting snow and the holly she had picked for the mantelpiece, he could see that with her eyes, and Jocko, bent and crooked, whistling in the dusk at the river's edge for their dog . . . and Tex Farrel walking up the castle road again to see the girl Sonny Laurel had loved there. . . . Docker had thought that when the hearings were over he would return to the battery by way of Lepont, but when he read the last paragraph of Denise's letter he knew he would never do that, and knew that the village of the Salm was one more place that was gone from him. She had written:

"My husband is alive. I have a letter from him. It may be a long time but he is free and will be coming home. As I look at these words, I must say to you I feel they are like the broken links of a circle and I am able to believe my life can be whole again . . ."

There were a few more words, the gentle and falling close to all such letters, and then her signature, the first letters clear and precise, the rest running into jagged scratches.

Chapter Thirty-One

February 15, 1945. Hotel Empire, Liège,
Belgium. Thursday, 1000 Hours.

A heavy-weather front moved toward Liège that night.
Dark clouds drifted over the city the following day and
the ballroom of the Empire Hotel was gloomy with
shadows, the light from the chandeliers shining palely
on the faded carpets.

Lieutenant Bart Whitter sat in a chair between Sergeant Corey's desk and the conference table, dressed for
his appearance at First Army's board of special inquiry
in a carefully pressed class-A uniform that included an
olive drab tunic with light tan trousers and polished
brown oxfords secured by leather straps.

In giving testimony Whitter frequently consulted a
small black notebook and, on occasion, spoke in pronounced southern accents, apparently in deference to
the major's oak leaves and the faded swank of the ballroom.

"Ah can assure the members of this inquiry I'm clear
on that point, crystal clear," he said, in answer to a
question from Captain Walton. "My orders to Docker
were to proceed due east with his gun section."

"Lieutenant Whitter, would you give us the time and
date of those orders," Karsh said.

"Yes, sir. I got that information in writing. It was
about six-fifteen A.M. on December thirteenth."

Walton said, "Did you always keep a written record of such orders?"

"When they were important, I surely did, captain. March orders to my gun sections, changes in Air Corps ID signals—things like that, they're all written down in the book. But if it was just a piffling matter, I didn't bother."

"I'd like you to identify that book for the record," Karsh said.

Whitter approached the conference table and gave the book to Walton, who flipped through it and said, "Sergeant, take this down. 'Lieutenant Whitter referred to a personal notebook in answering questions relating to orders he gave Lieutenant Docker on thirteen December. Said questions and answers are included in transcript. The notebook pages are numbered consecutively, contain handwritten notations of orders given by the lieutenant to gun sections covering the time from' "—Walton looked at the first and last pages of the notebook—" 'from the middle of September, 1944 through January of the following year. Notes are made in both pen and pencil. The notebook is a blue-covered Cerberus, number fifty-two.' "

"Lieutenant Docker, you heard Lieutenant Whitter's testimony," Karsh said. "Did he give you such orders?"

"Yes, sir."

"But after reaching the town of Werpen, isn't it a fact that you withdrew several thousand yards to the *west*?"

"Yes, sir."

"On whose orders?"

"Lieutenant Longworth's, sir, second-in-command of our platoon."

"Were his orders in writing?"

"No, sir."

"Did any of the men in your section hear Lieutenant Longworth give you those orders?"

"No, sir, they didn't."

"So it follows they can't confirm their existence."

"That's right, sir. Lieutenant Longworth and I were alone when he countermanded my original orders."

Major Karsh turned to Whitter. "Lieutenant, did Lieutenant Longworth advise you that he'd given Section Eight a change of orders?"

"No, sir, he did not."

"Did Lieutenant Longworth discuss the situation at Werpen with you in any way at all?"

"No, sir. But you got to understand, major, we were damned busy at Battery with them V-4 sightings to check out for Battalion and the Ninth Air Defense Command. But I can say this, major, I don't know nothin' about why Docker here went high-tailin' it out of Werpen, contrary to my orders."

Karsh turned to Docker. "Lieutenant, let's look at the facts. One, you didn't follow the orders Lieutenant Whitter gave you. Two, we have only your word that Lieutenant Longworth countermanded those orders. Three, Lieutenant Longworth is dead and can't confirm your story. Therefore—unless we accept your unsupported version of the incident—it would be difficult to blame anyone for concluding that you had retreated from a combat area without authorization. Would you disagree with that conclusion?"

"Am I restricted to a yes or no answer?"

"It seems to me a yes or no would be sufficient, but I'll allow you any leeway you feel necessary."

"Thank you, sir. Unless I'm mistaken, this line of questions is aimed at establishing a parallel between what I did at Werpen and what Jackson Baird told me he did on December sixteenth, the first day of the German offensive."

"For the record, I must state that you're making a not necessarily accurate evaluation of Lieutenant Whitter's testimony."

"Perhaps that's true, sir, but to be as objective as I can, I'd like to review what happened before we got to Werpen. And to do that, I need to ask Lieutenant Whitter a few questions."

Whitter jerked around as if he'd been jabbed with a cattle prod. "That's just like you, trying to drag me into it. I'm not on trial here, *you* are, Docker."

"Lieutenant Whitter, you will be in order," Karsh said.

"I'll answer any damn question he's got the guts to ask—"

"Lieutenant *Whitter*."

"You ain't dumpin' on me like you did Korbick, Docker, 'cause *I* got nothin' to hide."

Karsh banged his fist on the table. "Goddamn it, I will not tolerate—" He drew a deep breath and said, "Sergeant, strike the profanity. Lieutenant Whitter, *no* one is on trial here, and you *will* conduct yourself in a manner consistent with those silver bars on your shoulders. Is that clear?"

"It's crystal clear," Whitter said. "My daddy was a county sheriff in Alabama and I don't take a back seat to anybody far as respecting the law is concerned." Squaring his shoulders, he looked stonily at a point about two feet above Major Karsh's head.

"Lieutenant Docker, you may question Lieutenant Whitter, but I'll be the judge of the relevance of your line of inquiry. Understood?"

"Yes, sir."

Docker stood and walked to where Whitter sat stiffly in a straight-back wooden chair, fists braced on his knees.

"Lieutenant, the day you gave me those orders, do you remember telling my gun section anything else?"

"I might or might not, Docker. But if it's important, you can bet I've got it written down."

"Let me help you out," Docker said. "Do you remember telling my section they'd be starting home by Christmas? And that we had the Krauts in a meat grinder?"

"So what if I did? That was just my way of boosting morale, putting a little starch in their backbones."

"You remember I objected to it?"

"What if I do? . . . Okay, sure, you thought it would make them overconfident or some such damn fool thing. If that's what you want me to say, I'll say it. But it's a fact, if you had your men on the ball, a pat on the back from me wouldn't hurt 'em."

"You also gave us a fall-back position. Do you remember the name of the town?"

"You can bet I got it written down, Docker. The name of that place was Lepont."

"So you had quite a lot to say that morning, Whitter. You told us we'd be home for Christmas and like a Horace Greeley in rear gear, you kept saying, head east, head east, and at the same time you gave us a fall-back position to defend if we ran into enemy strength we couldn't handle—"

"That's right, make it sound like some Joe College joke. But the fact is, Docker, you didn't follow orders. You turned tail at Werpen before running into any Germans." Whitter's eyes narrowed, a small smile on his lips. "I see what you're after. Three of your men got killed in an empty town looking for souvenirs in a booby-trapped house like a bunch of recruits. Now you're trying to twist it around to look like it was my fault, because I got 'em relaxed and off guard, talking about getting home for Christmas."

Docker felt an involuntary stir of pity for Whitter, a man so paranoid he couldn't wait to put the nails in his own coffin. But this was no time for pity . . . he might be paranoid, but he was also a lying son of a bitch who was trying to destroy him.

"How did you know the town was empty?"

"What're you talking about?"

"I'm talking about how you knew the town of Werpen was empty when my section got there. You testified to that effect. Would you like the sergeant to refresh your memory?"

He glanced at Sergeant Corey, but to his surprise she was already flipping back through her notebook and before Karsh could direct her to repeat Whitter's testimony, she had begun reading: "Three of your men got killed in an empty town looking for souvenirs . . ."

She looked intently at Docker. "Is that enough, sir?"

He nodded, realizing that she had slightly accented the word "empty."

The major cleared his throat. "Young lady, you will wait for permission from an officer of this board to recap testimony. Is that clear?"

"I'm sorry, sir."

Docker turned to Whitter. "My question was, how did you know Werpen was empty?"

"How in hell you expect me to keep track of things like that?"

"You couldn't have known firsthand because you weren't there. I didn't tell you and no one else in my section had an opportunity to. And you've testified you didn't discuss the matter with Longworth. So who told you?"

"Well, maybe I heard somebody talking about it at the battery—"

"Then that had to be First Sergeant Miles Korbick. He was at Werpen driving Longworth's jeep."

Whitter looked suddenly relieved. He crossed his legs and smiled quickly at the officers of the board. "I'm sorry about wasting everybody's time with something that frankly don't make a doodly-do bit of difference. But it was Sergeant Korbick, all right."

"Did Korbick tell you about the meals left on the tables? And the pots that were still warm on the stoves?"

"Yeah, he mentioned that."

"So what action did you take?"

"What's that supposed to mean? I didn't take any action at all, Docker. I didn't have to."

"Why not?"

"What the hell you mean—why not? Docker, you got something on your mind, I wish you'd say it—"

"You knew my gun section was in an exposed and vulnerable position, didn't you?"

"I'm no mindreader, Docker. But if I did, you're for-

getting one little thing." Whitter's smile, embracing Sergeant Corey and the officers at the table, had become
more confident. "There was a shootin' war goin' on,
and lots of line troops were in exposed and vulnerable
situations—"

"But you're too smart a soldier not to know what we
were up against. Plain common sense would tell you
how many German troops would be needed to evacuate
a town like that, every man, woman and child pulled
out only a half hour or so before we got there. But
you've testified not that you *didn't* take any action, but
that you *didn't have to* take any action. Why, lieutenant? *Why* didn't you have to take any action?"

"Because you already had your orders, Docker, and
you damn well know it."

"Whose orders? Yours—or Longworth's?"

"It don't make no never-no-mind. You had all the
damn orders you needed—"

"I'm going to suggest *why* you didn't have to take
any action, lieutenant. Isn't it because you *knew* that
Lieutenant Longworth had already given my gun section new orders?"

"Now hold on, you're goin' just a mite too fast"—
Whitter uncrossed his legs, squirmed around in the
chair—"thing is, Docker, there's an understanding between officers. When I said Longworth didn't talk to
me about you pulling back that was another way of saying we didn't have to spell everything out in so many
words. You got to trust each other, trust the men under
you to figure out a situation and take care of it, so I
know Longworth was doing what's right even if he
doesn't tell me every little thing because he was gone
from the battery a lot with those V-4 sightings anyway
and I . . ."

Whitter lost the thread of his thought, but in searching for a connecting pattern he blundered onto another
tangent, saying, " . . . But you never believed we
were any good, did you, Docker? Thought we were all
layin' around the battery in our fart sacks, ninety-day

wonders . . ." He frowned at his hands. "It ain't easy, which is something people always forgot." Whitter's tone had become almost conversational, and the conversation could have been as much with himself as with Docker or anybody else in the room.

Major Karsh shifted his papers about, pausing now and then to make penciled notes on his legal pad. Finally he cleared his throat, looked at Weiffel and Captain Walton. "You gentlemen have any questions?"

Lieutenant Weiffel shook his head. "I have no questions," Walton said.

Whitter seemed puzzled by the silence in the room. He smiled at the officers and Sergeant Corey, rubbed his hands together and looked at Docker.

Karsh said, "Lieutenant Whitter, you're excused now. But before you leave, I'd like to express my thanks to you for appearing before this board."

"I appreciate that, major, but I don't expect any commendation for doing my plain duty. I learned that at my daddy's knee, and sometimes over it."

Whitter, Docker realized, wasn't aware of the dismissal in Karsh's tone and eyes; in fact, he seemed to have accepted the major's cool words as a generous tribute. His mood was once again expansive as he relaxed and presented the officers at the table with a friendly, conspiratorial smile.

"If you don't mind, I'd like to mention one other little incident I guess hasn't come to the attention of you gentlemen."

"Is it relevant to these hearings?" Karsh said.

"Well, sir, I think it is."

"Then let's have it, lieutenant."

"We had a mighty fine top kick in Battery D, major. Korbick, Miles Korbick. I'd like to tell you why he's no longer with the battery and who's responsible for it . . ."

As Whitter began to talk about that particular night at Battery headquarters, to tell it as he saw it, Docker remembered it as he saw it . . . the clerk from Graves

Registration (was his name Nessel?) fretting over Spinelli's missing poncho and hood, and Corporal Haskell
backing away and raising the empty hands he had
bloodied on Larkin, and Kohler dumping a helmetful of
waste over Korbick's head while the first sergeant sat in
his sudsy metal bath . . . and as Docker listened to
Whitter's voice rising with his conviction and indignation, it occurred to him again that one of war's most
upsetting—most dangerous—legacies was the confusion
forced on even tolerant men about where the truth,
where the reality of it was . . .

"Korbick worked his ankle off," Whitter was saying,
"trying to make a soldier out of a New York character,
a boy name of Sam Gelnick. But Docker always stood
up for Gelnick. Did his level best, level *worst* would be
more like it, to keep Korbick from making a man out of
him."

"If there's a point to all this," Karsh said, "I'd appreciate it if the lieutenant would—"

"There's a point to it, sir," Whitter said. "Naturally,
Docker's men took their cue from him. They made
jokes about Korbick, not to his face but behind his
back. And one night, sir, they took out their spite
against him in a way you wouldn't think white men
were capable of." He fixed a righteous stare on Docker.
"While he was sitting in the tin barrel he took baths in,
I hate to say this in front of the lady here, they dumped
a helmetful of latrine dirt over Sergeant Korbick's head.
Ruined a fine man's army career, turned him into the
kind of person you see and laugh at in some nuthouse.
And all that because he was putting the blocks to that
Jew-boy, Gelnick, trying to make it plain to him that
the things he got away with where he came from just
didn't sit right with the people running this man's
army . . ."

There was a mindless anger in Whitter's voice now, a
gleam of sweat like oil on his forehead. He paused to
take a deep breath but before he could say another

word Major Karsh removed his glasses and looked
evenly at him, the rictus smile back. And as Whitter
opened and closed his mouth soundlessly, once again
glancing nervously toward Docker, Karsh sighed,
dropped his pencil on the table and said, "The board
has expressed its appreciation for your earlier testimony, lieutenant."

He rapped gently on the table with his knuckles.
"We'll recess now, gentlemen, and reconvene at fourteen hundred hours."

The weather had turned colder. A feathery snow was
dissolving on the surface of the river. Docker sat on an
iron bench under bare poplar trees and looked through
the tracery of a bridge toward buildings that had been
battered into rubble by bombs and rockets.

He smoked a cigarette and thought of Gelnick, the
Hogman, with his squinting, suspicious eyes (and what
good reasons he had to be suspicious) and the flecks
and crumbs of food that frequently ringed his mustache,
and he thought of Gelnick's wife, Doris, whom he had
never met or even seen a picture of, and remembered
the way Larkin had described her, and the ache (intended or not, you couldn't tell with Larkin) there had
been in the words he had used. Not your all-American
cheerleader type, Larkin had said, little, almost thin,
but great legs and great black hair and brown eyes that
made you think she could be Spanish or something . . .
When he looked away from the river he saw Elspeth
Corey walking through a park on the opposite side of
the boulevard. He had an impulse to join her but hesitated because he felt it probably wouldn't be proper under the circumstances . . . A military convoy pulling
75-millimeter cannons rolled past, and when it was
gone, the big tires grinding solidly through the grime of
sleet and ice in the street, Docker saw no one in the
park, except two old women in black coats gathering
fallen twigs under the trees.

When Docker returned to the Hotel Empire an hour later, the double doors to the ballroom were open and the MP corporal was not at his post. Karsh was seated alone at the conference table, glancing through a sheaf of typewritten pages. There were no other papers on the table or on the desk that Sergeant Corey had been using. Everything else was gone, too—note pads, files, coffee cups and even the mason jars that had held sharpened pencils.

Major Karsh observed Docker's reactions and smiled. "Sit down, lieutenant," he said. "Have a cigarette, if you like. This is no longer the seat of First Army's special board of inquiry." The major glanced around and snapped his fingers. "Like that, the hearings are over and we have only a few last details to check out."

Docker took off his overcoat, folded it on Sergeant Corey's desk and sat down facing the major.

"You're surprised, I'm sure," Karsh said.

"In addition to that, I'm pretty damn curious."

"That's a normal reaction, but the explanation is simple. During our recess I telephoned Colonel Rankin. After we discussed the matter, he agreed with my recommendation to terminate the hearings."

"Then you and the colonel agreed on a verdict?"

"No, we didn't," Karsh said. He took a leather cigarette case and a Zippo lighter from a pocket of his tunic and put them on the table. "There is no verdict, lieutenant. No conclusions or recommendations, not even any educated guesses."

"Then can I ask you what the hell this charade was all about?"

"Of course, you can. But it was *no* charade. I can assure you this board of inquiry wasn't convened for trivial or ulterior reasons. We hoped to get the truth, or a good piece of the truth in regard to Private Jackson Baird. I've now decided that isn't possible. You and I could sit across this table exchanging questions and answers for"—Karsh paused to light a cigarette—"for another week or another month, but we still wouldn't be any closer to agreeing on the truth of these issues. It's like that black whiskey your gunner cooked up for Section Eight. Personally, I'd accept your version of what occurred at Utah Beach. But do you think you could convince Lieutenant Whitter of that?"

"I wouldn't bother—"

"Then you see my point."

"Yes, but I don't think you see mine, major. I wouldn't bother because it doesn't make a damn bit of difference one way or the other, that whiskey is no more important than the sears we filed off our rifles, or the helmet of crap dumped over Korbick's head. The important question from the start was whether or not Jackson Baird deserted his post under fire. And now you've called the hearings off because you say there's no answer to it."

Karsh frowned down at his Zippo lighter, which was decorated on each side with tiny replicas of the First Army shoulder patch—the letter A in black on a field of gray.

"It's a difficult question, lieutenant." He blew a fat smoke ring then, and broke its symmetry with a flick of his finger.

"However, I didn't say I couldn't answer it. What I suggested was that *we* probably couldn't find an answer we could agree on. If you want my opinion, based on the boy's bloodlines, I would say *no* to the question. The Baird family didn't put its name in the history books and on grave markers across the country's bloodiest battlefields by breeding cowards. But we're not talking about something as uncomplicated as studs and mares and bloodlines—"

"No, I presume we are still talking about your gray areas," Docker said.

"You can disparage that legal and moral no-man's-land if you want, but in all warfare, and that includes business and politics and every other form of human competition I know about, there are very few blacks and whites, Docker. Which is why the world needs judges and juries who can hear both sides of an argument and establish some ground rules for compromise."

Docker didn't entirely disagree, but wasn't sure he needed the lecture.

Major Karsh blew another smoke ring, seemed pleased by its completeness, and poked a finger through it. "Practically everything we touched on in these hearings had a couple of different shadings to it. We know the Baird youngster soldiered well in your section, and that he fought and died, not just honorably but even heroically. That's a series of events we can call facts. As for the rest of it . . . who's to say? Matter of fact, who's to say about your friend Larkin? . . ."

Larkin? What the hell, Docker thought. He suspected Karsh had been talking, at least partly, to justify himself for the way he'd grilled him. It had been pretty clear to him, after a while, that the hearing was designed to reach one conclusion—the exoneration of Baird— regardless of what he or anybody else said, and Karsh seemed to need to make this right—for himself as well as Docker. . . .

Karsh pointed the tip of his cigarette at Docker. "Yes, Larkin, lieutenant. He's somebody else who told you something incriminating about himself—I'm accepting for the moment what you said Baird told you. But take it a few steps further. You also said Larkin had never been involved in anything like blackmarketing. The Germans were on their way. You gave him a mission to take a little Jewish girl to a safe place. Who's to say he didn't change his mind about the black market goods, decide not to go through with it after, or maybe even before, he delivered that little girl? Are we supposed to take the word of Bonnard, a known dealer in contraband and probably a German collaborator? Maybe Larkin was no more guilty of what even you, his good friend, thought he was, than Baird. I'm willing to consider that possibility, are you? You wanted to know what this so-called charade was all about. A fair shake for a couple of good soldiers . . . that's what it was about . . . at least for me . . ."

That last was said mostly under his breath, but Docker caught it. He didn't buy any more than before that that was *all* there was behind it, but still, the underlying point was the same one that had occurred to him during the hearings, and it wouldn't go away. He picked up Karsh's cigarette lighter, watched the light gleaming on the square black *A* painted on its side. He put it down, looked at Karsh. "Major, could I have another look at the statement I gave to Captain Grant?" Docker suddenly felt very tired. "The one we decided to call File A, I believe."

"Of course," Karsh said. "I'll call Brabant Park and have a copy sent over by courier. May I ask why?"

"I'm not really sure. Can you understand that?"

"I think so. You want to be *very* sure. Isn't that it?"

Docker nodded slowly. "I remember the words Baird used, and how his voice sounded. I understood the words, but I'm not sure now that he did."

Karsh looked at him. "Do you want to make what you've just told me a part of the record, lieutenant?"

"Yes," Docker said. "If I can get it straight in my own mind."

"But why rip at yourself this way? I believe I know what you're thinking, and writing briefs is my line of country. Why not let me put your thoughts in an amendment to File A? And to adjust the transcript of the hearings? I could have both documents delivered to your hotel within a few hours. You just sign them and we'll put an end to this business." Karsh stood and came around the table. "Doesn't that make sense, lieutenant?"

Docker nodded because it did make sense, he thought, standing and pulling on his overcoat.

The major walked across the room with Docker, a hand resting lightly on his shoulder in a gesture of support and encouragement.

"I'm hosting a little party here at the hotel tonight," he said. "Some of General Adamson's people and a few local bureaucrats. Would you care to stop by after supper?"

"Thanks, but I'd better get back to my unit."

"Then I'll say good-bye to you here." Karsh smiled, not the rictus—this time—and took the cigarette lighter from his pocket. "I saw you looking at this. A driver in our motor pool makes them up for us. Would you care to have one as a souvenir of the hearings?"

"Thanks, but why not give it to Sergeant Corey? I noticed that she smokes."

Karsh nodded. "All right. I'll do that tonight. With the lieutenant's compliments."

They had stopped under the tall arch of the double doors. Docker turned and looked back into the ballroom, where the light from the windows and chandeliers caught sparks in the golden ceiling and fell softly across the old carpets and empty tables and chairs.

He stepped back a pace, gave Karsh a salute and went down to the lobby and out into the snow blowing through the streets.

Chapter Thirty-Two

February 15, 1945. Hotel Leopold, Liège,
Belgium. Thursday, 2200 Hours.

Buell Docker packed his gear that night after initialing
a revised transcript of the board of inquiry hearings and
an amendment to his original statement to Captain
Grant. When he finally signed both documents under
Lieutenant Weiffel's careful eye, he had assisted in the
transformation of Private Jackson Baird from a frightened recruit into a certified hero, the statement and
transcript now only stressing Baird's disregard for his
personal safety, his bravery under enemy fire, and the
fact that his death in the line of duty had been in the
highest traditions of the service and reflected credit on
his family, his country and the United States Army.
Baird's defection from his unit and subsequent attach-
ment to Gun Section Eight was explained, defended and
praised in a single sentence which, Docker thought,
mostly demonstrated the major's virtuoso forensic tech-
niques:

"In the confusion and disruption created by the massive German counterattack in the Ardennes, Private
Jackson Baird became separated from his unit, but dis-
played courage and resourcefulness in finding and at-
taching himself to a 40-millimeter gun section which
had been battered by the first waves of the enemy at-

tack and was retreating to regroup at a defendable position."

Well, Docker had thought as he signed the last of the papers, who was to say it wasn't at least "a defendable position"? . . .

Docker told the clerk at the desk to send someone to wake him at four in the morning. He put out clean linen and shaving gear and was mentally flipping a coin to decide whether or not to go out for a good-night bottle of beer when there was a knock on the door. He opened it and smiled when he saw Trankic's wide bulk in the doorway.

"Come the hell in. But if you want a drink, we'll have to go out."

"Then what're we hanging around here for?"

"There's a bar down the block with pretty good brandy. Let me get a coat."

They went down the stairs to the lobby and walked through heavy snow along a blacked-out street.

"What are you doing over here?"

"I brought some news for you, Bull."

"Anything wrong?"

"No, nothing's wrong."

"Who did you leave in charge of your section?"

"Well, Solvis and Farrel are looking after things, showing the new guys how everything works."

They pushed through the doors of a bar crowded with soldiers. The air was heavy and noisy with cigarette smoke and accordion music and bursts of talk and laughter. At a table in the rear, as far from the music as they could get, they ordered brandies and water.

Trankic wore a fatigue uniform and the rim of his helmet shaded his broad, weather-rough cheeks and worried eyes.

"So what is it?" Docker said.

"Blame that ginney Linari and that flannel-mouth Kohler if you want to blame anybody." Trankic took a worn and soiled envelope from his pocket and placed it on the table in front of Docker. "Dumb fuckers, they told Dormund he'd get his ass in a sling for not giving it to you after Baird got racked up."

Docker glanced at the envelope, which was addressed to him in block capitals.

"This is from Baird?"

Trankic nodded and sipped his brandy. "He wrote it the night before that tank hit us. Gave it to Dormund to give to you if anything happened to him. So naturally, Dormund forgot about it. I should have made him a new fucking head out of that tin can after all. Linari and Kohler found out he had it and got riding him about it. Told him he'd do time in Leavenworth, shit like that. He got so scared, he hid it in his duffel bag. Shorty finally told me about it and that's how I got hold of it. Just last night."

The waiter put two brandies on the table and stood watching them until Trankic gave him a hundred francs.

Docker opened the envelope and removed two sheets of ruled notebook paper, the kind Solvis used for his diaries. The overhead light was dim and obscured by the heavy layers of smoke. Docker turned the sheets of paper toward the bare bulb to make out Baird's cramped handwriting.

He drank the brandy, following it with a sip of water, but the liquor didn't reach the coldness in his stomach that had been gathering there since he had first glanced at the envelope with his name on it.

Jackson Baird's letter read:

"Dear Sergeant Docker:

I'm writing this without much light, the fire's about out. So if you have trouble reading it, you'll know why. I'll give it to Dormund when I'm through and if he gives it to you in the next few days, well—that's that.

I guess you knew from the beginning I was lying to you. I think Corporal Trankic did too. So it was a relief to talk to you tonight and finally tell you what happened. But I'd also like you to understand a little about why I lied. Maybe you can forgive me for that.

When I first saw German troops and heard artillery fire, it was like a nightmare. It was that kind of feeling, like something was coming for me and I couldn't move a hand or foot, couldn't even scream for help. Then I threw my rifle away and ran. The other guys in my company stayed at their posts. I've thought about them a lot, sergeant. In those first few days I thought I was the only soldier alive who was a coward. It was the loneliest feeling I ever had. The worst thing about it was that I felt it was so final, that there was nothing I could ever do to change it. And then you and the other men in the section helped me to settle down, to get hold of myself. And I began to pray to God I'd get another chance. I realized a person just can't be ashamed of being afraid, you've got to get over it. Farrel and Sonny Laurel talked with me about it, and I didn't feel so alone then. Kohler even told me to call him Shorty after a while.

But there was no room for weakness—no, that's not the right word. When I was growing up, there was no interest in weakness. To be afraid of things— that was for other people, not the Bairds. And there was no interest either in losing or coming in second. If I won something, that was fine. But it was only at times like that—for instance, I was pretty good with horses and I always got top grades—that I felt like I was part of things. If my mother had lived, it might have been different. Maybe for my father, too. But if anything happens to me, sergeant, the only way my life will have any meaning is if he knows about me and can accept it. The guys who didn't run deserve that. My father has got to live with what happened to me that first day, because I have. Then he should know I tried to get over it, tried to be a good soldier. That's why I'm writing this to you. I didn't know I could ever feel so sad. Maybe I'll never see him

*again. It seems to me I wanted very little in my life. I
still don't think I asked for too much. I'm going to
sign this now but I'm hoping you'll never read it. If
everything works out tonight, I think I'll be able to
speak for myself. But if it doesn't, I'd like to ask one
last favor, sergeant. Please, and this means something
to me that you may not understand, I want you to
make sure my father sees this letter. In some way, it
could help him too, when he thinks about me."*

The signature, which he had written in full—Private
Jackson Baird, United States Army—was close to the
bottom of the page, letters small and crowded together.

Docker gave the letter to Trankic and sipped his
drink.

His hands still trembled. Every word of the letter had
sent a chill through him.

"Christ!" Trankic said, and looked up at Docker.
"You know I *had* to hit him that time, Bull. You know
there was nothing else to do . . ."

"Sure, Trank . . . you got a place to stay tonight?"

Trankic glanced at the girls seated along the bar,
laughing with the soldiers. "I'll find someplace. Where
you going?"

Docker put Baird's letter in the pocket of his tunic.
"I've got to see a man."

"Want one for the road?"

"Rain check on that." Docker stood and pushed his
way through the crowded bar to the street.

In the lobby of the Empire he asked for Major
Karsh's room number, took an elevator to the sixth
floor and walked along a corridor whose decor had
once been grand, lofty ceilings with original gold and
silver wallpaper now faded and discolored, blending in
softly with the worn carpets and stiff brocade draperies.

He stopped at the number the desk clerk had given
him and knocked on the door.

Sergeant Elspeth Corey opened it. In the light from
an overhead fixture he saw that she wore makeup and

that her light hair was held back by a brown velvet ribbon. Noisy conversation sounded in the room behind her, and from the radio a chorus was singing, "Oh, What a Beautiful Morning."

"Is Major Karsh here?" he said.

"Yes, he is, lieutenant. Shall I tell him you're—"

"I'll find him," he said, and walked past her into the parlor of a suite furnished with worn velour chairs and sofas. The air was blue with cigarette smoke, sharp with the smell of gin and whiskey. A bar had been set up with card tables covered with a linen bed sheet. Several Belgian civilians were talking with Captain Walton and General Adamson's aide, Colonel Rankin. At the bay windows, blacked out by coarse navy sacking, Karsh and Lieutenant Weiffel stood beside two matronly ladies and a newspaperman with a correspondent's patch on the sleeve of his uniform. An enlisted man stood behind the bar with a towel over his shoulder.

Major Karsh turned from the group near the window and smiled when he saw Docker. He excused himself and crossed the room to join him, stopping to collect a fresh drink on the way and to exchange a nod with the civilians and Colonel Rankin.

"Well, I'm glad you've changed your mind, lieutenant," he said. "The bartender's name is Billy and what more does a thirsty guest need to know?"

"Thanks, but I don't want a drink, major."

Karsh looked closely at him. "What is it, Docker?"

"I'd like to talk to you alone, sir."

"About what, if I may ask?"

"The Baird transcript, sir."

Karsh glanced quickly, almost reflexively toward Colonel Rankin, and said casually, "I can't imagine there's anything more to say on that subject."

"Not true, sir. Is there someplace we can talk?"

The colonel joined them, a dark brown whiskey and water held loosely in his hand. He looked deliberately from Karsh to Docker, his wide-set eyes seeming to gather them together in one quick, appraising glance.

"Lieutenant, I've been pleased with your cooperation," Rankin said. "For a while I thought you were coming down with what we call 'the myopia of junior officers.' " Rankin rattled the ice in the glass. "Do you get my meaning?"

"I'm afraid not, sir."

"I mean the nearsightedness that afflicts troops too close to the action. They have their eyes fixed on the ground so hard that they seldom see the horizon, the larger picture . . . Billy, get me another one of these."

The barman gave the colonel a smiling nod and began pouring a fresh drink.

"Colonel, would you excuse us for a moment? We've got a couple of details to clear up," Karsh said.

The colonel took a full glass from the barman, turned back to Karsh.

"Nothing myopic, I hope, because if there is, I want to know about it. We've had our procedural differences in this matter and I've deferred to you so far." The colonel's eyes focused on the drink in his hand. "You've done a good job, Karsh. Keep it that way."

"I intend to, colonel." Karsh took Docker's arm and escorted him past the Belgian civilians into an adjacent bedroom where, after snapping on the lights, he closed the door with a decisive gesture and looked coldly at Docker.

"All right, what's on your mind, lieutenant?"

"The transcript isn't complete yet," Docker said. "It doesn't speak for Jackson Baird. That's what we've got to talk about, major."

"We don't have to talk about one goddamn thing. We've talked enough, too much." Karsh's voice was tight with exasperation. "And by God you had better understand this . . . the final transcript of those hearings—repeat, *final*, complete with decorative sealing wax and appropriate endorsements and signatures, including *yours*, lieutenant—is on a plane this very moment for SHAEF in Paris, and from there it will go by special courier to General Jonathan Baird at Mac-

Arthur's headquarters at Leyte. And nobody is going to change one sentence, word or comma in that transcript, now or at any time in the future. Do I make myself clear, Docker?"

"I think you'd better read this," Docker said, and handed him Jackson Baird's letter.

Karsh's eyes swept across the page like guns tracking enemy positions. When he finished reading, he walked around the room in an aimless circle, pausing occasionally to press his fingers tightly against his temples. Finally he stopped and started at the letter again, frowning and shaking his head slowly, as if not quite able to believe what was in front of his eyes.

"All right, I've read it," he said, and looked grimly at Docker. "Are you familiar with Jackson Baird's handwriting?"

"Yes, sir. I've seen it before. He wrote a detailed memo on the defense of our position on Mont Reynard—"

Karsh cut him off. "All right, all right. You're sure this is his handwriting?"

"Yes, sir, I am."

"Then supposing you tell me just what you expect me to do with this letter."

For an instant Docker didn't understand what Karsh meant; the literal sense was clear, but he was puzzled by the tone of dismissal, a sarcasm in Karsh's voice.

"I should think that's pretty obvious."

"If it were obvious, I wouldn't have asked the question."

"Then you're either making a debater's point, major, or you're pretty stupid—"

"Now watch yourself, Docker. We aren't a pair of hack drivers exchanging dim-witted philosophies in a Third Avenue bar. You're a buck lieutenant and I'm a major, and I would strongly advise you not to forget that—"

"I expect you'd also like me to forget those gray areas we discussed, *major*. Or do you even remember them now? We aren't talking about a matter of opinion, or a matter of viewpoint. What you're holding in your hands now is the truth. So why do you need *me* to tell you what to do with it?"

Karsh pointed a finger at him. "I'm warning you for the last time, Docker, I won't tolerate—"

The door opened and Captain Walton looked into the room, making quick, silencing gestures with his hands. "Major, the colonel suggests you gentlemen tone it down."

"Yes, right . . . tell the colonel there's nothing to worry about, we'll be through shortly."

When Walton closed the door, Karsh's attitude changed abruptly. He sighed and sat down heavily on the arm of an overstuffed chair, his hands hanging at his sides. "I'm sorry, Docker," he said. "I'm not Army, for Christ's sake, I'm civilian with a law degree from Columbia who was writing briefs for labor unions until he got salutations a few years back from his draft board. An officer and gentleman by an act of Congress."

He sighed again, wearily, and stared at Baird's letter. "Where in hell did you get this?"

After Docker explained, Karsh stood and paced the floor again, finally said quietly but intently, "I want you to listen to me, Docker, and I advise you to listen carefully, although you're a smart man and may already have gotten the idea, but here it is from the horse's mouth . . . there was only one conclusion, one acceptable judgment from the board of inquiry convened to investigate the matters relating to Private Jackson Baird. Your original statement to Captain Grant— never mind your good motives—started the wheels turning, you must know that. The report went up to First Army, then to Corps and Group and SHAEF and on its way it was read by many high-ranking officers who were classmates or close personal friends of Major General Jonathan Baird. Your report then went to General Baird himself, and he demanded an investigation into the circumstances of his boy's death. Not a white-

wash, Docker, an investigation. But the *a priori* deter-
mination of those same personal friends and classmates
was that extenuating circumstances must have contributed to Jackson Baird's alleged desertion under fire,
and it was agreed that the function of the board was to
discover those circumstances, and it was further agreed
that whatever other facts were developed would be irrelevant to the primary mission of the board."

"Are you telling me that Baird's letter is irrelevant?"

"Goddamn it, *listen* to me. I tried as forcefully as I
knew how, Docker, to dramatize all those extenuating
circumstances." There was an entreaty in Karsh's voice
then, a clear appeal for understanding, which had begun
in that earlier unofficial discussion after the hearing.
"I'm talking about the boy's emotional condition, the
physical battering he received, the other gray areas you
now seem to think have turned to black or white. I attempted to draw parallels between Larkin's black market deals, the sears you filed from your rifles, even your
goddamned black whiskey, trying my damndest to make
you see the ambiguities of those situations, hoping to
God you would understand that no man should try to
function as a judge when the judicial arena is a battlefield . . . I gave you the opportunity to exonerate
your friend Larkin, *and* Jackson Baird, without any
mental reservations. And, damn it, that's exactly what
you did, Docker."

"I know what I did, and I think I know why I did it,"
Docker said. "But I'd like to hear what your reasons
were, major."

Karsh sat down again on the arm of a chair, put a
cigarette in his mouth but didn't light it. He looked at
Baird's letter and smoothed its surface with his fingertips. "I can give you several explanations for what I
did," he said quietly. "They range from cynicism to
plain self-interest to what you could call a vague ideal-
ism. First, I *wanted* to find that boy as pure and innocent as driven snow, Docker. When those hearings were
over, I hoped to announce with full judicial authority

that Jackson Baird was an authentic American hero and
patriot, because"—his smile flared—"because . . .
maybe it sounds corny . . . they were all heroes to me,
Docker. Whether they sacked oats in Fort Riley or
pushed a pencil in a supply depot five thousand miles
from the front. Do I have to tell you that *anybody* wearing the uniform that went up against the Nazis was special to me? . . . And secondly, since the case of Jackson Baird was so threaded with contradictions and
question marks, I saw no purpose in returning findings
that would only do a disservice to the discipline and
morale of the whole Army. And third, I knew there was
only one acceptable judgment, and trying to be a good
soldier, I went out and got it."

"Your last point makes sense, I think the rest is a lot
of bullshit, major—"

"Damn it, Docker, I won't—"

"You're forgetting that Sam Gelnick was also one of
your special people who wore the uniform that went up
against the Nazis. Yet you let that asshole Whitter characterize him without reprimand as an incompetent Jew-
boy, and you didn't back away from the rest of Whitter's garbage until I proved he was lying. So just how
far were you and Rankin prepared to go to get the verdict you think General Baird and his friends wanted?"

"If all that makes you feel better, fine," Karsh said.
"Frankly, I don't know what the final tab might have
come to. Just be grateful you didn't have to pay it."

"It may come to that yet."

Karsh looked at him sharply. "I've told you as flat-
out as I can that this business is over, Docker. As a
lawyer and as a man who knows how this system works,
I'd advise you to accept that."

The door opened and Colonel Rankin walked into
the room. "Now just what the hell's going on in here?
That correspondent from London, his ears are coming
up to a point."

"I'm sorry, sir." Karsh hesitated, then let out his

breath slowly. "The lieutenant has reservations about the Baird transcript."

The colonel closed the door and looked with a puzzled smile at Karsh and Docker. "I just plain don't understand this," he said. "But I'd like you gentlemen to satisfy my curiosity on the double. Your board of inquiry, major, has fulfilled its function. As of about fourteen hundred hours today, it closed down shop. The areas you investigated are no longer subject to discussion. So what's all this piss, shit and corruption about reservations, lieutenant?"

"Colonel, I received a letter only an hour or so ago written by Baird the night before he was killed. I think you should read it, sir."

Rankin put his half-empty glass on a chest of drawers. "All right, where the hell is it?"

He accepted the pages from Karsh and read through them quickly, a frown darkening his blunt, flushed features. Then he read them again, but more slowly this time, and when he'd finished he looked directly at Docker and crumpled both pages in his big hands and tossed them in the direction of a frayed leather wastebasket.

"That won't do it, sir," Docker said.

"I'll tell you something, soldier," Colonel Rankin said. "Don't ever use that tone to me again or you'll fucking well regret it. Now I'll tell you what *I* think. There's no date on that letter so we don't know *when* it was written. Lots of it's smeared and smudged, so we don't know for sure *who* wrote it. So that's the end of this business, gentlemen. I don't want to hear another word about it."

"Sir, don't you think General Baird should make that decision?" Docker said.

Rankin stared at him. "Jesus, boy, you are a dummy. I respect your combat record, lieutenant, and because of that and *only* because of that, I'll overlook that last remark. But you'll return to your unit immediately. And that's an order."

Docker looked around the room, feeling for an instant a strange loss of orientation, even identity. It wasn't an alarming sensation, it was a rather comfortable one, in fact, because it seemed to place him at a safe remove from Rankin's authority . . . He saw that Baird's balled-up letter had struck the side of the wastebasket and lay on the rug beside it. He went over and picked it up, smoothed out the pages. The look of Baird's handwriting reminded him acutely of the night of the attack and the overwhelming noise the German tank had made coming up the hill to their position . . .

Colonel Rankin and Karsh watched him expectantly. The moment had a certain finality about it, Docker knew.

"I've got just one question, colonel," he said, and heard with some surprise the deceptive mildness in his voice. "How far do you want to take this, sir?"

"Docker, you're buying yourself a whole shithouse full of trouble."

"Maybe. But that doesn't answer my question, sir."

"I don't intend to answer your question." Colonel Rankin's face was as red as a fresh burn. "What I will do, soldier, is nail your ass to the floor for insubordination."

Karsh cleared his throat. "Sir, I think we might consider the fact that Lieutenant Docker has been under a severe emotional strain—"

"Goddamn it, Karsh, keep your mouth shut until I ask you to open it. Is that clear?"

"Yes, sir, that's very clear."

"Good. I'm pleased to find there's some courtesy and discipline left in this man's army, although I'm not optimistic about finding any efficiency and competence to go along with it." Rankin turned to the chest of drawers, picked up his drink and took a long pull, then stared at Docker and Karsh, once again, apparently in control of his temper and emotions.

"I'll tell you something, Docker. You're not Army. And neither is Sid Karsh here. You're just a pair of goddamn civilians we lent some uniforms to. When the war's over, you pack 'em away in mothballs, air 'em out for Armistice Day or a Legion convention. That's all the army means to you. But it's not your life." There was a raw, honest anger in the colonel's words, though the only physical manifestation of his feelings was the white of his knuckles against the weathered tan of his clenched fists . . . "We shot a man in Paris two weeks ago for desertion," he went on. "A private soldier name of Slovik. But mark this, and mark it well, he's the first soldier court-martialed and executed for that offense since the goddamn Civil War. But in the Baird matter I find officers bandying that charge around as if it's no more significant than a recruit throwing a cigarette butt on a parade ground."

The colonel finished his drink and put the glass down so hard that a piece of ice bounced out and rolled across the top of the chest of drawers. "Well, I've got some news for you gentlemen. When this war is over and done with, when you're back getting tanked-up on Saturday nights at your country clubs and telling everybody how you won the damn thing, when the time comes, there will still be an Army of the United States standing ready to defend America in any part of the world it's called on to, and *that* army doesn't need help from any Lieutenant Dockers or Sid Karshes . . . And I'll tell you one last thing. This army isn't going to let either one of you soil its reputation or the good name of the officers who care about its principles in war and in peace, not just your damn summer soldiers but winter soldiers too . . ." He jabbed a finger at Karsh. "You told me you could wrap up the inquiry your way, and I let you try, although I had a feeling in my goddamn gut we should prepare a transcript of what we wanted and call the witnesses to attention and order them to sign the goddamn thing."

"I'd like to point out, sir," Karsh said, "that when we discussed procedure none of us knew about this letter from Jackson Baird."

Rankin looked steadily at Karsh. "What letter are you talking about, major?"

There were always two separate wars going on, Docker thought. He preferred the one with guns . . . "This is the letter Major Karsh referred to, sir." Docker folded the two pages of Baird's letter and put them in the breast pocket of his tunic. "I think General Adamson might want to see it. If not, I'll try General Middleton and General Bradley. And if that doesn't do the job, I might interest that newsman outside drinking your whiskey."

"Major Karsh, you're a witness to every goddamn word of this," Rankin said. "Now you want to know how far *I'll* take it, Docker? Just as far as it takes to lock your wise ass away in a military stockade for about twenty years."

Docker opened the door that divided the suite and saw that the group in the living room was staring at him and Colonel Rankin. He said quietly, "With respect, sir, I believe my orders from Major Karsh take precedence here. He told me that my job and the responsibility of First Army's board was to get the truth. I've been following those orders to the best of my ability. I intend to continue following them, sir. I also don't give one damn about these gold bars or a court-martial, colonel, if that's where you want to take it."

Docker came to attention then, snapped a salute at Karsh and Colonel Rankin and walked out of the room.

"Goddamn it, soldier, you leave this hotel, you're under arrest," Rankin shouted after him.

Docker crossed the slippery brick driveway outside the Hotel Empire and turned into the street where his jeep was parked behind a row of American command cars.

He felt nothing at all, and was grateful for that; for the relief from the insistent pain he'd felt when he'd looked at Baird's cramped handwriting. Someone called his name, the voice light on the churning winds, and he turned and saw Elspeth Corey running toward him on the snow-packed sidewalk. She wasn't wearing an over-coat and when she stopped she hugged her elbows tightly against the gale pounding through the narrow street.

"The major told me to ask you to wait for him," she said.

"You'd better get back inside."

"Will you wait for him?"

"Did he say why?"

She shook her head. "The colonel is phoning for the MPs. Major Karsh asked me to try to catch up with you and tell you to wait for him."

"I don't see any point in that."

A few strands of hair heavy with snow fell across her forehead. She pushed them away. "Do you always have to be so stubborn?"

Docker glanced past her and saw Karsh turning into the street from the driveway of the hotel. He was strug-gling to thrust his arms into his overcoat, but the wind had caught the tails and sleeves of the garment and the erratic flappings sent dim shadows leaping ahead of him on the sidewalk.

When he joined them, Docker saw the tension in his eyes. "I'll take you to General Adamson," he said. "I can get you in to see him, but you'd better be damned sure what you want to say."

Docker got behind the wheel of his jeep. "Get in, ma-jor."

He stepped on the starter and said to the girl, "Thanks, sergeant. Now for Christ's sake get back to the hotel."

However, when he accelerated past the curved drive-way, he checked the rear vision mirror and saw that she was still standing there looking after them, arms tightly hugging her body.

Chapter Thirty-Three

February 16, 1945. Brabant Hall, Liège,
Belgium. Friday, 0100 Hours.

General Adamson asked Major Karsh to wait in the
anteroom of his office, a converted drawing room in
one of the châteaus at Brabant Park. The general sat
on a divan facing a marble fireplace topped by a dark
wooden mantelpiece that held an ormolu clock and
clusters of diminutive jade animals arranged among
fronds of fir branches.

He adjusted his reading glasses and examined the envelope that Jackson Baird had addressed to Buell
Docker. After studying the grain of the paper and
Baird's handwriting, he lifted the flap and removed the
two sheets of ruled paper. "Lieutenant, there's coffee on
my desk. Also some brandy. Now let's see what we've
got here." The general began reading Baird's letter.

Docker poured himself a canteen cup of coffee.
There had been an interval of cold tension when they
first arrived. Colonel Rankin's telephone call had pre-
ceded them by several minutes, and it was only after
Docker, at the general's insistence, had repeated his
story a second and a third time that General Adamson
waved Karsh from the office and agreed to read Baird's
letter.

Sipping the strong black coffee, Docker glanced
around the large room, which was hung with faded tap-

estries and furnished with a clutter of civilian and military effects. Overstuffed furniture, hunting prints, portraits topped by gallery lights shared space with flag-dotted situation maps, field telephones, a short wave radio transmitter and the general's carbine and gas mask.

When General Adamson finished reading Baird's letter, and after checking the blank sides of the pages to make sure he had missed nothing, he stood up and paced in front of the fire. Finally he said, "Well, lieutenant, if all my decisions were this simple, I could probably log four to six hours sleep every night." He turned and walked to a situation map that was propped up on a tripod in front of a wall of books.

"I was pretty damn good at running a division," he said, and nothing in his tone or manner marked the transition. "That's pretty much like riding a horse—one source of power, one target to aim it at. But a corps—that's like riding two horses, with one foot on each of their backs. Up at Army and Group you need to be a politician more than anything else. You've got to pussy-foot around the government-in-exile people, stand back and let de Gaulle go first up that big street to liberate Paris, make sure the VIPs have comfortable quarters and a safe look at the action. Imagine an army commander destroying a town like Lourdes because it was the best and quickest way to save lives. They'd crucify him for it. Lieutenant, the closer I get to that kind of decision, the less I feel like a soldier. Take Dresden . . ."

Docker heard a new tone in the general's voice, a bitterness as his eyes moved across the flags on the situation maps, gaudy little pennants signaling death and victory.

Docker carefully put the canteen cup on a desk and stood watching General Adamson, but his thoughts had turned to the German officer who had died on Mont Reynard . . .

"There wasn't any military reason to hit Dresden,"

the general was saying. "No industry there, no depots, no troops, no logistical significance. But we killed about one hundred and thirty thousand people in twenty-four hours, old men and women and children, and do you know why, lieutenant? We killed those people because Uncle Joe Stalin told us to. He chewed the ass out of Churchill and Roosevelt at Yalta because of the way we fell apart in that German counteroffensive in the Ardennes. And so to shut him up Churchill turned Bomber Harris loose and, of course, we had to go along with him. Ike was against it all along. Vaporizing those civilian cities wasn't warfare, he said. It was just terrorism, and Ike wanted no part of it. Hell, it was a holiday in Dresden when our raids began, some kind of religious celebration that tied in with Lent. The children were in the streets in carnival costumes when the bombers came over . . . Maybe every soldier's got just one good war in him. If that's true, I'm glad this one's about over."

"Do you believe that, sir? That it's about over?"

"Well, I hope so. Take a look." The general pointed to the map. "The Russians are ready to strike on a line stretching seven hundred and fifty miles from East Prussia into Poland and clear down to the northern frontiers of Hungary. They've got fifty artillery divisions and about five *hundred* infantry divisions out there. Five million soldiers ready to pull the noose tight. We've beaten Hitler and the Nazis, something thirteen countries in Europe couldn't do. MacArthur will be having his uniforms made in Tokyo within a few months. What happens then, God only knows. So let's take care of a *simple* problem, lieutenant." He picked up a telephone. "Corporal, put me through to Colonel Rankin."

The general sat on the edge of his desk to wait for the connection, but his eyes stayed fixed on the situation map. "But you can count on this, lieutenant, the Germans won't surrender. They'll fight until every building in Berlin falls down on their heads. I read this somewhere, I don't know which of them said it, Goebbels or maybe Goering, but one of them said that when the Nazis left the scene of history they'd slam the door on themselves so hard the rest of the world would hear the echo for a thousand years. I think I believe that . . ."

The general straightened and spoke into the mouthpiece. "Yes, I'm waiting for Colonel Rankin." Then: "George, I'm sending a driver to the hotel with Private Jackson Baird's letter. The driver will also have a personal note from me to his father. I want you to put a hold on that transcript that's on its way to SHAEF. You will send the original transcript in its place by tomorrow morning's courier plane, with the two letters I've mentioned—mine and young Baird's."

Adamson listened for a moment or so then, nodding occasionally and glancing at Docker. Then he said, "George, I understand your concern. And I appreciate your opinion. But I don't intend to pursue the matter. So we'll consider it settled. Now there's one other thing you can do for me. I'm going to write a supporting recommendation for young Baird's decoration. But I'd like you to put it into good, clear English for me. Will you do that? Fine."

The general replaced the receiver, walked to the fireplace and stood with his back to it. "You see, lieutenant, that was a real simple decision. Simpler for me than Colonel Rankin because General Baird is a friend of mine. We were classmates at the Point. Rankin's like a guard dog. He wants to protect us. And maybe that kind of loyalty serves a useful function. But I believe General Baird would prefer the truth to anything else. He asked courage from his sons. He wouldn't want us to ask anything less of him."

Adamson's mood changed now. "But we're still soldiers, lieutenant, and there's still a war on, so I think you'd better get started back to your outfit."

"Yes, sir. And thank you, sir."

Docker saluted and joined Major Karsh for the ride back through the snowy countryside to Liège.

They drove back to the city on roads flanked at intervals by First Army sentries. It was two o'clock in the morning and bitterly cold, winds from the stubbled fields and frozen ground twisting and gusting inside the jeep.

They didn't speak until the dark outlines of Liège loomed ahead of them. "How come, major?" Docker said then. "Did we finally run out of gray areas?"

Karsh lit a cigarette and put the box of GI matches back in his pocket. Settling himself deeper in the hard canvas seats, he fastened the top button on his overcoat and looked out at the spray of ice frothing up from the wheels of the jeep. When he finally turned to speak to Docker, his faint smile was reflected in the slick icy windshield. "No, it wasn't any shortage of gray areas, Docker. At any rate, I don't think so. Maybe I realized I would have to live with myself as a civilian longer than I would as a soldier. Or maybe it's what you said about Gelnick. Or a combination of things." He sounded tired then. "But who knows, Docker? Not even my mother calls me Sid."

Karsh flipped his cigarette from the jeep, and when it struck the ground, tiny sparks flared in the darkness behind them.

At five-fifteen the following morning, Docker came downstairs from his room in the Hotel Leopold. The lobby was cold and dimly lit and two old men in heavy sweaters were sweeping the marble floors.

Sergeant Trankic got up from a sofa and came to meet him. His helmet was pulled down over his forehead and a cigarette slanted up from his mouth. "I found a mess open, Bull. I got coffee and some fried eggs on bread. They're in the jeep. Want to eat here or on the road?"

"Let's hit it," Docker said.

They drove through the city with Docker at the wheel, the jeep moving slowly in a column of heavy trucks. As they approached the river, Docker swung off the road and slowed near the courtyard of the Hotel Empire, where several ancient civilian cars were parked in the drive near the doorman's empty kiosk.

Docker knew the look of this place would always be with him, like the fields and towns of the war, one more place where a piece of him would remain when he set out on the last road home. He felt like he had won some kind of victory for Jackson Baird here, and maybe for all of them, and now he could leave that young man in peace, linked with the memories of the other men whose lives, and deaths, had formed a brotherhood on the peaks of Mont Reynard.

"What are we stopping for?"

"We're not," Docker said.

He turned back into the traffic and soon they were winding through the foothills that led from the city into the forests of the Ardennes.

Chapter Thirty-Four

May 8, 1945. Near Ludendorff Bridge on
the Rhine. Tuesday, 1300 Hours.

The war ended for Section Eight on the banks of the
Rhine a dozen miles from the Ludendorff railroad
bridge where it spanned the river at Remagen.

There were eight survivors from the original unit.
Sergeant John Trankic, corporals Ed Solvis and Harlan
("Tex") Farrel, privates Chet Dormund, Guido Linari
and Shorty Kohler. Corporal Schmitzer had been transferred to an inactive unit in England to be processed for
an honorable discharge. The eighth survivor, Buell
Docker, was in command of Dog Battery's second platoon since Lieutenant Whitter had been assigned to an
administrative post at Battalion headquarters. The
group was again at full strength with the addition of
seven privates from a redeployment depot near Paris.

On the opposite side of the river lay the ruin of an
industrial town, now a waist-high crust of twisted girders and powdered mortar and brick, flattened and com-
pacted by months of aerial bombardment and artillery
fire. Only one feature in that dismal landscape had escaped destruction from Allied bombardment; a tall,
black smokestack remained standing, rising like a dark
exclamation point above the heaps of rubble. It had not
gone completely unscarred, however; a shell fragment

had scored a hit near the top of the chimney, creating a narrow hole there like the eye of a needle.

Shorty Kohler called to tell Trankic the battery jeep was coming toward their position.

Docker parked on the roadside and walked to the revetment, the men gathering around him as he distributed mail and packages. Trankic put two canteen cups on the sandbags and splashed whiskey into them. Farrel unhooked the cup from his cartridge belt but Trankic said, "Tex, you're too young for this stuff."

"Goddamn it, I'm practically a married man."

"When were you in Lepont?" Docker said to Farrel.

"Just last month. I stopped by Jocko's place on the way to Bonnard's. The damndest thing, sarge, I mean lieutenant, he found that big old dog of ours. It was lying by the stove like it owned the place, and I saw the schoolteacher. She was with her husband . . ."

Trankic sipped his whiskey and stared across the river. "That goddamn smokestack bothers me."

"What bothers you about it?" Docker said.

"I don't know, unfinished business maybe."

"She told me to say hello to you, sarge," Tex said.

Docker leaned against the revetment and looked at the river, the surface broken in delicate patterns by the hazy sunlight. There was a nice finality in thinking of her at ease in La Chance, her husband beside her, the bombs and enemy soldiers only a bitterness in the past, and Radar, taking a soldier's rest in front of the big iron stove . . .

Kohler came down the riverbank from the jeep and joined the others standing around with Trankic and Docker. There was a strange look on his face.

"Hey, listen to this, you guys," he said. "The fucking war is over."

"Yeah, says who?" Trankic said.

"I just heard it on Docker's radio. The guy on the radio says it's all over." Kohler looked at Docker. "I just heard it, on the radio in the fucking jeep."

Chet Dormund let out a whoop of laughter and

clapped his hands together, then subsided almost immediately, it being apparent even to him that no one else
shared his mood.

Linari said, "Hey, Shorty, you sure you heard it
right?"

"Go listen to it yourself," Kohler said. "Why should
he lie about it? Get it through your head, Guido. It's
over."

Docker walked to the jeep and fine-tuned the radio.
As the men joined him, a British announcer was describing the scene in London's Piccadilly Circus, his
voice broken up by static and lost completely at times in
the sound of church bells.

They listened to an announcer speaking in French
from Paris, and a U.S. Armed Forces reporter repeating
the first comments on the cease-fire from General Eisenhower in France and President Truman at the White
House. There were bursts of music and a recapitulation
of the sequence of events by Armed Forces announcers,
details of the German surrender and snatches of interviews with soldiers and civilians in the streets of London and New York. In a final interval of windy silence,
there was a hush, an almost reverent stillness, and then,
suddenly and jubilantly, came the sound of the big bells
tolling from Westminster Abbey and Notre Dame in
Paris.

Docker went back to the cannon and listened to the
thin music of whistles drifting toward them now from
captured German cities on both sides of the Rhine. He
lit a cigarette from Karsh's lighter with First Army insignia on its sides—a square black *A* on a gray field—
and looked at Trankic.

"Let's take care of that unfinished business now."

"I guess we'd better," Trankic said.

Picking up a clip of ammunition, Docker climbed
onto the loading platform of the cannon. Tex Farrel
joined him inside the revetment and secured the lever
that locked the cannon into the directional apparatus.
Trankic adjusted the azimuth and elevation scopes to

the smokestack, and the barrel swung swiftly around to focus on it.

Docker looked across the river and studied the thin patch of daylight at the top of the chimney. "What about it?" he said to Trankic.

"What about what, Bull?"

"Think we could put a few rounds through that hole up there?"

"Sure," Trankic said, and turned the operation wheels slowly, bringing the cross hairs of the sights in line with the jagged hole at the top of the smokestack.

The rest of the men had crowded around the rear of the revetment. "You guys are fucking gonna see something now," Kohler said to the recruits who were bunched together in defensive isolation from the veterans.

"They'll see it but it's not like the wretched way it was," Dormund said.

Docker slammed his foot down on the firing pedal. The sound of the cannon was all around them, the glowing tracers describing high arches of fire as they crossed the river toward the smokestack standing above the debris on the opposite shore of the Rhine.

When the first six rounds of ammunition, tracking each other at fifty-yard intervals, flashed through the circle at the top of the black chimney, there was a cheer from the soldiers, and another when the projectiles curved to the ground thousands of yards beyond the river to explode like strings of big firecrackers.

Docker called to Trankic, "Let's take it down now!"

Trankic fed the adjustments into the director and the gun barrel dropped sharply, its flared muzzle zeroing in on the base of the smokestack, and when it locked there Docker hit the firing pedal and another stream of tracers soared over the river.

They struck the base of the chimney, the warheads exploding in rapid bursts, and the length of the stack shuddered as if the ground beneath it had twisted violently, and then the huge chimney began to tumble and fall in graceful patterns as slowly as if it were melting toward the ground, the bricks detaching themselves from the main shaft and spinning lazily through smoke rising from the exploding artillery shells.

Docker put the cannon on safe and listened to the sound of bells and whistles in the winds and watched the huge smokestack collapse in powdered heaps along the far bank of the river.

When the last of the explosions had come like winter thunder through the settling dust and smoke, when the air was clear again, Docker and his men saw that the distant stretches of earth were flat as a man's hand from the silver shores of the Rhine to as far as they could see into the heart of Germany.

A Roll Call

CORPORAL EDWARD G. SOLVIS was honorably discharged from the United States Army at Camp Grant, Illinois, four months after the end of the World War II. At a Lions Club luncheon given in his honor by the president of Citizens' Trust of Davenport, Iowa, Solvis was informed that he had been promoted to assistant cashier and appointed to the bank's pension and credit union committees. As an additional gesture of appreciation, his years of wartime service were credited to his seniority at Citizens' Trust.

After adjusting himself to the routines of civilian life, Solvis assembled his notes and wartime diaries in chronological order and began to prepare an informal history of the unit in which he had served.

He corresponded with the surviving members of Section Eight, sent them questionnaires to fill out and, as his original design expanded, addressed inquiries to other individuals and organizations who might have had information about or related in any way to the section. When this work was as complete as he could make it, Solvis asked Buell Docker to assist him in finding a permanent repository for his files and records and diaries. It was through Docker's contacts that the permanent

Edward G. Solvis Collection was established at the College of Pennsylvania.

The following information is from the Solvis Collection in the archives of the college at Ardmore, Pennsylvania.

PRIVATE FIRST CLASS JOSEPH PITKO: His body was never recovered or accounted for by Graves Registration. Private First Class Pitko is still carried on the battalion roster as MIA (Missing in Action) in the Ardennes Campaign.

PAUL BONNARD: Widowed, with three grandchildren, Bonnard lives at the gatehouse and continues to tend the grounds of Château Rêve, converted now into a retirement home for the Order of the Sisters of the Sacred Heart.

PRIVATE FIRST CLASS IRVING GRUBER: Gruber is buried in the family plot at the Beth Shalom Cemetery in the borough of Brooklyn, New York. His headstone lies between that of his mother and his older sister, Hilary.

PRIVATES FIRST CLASS LEO PIERCE AND CARMINE SPINELLI: They are buried in the Netherlands-American Military Cemetery in Margraten, Holland.

JOCKO BERTHIER: Under a war reparations act, Berthier was granted fifty thousand Belgian francs as compensation for the injuries he suffered during the German occupation of Lepont. He was later awarded Belgium's third highest civilian decoration for his voluntary assistance to the American gun crew at Lepont during the Battle of the Bulge. Berthier sent Solvis several photographs of his enlarged and renovated café-bar, which now occupies two additional storefronts facing Lepont's old church.

PRIVATE FIRST CLASS CHESTER DORMUND:
Answered only one inquiry. After his discharge from
the Army, Dormund worked as a short-order cook in
Sweetwater, Texas. On his nights off, he wrote, he liked
to watch the harness races and "bet a little money on
the wretched trotters."

CAPTAIN WALTER "DER HENKER" BRECHT:
Captain Brecht left a widow and two sons in Frankfurt-
am-Main, Germany. During the Allied occupation, Frau
Brecht contributed her husband's library of Spanish and
Portuguese plays to the American Armed Forces Library at Munich. Solvis learned of this from an article
in the service newspaper, *Stars and Stripes*, which listed
the specifics of Frau Brecht's bequest in a story outlin-
ing the cultural opportunities available to GI wives in
Germany.

FIRST SERGEANT MILES KORBICK: Released
from an Army hospital in Georgia in 1947, Korbick
was discharged from the army the same year. He
opened one of the first laundromats in Florida—
"Korbick's Korner"—which was the beginning of a
chain that has expanded into seven southern states.

PRIVATE FIRST CLASS SAMUEL GELNICK: His
body was returned to the United States at the request of
his wife, Doris. Gelnick is buried in the Star of David
Cemetery in the borough of the Bronx in New York.

PRIVATE FIRST CLASS GUIDO LINARI: Linari
never replied to Solvis' requests for information. Solvis'
third letter was returned from Linari's former home on
Pell Street in New York City stamped "Not Known at
This Address."

LIEUTENANT GENERAL WALTER ADAMSON:
Adamson retired from the army in 1954. He captained

a senior officers' polo team at Boca Raton, Florida, and
contributed articles to leading military journals. His extensive memoirs, *The Last Great War,* were published
posthumously in 1970.

GENERAL JOSEF "SEPP" DIETRICH: The commander of the Sixth SS Panzer Army was sentenced to
life imprisonment for war crimes in 1946, but was pa-
roled and released in 1955. In 1957, General Dietrich
was sentenced by a German court to eighteen months in
prison for complicity in the deaths of Captain Ernest
Röhm and other SA (Sturmabteilungen) officers in
1934. The general died in Germany in 1966.

PRIVATE FIRST CLASS SONNY LAUREL: Laurel
is buried in the Mount Olivet Home of Eternal Rest in
a suburb of South Chicago. Funds for a Little League
baseball park were donated to the city by his parents,
the Wellington Laurels. The Sonny Laurel Memorial
Field was constructed in Rogers Park on the north side
of Chicago on land contributed jointly by the Laurel
family and Loyola Academy.

COLONEL OTTO SKORZENY: Skorzeny, sixty-
seven, died of bronchial cancer in Madrid, Spain, on
July 8, 1975. After World War II Skorzeny was acquit-
ted by an Allied War Crimes Tribunal. While awaiting
a denazification trial, Skorzeny escaped from a German
prison camp at Darmstadt and spent the remaining
years in Spain, where he worked as an industrial engi-
neer. In the 1960s he was accused by official sources in
Israel of organizing a network of ex-Nazis called Die
Spinne ("The Spider") whose goals were said to be the
resurrection of the Nazi Party and the destruction of the
state of Israel. In 1973 it was reported by an Italian
magazine that he had served as a consultant to a group
planning the assassination of Premier Fidel Castro of
Cuba.

COLONEL GEORGE RANKIN: Promoted to Brigadier General four years after World War II, George Rankin was killed in action in the first months of the war in Korea.

MAJOR SYDNEY KARSH : Discharged from the Army in January, 1946, Karsh served for twenty years as a senior partner in the New York law firm of Masterson, Karsh and Nevins. Specializing originally in international labor legislation, Karsh and his associates have in recent years devoted their full time to the International Amnesty Movement, in cooperation with the United Nations Human Rights Committee.

CORPORAL WALTER SCHMITZER: Schmitzer was discharged from the United States Army with a seventy percent disability, suffering from a variety of nervous disorders adjudged directly connected to his combat experiences in the Ardennes. Schmitzer supplemented his Army pension by working as a dispatcher for Goodwill Industries in Detroit, Michigan. In 1967 he moved to Laguna Beach, California, and answered only one subsequent inquiry from Solvis. "I haven't married and don't expect to now."

FRITZ WENDEL: Wendel, who test-piloted the first model of the Messerschmitt-262 on July 18th, 1942, was found dead of gunshot wounds at his home in Augsburg, West Germany, in February of 1975. A hunting rifle was at his side. Police would not comment on whether the death of Wendel, fifty-nine, was a suicide or an accident.

LIEUTENANT BART WHITTER: Discharged from the army at Fort Benning, Georgia, on February 10th, 1946, Whitter returned to Mobile, Alabama, and entered the real estate business. He was a responsive correspondent. He ran for the office of sheriff, but was defeated by several thousand votes. His wife divorced him

in 1956. Whitter remarried the same year. In his brief
political campaign, his slogan had been: "Vote for the
Man!" In a recent letter to Solvis, Whitter appraised
his defeat at the polls in these words: "I never changed.
The people knew where I stood, but they changed. The
whole damned South is changed. People think change is
the same thing as progress, but I can tell you this—
they're dead wrong."

PRIVATE FIRST CLASS VALENTINO "SHORTY"
KOHLER: Kohler sent Solvis Christmas cards over the
years. Additional news of Kohler came in a letter from
Buell Docker dated March 17, 1963. The following ex-
cerpt is relevant: "I thought the man looked familiar
when I went into P.J. Clarke's pub about ten last night.
He was standing beside his cab across the street. When
I came out an hour or so later, he was still there and
there was no doubt about it. He'd been waiting for me,
and insisted on driving me back to the hotel. He
wouldn't throw the flag even though I reminded him a
hack inspector could ground him a month for that. No,
the ride was on him. Shorty's put on weight and lost
most of his hair but he's still ready to tell the world
where to shove it. When we shook hands at the hotel,
he said, 'I just wish to hell the guys hadn't called me
Shorty. Because I wasn't near as short as them rupture-
heads thought I was.' I asked him if he'd meet me for
lunch the next day, but he told me he'd be working over
in Brooklyn and couldn't make it."

COLONEL JOACHIM PEIPER: Peiper commanded
the "Kampfgruppe Peiper," which was responsible for
executing eighty-six American military prisoners of war
in a field near the town of Malmédy during the Ardennes offensive. Colonel Peiper was sentenced to death
by an Allied War Crimes Tribunal, but the sentence
was commuted and he was released from Landsberg
Prison in 1956. In 1964 Peiper purchased a vacation
home in the village of Traves in the Vosges Mountains

of France. On the night of July 20th, 1976, the villa
was destroyed by explosions and flames. Firemen later
recovered the charred body of Joachim Peiper from the
wreckage. The words "Peiper SS" were discovered
painted on roads leading to and from the village of
Traves. Other members of the Peiper family were not in
France on the night of the explosion.

DAVID HAMLIN: Hamlin, Buell Docker's good
friend, is a professor of history at the College of Pennsylvania. He was married to Elaine Riley in 1948. Their
son, Charles, was born in 1952. Professor Hamlin received a Pulitzer Prize in 1961 for his three-volume
study of epic poetry in relation to the concept of the
war hero in various European cultures. Charles Hamlin
enlisted in the United States Army and was killed in
1972 on his twentieth birthday in a helicopter crash
near Hon Quan in South Vietnam.

JOHN TRANKIC: After his discharge from the Army,
Trankic operated a machine and welding shop in Calu-
met City, Illinois, for twenty years. In 1967 he moved
his family to northern Wisconsin and opened a gasoline
station and bait shop near Crawling Stone Lake. As a
hobby, Trankic teaches automobile repair and mainte-
nance to the Chippewa Indians on the Lac de Flambeau
reservation.

MARGRET GAUTIER: Mademoiselle Gautier lived
with her aunt and uncle, the Etienne Francoeurs, until
she enrolled in a pre-medical course at the University of
Louvain. At twenty-four, Dr. Gautier emigrated to Israel. She wrote one letter to Mrs. Agnes Larkin, for-
warded by the United States Army. The letter closed
with this sentence: "I remember now only the coldness
in the cab of the truck and your husband's words, which
I didn't understand but which were so comforting to the
very frightened child I was then." Agnes Larkin sent a
copy to Solvis, asking his advice on how best to answer

it. Solvis explained certain events of that distant night, but omitted any mention of the German supplies Larkin had taken from Castle Rêve.

LIEUTENANT COLONEL KARL JAEGER: In the spring of 1945, United States Army Graves Registration teams collected the bodies of hundreds of German soldiers who had fallen in the Ardennes in the last great German offensive of World War II. These soldiers were buried in mass graves in unmarked fields near the battle sites where they had met their deaths. Among the German dead buried outside Lepont was Lieutenant Colonel Karl Jaeger. Solvis received this information from Father Emile Juneau, pastor of the Eglise de Saint Esprit in that village. The priest had attempted to locate Karl Jaeger's wife and family in Dresden, but their apartment building was among the thousands destroyed in the fire bombing of that city in February of 1945.

CORPORAL MATTHEW LARKIN: Larkin's remains are buried in Saint John's Catholic Cemetery in the borough of Queens, New York. Prior to the return of his body to the United States, his wife wrote the Department of the Army in Washington requesting a military funeral for her husband. The request was granted. His service record contains the notation that he was "killed in action in the service of his country." In 1962 Agnes Larkin sent invitations to Solvis and Buell Docker to her daughter's graduation from the College of the City of New York.

PRIVATE FIRST CLASS JACKSON BAIRD: Baird's body was returned to the United States at his family's request and is buried in Arlington National Cemetery in Virginia on the shores of the Potomac, where his grave is linked with those of all the other soldiers in the Fields of Dead, those vistas of endless stone markers used for more than a century in the military cemeteries of America. Baird's photograph hangs in the library of the Baird family home in Middleburg, Virginia. Flanking it are the soiled letter Baird wrote to Buell Docker on the last night of his life, and the commendation which accompanied his posthumous award of the Silver Star, mounted in antique enamel frames inset with miniature American flags. The Silver Star itself was buried with Jackson Baird at his father's request.

LIEUTENANT BUELL DOCKER: Docker was elected to the state legislature of Pennsylvania shortly before his thirty-ninth birthday, after practicing law for seven years in Philadelphia. At that time, Docker moved to the capital city of Harrisburg with his wife, Elspeth, his daughter, Martha, and his son, Corey. On the wall of his office in the State House are two framed cables of congratulations which he received the night of his election. One is from Harlan "Tex" Farrel and his wife, Felice Bonnard Farrel, of Herstal, Belgium. The other is from Denise and Etienne Francoeur who still live in the village of Lepont, a block from the church and Jocko's café, on the banks of the River Salm.